HONOUR REDEEMED

With his fiery Irish blood and well-known reputation for trouble, Lieutenant George Markham leads his embattled Royal Marines against the French in Corsica. His mission: to seize the island. His problem: not just the French, but spies, traitors, and jealous rivals – including jealous husbands. Enemies abound – in both French blue and British red – and the only men Markham can rely on are grim, taciturn Sergeant Rannoch and a man who owes Markham his life – Bellamy, the educated, black Marine.

HONOUR REDEEMED

HONOUR REDEEMED

by

David Donachie
writing as Tom Connery

Magna Large Print Books
Long Preston, North Yorkshire,
BD23 4ND, England.

British Library Cataloguing in Publication Data.

Donachie, David writing as Connery, Tom
   Honour redeemed.

   A catalogue record of this book is
   available from the British Library

   ISBN   978-0-7505-4180-0

First published in Great Britain in 1997 by Orion

Cover illustration © Misty Fugate by arrangement with
Arcangel Images

Published in Large Print 2016 by arrangement with
David Donachie

Magna Large Print is an imprint of Library Magna Books Ltd.

Printed and bound in Great Britain by
T.J. (International) Ltd., Cornwall, PL28 8RW

This book is dedicated to
Peter Wright, Kevin, Pat
and all the staff at the
Midland Bank, Deal

For their unfailing good humour!

Chapter one

Even low in the water George Markham could see the French artillery shells arcing through the sharp dawn sky towards the heavily-laden boats, the swell off the coast of Cap Corse seeming to lift the cutter to meet them halfway. To the south, that portion of Admiral Hood's fleet sent to bombard the Fornali fort and the town of San Fiorenzo blazed away, the flash of their great guns followed seconds later by a succession of dull thuds, these mixed with boom from the land-based cannon, some of which had turned their attention to the approaching boats. The knot in Markham's stomach, on this, his first amphibious operation, was made up of apprehension mixed with a great deal of uncertainty. It proved of little comfort to recall that, amongst the mixed bag of men he commanded, not one had experienced this particular form of warfare: an opposed landing on a hostile beach!

For what they were required to do, when they did reach dry land, he had received none of the instructions to which, as an ex-army officer, he was accustomed. Any conferences about tactics had been confined to the higher commanders, naval and military. It was the complete opposite of regimental warfare, where the conclusions of such councils filtered down to the line officers, with clear objectives outlined, plus abundant

9

information about the terrain they must cover and the enemy they faced.

Captain de Lisle, the commander of his ship *Hebe,* had been vague to the point of opacity, his orders an airy instruction to get ashore and take Fornali, as though that bastion had neither walls, guns nor a French garrison. Markham had no idea of the quality of that defence. And who would be there to support him on his right or his left?

The shells heading their way were the first indication, a calling card to say that, at about eight hundred yards from the shore, the first wave of attackers were well within range. Dozens of boats were spread out in the bay, each moving at its own maximum pace. But all were converging on a limited strip of beach, so every stroke of the oar brought them closer together, giving Markham, who was somewhere close to the centre, a feeling of being hemmed in.

For a nation that prided itself on the efficiency of its artillery, this first salvo was less than perfect. Some of the fuses were too short, and the projectiles burst harmlessly, well above their heads, puffs of black powder in a rapidly brightening sky, sprouting and thinning until they were dispersed on the wind. Others, too long, landed fizzing in the still black water, sending up great white plumes to soak both passengers and crew of any downwind boat.

But one did terrible damage, detonating a few feet above the waves, the blast rocking Markham's boat, and wrought havoc on the nearby launch. The marine officer in that boat, sitting to one side of the tiller, was cut in two, a great fount of frothy

10

blood shooting up from his lower trunk as the top half spilled over the side. The midshipman beside him was blown back over the stern. Several of the rowers were smashed into the thwarts, their screams adding to the roar of the blast.

The launch lifted and span as explosive and chain shattered her flimsy side planking, sending deadly wooden splinters into weak and yielding flesh. The craft was broken in two long before she dropped back into the water, the occupants, the majority already wounded, spilling out into the sea. Those marines dead or too seriously harmed to discard their heavy packs sank like stones. Others fell to the same fate through blind panic, trying to swim with fifty-pound weights on their backs. A few, sailors and marines, had the sense to cling to life, using the wreckage of the boat to stay afloat, one hand struggling, in the Lobsters' case, to release the straps that held their equipment.

Most of the men in *Hebe*'s cutter stared straight ahead, those rowing trying to get them to the shore with as much haste as they could muster, the rest not wishing to observe too closely a fate that might well await them after the next salvo. But Markham was transfixed, his body stretching over the side as if he could hold out a helping hand to the lower section of a fellow officer, still sitting, legs twitching, in the only piece of the launch that looked whole. Midshipman Bernard, a pimply, pallid-faced slip of a youth who looked as if he were barely breeched, turned as well, though the hand that held the tiller remained steady, his eyes examining the carnage with a studied lack of passion.

'There are survivors,' said Markham, still pointing.

'May God grant them mercy,' Bernard replied.

'God be damned,' Markham growled. 'Steer for the poor sods.'

'We have our orders, sir,' piped the midshipman.

The seconds for which their eyes locked spoke volumes. That a sprog like Bernard should even dream of questioning a superior officer was singular. But the look on the boy's face, a sort of superior half-smile, showed an insolence as wounding as it was unwelcome. The youngster knew that aboard the frigate, being impertinent to Lieutenant George Markham was more likely to earn him discreet praise than a public rebuke.

But the object of his condescension wasn't on the ship; he was in command of the marines in the cutter. The level of his anger exaggerated the Irish inflection in his voice.

'Put down your helm, you stinking, short-arsed little bugger, or sure as hell is hot, I'll tip you into the bloody water myself.'

'Sir,' Bernard protested.

Markham's face, red enough with passion to match his coat, came towards him so fast that Bernard thought he was about to be head-butted. Fear mingled with disgust at the sight of a King's officer, even one with Markham's reputation, behaving in such a demeaning fashion.

'Do as you're damn well told, boy.'

Still Bernard hesitated. It was a safe bet that Captain de Lisle would back him if he disobeyed, since he took every opportunity to remind Markham how much he disliked having him aboard.

But his captain wasn't here, and the marine officer was, looking as if he would be as good as his word.

'Ship the larboard oars,' Bernard croaked, as he put down the tiller. The cutter swung in an arc until the prow was pointing towards the centre of the wreckage. 'Haul away, even.'

'Rannoch!' Markham yelled. His sergeant, huge, square-shouldered, half turned from his position in the centre of the boat. 'Get Ettrick and Dornan stripped of their packs and ready to go over the side.'

'They are floaters, sir, not real swimmers.'

Markham carried on as if Rannoch hadn't spoken. 'We can't get the survivors into the cutter. But try to get a hold on them, every man who can't swim between the oars to take one survivor.'

'Sir,' Rannoch replied crisply, before issuing his orders in a quiet tone. Ettrick and Dornan began to divest themselves of packs, belts, headgear and coats. The sergeant removed his own tricorne hat to wipe the sweat from his brow, revealing the blond, near-white hair that, with his strong, square face and blue eyes, gave him an almost Viking appearance. The hat was lifted above his head, pointing as the second salvo came over. If fuse adjustments had been made, they produced little difference in the result. But one pair of guns had certainly been re-aimed, since those shells that did burst at a proper height landed right in the course that Midshipman Bernard had previously been steering. He had spun round to look, and when they exploded what little blood he had left drained from his face completely. Then he turned to look at Markham, mouth moving in speechless shock.

'Paddy's luck, boyo,' Markham said, following that with a disarming grin. Angry as he'd been, he knew that Bernard's attitude merely aped that of every officer on the ship. They'd hated him enough before they'd ever reached the Mediterranean. After Toulon that was magnified tenfold. His mere presence within earshot was enough to set off a string of comments about jobs less than half done. These were larded with Paddy jokes, or allusions to the iniquity of illegitimacy, biased courts martial or the coruscating stain, regardless of subsequent good fortune, of being branded a coward.

As the disturbed water settled behind them, he unbuckled his own swordbelt and slipped the brass gorget over his head. Whatever reserve the midshipman had harboured quickly evaporated, respect in his eyes replacing the wonder that had taken over from fear. He craned forward now, calling out to the oarsmen for adjustments that would take the cutter alongside the wreckage without harming the men in the water. The two Lobsters who could swim slipped over the side, guiding the survivors towards the hands reaching for them, most too afraid to let go of the wood that had kept them afloat.

Markham had already thrown his hat into the bottom of the cutter, and had raised himself just enough to remove his coat, calling to the nearest men, 'Tully, Hollick, help me with my damned boots.'

As the two men facing the stern grabbed at the fine, polished leather, Markham had a moment to look round the deep, cliff-lined bay. Behind him, blocking the exit to the Mediterranean, lay half of

14

Admiral Hood's fleet, six line-of-battle ships that were a major part of Britain's wooden walls. The rest were engaged in bombarding the Fornali fort, and further down the bay, the town of San Fiorenzo, the boom of the huge naval cannon rolling like continuous thunder. The transports, carrying troops, were now inshore of the frigates that had disgorged the marines, the soldiers who would form the second wave lined up on deck, waiting for the boats to return and take them ashore. The water between ships and shore was chock-full, a veritable armada of boats, cutters, launches, barges, plus a pair of bomb ketches well forward.

The Fornali fort which they intended to envelop, massive walls built square round an old circular Genoese tower, lay just to the south, on a promontory that jutted out from a coombe nestled between low limestone hills. Further down the bay, behind San Fiorenzo, more hills rose, tier upon tier, towards the central mountains of Corsica, now bathed in full morning light, the very highest streaked with snow and shrouded at the peak in dense cloud. This panoramic backdrop suggested an illusory serenity, which was immediately shattered by the arrival of the third salvo.

'The guns have shifted again, sir,' said Bernard, pointing to the spouts of water now bracketing the boats laden with the small number of artillerymen and engineers who had been allotted to the first wave of the attack.

'Then you sailors are doing your job,' Markham replied. He stood up unsteadily and put one foot on the bulwark, which made it hard for him to sound as confident as he wished to. 'Most of the cannon in the fort are trying to sink them. And if the few they can spare to keep us warm have to lever and elevate endlessly, they'll never get the range right.'

'Backwards, sir,' yelled Bernard, throwing out a hand to stop Markham. 'If you try to dive you'll tip the lot of us out.'

Slightly abashed, Markham span round, sitting on the edge and falling back into the water. It was the Mediterranean, and warmer by far than the sea around Wexford Sound. But on a late February morning it still had the power to shock with sudden chill. Coming back to the surface, he saw that *Hebe*'s crew had oars and a boathook out, to haul in those being aided by Dornan and Ettrick. He twisted quickly and swam underwater, heading towards the furthest floundering marine, who was hanging on to a piece of the launch's shattered counter that didn't look big enough to support him. Head bobbing up and down, he registered that the fellow was different, without quite establishing why. All he really observed were the curls on the man's head, so tight as to be proof against a soaking.

At first he thought the object that he'd bumped into, dark and wet, was a piece of wood. But then he saw the flash of red as he surfaced and it span over. Markham felt his heart stop as he stared into the wide open eyes of the dead marine officer, the half of him that had been blown overboard still with enough air trapped inside the trunk to float. They were wide open, still registering the shock that had come to the man at the moment when

16

the piece of jagged steel from the shell casing had sliced through his vital organs. The mouth was open too, in a silent scream of terror. The last time he'd seen that face it had been red with wine and merriment, laughing across the dining table in the great cabin of Nelson's ship, *Agamemnon*. Gently, with his own eyes now closed, Markham pushed the body away.

'Lie back on me, man,' he gasped, as he came close, before spitting out the mouthful of salty water this remark had earned him. 'If I take your weight, we can make the cutter easily.'

That the fellow didn't believe him was obvious as the head came round. The furious shake, given the panic in the man's huge eyes, was super-fluous. He looked past Markham to where those lucky enough to get close to the boat were now being firmly held by their redcoated compatriots. Bernard had steered on to close the gap with him. Now no more than ten feet separated them from safety, but to this fellow it was too far. As soon as Markham tried to grab him, the man went crazy, yelling and kicking and demanding to be left to float.

In his panic, and a blind attempt to drive Markham away, he did let go, the free hands now scrabbling to take hold of the only thing that would save him. Markham felt himself go down as the man's weight landed on his shoulders. He tried to yell a command but that was stopped by the inrush of water. A knee took him in the groin, even slowed by the water having enough force to send a screaming ache through his lower body.

They were both under now, every limb of the

survivor flailing back and forth, with one hand firmly gripping Markham's shirt. Trying to hit the fellow to calm him down was impossible in water, and they went on sinking, the survivor continuing to flail wildly, though with less force, since he was running out of breath. Markham was in a similar state. Already he could feel the pressure building up in his chest, the tightness that precedes the desire to breath. All thoughts of rescue were gone now, the yearning to survive becoming paramount.

Try as he might, he could not prise the man's thick fingers open enough to release his shirt, and instinctively he knew that grip would be the last thing the other marine would relinquish. Nor did he have any chance of slipping out of the garment. His only hope was that by going limp he could at least preserve his wind. Indeed, he might just save himself from drowning, if the man clutching him would let him go as useless. Above he could see the light refracted in the surface of the water, the dark shape of the cutter's hull, surrounded by kicking legs, moving to block it off.

The lead line, dropping through the light, missed Markham by a fraction, catching the other marine on the ear. His struggles ceased for a split-second, which allowed his rescuer to catch hold of the line and wrap it round his wrist. Someone above had the sense to haul the rope back up, instead of just letting it endlessly descend, and that allowed Markham to tug hard, letting them know they had a weight greater than the lead on the line. The water had cleared enough to show some of the victim's features now his struggles had stilled:

18

round, dark face, and still those huge, terrified eyes. As Markham looked the mouth began to open, as the marine did the only thing his body would countenance when the lungs had run out of air.

Above, they began to pull, so Markham pushed his free hand under the fellow's chin, to try and stop him taking in more water. The stuff he'd already swallowed he spat into his rescuer's face as soon as they surfaced. Markham couldn't care, too busy himself sucking in great gulps of air. Hands were reaching out to grab his shirt, this time the welcome ones of his own men, and as they hauled the pair towards the cutter, the officer heard one of Bernard's sailors exclaim, 'Christ almighty, Lieutenant Croppie has gone and bagged himself a darkie.'

Bernard had the cutter back on course for the shore long before Markham could raise his head from between his knees, with Rannoch issuing orders to loop the lead line round the rowlocks so that the men they'd rescued could hang onto the boat themselves. He also heard the sergeant remind them of what they were about, and to get back to being fully prepared to land, weapons at the ready.

'There's an army officer on the beach, Lieutenant Markham,' said Bernard softly. 'Might I suggest that you replace your coat and boots?'

Markham nodded and raised his head, looking over the prow. The strand was a mass of boats, each one disgorging its quota of marine passengers before spinning away to get back and pick up the soldiers. The marines they'd put ashore moved forward into line to engage the enemy, who occupied the grass-covered dunes that rose between the beach and land proper. Several red-coated bodies floated at the tidal edge. Others lay face down a few feet from the water, on the blindingly white sand. But an attack was in progress, with the British marines moving forward in a disciplined way to engage the French defenders.

Two things made Markham's heart sink as he contemplated the scene. The first was that *Hebe*'s cutter would be the last vessel to arrive. The survivors were hanging off the side of the boat, ten men who could prove valuable in the future. This might have served as a decent excuse for tardiness, if it hadn't been for the second depressing fact; the identity of the officer in command who, having directed those already ashore towards the enemy, now stood glowering, facing the sea, peering through a telescope as he watched the last boat approach.

'Is that colonel who I think it is, sir?' called Rannoch, when the spyglass dropped.

'It is,' Markham replied, as he struggled in vain to pull boots on over soaking wet stockings and breeches.

'Christ, I can see the scar, which I take to mean we are in for a bollocking.'

Markham could see it too; a livid, ragged white streak across an otherwise puce face. Some of the balls from the French muskets were sending up spurts of water and sand around him, but he ignored the danger. Unwilling to give his old adversary any credit for bravery, Markham told himself that at such extreme range, shots like those were flukes, balls with dying velocity that would probably inflict little harm.

'I'll have to ease off, sir,' said Bernard. 'With those men in the water I can't run up the sand for fear of trapping their legs.'

'Then do so.' Suddenly the cutter slowed, which earned them a bellow from shore to 'put their damned backs into it'.

'What shall I do, sir?' asked the nervous mid-shipman.

'Ignore him,' Markham replied.

'He looks to be a full colonel, sir.'

'He is, Bernard,' Markham said wearily. 'But I won't tell what he's full *of*, for fear of offending your sensibilities.'

'Damn you,' the hoarse, loud voice floated over the water, as the effect of Bernard's order to go easy on the rowing became apparent. 'I might have known, Markham, if there was a fight, that you'd be the last one into the action.'

'Sergeant Rannoch,' Markham said.

'Sir!'

'Get the men over the side as soon as we hit the shallows, if you please. Let's get the survivors ashore. It would be a pity to lose them now, especially with that bastard looking on.'

Rannoch replied in that clear, slow Highland lilt that could, in moments of stress, be so in-furiating. Now it seemed perfectly paced. 'I judge that he would enjoy watching men drown.'

'Me especially,' Markham replied.

'I take it you know the colonel, sir,' said Bernard.

'I do.' He turned to give the midshipman a wry

smile. 'I tried to kill him once, in America. He's been trying to do the same thing to me ever since.'

Rannoch led half the marines hatless, weaponless, into the rapidly shallowing water, each one taking the arm of a survivor. This sent the Colonel into a paroxysm of rage. He was thumping his boots with his riding crop so hard that they looked set to split, the loud cracks floating across the water every bit as noisy as the gunshots behind them. Markham jumped out as the keel finally ground into the sand, coat over one arm, and carrying his boots. But he had his hat on, which allowed him to lift the thing in an insolent salute.

'The detachment from the *Hebe*, Colonel Hanger, at your service.'

Chapter two

The Honourable Augustus Hanger was an experienced soldier, even if George Markham had no great appreciation of either his manners or his abilities. Berating an improperly dressed lieutenant, even one he hated with a passion, would have to wait while there was a battle in progress. Barking an order to 'get properly attired and follow on', he turned on his heel and headed back up the beach to take charge of an assault in which, given the numbers engaged, most of the advantage lay with the defenders.

Fortunately, since the French commander had been vouchsafed no notion of where the British intended to land, his troops were thinly spread, most between San Fiorenzo and the Fornali defences, with only a screen of infantrymen to contest the vulnerable northern beaches. But the enemy held the advantage of cover. And now that the British had shown their intentions, General Lacombe had the chance to concentrate while the landing party was held in check. Coming ashore piecemeal, with no clear command structure, and faced with a fire to which they couldn't effectively respond, the assault had broken down. The marines were now lying, individually and in small knots, on the white strand of the exposed beach, flinching as the spurts of sand from patiently aimed muskets fired from the crest of the line of dunes covered their backs.

Markham's first thought was that they were lucky. Clearly Lacombe lacked field ordnance, mortars or mobile cannon which, firing grenades, could turn this beach into a charnel house. Boots in hand, he was about to advance barefoot in Hanger's footsteps, when he heard the colonel bellowing for the men to get to their feet and move forward – a wise notion, since out in the open they were sitting ducks. But Hanger seemed content to move straight up the beach, to concentrate his forces and take the enemy by frontal assault, seemingly unconcerned for the flanks, which would, surely, be reinforced the longer the action went on.

'Rannoch, get the survivors armed.'

'Two of them are sailors, sir.'

'Mr Bernard will return them to the fleet,' Markham barked. 'They're no use here.'

The Highlander might talk slowly, but he could move swiftly enough when the need arose. Within seconds he had the two tars aboard and was taking the marine survivors along the beach, ordering them to strip the nearest dead and wounded of their equipment. Markham ordered the rest of his men to kneel, and taking advantage of the limited amount of fire coming in their direction, struggled to get into first his boots, then his coat. That achieved, he took out his small telescope, ranging it up and down the long strand.

A mile to the south lay the Fornali fort itself, on its rocky promontory, the ramparts facing the beach bristling with silent cannon. They were useless against a British force coming ashore out of range. But, if they couldn't invest it properly, and were forced to attack from their present positions, they'd be brought into action, to play along a crowded shore that offered little cover. More rocks enclosed the northern arm of the shallow bay, while behind the long line of un-dulating dunes he could see the tops of a whole forest of pine trees. The upper branches, bent to accommodate the strong winds that blew around Cap Corse, were ablaze with the morning. It was the angle of that, edging over the top of the pines, that showed the very slight depression in the unbroken ridge of sand, a small but significant dip, and led his eye to what appeared to be a thick clump of tangled gorse fronting the dune.

There was something odd about the colour of the bushes, a sort of dead, greying quality that contrasted sharply with the deep green of the treetops. Not visible while in shadow, it was more obvious now. Adjusting his glass to concentrate on the area in front, he could see that rather than being smooth, the sand seemed to be disturbed, as though it had been well trodden. The more he looked, the more unnatural it seemed, making him wonder if those bushes were camouflage, designed to cover up the one real gap in the main line of sandhills. He looked round for Rannoch, only to observe that he was still occupied.

'Halsey.'

'Sir!' the corporal replied, coming to his feet and standing to attention, musket at his side, as if he were on a parade ground. Markham pointed along the seashore, convinced that what he was seeing was a point where the dunes broke, to provide an avenue to the firm, forested ground behind. Yet there was a very good chance that it could be a blind hollow that would lead nowhere.

'Take four men along towards those rocks to the north. You'll observe, about halfway, a great crop of bushes, covering what might be a gap in the dunes. Stay near to the waterline till you get abreast of it, then stop and face it. If nothing happens then, march slowly up the beach. I want to see if you draw any fire.'

The brown eyes didn't blink, but Markham saw the soft nose dilate slightly. Halsey was an experienced marine, a man who'd served for years both ashore and afloat. He would know that if it was a gully, a chink in the line of defence, then it was likely to be well protected. Lieutenant Markham had come aboard *Hebe* in an Army uniform, leading a detachment of soldiers, anathema to proper Lobsters, which had caused no end of trouble on the voyage out. Even although they, along with the ship's marines, had been through the siege of Toulon together, and all that resentment should have been laid to rest, it showed for a fleeting second.

'Don't march more than twenty paces from the waterline. The range looks to be well over a hundred yards, so unless they are proper marksmen, you should be reasonably safe. But if you attract heavy fire, you may retire into the water. Just keep your muskets and powder well above your heads.'

'And if they have a cannon, sir?'

Markham's first impulse was to bark at him, to say that this was neither the time nor the place for a speculative discussion that Halsey had no right, anyway, to indulge in. That if there had been any cannon they'd know by now, since shells would be exploding about their ears. But this was a man who, if a touch uninspired, was obedient and, in some desperate actions, had never let him down. So he dissipated his anger by shouting for Rannoch to return. With Halsey he tried to sound reassuring.

'Then get the hell out of there as quick as you can. Make for those rocks at the head of the bay, get in amongst them, and stay there until the whole bloody army has landed.'

The pale, slightly pasty face nearly broke into a grin, the corporal, through ingrained discipline, just managing to smother the impulse. He span away, calling the names of the men he wanted, before heading off in the required direction. Now fully dressed, Markham looked up the beach, to where the attacking troops had reached the seaward side of the dunes. The steep slopes gave them protection from the enemy fire, but every man who tried to advance struggled to find any footing in the soft, dry sand.

There was a moment's hesitation as he stood there, half listening to Rannoch as he pushed the rearmed marines, new to his ways, into some form of order. The man in command of the landing had given him quite specific instructions, and he was about to disobey them – bad enough in itself, but made ten times more dangerous by his relationship to the colonel. Augustus Hanger, always assuming he couldn't contrive a way to get him killed, would love nothing more than to get George Markham in front of a court martial. There, the chance would exist to redress what he saw as the mistakes of New York, and kick this one time Lieutenant of the 65th foot, masquerading as a Lobster, out of both services.

But looking up the beach, Markham knew he had two choices: to prolong the folly of a frontal assault, or to make some kind of effort to go round the enemy before the French commander could bring up more defenders. It might be his first amphibious landing, but he'd heard often enough how awkward they were. Timing was everything; the ability to get enough troops ashore to secure the landing area before the enemy could gather the strength to throw the assault back into the sea.

And things on this beach were at a critical juncture. Did General Lacombe have field artillery at his disposal, guns which, at this very moment, were being wheeled into position? If he had, and could concentrate enough troops, he would impose himself on the second wave of soldiers, now being loaded offshore into the returned boats. Discipline and the burden of his reputation tugged him one way, while everything he'd ever learned, fighting in both America and Russia, pulled him inexorably towards the other.

In total, including himself, he had twenty men, eleven of his own, plus eight from the sunken launch. These showed little or no fighting spirit, but he put that down to the fact that not one of them had a whole uniform and they'd all received a fright.

The crack of ordered musketry, so different from the individual shots being fired from behind the dunes, made him turn back to look towards Halsey, just in time to see the spurts of sand that seemed to spring up around his feet. The corporal was only too eager to obey his officer's orders, and lifting both musket and powder horn above his head, he turned round and plunged into the sea, followed by his men, until the protective water was up to his chest. That salvo of musket fire had told Markham all he needed to know. If the spot was defended it must represent a weakness that the French feared might be exploited.

'Rannoch, we'll close on Halsey. No packs. Just muskets, bayonets, a bag of grenades and entrenching tools.'

It would be best to advance diagonally across the beach to the edge of the dunes, just below the spot where Halsey had attracted fire. Beyond that lay the clump of bushes which hinted at a possible way through. If they could throw up enough sand to protect themselves, they could move up on the enemy position.

'With respect, sir,' said Rannoch slowly, looking straight up the beach to where Hanger, half crouched in the sand, was waving his sword and berating his men, urging them forward, 'we have been given our orders.'

Markham smiled, having become accustomed to the way Rannoch felt free to question him. His sergeant was trying to tell him, without saying so in front of the others, what he was risking.

'We are joining Colonel Hanger, Sergeant, but just a tad left of where he thinks. Bring up the rear. And try and keep those Agamemnons in some form of order.'

'We're not Agamemnons, sir,' said the Negro marine, his voice deep, resonant, and surprisingly cultured. 'They took us out of *Seahorse* to make up the numbers for the attack.'

'Shut it, you black bastard,' growled another man. Tall, hollow-chested, with thick eyebrows over angry eyes, he clearly exerted some leadership over the Seahorses, given the way they looked at him. 'Who asked you to speak up fer us?'

The still damp survivors had enough spark to add a growl to that, as though they heartily approved of the sentiment. Markham was watching the Negro's eyes: large, a deep fluid brown, and so much more expressive than his face. The man who'd snapped at him turned to Markham, ducking slightly as a musket ball cracked in passing, making no attempt to defer to his rank or soften his voice.

'We lost the officer, along with our sergeant and

29

corporal, in that blast. But that don't mean we're free to be ordered about by any Tom or Dick that fancies it.'

'Sergeant Rannoch,' said Markham, moving closer, 'if this bastard opens his mouth again, put a bullet through what passes for his brain.'

Out of the corner of his eye, he saw the row of startlingly white teeth, and heard the low, warm chuckle. Another ball cracked as it sped past, underlining that wherever they went, it was time to move. He didn't know what impulse made him act as he did then, and analysing it later he could only believe that he had suffered so much condescension himself in his chequered life that he was naturally in sympathy with anyone likewise afflicted. Spinning quickly, he looked the Negro in the eye.

'Name?'

'Eboluh Bellamy, sir.'

'Well, Mr Bellamy, you are, while we are on the beach, in temporary charge of the Seahorses. I expect the men you lead will not disappoint me.'

'I'm not taking orders from no darkie.'

'Name?' Markham barked, spinning round, as Rannoch's musket came up to the hollow-chested marine's ear.

'Sharland, sir,' the man replied, the anger in his eyes replaced by fear.

'Well, Sharland, you will lead us across the beach. And the only way you'll avoid being broken at the wheel after we're finished is to ensure that I don't see one scrap of your ugly face. Now move!'

There was no choice and he knew it. An officer could shoot him where he stood for disobeying an order, and his superiors would praise him. And that might be the better fate than a thousand lashes tied to a wagon wheel. Sharland turned towards the dunes and, growling at the rest of the Seahorses to join him, started to jog across the beach in the direction set by Markham's sword. The Hebes, and his new corporal, were behind him. Their actions didn't go unnoticed, and since the men crouching behind the dunes presented few targets, most of the French fire from the crest of the dunes came their way. The musket balls kicking up the sand around their feet added some urgency to the manoeuvre. Hanger, alerted by the change of target, was bellowing for them to join him, which Markham studiously ignored. Difficult as it was to run properly on sand, they made good speed, with Markham frantically signalling to Halsey and his party to get out of the water, then come up to the southern edge of the clump of gorse.

'Dig,' Markham gasped, as soon as they reached the point he'd chosen, a shallow depression caused by swirling winds that ran along the very base of the dune. Behind them the beach lay flat and smooth to the water's edge, in front was a steep wall of sand topped with sea grasses. Close to this they were, like Hanger's men, relatively safe, since anyone wanting to fire on them would risk exposure as they leant out to aim. The problem was how to get past it.

'Bellamy, get your Seahorses to throw up a breastwork facing those bushes. Nothing special, just enough to protect you from musketry when you're lying flat.'

31

'It's too soft,' moaned Sharland, kicking at it with one boot.

'It isn't underneath,' Bellamy replied, in a gentle voice. 'There will be damp sand below.'

'How the fuck would you know, soot face?'

Markham hit him then, using the flat of his blade. For a second the marine, shovel in hand, looked set to retaliate, but good sense stopped him, since the officer's sword was lifted once more, this time with the sharp edge threatening him. But he did snort and spit before he started to dig, a long streak of dirty saliva, aiming it close enough to Bellamy so that the black man would know who it was intended for.

Rannoch's voice was in Markham's ear, earnest, but in no way anxious. 'They will not sit still, sir, when they see the first spade full of sand.'

'I never thought they would, Sergeant.' Markham called for his Hebes to gather round, then pointed towards the steep slope of the dune. 'Dornan, lie back on the slope. Tully, you climb up him and do the same. We'll make a human ladder to the top. If you get near the rim keep your musket out of sight. Everyone else on your knees, aiming for the fringes of sea grass on either side. If you see so much as a sandfly, shoot it.'

Pushing past the digging marines, Markham poked his nose round the side of the dune. He immediately drew fire, forcing him to pull back quickly. 'Halsey, get your muskets trained on the opposite side of the gully, and put one round through the grass. Reload at the double. From where you are you'll have a better view of the rim. Bellamy, any man not digging to do the same to the grass above Halsey.'

'They won't obey me, sir, if I tell them.'

'They will if you learn to shout,' Markham snapped. 'Rannoch, a couple of grenades, if you please.'

Dornan had Tully's feet on his shoulders. Hollick had clambered up them both, followed by Leech and one of the Seahorses, who was now very near to the top. Rannoch laid the fuse on one grenade in the firing pan of his musket, and fired, setting it alight. He waited until it burnt down a fraction, and, holding his arm out wide, lobbed it at the piles of gorse, some thirty feet away, before throwing himself back to avoid the blast. He was halfway through reloading his musket when the grenade went off, the thud of the explosion dulled by the effect of the soft ground.

'Keep that up, Bellamy, in exactly the same way as Sergeant Rannoch. You might, if you can get it in the bush, be able to set the wood alight.' Easing his pistols from his belt, Markham put one foot in the outstretched hands of Private Dornan. 'Ready, Sergeant Rannoch?'

'You cannot leave that black man in charge down here, sir,' said Rannoch, softly but insistently, into his officer's ear.

'Why not?'

'Well, first it is not right, and second they will likely shoot him before they ever aim a gun at a Frenchman.'

'Take a close look. Bellamy is no fool. Look where he's sitting.'

The Negro was at the rear of the digging Seahorses, his own musket resting on his knees,

33

levelled at the straining backs of the party shovelling for damp sand. While he worked to set a grenade alight with Sharland's weapon, his eyes were fixed on the men aiming their muskets at the dune above Halsey's head. Even when he stood up to throw, he hardly took his eyes off his fellow Seahorses. Markham's voice, hitherto friendly, suddenly became harsh as he responded to Rannoch, which had been a rare thing since the shared danger of Toulon.

'And Sergeant, I will decide what is right, not you.'

'Sir.'

The blue eyes had gone blank, and a look of dumb insolence spread across the Highlander's face, which on the face of a man who had saved his life, made Markham feel ashamed.

'You may stay here if you think it best,' he added, though given that he was not one to apologise, he did so through gritted teeth. 'As soon as I secure the rim, get the rest to follow me, and bring up the rear.'

'What about the breastwork?' asked Rannoch.

'Bluff, just like the grenades. I want them to think we're coming in the front door. But we're not!'

Chapter three

It was impossible to clamber up without stepping on some sensitive part of the men who made up the human ladder, so Markham heard a goodly number of the curses usually only employed when officers were out of earshot. And he kept his eyes fixed firmly on his destination, every nerve strained for the first sight of the grass being moved by anything other than the gentle breeze. The salvo from Halsey came just as he saw the grass part, and the end of a musket protrude. The balls whistled harmlessly over the Frenchman's head. Assuming that he had at least twenty seconds before those guns could reload, he stood upright, and leant over, his weapon aimed at the climbing redcoat officer.

Rannoch's ball, fired from a mere twenty paces, took him in the middle of the face. The Brown Bess used a large-calibre ball, and being lead it expanded when fired. Even though the Frenchman was thrown back by the shot, Markham could see the way his face just caved in, a black expanding hole which suddenly went bright red at the edges, as his blood and brains were pushed out the sides of his shattered skull. Any attempt at gentleness was abandoned, and he heard Leech screech with pain as, searching for sudden purchase, his foot dug into the recumbent marine's groin. Behind him he could hear the yells of rage as those following him copied his example.

Using his free hand, he grabbed at a thick tuft of grass just as another musket tip poked through. In their desire to stay concealed, the defenders had removed their bayonets, which was just as well, since a quick downward thrust would have speared Markham before he could raise his pistol. And the defender, instead of just firing as soon as he saw the British officer's face, tried to elevate himself slightly to improve the angle of fire, which gave Markham the split-second he needed to pull himself up and fire at the hat. This time the ball took the Frenchman in the temple, but being smaller it left nothing but a small entry hole as the light of life died in the eyes.

Then Markham was on the top of the dune, lying flat so that the grass would afford him some protection. If he so much as got to his knees, he'd present a target to every French musket within range. That included those who still had Hanger and his men pinned down. In fact, even with half a dozen marines up here he was dangerously exposed, since the colonel seemed content to hold his position, and wait for the reinforcements now coming ashore.

The whoosh of the shell passing overhead made him push himself even further down into the soft sand, until, realising the direction of the shot, he turned his head towards the open sea.

The bomb ketches had come close in ahead of the second wave of soldiers, with one boat, a decorated captain's barge, well to the fore. A solitary officer, a post captain, stood in the bows, telescope in his hand, clearly directing the fire, oblivious to the French cannonfire which was sending up great plumes of water around all three boats. Even at this distance, Markham was sure the captain, rather smaller than those close to him, was Nelson.

With springs on their cables, the bomb ketches, each with a pair of guns, were firing at differing targets, the deep boom of their mortars mingling with the counter-battery fire still being applied by the fleet to suppress the main French batteries. The one closest to the fort was aiming at a point between the Fornali and the landing ground, the probable route of any reinforcements. The other, which had fired the shot that had just passed over Markham's head, was being used to support the assault, its first target aimed at what must seem, from the sea, to be the very northern tip of the marine attack.

The shell from the second gun was fired just after the first shot landed, making no more than a dull thud as it hit the sand. Then it went off, a great boom that sent a plume of grit, wood and pieces of rock into the air, into which the second shell dropped. That exploded before impact, and added human flesh to the mixture which still hung in the air. These mortars were the perfect weapons for the task, able to fire in a high trajectory over the attacking troops, with enough elevation to land lethally amongst the defenders.

His men, who had frozen at the first salvo, scurried on to join him, the last and youngest, Yelland, bearing a whole mass of belts buckled together. His hat tipped off as he fell forward, exposing the fine blond hair. Then he raised his handsome, innocent-looking countenance towards his officer, who had to remind himself, for the hundredth time, that this was probably the face of a double murderer.

'That sambo's notion, your honour,' he gasped. 'He took them off the Seahorses so we can pull the rest of the lads up.'

'A good idea.'

'Ain't it, though. An' here's me thinking they was no smarter than tree-swingin' apes.'

The next pair of mortar shells, fired together, swooshed over their heads again, to explode just below the backward slope of the dunes a mere fifty feet south. Even at that distance, with the blast driven up, they still felt it, a wall of sand-filled air that hit them hard enough to make everyone spin away.

'Jesus Christ, that was close,' hissed Hollick, who was busy trying to pull Leech up to the top.

Yelland had leant over to pass the makeshift rope to Tully, and was only saved from tipping back down the slope by Markham, who grabbed the youngster's belt. Looking straight down he saw Rannoch, who was making no attempt to climb up to join them. Instead he was directing the remaining Seahorses, who were now throwing a continuous stream of dark brown sand out to form the required breastwork. The pile of gorse off to Markham's left was well alight from grenades which Markham hadn't even noticed go off, and Rannoch seemed too intent on the task in front of him to obey his orders.

In the time it took to get Dornan, as bovine as ever, up to the top, he was free to ponder on why his sergeant, whom he'd come to trust absolutely, had failed to support him. But such thoughts had to be put aside. The next salvo from the guns came nowhere near his party, having shifted along the beach towards Hanger and his men. If those shells had done any damage, the French would be disorganised. But not for long, and Markham knew that whatever had happened he'd still be outnumbered. Jumping to his feet, he yelled for his small party to follow, and ran for the point at which the dune sloped down again.

The sight that greeted his eyes nearly made him stop dead, aware of how lucky he had been. The low wooden palisade, well back from the dunes on the very edge of the treeline, behind which the enemy had been arranged, was blown asunder, bits of log mingling with the shattered bodies of the Frenchmen. Those who had survived were either crawling or staggering around in a daze, so taking the position was simple. But he shuddered as he contemplated what might have happened had that defence still been intact. He would have charged into full view, to be cut down for certain by a deadly, well-prepared salvo from the defending muskets.

Whatever Rannoch's reservations had been about climbing up the dunes, he showed enough zeal in the way he led the rest of the men up the gully. The blast had raced through the gap, partially destroying the camouflage. He'd used bayonets to pull the flaming remainder clear, and as soon as there was sufficient space, charged through with Halsey at his heels. Even the Sea-horses, their beltless coats flapping wildly, seemed imbued with the right spirit, screaming as they stumbled though the dense smoke, their feet slipping and slithering in the sand.

They too stopped when they saw the destruction visited on the French by those mortar shells. As the billowing fumes cleared, Markham was aware that Bellamy was missing. But there was no time to ask what had happened to him, not with battle still in progress. And the prospect of what he was about to do pleased him immensely, since it was clear that the main attack was still bogged down on the seaward side of the dunes.

'Right, Rannoch, form the men up, and take them in amongst the trees. Spread out four abreast, and let's see if we can outflank the enemy and save Hanger's reputation.'

Said with a laugh, it was no joke when Markham and his men tried to implement it. The briefing he'd received aboard *Hebe* had not only been useless; it had been short and unpleasant. But one salient fact he could remember. Captain de Lisle had referred to the garrison numbers holding San Fiorenzo and Fornali as being barely more than a thousand men. With the fleet putting twice that number ashore at a point of their choosing, and able to bombard any position they wanted in support, there was enough reason to be sanguine. The enemy was required to split his forces, while the besiegers could concentrate theirs.

Not that Markham was in much doubt about the ability of the French troops to hold their ground where possible. They were mostly men who'd served in Royal regiments before the revolution,

40

soldiers who had repelled an attack on the Mortella fort the previous year by some of the very same men they were facing now. And Lacombe St Michel, their commanding officer, had a reputation for terrier-like tenacity when it came to defending a position. Against that, the vicissitudes of three years of political turmoil should have weakened both their numbers and morale.

With a slight feeling of embarrassment, he recalled that meal aboard *Agamemnon*. Full of wine, he'd drunk the toast at dinner with gusto, as sure as his fellow guests that British arms could drive back a couple of French regiments, lock them into town and fort, besiege then overcome them, in a situation where they could expect no exterior assistance. But battling his way along the line of the dunes, using the tall pines on the edge of the forest for cover, Markham wasn't quite so confident.

He sensed that whatever he'd been told about the enemy strength was faulty. No general in Lacombe's position would risk his entire force outside the protection of his main defensive perimeter, which had to end at the Fornali fort. Yet not only did the defenders have parity, now that the landing site had been identified, but more troops could well be arriving, reaching the point where they might actually outnumber the attackers. Under Hanger's command, the men on the beach had been content to wait for reinforcements. Yet they were being pressed with such force that they risked being pushed back, their sole support the mortar shells ranging up and down the beach.

All Markham and his men could do was probe on the flank, trying to pick off those holding the high ground above Hanger's head. And it was bloody work. He lost two of the Seahorses, who lacked his own men's battle experience, before they'd managed fifty yards, then found himself pinned down as the French, realising the threat, concentrated enough firepower against this attack to halt his advance – not difficult, given his limited, and diminishing, numbers.

'Could we go further into the wood?' asked Rannoch, his back pressed against a tree. 'The cover is thicker the more trees we have between them and us.'

Markham shook his head. 'We must keep contact with the line of dunes. If we separate from that, the French will just cut us off and drive us so deep we'd be useless.'

There was no mistaking the sound of the approaching mortar shell, even if the sight of the huge black ball was obscured by the high canopy of trees. The barrage had shifted to the northern end again, and with the Hebes out of sight, the navy was laying down fire right on the perimeter of Hanger's position. Every man in Markham's party threw himself into the pine needles, covering his head with his hands as the projectile burst above and behind them. Even as he cursed the pain in his ears, Markham couldn't blame the gunners. Their job was to support the landing, and as far as they knew the northern limit of the position was designated by the red coats of Hanger's men on the beach.

The second salvo came over, driving them all, if

that was possible, even deeper into the ground. Above their head, branches snapped, cracks that rent the air with enough force to drown out the popping of musket fire. Then whole trunks went, groaning like bereaved humans as they fell through the nearest trees, tearing off even more wood and foliage. Then silence descended. But it didn't last long. The mortars shifted, landing now just ahead of their position, amongst what Markham hoped were the Frenchmen holding him up.

He was on his knees now, using a decent-sized trunk as cover, just about to order his men forward behind the guns, when Quinlan's voice, a hoarse whisper, came from the very edge of the forest, the point where the line of the trees gave way to mixed pine needles and sand.

'Party crawling along the top of the dunes, sir, in the long grass.'

'Where?' demanded Markham, spinning away from his own tree, then scurrying across to take a look, vaguely aware that Rannoch was following him.

'Only saw the bugger's hat. I think he lifted it to take a bearing.'

'There will be more than one,' said Rannoch.

It was logical. With more troops coming ashore, that gully had to be held. Rather than fight his way back to the head of it, the French commander was trying to sneak some men past them, probably enough to reconstruct a defence and nullify what Markham had achieved. Then he could keep them pinned down where they were, isolated and useless.

Markham felt stymied. The trees offered little

help. They were like the birches that he remembered from fighting in Russia, lacking the lower branches which would make climbing them possible, so the notion of getting men and muskets level with the top of the dunes had to be discounted. Racking his brain for a solution, Markham glanced up at the sun filtering through the canopy, so thick that only a fraction of the light penetrated to the soft, pine-covered ground.

He tried to calculate the arc of those trees falling across the route of the Frenchmen. Certainly pines barring their line of advance would force them to expose themselves, but whoever among his own men wielded an axe, always assuming they had one, could hardly survive the salvos that would be aimed in his direction as he cleaved away at the resinous wood.

Even if it was no more than an attempt to bluff, he had to get his men in some kind of position where they could make their presence felt. His Hebes were well spread out, some level with him, but mostly behind and to his right. He could see Sharland hugging a tree, in close proximity to the remaining five Seahorses. Corporal Halsey was to the rear of them to make sure that they didn't run if things got too hot.

'Seahorses, move up alongside me to the left and spread out.' It was infuriating the way Sharland hesitated, as though any command had to be filtered through his insubordinate brain before it could be obeyed. Even more annoying was the way the others were looking to him for guidance. 'Quickly man!'

Rannoch gestured furiously, exposing himself

to do so, then glared at Sharland as he ducked quickly back behind his tree. The musket balls that whipped through the still, warm air of the forest a split-second after he disappeared showed both in their accuracy and their number just how close they were to the enemy. One ball took a lump out of Rannoch's tree, covering his head and shoulders in fine wooden chips.

'I would say we are outnumbered,' he called, calmly brushing his uniform coat as the Seahorses, taking advantage of the enemy's need to reload, finally obeyed the command.

'I doubt they'll come for us,' replied Markham grimly. 'All they have to do is keep us where we are.'

'Not if they are on both sides of us, sir,' growled Rannoch, nodding towards the top of the dunes. 'The colonists always tried to do that when they caught us in wooded country.'

Markham didn't answer for a moment, reminded yet again of how little he really knew about the Highlander. He'd been a soldier a long time, and had served in the Americas before and during the War of Independence. And then there was that M burnt into his thumb, the sign of a man who had been tried and convicted of manslaughter.

'Some return fire, if you please, while the remainder of the men deploy. Two rounds through the trees to keep the enemy heads down.'

Sensibly, Rannoch ordered half the muskets to discharge, then the rest while the first section moved. Annoyingly, the men took no real aim, but just blazed away in the general direction of the

45

target. Not that aiming was easy with a Brown Bess, which had a recoil like the kick of a mule. But Markham and Rannoch had spent a lot of time on that in Toulon, and the Hebes had seen what dividends could be gained from disciplined musketry. Now, it seemed, having been at sea for a few months, they'd forgotten everything they'd been taught.

The balls started to fly as soon as the first man moved, and what was intended as a smooth re-deployment was instead an undignified scramble that fortunately passed without loss. With his men now strung out in a long line facing the dunes, Markham was left to ponder the difference between theory and practice. He had an enemy on his right, certainly more numerous than he'd originally supposed. In front was a wall of sand manned by Frenchmen who were above them, and would, unless stopped, take up positions on his left. The only way to put a definite check on the enemy was to attempt the near impossible, and get his men back on the top of the dunes to drive them back.

Logic demanded that, cut off from support, he withdraw to a position and try to mount a defence. But that would eventually be futile given the numbers he faced, leading to a ignominious sur-render when either his ammunition expired or his casualties became unbearable. To stay here and do nothing would lead to just as much useless sacrifice, and he knew that the needs of the men about to land on the beach called for an assault, which, even if it failed, would occupy some of their potential opponents. It was hard to discern which was the lesser of the two evils. And there had to be a moment, given his past, when he examined his motives, to reassure himself that his reluctance to withdraw had no connection to his own vanity.

Duty demanded that they at least make the attempt. But one thing was certain. The first marine to try and scale the dunes would attract the fire of every French musket in range. It was not something he could bring himself to order any man to do, so he would have to do it himself.

Chapter four

He'd just put one foot out from behind the tree when the first field gun fired, the sharp crack of the discharge so very different from the great guns of either fort or ship. Markham span round as a second went off, followed by a rippling fire as the whole battery sent a salvo of shells over the dunes. He listened for the sound of the explosion, dreading what he was going to hear, saddened when his fears were confirmed. There was no mistaking the noise of canister, an almost dull, popping sound compared to the reverberating boom of an explosive shell.

The second wave, the soldiers from the transports, must be coming ashore. General Lacombe had been shrewd enough to place his field pieces well back, far enough from the dunes to allow enough elevation to clear both them and the trees. And he'd kept them silent, till they could wreak havoc on a beach crowded with redcoats, doing terminal damage to the assault before the navy could deploy enough firepower to suppress his cannon. The wind which had carried them onshore, and had ruffled the top branches of the pines, seemed to have died away in the last quarter of an hour, becoming no more than a slight breath. A mystery to him, it was something which would make the sailors curse. Without it, they'd have the very devil of a task to get their ships inshore to aid the landing.

'Attack coming,' yelled Rannoch, raising his musket. Markham, following the line of the barrel, could just see the blue coats of the enemy as they moved from tree to tree in a line at right angles to the beach. A careful examination showed no great numbers, nor did they seem to be advancing as fast as they might.

'Hebes, fall back and face,' Rannoch continued. 'Not one of you to fire until the order is given, do you hear me now? And we will have none of that blazing away regardless. Remember what you were taught, and discharge your weapons properly.'

'What's the state of our ammunition, Sergeant?'

Rannoch called on each man to report, which told Markham what he feared; that not one of them had more than ten rounds left, and several had only half of that. They could neither defend this position, nor mount a counter-attack that would not depend on bayonets, something given that they were a small band striking against the flank of what he knew to be a vastly superior force. All the time he was thinking, he never took his eyes off the French, who still seemed intent on drawing fire, rather than mounting an all-out assault.

'They cannot keep that up forever,' said Rannoch. 'Permission to remind them that we have a sting, sir?'

'Do you have the means?'

'I always carry an extra ration of my own manufactures.'

'Granted,' Markham replied, as the second salvo from the field guns screamed overhead.

He watched as Rannoch moved back from his tree, towards another with a small bush at its base, which had somehow survived the lack of sunlight from above. Once there he lay down, elbow crooked, and settled himself, the barrel of his Brown Bess pushed hard back into his shoulder. He'd already picked his target, Markham knew that. Some poor sod who thought his dodging from tree to tree would keep him alive was about to pay the ultimate price of not varying his movements.

Rannoch was a remarkable shot. Not willing to rely on issued musket balls for his weapon, he cast his own. The Brown Bess he owned was old, a prized possession that the Highlander loved almost more than his life. With a stock shaped to fit his shoulder, and lead balls already tested through his own barrel, he was able to reduce the normal problems caused by the notoriously inaccurate Brown Bess musket. It fired a large-calibre ball, whose route to target was easily affected by windage which, with an improperly cast ball – the case with most standard issue – could carry the shot a dozen yards off true. It was a weapon designed to do better. But, typically, British officers marched their men so close to the enemy that accuracy didn't count. Concentrated fire at close range, with reloading in twenty seconds, was the aim, therefore no attempt was generally made to improve effective long-range musketry amongst either land or sea forces.

Rannoch fired, the sound of his discharge drowned out by the shells flying overhead. But Markham saw the flash in the pan as the flintlock struck, plus, in the gloom caused by the forest canopy, the long streak of flame as the ball left the barrel. Turning to examine the result, he saw the French soldier, who had just reached the edge of the tree of safety. He jerked away from it like a rag doll, as Rannoch's shot, which at something approaching eighty yards was practically point blank to the Scotsman, smashed into his chest.

The Highlander rolled behind the trunk at his right elbow long before anyone returned a shot, pushing himself up to his feet, his hands moving automatically to reload. Wormer in and out, cartridge ripped, powder and ball rammed home. Flintlock back, horn up and tipped into the pan, with the excess gently blown clear. Rannoch was back down, elbowing into position for a second shot, within twelve seconds. Markham knew it was that long, because he'd timed him before. And another Frenchman died because he didn't think it could be done, so was standing out to fire in the gap when Rannoch killed him.

The movement of reloading was repeated, but this time Rannoch threw his hat behind the bush, then dropped down and rolled the other way, to the right of his tree, into the open. His third victim, who'd been waiting for him to appear, was showing no more than half his shoulder. But he moved out further, fatally, as he tried and failed to readjust his aim. His ball went way over Rannoch's head. The shot the Highlander fired took off the Frenchman's hat, and the top of his head with it.

'Enough!' Markham called, as Rannoch stood up again. But he didn't reload this time. He shouted for the Hebes to stand by to fire, then stuck the barrel of his musket out to drag back his hat. The fusillade of shots that kicked up the earth close to the muzzle showed just how many of the enemy were poised, nervous fingers itching at triggers, eager for him to appear. Every gun that opposed them was aimed at his tree in anticipation of his next shot. But the reply didn't come from there. As if to show they hadn't entirely forgotten how to aim, the Hebes, judging by the number of human screams that rose above those of the shells, made the enemy pay from their concentration on Rannoch.

'That was neatly done, Sergeant,' said Markham.

'It pays to learn from those you fight,' the Highlander replied. 'If you had ever seen service in the forests of North America, you would have seen a Jonathan do that in half the time. Not that officers were much given to education. They used to line us up on the roads in close order to return fire.'

A slight grin had become evident on his square face as he said those last few words, though he couldn't keep the bitterness out of his tone. The sergeant didn't like officers, a fact which he made no attempt to hide from his own.

Throughout Rannoch's firing, Markham had been trying to imagine what was happening on the beach. If his impression was correct, then the French general had used his troops and artillery wisely. He could have employed them earlier, as soon as he'd seen the route of the landing. Instead, he'd held their fire until the main body of the attackers were committed, no doubt waiting till they actually began to land before letting fly with canister. The small deadly balls would scythe through the packed troops on the shoreline, while the infantry would make sure that any attack from the marines already up the beach was held in check. The whole landing was thus in jeopardy.

It was his turn to adopt a grim smile, recalling the one adage that would cross all borders as far as soldiers were concerned. That was the simple axiom that you could never do wrong if you marched towards the sound of the guns. But Markham had his own maxims, the greatest of which was to create surprise; to do that which the enemy least expected. They were facing a French officer who knew the redcoats were in a position which was, by the minute, becoming less tenable. He would anticipate withdrawal. The last thing he would expect is to see the redcoats heading off in a new direction, on a mission every bit as suicidal as an assault on the dunes. What could twenty men achieve against the whole French defence?

Markham knew it was madness. But he also

knew it was necessary. Even if he could stop those field guns firing one or two salvos, and sacrificed everyone present to the task, he would be saving many more men on the beach. He was on the move quickly, taking advantage of the disorganisation that Rannoch had initiated and the Hebes completed, running across the face of the French, calling on his men to do likewise. Each move from tree to tree was accompanied by ragged, individual musket shots from an enemy that seemed, inexplicably, too shocked to react. That was a blessing which could not last. As soon as Markham thought them out of effective range he yelled for the party to form up more closely, using the sun, glinting through the trees above his head, to guide his course.

The line of forest wasn't deep, and as they approached open country, Markham could see the hard-packed earth of a road that stood be-tween them and the flat fields beyond, an artery that probably ran all the way along the rear of the French position. This had allowed Lacombe to deploy his field guns quickly opposite the chosen landing site. It said a great deal about the plan for the attack that, in the topography he'd been given before coming ashore, such a vital piece of in-formation had not been mentioned.

There was no time to ponder on that, but it made him turn sharp left, and he called back for everyone to move quickly and keep a sharp look-out, before sending Yelland, his fastest runner, on ahead as point. Markham had no illusions about those he'd just faced. The officer who commanded them, always assuming that he wasn't among the casualties, must guess his intentions. There was no reason for a small party of troops to head inland unless they were after the field guns, so the only chance he had of reaching them was to do so before the pursuit could get between him and his target.

'Enemy,' gasped Yelland, his chest heaving, 'at around ten of the clock, moving quick through the trees.'

The boy had stopped to impart this, which earned him a shove and a wheezing rebuke, followed by a question, from his officer. 'How close?'

''Bout three hundred yards.'

The guns were near at hand now, the sound so loud that each tree magnified the report. The still air was full of the smell of discharged powder, and Markham was sure he could actually hear the artillery officers shouting their commands. That fleeting impression was washed away by the crack of musket balls as the enemy infantry tried a long-range salvo through the trees just to slow them down.

'Bayonets, Sergeant Rannoch,' he yelled, slowing a fraction. Even with all the other sounds that assailed him, he heard the deadly scrape as well over a dozen bayonets were pulled from their scabbards, on the run, and slotted home. 'I'm going to push out onto the roadway. We have about three seconds to form up in a line, two ranks. Then it's one volley each followed by the charge, bayonets out, and screaming like fiends from hell.'

Rannoch couldn't wait. His first yell, a Highland battle cry that only he understood, rent the air as they emerged into clear country and brilliant sunlight. Yet he had the presence of mind to order that line of Hebes into place and get off the salvo Markham wanted within seconds. The Seahorses followed suit, most of them fumbling, and sending off a wild discharge that threatened their own more than the enemy.

But they followed fast enough, through fear as much as excitement, when the Hebes lowered their bayonets. They'd already run a long way, so the rush that Markham intended could not be achieved. Nor did they pause to form an unbroken line. But as soon as the gunners saw their red coats, the cry of 'Sauve qui peut' went up, especially from those nearest to the marines. Markham was at the head, sword and pistol fully extended, blessing silently one fact; that despite his fears, General Lacombe had not deemed it necessary to detach any infantry to protect his cannon.

Some gunners, even those who'd been in the act of loading, stood to fight, grabbing anything they could to protect themselves; swords, rammers, with one having the presence of mind to roll an empty barrel towards them in an attempt to slow the charge. The artillery officers came to the fore, two men, a captain and a lieutenant, trying to shout and steady their troopers at the same time as they aimed their pistols. Markham, his scarlet coat too obviously different from the red of his men's, was their target. He had to start weaving, though in doing so he exposed the men running behind him. The unwelcome yell of pain reached his ears as he jumped over the barrel, unsure of who had been hit – and not much concerned, since he looked set to run right onto one of the officers' swords.

The push in the back sent him flying, tripping over his own boots, and unable to stay upright, tumbling in a heap at the feet of the two Frenchmen. In the act of rolling to rise up, he saw in their eyes the fear that must have been present in his, as faced with a line of charging bayonets they stared death in the face. The younger of the pair had the sense to drop both his weapon and to his knees. But the captain stood his ground, and the Brown Bess, over five feet long with bayonet attached, skewered him long before he could sweep his sword down to cut at the marine officer, now struggling to rise.

The thud, as Tully clubbed the lieutenant with his butt, was right beside Markham's ear. He was on his feet just in time to yell at the marine to stop, as he raised his bayonet over the recumbent officer. For a second, he was convinced that Tully would not obey, the light of battle in his pig-like eyes was so strong. But the point stopped half an inch from the Frenchman's breast, and a shove from Markham sent Tully after his mates.

'Face left and reload.'

Markham's command was understood by only half his own men, and none of the Seahorses. Dornan, even when it was repeated, still laid about him, for once his strength an advantage over his habitual ponderous behaviour. Tully, with his best friend Hollick by his side, was stabbing right and left, even bayonetting Frenchmen who were clearly out of the combat. But Rannoch had halted, lining up Quinlan, Ettrick, Yelland and

Leech, while Halsey, sensibly, had taken Dymock and Gibbons to examine the guns, and finding one loaded, was already smashing at the elevating screw to drop the muzzle.

So, when the line of French infantry showed through the thinning trees before the gun position, there was very little to oppose them. Markham had anticipated this, just as he knew he'd be out-numbered, his only hope that they could sell their lives so dearly that the soldiers could get off that beach before the guns could be brought back into play. Rannoch had them firing at long range, just to slow the enemy down, as he yelled at the Sea-horses, milling about in confusion, to form up, while simultaneously lambasting the remaining Hebes.

It was only partially successful, not delaying the enemy for more than the time it took for their officer to get them to their feet again. They let off a fusillade of their own, at extreme range, which was rendered useless by the protection afforded to the British by the captured cannon. It was hard, given the pine trees, to make out how many of them were in the attack, but Markham was sure they were outnumbered ten times at least, with plenty more Frenchmen behind this lot should they succeed in checking them. While Rannoch controlled the reloading, he jumped on one of the rear limbers, looking desperately for a position they might retire to if they could. Re-solving to do or die was one thing, actually carry-ing it through quite another. His heart sank when he saw the terrain, though: open fields, flat and devoid of ditch or embankment.

Rannoch's voice rose over all the other noises, calling on the marines to aim, then shouting the command to fire. It was probably the first proper, controlled, volley the enemy had faced that morning, and even with so few weapons it had an effect. Even the officers out in front of their men, brandishing their swords and calling them on, hesitated. Rannoch had killed one of them before they got moving again.

Markham was about to run to join the line, his heart beating, it seemed, in time to the reloading orders, when he caught sight of Halsey out of the corner of his eye. The corporal was bent over, looking down the barrel of a cannon, a length of smouldering match in his hand. That dropped almost immediately, and the gun fired, shooting back in a recoil that lifted the front of it right off the ground. The shell, originally aimed at the beach, scythed through the trees, taking lumps out of several as it pursued an erratic course, until it ran full tilt into one trunk and exploded, sending a shower of tiny canister shot in all directions.

That was when he saw Dymock, just beyond Halsey, hacking at another elevating screw. The marine was so occupied, he didn't see the wounded artilleryman who'd risen unsteadily to his feet behind him. The Frenchman had a sword in his hand, which he raised slowly, and with difficulty, until it was above his head. Markham raised his pistol at the same time. He fired at some twenty-five feet, and took the artilleryman right in the neck. Both he and Dymock span round, the surprise on one face mirrored on the other, the difference only becoming plain when one of the pair crumpled to the ground.

Markham was already running, his eyes searching the debris of the gun position for something heavier than a musket butt. Halsey had moved too, closer to the gun Dymock was working on, and he was carrying a hammer. Rannoch was calling for his men to shoot at individual targets, taking advantage of the confusion caused amongst the French infantry by the unexpected round of canister arriving in their midst. Freed from any pressing task, Markham looked down the road along which the fleeing artillerymen had disappeared. And there he saw the first hint of another force of infantry, forming up before moving forward to retake the position and the guns.

Halsey didn't aim a second time; he just jammed the slow-match into the touch hole as soon as the muzzle dropped. This time the shell struck a tree just fifty yards away from the road, before dropping, unexploded onto the ground, the fuse still fizzing as it rolled on further. It could not have achieved more if it had been aimed, since it brought the French advance to a halt, with infantrymen diving in all directions trying to find some protection, while musket balls whistled around their ears as they did so.

'Never mind firing another gun, Halsey,' Markham cried, crouched down himself as the shell exploded. 'Use that hammer to smash the wheel.'

Then he ran over to the line of marines, calling to the remaining Seahorses to join him in tipping the guns on their sides. They were useless at musketry, from what he could see, so that was better left to his own men, few as they were. The first thing they turned on end was a limber, and Markham ordered Rannoch to get his men behind it. He had six guns to disable, and that would take at least ten minutes. Not that they'd be useless for long once the French re-took the position. But they would do what they could, and as soon as it appeared that the defence would be overwhelmed, he'd do his best to surrender with whatever men survived the coming assault.

The threat from the woods was now less than that from the road. But Markham lacked the men to suppress both, and since those amongst the trees were the closest, he let Rannoch be. Not that his sergeant wasn't aware of the danger: taller than most of his men, he could see quite clearly what was coming their way.

'Another limber across the road, sir,' he called, 'will give us more time.'

He was right, of course. But in the calculations Markham was making, it would gain them five minutes at the most. Four of the guns were now disabled, Halsey having smashed the wheel on one, while the Seahorses had tipped three others onto their sides, the top wheels spinning uselessly. But the task was taking longer than he thought. He'd done what he could, and even if the remaining artillerymen came hard on the heels of the approaching infantry they'd not get off a salvo with the two remaining pieces for a while. So he ordered the Seahorses to pull back, and started to search for something that would do as a white flag.

'French are pulling out, sir.'

'What!' Markham replied, spinning round to

look at his sergeant.

'They're moving diagonally across our front, retiring towards the fort.'

Markham looked down the road again, his heart lifting as he saw the column of infantry had stopped. Their officers were shouting and waving their swords, and over the morning air came the sound of a trumpet ordering the retreat, an order which was obeyed with steady discipline. The Frenchmen in front of Rannoch had no such luxury. They broke and ran as the first redcoats of the approaching British assault force showed through the pine trees.

Chapter five

The luxury of rest was not available, since a quick strike on the retreating enemy might sweep them past their own defences. And the senior officers who'd come ashore with the second wave were right up with the forward troops, urging them on. General d'Aubent, the army second in command, stopped to survey the damage that Markham and his small party had done to the artillery position. A taciturn man, he awarded their efforts no more than a grunt of approval, before they were ordered to join the troops under a Major Lanester who were fanning out in the fields to the rear of the road, intent on attacking the enemy flank.

Lanester, fat and red-faced, had commandeered the artillery horses, so he and his officers were now mounted, albeit bareback, and able to ride ahead. Markham, cursing, was left to walk with the infantry, so it was with some satisfaction that he saw them haul up short as they received a volley from what looked like a strong trench line. Lacombe might be short of troops, but he'd known that an invasion was possible for some time, and with only three major centres to defend, San Fiorenzo, Bastia and Calvi, he'd used the time wisely, strengthening their perimeters so that his troops fell back into prepared positions.

Lanester sent one of his captains back to organise an immediate assault, and in the confusion that followed, as the regimental officers lined up their soldiers, the small party of marines was temporarily forgotten, for which Markham was extremely grateful. He was tired and so were the men he led. Added to that they had little or no ammunition left. A further factor in holding back was that lassitude that comes after any action, a feeling of almost total sorrow, the 'black dog' which has nothing to do with success or failure.

Markham felt it the most. He'd taken terrible risks, and only the most tremendous luck had saved his little force from annihilation. Standing in the shade of an olive tree, he mentally recalled everything that had happened in the last two hours, cursing himself for the bone-headed decisions that had cost lives. It was with only half his attention that he watched the soldiers go into action, two long lines of redcoats marching across the unsown fields, trying to hold formation on the uneven ground. It had all the foolishness for which the British Army was famous, offering easy targets to even the most indifferent French shot once the men were within range.

He could see Lanester, seeming more plump now that he was mounted, waving his men forward with his hat. The questions filled Markham's mind. Why had he not waited, examined the position so that both he and his junior officers knew what they were facing; sent forward skirmishers to locate the French fire points and probe the strength of the defences?

The order to halt took him by surprise, and he wasn't alone. Whoever commanded the French troops had called on every man to aim his weapon and wait. Yet just before the point when he would have been certain to order the opening fusillade, the enemy had stopped. Several muskets, no doubt held by men too keyed up to resist, went off, and that was followed by an uneven rippling fire all along the perimeter. Lanester had his sword out now, and he waved it in a wide sweep that had his men falling back in a line just as disciplined as it had been when they were going forward.

Once they'd covered about thirty paces, they stopped again. Packs were discarded and piled to form a temporary fire point for one section, while the rest took out their entrenching tools and began to dig, oblivious to the popping fire which came from the enemy, musket balls that very occasionally found a British target. Lanester, meanwhile, rode back towards the tree under which Markham and his men rested, one officer peeling off, no doubt with a message, and heading inland to where the troops under General d'Aubent were held up on the road.

'Now that's not something I would have tried if some angel hadn't taken care of those field pieces.'

The voice was soft, American, and close up, Markham could see that Lanester was no spring chicken. Indeed he was old for his rank, the red face caused more by long exposure to the elements than what the marine officer had supposed was just over indulgence in food and drink.

'I believe I have you to thank for that, sir?'

'Lieutenant Markham, sir, and a contingent of marines from *Hebe* and *Seahorse*.' This was said as he pulled himself upright, his eyes fixed on those of the major, waiting to see if there was any reaction to the name. After a short pause, in which Lanester's face didn't move, Markham continued. 'That was neatly done, sir, the way you drew their fire.'

'Damnit,' Lanester replied, without much rancour, 'we shouldn't even be here. Our line of attack was across the beach and through the trees. This position was supposed to be taken by our Corsican allies. I'll be damned interested, and so will General Dundas, to know where they are. But that's war for you, boy, and with the slow rate of getting our own men ashore, it looks like all the plans made aboard ship are useless.'

He slid off his horse then, calling to his officers to do likewise. 'But since we look set to stay here, this tree will provide some shade for a regimental headquarters. Lieutenant Pearse.'

'Sir.'

'Mark out a defence line to fall back to if the French bring up more field guns. Deloitte, get a

64

party together and set the cannon our friend here destroyed back on their wheels, limbered up and over here. Forrest, take a messenger to General Dundas telling him what we've got and requesting new orders, plus some gunners to help us make use of the damn things. Then find the commissariat and get our supplies up here. Tell them we need everything – food, water, powder and shot.'

Lanester took a deep breath then, puffing himself up as if he was about to bellow. But what emerged did so softly, if vehemently. 'And someone find my servant and tell him if he doesn't get me some food within the next half hour, I'll skin him alive.'

As the officers rushed off to do his bidding, he turned back to Markham. 'You will join me in a late breakfast, and tell me how you found the battle quality of the enemy.'

He saw the marine officer look at his men, straggled around the field, some sitting, others lying, all exhausted. 'I'll get them fed too, never fear.'

'We should return to the beach, sir. That's where my own superiors are.'

'To do what? Act as a burial party or navvies hauling guns and stores ashore? Take my advice, Lieutenant. And if you think you need it, I will say I requested you to stay here.'

'They may be continuing with the assault.'

Lanester shook his head. 'No! We'll need to consolidate. The French have good defences round Fornali, certainly better than we thought. They also seem to possess more men than we were led to expect. And we are in double deficit thanks to our allies, extending our lines to face an enemy they should have tackled. There will be no *coup-de-main* stuff now, Markham. More'n likely we're in for a tad of a siege.'

Markham responded with a weary grin. 'We were at Toulon, sir. I don't think my men are going to be too enamoured of another siege.'

'Were you, by damn!' he exclaimed. 'Missed that action myself, which is a pity. I hear my fellow officers managed to evacuate some very valuable booty.'

The flash of distaste on Markham's face was so obvious Lanester quickly changed the subject, jerking a thumb towards Fornali. 'Well, this time you're on the outside trying to get in. A much better place to be, don't you reckon? Lacombe will have the devil's own job to hold his line even against us. And if the Corsicans do appear in strength, as they are damn well obliged to, he'll find himself having to surrender on whatever terms we choose to allow.'

The major's head jerked up and he looked past Markham's shoulder. 'Where in hell's name have you been?'

Markham turned round to see a lugubrious, long-faced individual, with grey-brown skin dotted with moles and full of wrinkles. A private, who was looking at the major as if he were tempted to strike him. He had a mule on a rope, and the animal was festooned with sacks, plus several chickens and two leather pouches which had wine bottles protruding from the top.

'If you wants fed faster, like, you'd best fetch along some decent vittles. If you don't, you waits till I's had a chance to scour.'

'Never mind your damned lip, Pavin. Get the fire alight and get cooking. And those marines in the field need tending, too. We'd still be stuck on the beach if they hadn't taken those guns.'

'I've got, like, brandy on the mule.'

'What's left of it, you mean. Time to put some work in for what you've purloined.' Pavin leant to one side, and spat slowly into the green thick grass under the tree. Then, having favoured his officer with another filthy look, he led the mule away. Lanester grinned at Markham. 'That man could find a feast and room to cook it in the Black Hole of Calcutta.'

'I take it that permits him some licence.'

'That and long acquaintance, sir. He's been with me over twenty years now.'

'Your accent is American, Major Lanester.'

'Not American, Lieutenant,' Lanester replied sharply. 'Virginian.'

Several soldiers arrived bearing used ammunition boxes, and these were arranged so that Lanester and his guest could sit down, while other were arranging stores, the collected rations of the troops still digging, which would be prepared in a makeshift field kitchen.

'I meant no offence,' Markham said.

'None taken.' The stream of messengers began then, officers and soldiers, either imparting information, requesting it, or reporting some task completed; one from General d'Aubent requiring lists of casualties, news of any Corsican reinforcement, plus information on the enemy defences and numbers, which had Lanester scribbling a long appreciation of his present position. By this time Markham had a cup of coffee in his hand, produced from the blazing fire on which Pavin was already cooking. In between he quizzed Markham, imparting as much information as he gleaned.

'Those guns should never have been allowed to deploy on that road. We were told that the Corsicans would keep Lacombe occupied, pen the French in their defences, so that we could get ashore and assault Fornali without too many casualties. We were also informed that we would face no more than five or six hundred of the enemy.'

'There were more than that deployed north of the fort this morning,' Markham said. 'And Lacombe must have other lines that need manpower. Unless he knew where we were going to land.'

'We didn't know that ourselves till last night, man. The Navy said it would depend on the wind, something they called the mezzogiorno, which blows on land in the early hours, then spins round and does the reverse at night.'

'Lacombe couldn't have guessed that, could he?'

'You'd think not,' Lanester replied, as a messenger arrived and handed him a note. He examined it for a moment, then opened his map case to study that. He looked up at Markham again, turning the case round so that he could see the outline of the deep bay, plus the contours of Cap Corse which ran north, the high range of mountains forming a spine down the middle. The major's finger moved as he spoke, pointing out the important features, plus the positions of the local forces.

'The Corsicans are still stuck on the other arm of the bay. They've now undertaken to attack towards Patrimonio and Barbaggio. That's the route to Bastia, which is the only way that Lacombe can get out of here, if he decides to go.'

'And if they close the pass?' Markham asked, pointing at a gap in the mountains called the Colla di Tregima. Lanester just raised his hand and ran a finger across his throat. Markham spread two fingers, to measure the distance between the present Corsican position, and where he and the major now sat. 'They're a long way from where they're supposed to be.'

Lanester waved the note he'd received, a hasty scribble on thin yellowing paper. 'Perhaps the locals are not much at anything other than slow marching. Anyway, this is their latest proposal. All we have to do, it seems, is drive the Frenchies into their arms.'

'Vittles,' shouted Pavin, 'by which if 'n you want them hot, you best shift.'

'What about those marines?'

'Saw to 'em first, as you damn well ordered, which is the first time I ever put a Lobster before a real soldier.'

'I subscribe to the theory that it is sometimes necessary to disobey orders, Colonel. If one sees an opportunity to affect the course of a battle, it is best taken, don't you think?'

Nelson was enjoying himself, and that statement only added to the fury evident in Hanger's face. This operation had given rise to the usual arguments between the two branches of the military.

Lord Hood had complete freedom to put a landing force wherever they wanted to go, but also a pressing need for a good safe anchorage. San Fiorenzo, in the deep bay created by the long arm of Cap Corse, provided that. The Army, under General Dundas, was happy to comply, seeing it as the weakest of the three towns the French held.

Hanger's actual position, here on the beach, was somewhat anomalous. Having professional soldiers to hand, Hood was shrewd enough to use them to take command when landing his marines. But with that successfully completed, and the commanding general still aboard *Victory*, he had no executive function. He'd already been informed that, since Lieutenant Markham was a marine officer, his disobedience of direct instructions should be seen in the light of their result, and in any case he lay beyond the jurisdiction of an army officer to question.

Unaware of what exactly had occurred after the evacuation of Toulon, Hanger had been ignorant of the fact that Markham was no longer a soldier. He'd been commissioned into the marines, and given his present rank, at the personal behest of Admiral Hood, based on the recommendation of his own nephew, the captain of the frigate *Juno*.

'Then may I say, Captain Nelson,' Hanger hissed, 'that if the right to disobedience is a tenet of seaborne warfare, the Navy has a strange way of going about its business.'

You had to look closely to see the face change, the narrowing of the eyes and shrinking of the cheeks almost imperceptible. Nelson turned away slightly, as if to check on the progress of the land-

70

ing, looking along a strand now full of marines and sailors, busy hauling the equipment necessary to besiege San Fiorenzo onto the shore.

'I don't think, as a service, sir, we have to apologise to anyone, especially King George's army.'

Markham didn't know Nelson well. If asked, he would have put him down as the co-operative type, more inclined to flatter a bullock officer than put him in his place. But he'd done just that in reminding Hanger that, if you excused the odd hiccup, the Navy had enjoyed almost continuous success in war for a hundred years. The way Hanger responded was typical, since he wasn't the type to stand condescension from anyone, and in doing so, he pricked on the greatest running sore in recent inter-service history.

'Not even for Chesapeake Bay?'

Markham, standing close to the scarred face of his old enemy, had a sudden vision of that campaign in the Carolinas. Of his own personal pain, mixed with the memory of the successes that General Cornwallis had enjoyed before being forced back, through lack of supplies and reinforcements, and his own casualties. Yorktown, the base he expected to hold, turned out to be the point of surrender, Cornwallis and his men trapped between the more numerous Continental Army, and a French fleet that the Royal Navy had been unable to dislodge.

'I daresay your new marine lieutenant remembers,' Hanger continued, glaring at Markham.

'I remember, sir, how the army behaved. Or, at least, the cavalry of Tarleton's British Legion.'

Hanger reddened then, and Markham was

about to continue, to elaborate on some of the disgraceful activities, not least rape and murder, that the British Legion had indulged in. But Nelson, unseen by Hanger, was shaking his head, in a way that looked like a direct order to desist. Luckily, Markham saw the black face, so obvious against the white canvas on the passing stretcher, which gave him an excuse to comply.

The men carrying the stretcher were heading to the point set up by a Navy surgeon, a temporary field hospital under an awning. The sawbones was already working with his assistants on those wounded in the attack. His detachment, both Hebes and Seahorses, well fed and rested, had formed another party under Rannoch's command to help with the unloading of the naval guns.

'With your permission, sir,' he said, addressing Nelson.

The captain followed his eye, then nodded. 'Carry on, Markham.'

Hanger hissed angrily again, and as he left them he could hear the colonel still complaining bitterly about his behaviour, a litany that his naval contemporary seemed determined to absorb in silence. Markham caught up with the stretcher, to find Bellamy suffering from a blow to the back of the skull that had probably rendered him unconscious. Now he was moaning softly, his eyes glazed and unfocused as he rolled his head back and forth.

Recalling what had happened during that attack, Markham could only remember one man standing to the rear of Bellamy, and that was Rannoch. The idea that his sergeant had inflicted such a blow was hard to believe. Certainly the Highlander was tough and uncompromising. But he was also, to Markham's certain knowledge, the type to care for any man placed under his command.

'What happened to you, Bellamy?'

'Don't know,' the Negro mumbled. 'Something hit me.'

Markham was crouched over him as they entered the shade of the awning, examining the wound more closely. Several inches long, the cut showed through the tight curls, which were matted with blood. He couldn't be sure, but it looked as though the marine had taken a hard blow from something very like the butt of a musket. The men carrying him put the stretcher down at the end of a row of casualties. Judging by the number, and the state of their wounds, it would be some time before the surgeon, bloodstained, cursing and swearing as he worked, would get round to this particular patient.

'Water, please,' he called to one of the loblolly boys, tending to those waiting as well as the men who'd already been under the knife. The sickbay attendant, a scarecrow with sunken cheeks, carried a leather water bucket and a ladle. He came over and looked down, first at the round black face, then at the officer. Markham reached into his uniform and produced a purse.

'Take this,' he said, holding out a couple of shillings. 'And make sure he's looked after till the surgeon's ready.'

'Thick skulled, them darkies,' the man replied, shaking his long, skeletal face as he indicated the

73

gash on Bellamy's head. 'And lazy, from what I've observed in the Sugar Islands. Scrimshanking, most like, and could get up and tend to himself if he had a mind.'

'He needs stitches in his head, and someone to make sure his skull isn't cracked.'

'Then he'll be here till doomsday, what with Mr Lewis lopping off legs and arms. Welsh he may be, but he'll not put no blackamoor afore one of his own. He'll be lancing boils before he gets round to this creature.'

Markham looked at the surgeon's back, at a filthy grey shirt streaked with the dark stain of excessive perspiration. To appeal to Lewis would probably be counter-productive. All he could do was leave Bellamy here, and drop by occasionally to see if he'd been treated. He stood up, passing over the coins.

'Then make sure he doesn't die of thirst.'

'Happily,' the loblolly boy replied, lifting his leather bucket and tipping it over Bellamy's face. The Negro sat up suddenly, shaking his head, and cursing in an unintelligible tongue. The medical attendant looked at Markham triumphantly, with a toothless grin. 'See, I told you he was lead-swingin', didn't I just?'

'Which ship are you off?' Markham demanded.

'*Agamemnon.*'

'Then I'll have you know that your captain is a personal friend. So if you don't want to find yourself out of this cushioned billet, digging trenches, you'll do as I ask.'

'I'll take care of him, all right, your honour,' the man replied, completely unabashed. Then he laughed, exposing his gums again. 'Can't let him pass over, can I. If a sweep brings you luck with a dirty face and hands, stands to reason this crow will bring on double.'

'Markham!'

He recognised the voice well before he turned to face Captain Richard de Lisle, the commanding officer of the *Hebe*. Standing in the entrance, against the white bright sand, he was no more than a tubby silhouette. Small, compact and a stickler for his *amour propre*, he didn't realise how such a position demeaned him.

'Sir.'

'I watched you disobey your orders coming ashore, and Bernard has confirmed that your deviation was deliberate. And what am I subjected to the minute I myself land? Colonel Hanger giving me chapter and verse about your damned insubordination.'

'Have you, sir?' Markham replied. He felt suddenly weary, too tired to stand to attention. The sun might be deflected by the awning, but the breeze had fallen away and the late afternoon heat was trapped and stifling in the confined space. Lanester's food, which had revived him originally, was now inducing its own postprandial torpor. Normally, facing de Lisle, he stood rigidly to attention and never looked the man in the eye. This was not through fear, but from a desire to avoid the little smirks that touched the captain's lips every time he delivered one of his insults.

Forced to weigh anchor from the Nore with the rest of the fleet, and told that he would have to take soldiers aboard to make up for his lack of

75

proper marines, de Lisle had hit the cabin roof when he'd found out the identity of the officer who led them. He was careful to avoid the word bastard, having already discovered such a barb might cause Markham to strike a blow. But there were plenty of other cracks in his locker for an illegitimate rake, a known duellist who clearly lacked two guineas to rub together. That applied even if his natural father had been a full general, since dead parents had no influence. Hints that Markham was a Papist, and should never have been given a commission in the first place, surfaced often, as did references to what had happened in the American war during and after the Battle of Guildford.

If George Markham had withstood these insults with seeming fortitude, it was only through long exposure. There had hardly been a time in his life when he'd not been vulnerable to such gibes from some source. His parentage, when he was a child, had been no mystery. With a wealthy Protestant father not married to a middling Catholic mother, he'd fallen foul of both religious groups, an outsider to one and a traitor to the other. That had at least taught him to fight from a very early age, especially since Sir John Markham refused to follow the practice of his ascendancy peers and ignore his very existence.

He not only acknowledged George as his child; he visited both him and his mother regularly, and such was his standing locally that he forced others to acknowledge them too, though the fact that they resented the need was ill disguised. School in Dublin had been little better than Wexford. He'd known peace when Sir John, as Governor of New York, had taken him to America, and allowed the boy to revel in the life of a Headquarters brat. To be gazetted an Ensign in the 65th foot was a dream come true, and he'd marched to war against the colonists, head high and proud. But that had all ended in his first real battle.

If relations with the ship's captain had been bad from the start, they were now even worse. Hood's intention to allow him a marine commission had sent de Lisle into a towering rage, during which he'd written an intemperate letter to the Admiral. The reply, couched with equal severity, and including a reminder to the captain of a 24-gun frigate of precisely where he stood in the naval hierarchy, had first cast him down. But it wasn't too long before it caused him to redouble his efforts to undermine the person he blamed for the whole affair, a task in which he was aided by every other officer aboard the *Hebe*. Personal dislike was now supported by the belief that Markham had, by making the Admiral angry, blighted all their prospects.

'I await an explanation, sir,' snapped de Lisle, dragging Markham back to reality.

'I did what all my experience suggested was correct, sir. If that displeases Colonel Hanger it can only be because he is ignorant of war, or a damned fool. I suggest you speak to either General d'Aubent or Major Lanester, who will give you a true appreciation of what we achieved.'

'According to Colonel Hanger, you sat uselessly on the enemy flank until the army attacked and took the French field guns. Then you appeared out

77

of the woods when the enemy was in retreat, and it was safe to do so.'

'And you, sir, like a fool, believed him.'

'How dare you speak to me in that tone! Might I remind you that you carried the honour of my ship in your actions? And once again you appear to have been found wanting.'

Markham blew then, the strength of his voice seeming to move the still air under the awning. 'The honour of your vessel, sir, is akin to your own, and would not comfortably reside in a flea carried by a ship's rat.'

'You will withdraw that remark!'

'No, sir, I will not.'

De Lisle didn't shout in reply. In fact, his voice was soft and silky, as if he had achieved some prior purpose. 'You will consider yourself under arrest, Lieutenant, until such time as I can convene a court. Colonel Hanger may not be able to haul you before the judgment of the Army, but given your present status, I will be able to see you brought before a naval hearing. I'll see you damned, Markham, as much for what you are as for the gross insubordination which you have demonstrated since we left Chatham.'

'Did Colonel Hanger hint at a reward for this, or actually promise you something tangible?'

De Lisle reacted as though he'd been slapped. Yet, once that shot in the dark had been fired, it was so obvious. His captain was a climber, with all the attributes of the type, which included an ability to sacrifice both principles and people to ambition. Hanger was very rich, and well connected in both London and the Mediterranean. At home, he caroused in the company of the Prince of Wales. Here, he'd lately become betrothed to Lizzie Gordon, the niece of another man of influence, the recently ennobled and promoted Admiral Lord Keith.

'I should be wary of him, Captain de Lisle,' Markham continued. 'Colonel Hanger has the morals of a snake.'

'I doubt your opinion of his moral standing would impress the colonel much.'

'This arrest, Captain. Does it confine me to the ship?'

'No, it does not,' snapped de Lisle. 'We are far too short-handed to have you skulking in your cabin. You may go about your duties. And if there is a god for a heathen like you, then perhaps he will see fit to arm a French ball to take off your insolent head.'

'There won't be one for you, sir. They do not have sufficient range.'

The silhouette turned sideways, and de Lisle spoke softly. 'Mr Bernard.'

The midshipman was outside, in the sunlight. Markham wasn't sure, as the boy stepped into view, if his face was red from excessive heat or embarrassment. And he kept his eyes resolutely on the face of the captain, not willing to engage those of the marine officer.

'You will have overheard every word exchanged here?' said de Lisle.

'Sir,' the boy replied noncommittally.

'Good,' the captain responded, unaware of Bernard's lack of enthusiasm. 'You will be called at Mr Markham's court, and you will be asked to repeat what he said.'

The silhouette was square-on again, but Markham didn't have to use much imagination to put a smirk on the pasty round face. 'We will see if half a dozen naval captains take kindly to the notion of a marine officer of this ilk. One who disobeys orders with impunity, and chooses also to call his commander's bravery into account.'

'Don't leave out your motives, sir,' said Markham.

'Have you turned in your army commission yet?'

'Yes,' Markham lied.

De Lisle, knowing how strapped he was for cash, must have supposed he'd done so. After all, he'd come aboard at Chatham with the bailiffs on his heels, further evidence of his raffish nature. Not that a lieutenant's commission was worth much, especially in a normal line regiment like the 65th. What the captain didn't know was that the commission in question was the last gift he had had from his late father. Since Sir John had died while he was serving in Russia, his half-sister Hannah had demanded back every penny that his natural father had gifted him. Even if he had no use for it, he'd keep that commission till his dying day.

For once de Lisle actually snorted, so great was his pleasure. And the irony in his tone was pitched too high to be anything other than contrived.

'That's a damned shame, Markham. You've gone and sold the only thing that might be of use to you. And God knows, you'll never get one back on your own account.'

De Lisle turned then and marched out into the bright light. As he stopped by Bernard he took a deep breath that made his whole frame swell up, as though to emphasise that he'd just concluded a very satisfactory interview.

Chapter six

There was a method to a siege which paid very little heed to notions of terrain and numbers. First, the enemy had to be denied any chance of sending out foraging parties to bring in food to the beleaguered garrison, which meant close investment of all means of escape. Then, having examined the perimeter defences, General Dundas picked the point at which he wished to attack. The beach area offered the best approach, since floating bomb vessels could give close flank support. Artillery, in this case naval guns and mortars, was brought up to bombard the walls and effect a breach, while the Army, with plenty of wood to hand, began to sap forward through the sand, to create revetted trench lines inching ever closer to the point at which the final assault would be launched.

Little glory could be expected in the preparation, only work: digging and sawing, dragging logs, carrying ammunition for the guns, or taking supplies of food and water up to the forward positions. Markham and his men were almost exclusively occupied with servicing the naval cannon, 32 pounders which had been put ashore with true naval efficiency. The officers of Hood's fleet had skills in moving heavy ordnance which drew quiet praise from General Dundas's engineering staff. They seemed to be able to construct no end of tripods, ropes and pulleys, so that getting the huge four-ton cannon out of heavily laden boats, then swinging them across the beach to the fascined roadway that Hanger had constructed, was made to appear like child's play.

Embankments had already been thrown up to house them, secure emplacements that were a mixture of pine logs and sand. With even more men from the fleet bringing ashore the gunners and ammunition, the 32-pounders were in action against Fornali at first light the next morning, aided by the line-of-battle ships which came inshore to bombard the seaward walls.

The general opinion was that Lacombe would have to ask for terms within a week at most. Confirmation of Corsican movements above the passes leading to Bastia, even if they hadn't actually invested Fornali, gave him no other option. The French were still fighting to hold it open, but it was a desperate task, only aided by the islanders' desire to avoid excessive casualties in an action which all believed would do little to affect the eventual outcome.

Markham seemed to have inherited the Sea-horses without anyone giving him specific orders to do so; not surprising with their own officer and NCOs dead, and their ship detached to carry dispatches to Admiral Hotham, Hood's second in command, cruising off Toulon. They set up a camp just inside the woods, retrieving their packs off the beach, then begging, borrowing and stealing those things which they didn't receive by right. Markham's own kit, completely forgotten about since the landing, had been slung ashore, probably by one of Bernard's sailors, who'd had no interest in the fact that Lieutenant Croppie's equipment landed in the water. Thankfully it contained very few perishables; an extra pistol, powder, balls and the necessaries for cleanliness. His spare shirts had dried fast enough, as had the powder, and Rannoch had undertaken to clean his weapons personally.

Once the bombardment commenced, with lines of seamen ready to resupply, there was little for the men to do but wait for the actual assault, and they were permitted some very well deserved rest. Markham, despite the noise of the cannon, slept like a log throughout the rest of the day, and only woke as it was getting dark. Exiting from the tent Rannoch had found him, he felt the wind coming off the land, a breeze which, for the second day running, had pushed the bombarding ships off their station. But still the orange glow of the shore-based fire lit the darkening sky, and awake, he could hear the balls crashing into the stone walls of the fort, slowly but surely creating a breach in the thick masonry. He watched for a while as the last of the light faded, until the guns were housed for the night, and the firing ceased.

Around him, his men slept or sat quietly talking round their fires, several of them bandaged where they'd suffered slight wounds. The Seahorses occupied one fire, separate from his Hebes. In both cases, their muskets, cleaned and gleaming, stood in orderly stacks ready for use. The smell that assailed his nostrils, a mixture of pine resin, warm gun oil and tobacco, was pleasant. That was, until it conjured up memories of other forests, and other encampments, where the same ingredients had been present, and death and destruction had come with the dawn.

'Dornan, some hot water, if you please.'

'Sir.'

The marine got to his feet and looked at him, while Markham waited for the information to seep into his brain. Round of face, with eyes that always seemed surprised, Dornan was sometimes more of a liability than an asset. Being slow-witted, he was often the butt of jokes from the sharper members of the unit, especially the two Londoners, Quinlan and Ettrick. Finally the marine bent and picked up a kid, which he dipped into the pot on the fire, spilling enough to kill half the flames and earn him a curse from his mates. Markham took the container off him and re-entered his tent. The small polished silver mirror, lit by one candle, gave off precious little light, and it threw his lean face into the kind of deep shadow that made him, not for the first time in his life, curse the shaving ritual.

But a hand across the square chin confirmed the need for the razor, the stubble thick and black in contrast to the dark brown of his tousled hair. The eyes were still full of sleep, grey pupils made cat-like as they picked up a flicker from the candle. He threw a handful of the hot water on his face before lathering up, and shaved round it, careful close to the numerous small scars that stood testimony to the number of wounds he'd sustained, not all of them from soldiering.

He knew he should really have an orderly, some-one to brush his coat, wash his shirts and breeches, clean his boots and shave him on de-mand. But servants, in his experience, were a venal crew, who engendered greater worry than they saved, more interested in what they could steal than in making their master comfortable. When they cooked, most of the food, chosen to suit their own palate, was wont to disappear down their throats, just like the wine. And woe betide the officer who left money or valuables lying around. There were exceptions to that, of course, personal attendants who would lay down life and limb for their master. But George Markham had never met one. Not in Ireland, England, America or Russia. So until he did, he'd see to his own needs, eating whatever food was put before him aboard ship, and joining his men on everyday rations in the field.

That thought made him smile, showing teeth white enough to match the creamy lather. There was a sort of hypocritical piety to such thoughts, given the life he'd led in London before being forced, by penury and the threat of arrest, to take up his army commission. Hard tack and salt beef it was not, though a wiser head might have made it so. But George Tenby Markham had lived high in his time, had a modicum of charm and Irish wit, and also believed in the old adage that it was necessary to speculate to accumulate. If he wan-ted to acquire a fortune, he felt he must spend as though he already owned one.

So he'd lived the life of a gentleman of the town, eating well, and sometimes drinking to excess, gambling just enough to be considered a player, attending balls, routs and rallies at Vauxhall and Ranelagh, and pursuing his love of all things gracious, especially the ladies, married and single, of the circles he'd moved in. He was drawn to the theatre especially, not only by a love of drama, but by the nature of the people who lived the thespian life. There was little hypocrisy in such a world, and much excitement.

The events of that period, when he'd returned from fighting the Turks on behalf of the Czarina Catherine, tended to break down into the duration of his romantic liaisons. Images of the women he'd made love to floated through his mind; faces, bodies and preferences in a joyful reverie. That ended abruptly when he recalled the unfortunate meeting at Finsbury Park, where he'd put a ball into the Comte des Ardres, a French emigré nobleman who, quite naturally, took great exception to finding George Markham in bed with his wife.

He swore, at the end of every affair, that it would be the last, a promise that had never yet survived a sideways glance or even a waft of seductive perfume. And as he removed the last of the lather from his ears and nose, he looked at a face now bronzed and lean instead of puffy and powdered. It was good to be here in Corsica, on active service, away from the temptations which had so often been his downfall.

The coat looked like what it was, a garment to fight in. It hadn't started that way, of course, although it had never been much in the way of finery. But crawling through dunes and pine forests and charging field gun emplacements had done little to improve the look of the thick scarlet cloth, even in weak candlelight. One of his gold aiguillettes had been clipped by a ball, and required to be trimmed with scissors. Grease from a cannon wheel had left a streak across the white facings, and there was a tear in his breeches which could only be hidden by pulling his stockings higher. With a final slap producing a puff of dust, he jammed his hat on his head and came out of the tent.

Looking around a second time he saw the Negro, Bellamy, perched on a log right on the edge of their encampment, stirring a pot over a small blaze. His head was swathed in a thick white bandage that contrasted sharply with his coal-black face, the skin so shiny that his cheeks picked up the orange from the dancing flames.

Rannoch was on his own too, bent over another fire, holding a tin pot in which he was melting the lead from standard issue musket balls. The cast he was using, which he'd scrounged off the *Hebe*'s armourer, lay to one side, by the bucket of water he needed to cool them. The first time he'd seen Rannoch at work, it had contained the old piece of barrel he used to test them. But that, along with everything else they'd owned, had been abandoned in Toulon, a place they'd escaped from with little more than their flapping shirts. Markham, out of the corner of his eye, watched Rannoch working as he moved through the rest of the men, checking on those who were awake, inquiring after wounds, hurts and lost equipment, until he was close enough to his sergeant to speak.

'Where are you going to get the barrel to test them?'

'I am using my own right now,' Rannoch replied, without looking up. 'Slipping it just home to see if it fits. It is not perfect but it will have to do.'

'The Army have supplies aboard the transports, muskets from every manufactuary in the land. And I am willing to bet that some of them are old stock.'

'But are they true to my barrel?' Rannoch said, looking at him. Then he picked up his own Brown Bess, the firelight picking out the sheen of the stock, and the gleam of polished brass on the firing plate. 'The piece I used before was cast by the same hand as this musket, though I will grant it was not at the same time. But they were true to each other. Only by luck will I find another like it.'

Markham was dying to ask where he'd got the originals, both musket and barrel. But that was just one of the dozens of questions which Rannoch did not care to answer. He kept his past to himself, which to a naturally inquiring mind was a form of torture. Was there a wife, a family somewhere, brothers, sisters? Where and why had he got that brand on his thumb, and what had happened to make his hatred of officers so deep and abiding? They'd become as friendly as a lieutenant and a sergeant could, Rannoch careful to preserve the necessary distinctions, so that he would not get too familiar with Markham. More importantly, this ensured his superior couldn't get too informal with him. This was fundamental for the proper maintenance of discipline. But inside those very essential constraints, they trusted each other, an accolade Markham had earned, and not one that the Highlander seemed prepared to bestow on any other superior.

'Why is Bellamy sitting alone?'

Rannoch's back stiffened slightly, as though he saw the question as a rebuke. 'When he came back, he took one look at the Seahorses around their fire, and moved away.'

'He could have sat with our men, could he not?'

'He did not ask them, sir, and neither did I.'

The check on Markham was in the 'sir', which was not an appellation often found on Rannoch's lips. And it was also in the stiff way his sergeant was holding himself, a plain statement that any further questions on the subject would be very unwelcome. That made Markham angry.

'At the moment, Sergeant, though I haven't asked for it, he's my responsibility.'

'Then do him a kindness and send him to run errands for the surgeon.'

'No!' Markham snapped, standing up.

'That is the right you have as an officer,' Rannoch replied, without looking up. 'Just as I have a duty as a sergeant to point out to you that the presence of that man could well make bother.'

'Did you see who hit him on the beach, Rannoch?'

It was a question he'd been determined not to ask, because it could do nothing but cause trouble. In some senses his own duty demanded that. The men had their own way of settling differences amongst themselves, and every officer worth his salt respected it. But now Rannoch pulled himself upright, to tower over his officer. And when their eyes locked there was neither deference nor fear in those of the Scotsman.

'I did.'

Markham was surprised rather than angry. 'Why?'

'Because if I had not, the Seahorses would never have followed me down that gully. And who knows what might have happened if they had sat still? I had no idea of the damage done by those mortars. You, and all the men we survived Toulon with, could now be dead.'

Markham turned away, totally at a loss. If Rannoch was anything, he was considerate to any man who served with him. Yet in his eyes, when he had answered, there had been a hint of something other than expediency. And Bellamy must know that the Highlander had cracked his skull with his musket. No wonder he was sitting alone. It seemed feeble, a mere gesture, to go and talk to Bellamy instead of reprimanding Rannoch, but that was all he could think of to do, firstly to re-assure the Negro, and secondly to let the High-lander know that should he fancy repeating the blow, Markham wouldn't tolerate it.

'I'm glad to see you have recovered,' he said, in-dicating that Bellamy, who'd started to rise, should stay seated. He was aware that behind him all conversation had ceased. 'I hope the surgeon did a proper job.'

When Bellamy replied, Markham was again struck by the quality of his speech. There was a minor colonial twang to it for sure, but it was no more than that, and certainly it was not the voice of an ignorant slave.

'He could hardly stand, he'd taken so much rum. I fear my head will resemble a patchwork quilt when it heals, of the variety made by country folk eager to fleece the unwary traveller.'

'Then let's hope the hair grows thick to cover it.'

'That is one thing I do not have to be concerned about. The hair on my head grows as thick as my skull.'

Now those eyes, dark brown with huge whites, were fixed on his. And that made Markham look away, since he knew he was being invited by Bellamy to comment on who had hit him. The marine could see his discomfort, and after only a short pause he continued.

'I have yet to thank you for saving my life before that.'

'I was happy to do it.'

The thick lips split into a wide, tooth-filled grin. 'Even if you nearly drowned yourself?'

'You should learn to swim, Bellamy.'

'That, sir, is to invite either crocodiles or sharks to feast off my flesh. The stuff of nightmares, I think, and I must own, because of it, to having an abhorrence of water any deeper than my ankles.'

'Yet you are a marine.' Bellamy's eyes dropped, and now it was Markham's turn to be introducing a subject that the other party didn't want to pursue. 'All in all, you've had a poor welcome to the island of Corsica.'

'A fitting one, if Seneca is to be believed.'

'Seneca?' asked Markham, unable to hide his

surprise at a soldier, let alone a Negro one, using the name.

'He was banished here. He said, *Quid tam nudum inveneri potest...*'

'Please Bellamy,' Markham protested, 'do not labour my weak Latin.'

The Negro grinned again. '"What could be so barren, so rugged all around as this rock? What more wanting of provisions, what more rude in its inhabitants?" There is more, much more, none of it flattering.'

'What are you doing here, Bellamy?'

For the first time, the marine adopted the voice that Markham had heard every other time he'd met a Negro. 'Ah fit for King George, boss.'

'And how often does King George fight you?'

Bellamy understood immediately. 'It is ignorance, sir, which brings retribution for slights imagined around my ears. I do not hold my place in the eyes of others as nature's gift. And I also own that I do not help matters by parading what erudition I have been blessed with.'

'It is unusual.'

That made him slightly angry. 'There is not a man I have served with, sir, even one blind with prejudice, who would not benefit from the education gifted to me.'

'By whom?'

'Archimedes Bellamy, my late master. A great human being. He schooled me in order to prove that a man of Africa was as good as any European, the only difference being in the teaching.'

'He seems to have succeeded remarkably well.'

'Thank you, sir.'

92

'Is his death anything to do with your presence here?'

Bellamy's eyes dropped, and the answer came in a whisper. 'Everything. And being of a scientific bent, I daresay he would be curious to see whether I will die at the hands of the King's enemies, or of the jealousy and prejudice of one of his subjects.'

Markham laid a hand on the black marine's shoulder. 'Do not fear to turn your back while you're under my command, Bellamy, regardless of what happened today.'

'That may cause you more difficulties than you can yet appreciate, sir.'

'Sergeant Rannoch.'

The response cut across the continuing silence at his back. 'Sir!'

'This marine is under my personal protection. No punishment is to be inflicted on him, by anyone, without my express permission. Do you understand?'

'I do, sir.'

Markham turned slowly, to allow those who'd been staring at him time to avert their gaze. All did so except Sharland, who was glaring with undisguised loathing. 'Bellamy will eat with us, march with us, fight with and possibly die with us. But if he receives so much as a scratch from anyone other than the enemy, the person who inflicts it will wish he was a leper.'

Both the Army and the Navy had set up facilities for the officers ashore. Neat rows of tents lay under the shade of the pines, the avenue that had been cut between them now part of the gun emplacements. Two long, high, canvas marquees near the dunes provided a mess for each service to dine in. Very close to each other, with long tables down the middle, the blaze of candles that illuminated the interiors showed the movement of every individual inside. Markham could see, as he approached, cups of wine being raised in toasts to the anticipated success of the siege.

The command posts were just in front of these, smaller affairs in the main, the only one to match the dimensions of the messes that of General Dundas himself. Under lanterns, staff officers busied themselves making lists and plans, each tent-front open to the cool night air, as well as the admiring gaze of those the occupants wished to impress with their zeal. As if to emphasise the duality of the enterprise, the navy had its own command post, with marine sentries at the door. The most striking feature of this was the fact that though the distance from one to the other wasn't great, there was no hint of traffic between them.

Organised as it looked, it was somewhat meagre compared with the tent cities he'd lived in when on campaign in Russia. There, the men who led the huge armies of the Czarina were great princes of the state. And they lived as such, their ententments made of silk, not canvas, the interiors floored with parquet, lit like royal palaces and filled with fine furniture. This display of oriental splendour was well matched by the glories of their table, feasts so splendid that, on the few occasions he'd tried to describe them to others, he'd not been believed.

Markham noticed some oddly dressed creatures at the end of the main tent, standing in a group: soldiers in short, dun-coloured serge jackets, tight black breeches and singular headgear. Red in colour, the caps they wore were tight-fitting, any excess above the crown flopping to one side like a rooster's coxcomb. The men themselves, conversing quietly, were compact, swarthy and moustached. He had just put out a foot to head for the naval marquee when the mellifluous Virginian voice of Major Lanester stopped him.

'This is a damn fine set up, ain't it, son? Just like being on spring manoeuvres.'

'It's a long time since I did any of that, sir.'

'Major André, as I recall, was rather fond of them.'

That made Markham stop dead. 'You knew André?'

'I did. Just as I knew your father. In fact, young 'un, I have more than half a feeling that you and I have met before, at a time when you were still a Headquarters brat. You'd yet to join the colours, of course.'

Markham was about to apologise. As Governor of New York, his father had been host to an endless stream of visitors, military and civilian. To remember them all was impossible, especially those loyalists, numerous and very vocal, who'd sided with King George against their fellow colonists. He'd suspected Lanester to be of that hue the minute he heard him speak, one of the hundreds of thousands of men, women and children who paid with everything for their adherence to the crown. But the idea of saying sorry died in his throat, the wistful look in Lanester's eyes making it superfluous.

'Unhappy days,' said Lanester.

Markham remembered them differently. First of all, there was the feeling of freedom bestowed on him merely by being away from the stifling hypocrisy of his background. For probably the only time in his life he felt he really belonged, and that he stood as an equal to the legitimate members of his father's family. In New York he, not half-brother Freddy, was General Markham's son. And if Sir John was a bit of a rough diamond, who'd himself risen from the ranks, he had ten times the power in the Americas that he'd enjoyed as the senior officer of the Wexford military district. To offend such a person was the height of foolishness, holding as he did the key to so much influence and wealth. With a fortune already under his belt, Sir John Markham grabbed the chance to make another. With a war in progress, and in control of the main manufacturing base in the colony, there was no lack of opportunity.

'How well did you know André?' asked Markham, feeling, with some guilt, that the question was posed merely to make conversation.

Lanester took his arm, pulling him gently towards the army marquee. 'Well enough to introduce him to an American General called Benedict Arnold.'

Markham stopped. That acquaintance had cost André, a man he'd liked enormously, his life. But Lanester just pulled a bit harder, as he continued talking, the glum look he'd had earlier replaced by a smile.

'I find it hard to face the past, young 'un. But it is best done. If you feel the same, come and dine with me.'

'Is Colonel Hanger in there?'

'He's rarely far from the open bottle, and that's a truth. But he just might be with General Dundas, who is entertaining several Corsican officers from across the bay.' He flicked a hand towards the group of strangely-dressed soldiers outside the general's tent. 'That there is the escort, and as rum-looking a bunch as their masters.'

Markham, while he hated Hanger, knew that the Colonel wasn't the only one who was aware of his past. The prospect of someone else baiting him was significant.

'I fear I must decline.'

'I learned years ago that you cannot run forever.'

Markham spat out his reply to that. 'I'm not running, Major Lanester. But neither do I welcome condescension from fellow officers who may well have drowned their manners in drink.'

'Especially Colonel Hanger, I suspect.'

'For a very good reason, sir. He may well be present, and one chance remark from that bastard and I might kill him where he sits.'

He was about to go on, to say that, while he was not prepared to swing for the action, he'd kill Hanger one day, regardless. All he needed was the colonel in an open field, preferably at dawn, with either a pistol or a sword in his hand. But even inside his own head, as the words formed, they sounded too much like bombast. He detached his arm from the hand of Major Lanester, pulled himself stiffly to attention, then saluted.

'Thank you, sir, but I really must decline.'

'As you wish, Markham,' Lanester replied, his voice full of sadness. 'But one day you must dine with me again. I have a feeling that with you, talking over old times might be less depressing than is the norm.'

Chapter seven

The major stopped, bending to brush the damp, sticky sand off his highly-polished boots, before lifting the heavy tent flap. The noise level grew as he did so, and a wall of warm, smoke-filled air touched both their faces. Then Lanester was gone, his voice loud and cheerful as he called for a bottle of claret to be brought to him at once. Markham turned away from both marquees, feeling that the welcome he'd receive in the naval one might well match that of the army, especially if any of *Hebe*'s officers were present. Besides, the celebratory noises coming from both tents suddenly seemed absurd, here in the middle of a battle, one that would see a pile of dead and maimed filling the breach that the cannon had spent the whole day attempting to create.

He made his way down to the beach, to the water's edge, looking at the well-lit ships that filled the anchorage, shivering slightly in the cold, late February air. The sky was clear above, a mass of stars that ended abruptly at the edge of a thick black cloud. Beyond the fleet he could see the other side of the bay, the western shore of Cap Corse, dotted with hundreds of pinpricks of light on the heights which overlooked San Fiorenzo. These must belong to the Corsican forces closing in from the east, whose officers were, at this moment, in the tent he'd just declined to enter.

Standing there, as the seawater lapped near his toecaps, it was easy to be introspective. Lanester had engendered unhappy memories in him, the kind of recollections that came all too easily when he thought about Augustus Hanger. The colonel's face had been a healthy, even pink before his broken sword had scarred it. But at times like these Markham wondered who'd inflicted the deepest wound. Before the day he met Hanger, everything in America had charmed and excited him. He had the right to wear an ensign's uniform, to march with a full belly through the warm forest of the Carolinas, marvelling at the organisation which could move several thousand men with such ease, and dreaming of one day being in command of such an army.

Even billeted on people who professed themselves opposed to his King and country had failed to dent that happiness. Flora Imrie's father had accepted his forced guest with equanimity, taking the opportunity to lecture a young, unformed mind on the rights and freedoms of mankind, the Irish included. In truth, the older man had dented some of Markham's youthful certainties. But most of his attention had been taken up by the man's daughter. Older and wiser, Markham knew he was too easily prone to romantic attachments. But this had been very different, made more so by being only fifteen years old. Love then was blissfully painful, new and exciting enough to make him physically tremble. The war, and the differences it created, so easily solved between him and Flora Imrie, seemed like trifles, a touch of madness from misguided grown-ups that would end in the same kind of harmony that they enjoyed.

After the pain of parting, he marched the ten miles from Salisbury to Guildford on a cloud of his own illusions. But then reality intruded. Battle was joined, men died in droves. His regiment, so fine, proud and smart, was shattered in two bloody assaults. With all his superiors dead, Ensign George Markham, filthy, lacking a gun, hat, or any experience, was the only officer left unscathed.

The shock and confusion of that was bad enough, but nothing to the state of his mind when he heard what Banastre Tarleton, and the cavalry of his British Legion, were doing back in Salisbury. He abandoned his post to rescue his first love, only to find that the town had been torched and Flora had died at the hands of men who were supposed to be on his side. And while he was absent, General Cornwallis, regardless of the casualties they'd already suffered, called on the 65th for one final effort, only to be told that there was no one to lead them into battle.

He kicked at the sand in an attempt to clear these thoughts from his mind, then set off towards the Fornali fort, quickening his pace along the beach. Thick black clouds had drifted in from the east to obscure the stars, and that somehow helped to alleviate such painful meditations.

Ahead the newly constructed gun emplacements loomed, great dark shadows like whales in the open sea. They were quiet now, the decision having been taken to conserve twenty-four-hour firing, so that when it was introduced, it would further reduce French morale. The gunners were asleep, the comatose bodies lit by wads of flaming tallow on the rear walls of the bastions, the shape of the odd sentry occasionally silhouetted by light as they paced to and fro. Out in front of them would be other marine guards, the screen of troops dug into sandy foxholes who would raise the alarm if the enemy tried to sally out from Fornali.

The darkness of the fort intrigued him. What should have been a hive of activity, as the enemy tried to repair the damage done by the guns, was instead peaceful. As he watched, some of the torches on the walls were extinguished, which, with the increasing cloud, plunged sections of the ramparts into total blackness. It was wrong; very, very wrong. The hairs on the back of his neck began to tingle, a sure sign of an unperceived danger. Straining his ears, he could hear the odd scrape of the forward piquet, as they moved to and fro, no doubt half asleep from too long on duty. Yet they'd be mindful that if they lost concentration, then they would be the first to die if the enemy sallied forth.

Markham stepped forward, climbing up the sandbags that lined the inner barrier, peering into the darkness, an act which alerted the marines actually protecting the guns. Right above the tallow wads, he was well lit, yet the sound of a musket moving, as it was brought from a weary shoulder to the guard position, was unmistakable.

'Who goes there, friend or foe?' demanded the gruff voice.

'Friend,' Markham replied, without turning round.

The next part of the challenge came automatically, the absurdity of the request lost on the approaching sentry. 'Advance and be recognised.'

'Sure, if I advance much further, friend, I'll be in Fornali.'

The sentry had come up behind him, the face, suspicious at first, reassured by both the uniform and the Irish lilt in the officer's voice. The weapon, dropped, was raised once more as he executed a sloppy salute. Another marine appeared, a corporal, who looked set to demand an explanation from Markham until the sharp tone of voice stopped him.

'Who commands the gun positions?'

'Captain Serocold, sir.'

'Would it be possible to rouse him out?'

The corporal shook his head slowly, the expression on his face turning from curiosity to doubt, 'He's at his pleasure, sir, with all the other officers.' He might have carried on to say the words 'and that's where you should be', since the sentiment was obvious in the look he gave this interloper. Markham was looking into the darkness again, sure he could hear sounds of the kind of movement that should be absent. Forward piquets didn't shift around unless they had to. They stayed in their foxholes, kept their eyes peeled, and shivered.

'So who is in charge?'

'My sergeant, an' he sound asleep.'

'Your muskets are all loaded and primed?'

''Course they is, sir.'

'Do we have any blue lights rigged?'

'They're by the great guns, primed and ready.'

'What is the order to set them off?'

'Anything suspicious out front that warrants it.'

He heard another sound then, like a gasp. 'Fire them!'

'What?'

'And get your entire guard detail up on the parapet, now!'

Ingrained obedience fought with propriety in the corporal's mind. He was being given a direct order by a marine officer. But it was one he didn't know from Adam, demanding of him he take a decision that should rightfully have rested elsewhere.

'Fire the damn things, man, and leave me to take the responsibility.'

'Liddle, do as the officer says,' the corporal barked, turning to the bemused sentry. That caused another second's delay while the private calculated the effect of this shift of accountability. But there was really no choice, and no time, in the face of the orders, to rouse out someone superior enough to question this strange lieutenant's rights.

'What's the procedure for calling the piquet back in?'

'There ain't one, sir. If Johnny Crapaud comes out to play they were to retire at once under the cover of our fire.'

The whoosh of the rocket, streaking into the night air, had Markham involuntarily hunching his shoulders. He watched the red trail as it shot skywards, then dropped his gaze as it burst forth, a blaze of blue light that illuminated the beach before him, turning it into a streak of white between the twin blacknesses of water and forest. The figures moving in the moonscape, no more than forty feet away, were shapeless, darkened faces under snug-fitting round hats, with nothing on their dress that picked up the light. For a second they froze, before one of them, more alert than his companions, fired off a pistol at the officer on the parapet. As he did so, he stood full face.

The ball came so close that Markham was sure he could feel the heat. He fell backwards, landing heavily on the surface of logs and compacted sand, his mind reeling in confusion, a major part of which was a disinclination to believe what he'd just seen – an outline of that floppy coxcomb he'd noticed earlier outside the general's tent. But he was yelling nevertheless, staccato orders to the corporal, who seemed as dumbstruck as the skirmishers in no man's land.

'Get everyone up onto the parapet and fire off a salvo!'

Pushing forward till he was against the foremost sandbag, he continued calling instructions as he gingerly raised his head. 'Rouse out your sergeant, then sound the general alarm and set off more rockets.'

The final command, as he peered over the rim, to get that damned captain out of the officers' mess, wasn't really necessary. Behind him, as he stood up, he could hear the trumpets blaring, summoning the entire landing force to arms. The sailors had come awake quicker than most, and with heartening discipline had set to preparing their cannon to fire without orders. The beach behind was full of men running towards the gun emplacements. But in the residue of the light from the flare, he could see the figures on the moonscape retiring, while the few marines who'd made their station hesitated to shoot at men who might be their own.

It must have dawned on some of them that the forward piquet were probably dead, since they began to fire, sporadically, at individual targets. Lifting his gaze, Markham looked at the fortress, still dark and even more brooding in the blue glow. There were no torches lit, no panic on the walls, no sign of any activity to either support an attack or repel one.

'Corporal, send a runner to General Dundas, at once. Tell him that the French are abandoning Fornali, and are in the process of retiring towards San Fiorenzo.'

'What in hell's name is happening!'

The officer, a naval captain, who rushed onto the firing platform was lacking both a hat and a weapon. Clearly this was Serocold. Markham took a deep breath, reported who he was and why he was there, and started to explain. The commander of the batteries lacked the patience to listen to his appreciation of the situation without interruption, and barked an order well before he was finished.

'Go back yourself, Markham, and tell the general. He'll need to send runners to alert all the other regiments and he won't do that on the word of a ranker.'

It was on the tip of his tongue to tell Serocold about the man he'd seen silhouetted against the flare, but he stopped himself, partly because there was not time, but more because he was beginning to doubt his own recollection. The naval officer was looking at him in a peculiar way, as if wondering why he was still there, which made Markham blurt out his clearly unwelcome advice.

'Can I suggest you move forward yourself, sir? The skirmishers are retiring, and I doubt they'll stand and fight.'

'I can't move from here without express written orders, you know that. My task is to protect the guns.'

He opened his mouth to protest, but shut it again. Serocold was quite right; regardless of what opportunities presented themselves, he had to stay put. If he lost the navy's great cannon, he might be beached.

'I have a section that has no fixed orders. Permission to send my men out, sir.'

'Granted,' Serocold snapped impatiently. 'Just as long as you do the first thing I asked of you, which is to rouse out Sir David Dundas.'

Though it would have been hard for even the best-disposed soul to spot it, there was some order in the chaos surrounding the command and mess tents. When he reported to Dundas, he found the general even less patient than Serocold. The silver-haired Scotsman, florid from the claret he'd consumed, was barking his instructions to all units to probe forward at once, following that with an injunction to pursue the enemy should they meet no resistance.

The Corsican generals, formally attired in full dress, stood waiting, looking perplexed, men dark skinned and moustached like their escorts, though no other feature registered. They'd been in the middle of their dinner. Now they were requested to take to their boats and alert their own forces, just in case Lacombe tried to push all the way through to Bastia.

By the time Markham got back to his own tent, Rannoch had the men fully dressed and ready, lined up for action, a sea of calm in an otherwise frenzied landscape. All around were rushing men, shouted commands, the odd blowing bugle, the whole scene made nightmarish by the combination of moonlight and waving torches. He grabbed his pistols and, with his men at his heels, headed back towards the gun emplacements. They were now back in action, the shells arcing towards the Fornali fort once more. The parapet, when he rejoined Serocold, was fully manned, the marines sensible enough to wrap bandanas around their ears so that the cannon firing over their heads wouldn't deafen them.

'I'd like to take my men forward, sir.'

'How many are you?'

'Eighteen in total.'

'What?' Serocold barked, his eyes lighting up in shock. 'The whole French force could be out there, man!'

'I think not, sir. In fact I would cease firing, since we are, very likely, now only damaging property which we will need to occupy.'

'You seem damn sure of yourself, Markham.'

107

Again he had to bite his tongue, unwilling to mention what was now an image plagued by uneasiness. 'I think I am right, sir.'

'Send up another blue light,' Serocold shouted. The rocket went aloft, to reveal a beach devoid of human life. 'Very well, Markham, you may proceed. But I will maintain fire on the walls till I am sure that it is wasted.'

It was eerie out on the strand of beach, close enough to the fort to attract gunfire, with the regular crash of the naval shells thudding into the ancient masonry. They found the bodies of Serocold's piquet. His men had died silently from knives that sliced their throats, or necks broken by powerful arms. The guns stopped suddenly, and an eerie quiet descended. Soon Markham and his party were joined by the remainder of Serocold's marines and, gingerly, they made their way towards the heavy studded gates. The French hadn't gone quite so far as to leave the door ajar, but it was almost like that, and taking possession of the Fornali fortress was easy.

Hanger, sent ahead by Dundas, arrived soon after with several officers, including Lanester, trailing in his wake. He was his usual abrasive self, quite prepared to blame Serocold and Markham for what he saw as a naval fiasco. But there was no time for long recrimination, nor for any explanations. The French were in full retreat, of that the was now no doubt, and every man who could be spared must partake in the pursuit. Each officer was asked to provide an appreciation of their readiness to move. It was clear, when they'd finished, that Major Lanester, with easy access to the road across open fields and an enemy who'd already vacated his defences, would be in prime position.

'What orders do you have, Markham?' Hanger demanded, spinning round to glare at him.

'None yet, Colonel,' he replied. He could easily have added that his duty was plain; to make his way to the beach headquarters set up by his naval masters and await instructions. But he would not oblige Hanger with anything that smacked of moving backwards.

'Good.' Hanger was looking over his shoulder, as if he could still see the fleeing enemy. 'Take your men forward and maintain contact with the French rearguards.'

'Sir.' Markham responded, aware of the glances being exchanged by the other officers present.

'Close contact, d'you hear?'

'With fewer than two dozen men, sir?' asked Lanester, the only one bold enough to speak out.

Hanger span back to face the American, scar white and eyes blazing. 'If you're so worried about Lieutenant Markham's ability to do as he is bid, sir, I suggest you would be better placed at the head of your regiment. Better, that is, than here, questioning me.'

Delivered to Lanester, it was clearly a rebuke to every officer present, all of whom took the hint and moved away to take charge of their units. The American's advice, nearly a whisper, was imparted as he slowly brushed past the marine officer.

'Don't get too close to them, young fella, or too far ahead of us. Long musket range should keep them on the move.'

Staying close to Lanester proved easy. Fully expecting to come up against a desperate rearguard action, Dundas decided to advance with caution, so that Markham's Lobsters soon found themselves acting as point to the American major's troops. It was Lanester's opinion that the wily old Scotsman was quite content to let the Corsicans entrap the French around Barbaggio, and keep them from the Colla di Teghima, through which ran the main road to Bastia.

Sound enough in theory. But Dundas must have realised as dawn broke, with his troops clearing San Fiorenzo and little sign of battle anywhere, that the Corsicans were not as far forward as had been hoped. Faced with the prospect that the enemy might slip away, leisurely probing was abandoned in favour of moving at the double, an order which was immediately greeted by the sound of field-cannon fire from the hills ahead. Throughout that day Sir David Dundas got his rearguard action, but it was from an army in motion, quite content to give ground every time the British troops mounted an assault.

Markham and his men tended to be forgotten when action was joined, Lanester too busy ordering his own troops into formation to bother with these supernumerary Lobsters, so that they were spectators to the mounting frustration of the pursuing soldiers. The French took advantage of every good defensive position, and deployed only long enough to force the British into battle order, exchanged one or two salvos for the sake of their honour, before decamping

110

to the next strong point.

Dundas was forced to stay on the road, hemmed in by the encroaching thick forests, and Lanester showed a fine sense of independence at the continual orders to press home his attacks, refusing to sacrifice men to what he suspected was a hopeless cause. He even stood up to Hanger, sent forward to inject some bite into the pursuit, a piece of insubordination that not only endeared him to Markham, but was resolved by another unit being pushed through to take up the front position.

'Damned right, too,' Lanester growled as he waved them through, his final wave of the hat a parting jibe to the fiery English colonel. 'He's in a stew now, Markham. But wait till the Frenchies have finished baiting him. God knows, he may oblige us with a seizure.'

As the pursuit lengthened, the temperature dropped, the wooded coastal plain giving way to ever rising hills, open country covered in low clumps of bush, where the wind added to the chill, until by nightfall those ahead of them were actually fighting in snow. With supply lines stretched to the limit, the Army command called a halt, the decision taken that Lacombe should be left to the Corsicans who must by now, with a whole day to deploy, be standing in their way.

Soon the slopes were dotted with campfires, each with its quota of soldiers huddling round the flames trying to keep warm. A kettle hung over each blaze, as the men tried to make something palatable out of their rations. This was not a problem that bothered Lanester. Pavin, his irascible cook and servant, proved his worth, providing chickens boiled whole in a sauce made of local wine, flavoured with herbs picked from the roadside.

Couriers passed to and fro, carrying news of the battle, which served to depress them regardless of the feast. Despite their allies holding good positions, it seemed that General Lacombe had succeeded in keeping his escape route open, with the Corsicans apparently unable to close the road.

'This is bad,' said Lanester, as he leant close to the fire to read the latest report. He sent off his belching, over-fed officers to make sure his men were ready, if required, to renew the pursuit. Pavin was clattering about, clearing up plates, when Markham returned after checking on his Lobsters. Both men stood for a moment, looking at the brooding snowcapped mountains, ghostly blue in the moonlight, as the sound of battle diminished.

'If Lacombe has managed to extract his entire force,' said Markham, 'you've got to admire him.'

'I can't believe they even disengaged.'

'I'm not sure they didn't have some help.'

Lanester slowly turned to look at him. 'What kind of help?'

Markham was now wishing he hadn't spoken. But having done so, and with the American staring inquisitively at him, he could hardly leave it there. As he explained, he was himself aware of the number of caveats he introduced: poor light, the brevity of the sighting, his own actual doubts about what he had seen.

'Should make an interesting report,' Lanester responded, his voice full of mockery.

Markham hadn't thought of that. But it was necessary, indeed required, that he write one. 'What do you think I should say?'

'Very little, if you're not sure.'

'I have to say something.'

Lanester was silent for some time, his head cocked, as though he were listening to the sound of his own men, grumbling as they settled down for a night made uncomfortable by the need to stay fully ready to move at an instant's notice.

'You must tell the truth, boy.'

'Which I would, if only I was sure of it.'

'Then the less said the better, I think, young fella, or you'll have every officer in Corsica, naval and Army, high and low, accusing the locals of treachery, for a notion you don't rightly hold to yourself.'

'Hood needs to be told.'

'And Dundas,' added Lanester swiftly, a sharp reminder of where his allegiances lay. 'After that, it will be up to them who they inform.'

'How in God's name am I to pass on such information in private?'

Lanester was silent again, a low growling in his throat the only evidence of his ruminations. 'Add a personal note for Hood, sealed and separate, to your report.'

'And the General?'

'Leave Dundas to me!'

The following morning found them in the same place, looking up at hills that were now silent. Gloom and despondency set in as everyone realised that if the French did elude them, the British forces would have to besiege Bastia, instead of just walking into the town as they'd anticipated. Hood would have his anchorage in the Bay of San Fiorenzo. But it would be untenable unless the French were expelled from the whole island.

Chapter eight

'Lieutenant Markham, sir,' said Captain Serocold, standing aside to allow the marine lieutenant to enter the great cabin of the *Victory*. 'As General Dundas requested.'

Hood looked at him with the steady, slightly bored gaze of a man accustomed to power. A long face, expressionless, under an old-fashioned wig, with a thick, slightly pendulous nose and bright blue eyes. To his left sat Sir David Dundas, resplendent in his much-braided general's coat, though the distracted look on his pink, smooth face failed to match the impression created by his attire. Two dozen other officers, Army and Navy, were present, including d'Aubent, Hanger, Lanester and Nelson. But Hood was the dominant figure, like the actor in a drama who casts all the others on stage into insignificance.

'We shall be with you in a moment, Lieutenant,' said Hood, before turning back to face the assembly. 'You were saying, General d'Aubent?'

'I only wish to repeat, sir, that the personal intervention of General Paoli seems essential. He cannot elect to hide himself away in his mountain fortress and ignore the whole campaign.'

'He won't budge from Corte,' Hood replied. 'Sir Gilbert Elliot tried to get him to be more active and failed. If a politico like him can't persuade the old goat to move, who can?'

A collective sigh seemed to sweep round the table as Hood lifted some papers, then turned to eye Markham. The object of the admiral's attention was trying to gauge the mood in the cabin, his train of thought broken by a sudden question from General Dundas.

'You were the officer who alerted the landing force to the French retirement?'

'I was, sir.'

'Not our finest hour,' Admiral Hood said, looking down at the sheaf of reports in his hand. 'I wonder what they will say in London when they hear of this? A French force slipping away unimpeded from beneath our very nose.'

Sir David Dundas shifted uncomfortably in his chair, the pink cheeks tightening as he looked anywhere but at the speaker. Instead he fired off another question at Markham.

'Admiral Hood has been kind enough to show me your report. You hinted that the men who silenced our forward piquet might not be French regulars.'

Markham knew that, unless Dundas had been shown the private addendum he'd included, that couldn't be true. He noticed Hood stiffen perceptibly, before he shot a sideways glance at Lanester, only to observe that the American was looking at the deck-beams above his head with an air of deep embarrassment. There was no time to gauge the reaction of anyone else, to see if what

115

had been imparted privately was now common knowledge. This forced Markham into an overly circumspect answer, designed to re-emphasis his doubts.

'My view of what occurred was brief, sir, while the whole affair was limited to the length of one flare.'

'Which is what you read in his report,' said Hood pointedly to Dundas.

'Had we shot one or two, Captain Serocold,' growled Dundas, clearly intent on covering himself, 'then we wouldn't have this damned conundrum.'

'Captain Serocold obeyed standing orders,' Hood snapped, 'and stayed with his guns.'

Dundas spoke again, pulling himself up in his chair to do so. 'I've listened to you, Lord Hood, and I have heard what you say about hot irons and the like. But surely you agree we can't trust 'em!'

Markham, ignored, had a chance to look around as Dundas continued, curious to know who'd been made privy to his private message. But that told him little. Those with the ability to dissemble wouldn't reveal their thoughts; the men lacking that gift would either look stupid, bored or both.

'The Corsicans misled us about Lacombe's troop strength before we landed,' added General d'Aubent, a pinched expression on his already stiff face, 'then failed to take up the positions they promised.'

'And how can we be sure,' Dundas murmured, a guileless look on his pink face, 'that someone in

116

their camp didn't contrive to let the French escape?'

Hood interrupted him, which also silenced a buzz of sudden conversation, to remind the General that at the very moment they were now discussing the Corsican commanders had been dining at his table. If it was intended to embarrass him into silence, it was a lamentable failure.

'That is so,' Dundas replied, slamming his hand on Hood's table with a force that earned him a reproving look. 'But there's been chicanery, sir. I will not accept that was coincidence. Even if it was, they were given a whole day to put matters right. Instead, they were made ten times worse. And now, when they should be investing Bastia, they've sat down in front of the redoubts at Cardo after one botched assault.'

'One made without our support, General.'

The Scotsman carried on as though Hood hadn't spoken. 'And what is the proposed solution to this fiasco? A hermit general named Paoli, who hasn't fought a campaign in twenty-five years. It's all stuff and nonsense. The locals at the very least lack zeal, sir. And I lack the strength to compensate for their manifest failings.'

Dundas had worked himself up into a passion, which caused him to appear to deflate when he ceased to shout. Nelson spoke suddenly. Among the other officers, he looked small in stature. But he had some of the same commodity as Hood, which compensated greatly for his lack of inches and girth.

'Might I remind you, sir, that these people have

117

fought the French before, and with some success.'

Hood was nodding in a sage fashion when Hanger cut in. 'Then it wasn't gained through wit or intelligence. Why tell us the French had five hundred men in Fornali when they had more than a thousand?'

There was an obvious response to that, even if no one was prepared to state it: that given the well-known reluctance of the Army command to undertake offensive operations, the truth might have kept the general and his men on Hood's ships. Nelson was equally diplomatic when he did reply.

'That estimate of Lacombe's troop strength may well have been a genuine error, Colonel. I doubt that forms a realistic presumption on which to base future operations. As you know, the naval opinion is...'

'That is not the subject of this part of the discussion, Captain Nelson.'

Hood had interrupted his junior in quite a friendly way, though Dundas and the rest of the Army contingent looked exceedingly annoyed. Nelson was obviously alluding to the conversations held before Markham had been ushered in, one that had clearly engendered a dispute between the two services. Judging by the hard set of most of the faces, he guessed it was still unresolved.

'Of course, sir.'

'I suppose, as well as forgiving Fornali, you have another explanation for the Colla di Teghima, Nelson?' demanded Dundas.

'It is not unknown, sir, for the military to be

118

taken by surprise.' Seeing both generals, as well as their attendant officers, swell up with indignation, Nelson added smoothly. 'And we in the Navy have been caught napping often enough to blush with equal vigour.'

'You didn't hear any of them speak, Markham, did you?' barked Hood, in what was more of a statement than a proper question, designed to bring matters back on the right track.

'No, sir.'

'And none of the forward piquet survived,' added Serocold.

'Damned thorough,' said Dundas, with a crafty look in his eye that served to annoy Markham. It was almost as if the general was trying to trap him into speaking out, something he was determined not to do.

'It's very necessary to be so, sir, if you wish to completely humbug your opponent.'

Sir David Dundas growled low in his throat, but it was Hanger who spoke. 'I am not one to give credence to the opinions of such a very junior officer, milord...'

He should have said nothing; kept his mouth shut and stared straight ahead. But he couldn't resist it, and his eyes were blazing as he cut right across Hanger.

'They're of more value, Colonel, than those of someone who was more interested in the fork in his hand than his duty. Had you bothered to leave the officers' mess, you might have observed something unusual yourself.'

The look in Hanger's eye was singular. Markham could see hate there, certainly, as well as anger, but there was also something else, altogether more enigmatic. Whatever it was never got aired, since Hood started shouting, which stopped everyone from speaking.

'How dare you, young man? Remember your station and apologise at once!'

He had to oblige, not only for the sake of the admiral's authority, but because there were officers who'd been in that same tent whom Markham held in some regard. Serocold himself had been wining, dining and gambling. So had Major Lanester. But he had to phrase it to exclude Hanger, since he'd rather expire than say sorry to him.

'My apologies are unreserved, sir.' Heads began to nod as he paused. But they stopped quickly enough when he added, 'To those officers who would grant that physical experience is better than ill-informed prejudice.'

'I would remind you where you are, sir,' said Hood coldly. 'I would also remind you that rank and title given can also be removed.'

'I had no wish to offend either you, or your office, sir.'

'That is not an apology,' barked Hanger.

'Really, Colonel Hanger, it sounded very much like one to me.' Hood's eyes changed. They were no longer flashing and angry, but amused and full of insincerity. He had no desire to hide his pleasure in his pun. It was often reported that the admiral had little regard for Bullocks, finding them timid, and always more prepared to object to some idea than to act upon it. Yet he lacked the strength in marines to proceed independently, so considered himself hamstrung by the army.

Markham could see both sides of the equation, could understand Dundas' disinclination to act without adequate force. Rumours were rife that he and Hood had exchanged warm words about investing Bastia, even going so far as to commit their quarrel to writing. The Army demanded two thousand more men before they'd move. And it wasn't just troops Dundas wanted. He needed a supply train that could cope with the rough terrain of the island. Hood, who took his bed and his guns with him wherever he went, and never went ashore to look at the ground he was asking the troops to fight on, had some difficulty in understanding the problems of land warfare.

'It's a damned nuisance,' Hood continued, addressing no one in particular. 'It's my turn to entertain every senior officer the Corsicans have tonight.'

'And we'll be sitting there wondering if one of them is working against us,' snapped Dundas.

'It would be very unwise to say anything, sir,' insisted Nelson.

This remark added to the manifest confusion on the faces of most of the assembly. No one looked more perplexed than d'Aubent, who took refuge in repeating what he'd said earlier.

'General Paoli's presence is essential. We will struggle to secure the island as a base without his willing co-operation.'

'We must rely on our own strengths,' said Nelson emphatically. 'And we must move with despatch.'

It was revealing the way the naval men nodded, while the Army, to a man, gave Nelson a hard

121

look. If they were at loggerheads, then this must be at the root of it. No one produced a colder glare than Hanger, and when he spoke, his tone was even more rasping and rude than normal.

'Does this occur to you, Captain? That the Corsican commanders know even better than we do they should have stopped Lacombe. They did not move with anything approaching enough speed.'

'I have already said, Colonel, there could be any number of mitigating factors.'

Hanger sneered. 'I have taken the trouble to read up on the history of this island, and have discovered that there is a long tradition of individual Corsicans playing Judas.'

'They claim to be as surprised as we were at the sudden withdrawal,' added Dundas, unnecessarily, and in a tone which left no doubt of his lack of belief in such a proposition. 'It is not beyond the bounds of possibility that someone was bribed.'

It was Hood who replied, looking to the deck-beams above his head to disguise his exasperation. 'Suspicion is one thing, proof quite another, and that applies to the Corsicans as much as it does to us.'

'What if the lieutenant were to attend your dinner tonight, Admiral?' said Hanger. Markham stared at him, completely puzzled, not least by the cold smile on the Colonel's scarred face. 'That will allow you to introduce him to our allies. It will be interesting to see how these Corsican leaders react when you tell them he is the officer who alerted us to the French withdrawal.'

Nelson responded swiftly, obviously worried.

'They might see that as tantamount to an accusation?'

'How could they, Captain, unless it is true?'

'It could be imparted as no more than mere information,' added Dundas. 'But what if one of them questions Markham, asking him if he saw anything untoward, presses him even?'

Hood's big hand slapped down hard on the table, a right he clearly allowed to himself while denying it to others. But Hanger was not to be deflected, and continued speaking in spite of the admiral's anger.

'If they have a Judas, he must be exposed. If not, we will be unable to plan anything, reinforced or not.'

'Tenuous, Colonel,' said Dundas, 'very tenuous. A man with the wit to deceive his close companions will hardly fall prey to a total stranger, and a mere Lobster lieutenant at that.'

'But worth a try, sir.'

'Certainly Colonel Hanger,' Dundas replied, looking keenly at Hood. 'It is worth a try.'

Markham was wondering if he, detached from the actual debate, was the only one to see how contrived the exchange between Hanger and Dundas had been. It had the air of something rehearsed. Hood drummed his fingers on his table, eyes fixed firmly on the papers before him, having ignored the general in the most blatant and insulting way. The sudden release of pent-up air left no one in any doubt that the words that followed were spoken by a man forced into a position he didn't relish.

'You will say nothing untoward, Markham, d'ye

123

hear? When you meet these Corsican coves you will be all innocence. They're a touchy crew, in the main. The last thing we want is every man jack of them feeling we're accusing them of treachery.'

'Sir.'

Markham replied automatically, as the realisation of the whole nature of this interview dawned on him. It was Dundas who'd requested his attendance at this gathering. Perhaps not everyone at the table had been informed of his speculations. Certainly the second in command, d'Aubent, had seemed perplexed on more than one occasion. But many had, including Hanger and very likely Nelson. There was a certain amount of amusement to be had from two things: their different interpretations, allied to the collective behaviour. In possession of a secret so comprehensively shared, they seemed debarred from any open allusion to it, which could only mean that such an act would be perceived as a breach of faith.

Dundas was determined, even if he was prevented from saying so, to blame the whole Fornali fiasco on the presence of Corsican traitors. It then followed that the same forces were at work as the French retreated. No great leap of imagination was required to see what effect that would have on any future operations. The General would have a perfect excuse to sit on his hands, regardless of what Hood urged on him. The wily Scotsman really didn't expect exposure from Hood's guests. He was just stalling, putting on pressure to compensate for the stress he was under himself, creating more obfuscation to avoid a prospect he abhorred: that he should be obliged to march on

Bastia without the required troops or supply train.

'Captain Serocold,' snapped Hood, 'take the lieutenant out and talk to him about that other matter.'

Markham saw Hanger's face move then, and he was in no doubt about what the admiral was referring to, which was confirmed as soon as they were on the maindeck.

'Captain de Lisle has asked that you be brought before a court martial for disobedience of specific orders, gross insubordination and a failure to honour his rank.'

'I'm aware of that, Captain.'

'Hood is against it,' Serocold replied, his saturnine complexion as hard as his dark eyes. 'He feels sure that, if he asks your captain, he can get him to drop the matter.'

'Why would he do that?'

'He knows that the Army's after-action reports concerning the taking of those field guns have diminished the role of the fleet marines in the affair, in favour of the deeds of the soldiers. According to the information he received privately, you and your men behaved well.'

'Who told him, sir?'

'I've just said it was private.'

'With respect, Captain Serocold, I should advise the admiral against interfering.'

Serocold smiled then, showing good teeth through the heavy black growth on his chin. 'That's not a set of words I'd care to put to someone like Admiral Hood.'

'I mean it, sir. Or at least let him enquire as to what witnesses Captain de Lisle intends to call.'

'I don't follow.'

'If Colonel Hanger is listed, in order to blacken my character, then the admiral will face an embarrassing rebuff.'

'Why?'

'Because it will confirm that Captain de Lisle is merely acting on the Colonel's behalf.' Serocold was looking into his eyes, a stare that Markham returned, one that told him that the naval officer knew all about his past. Suddenly Serocold grinned.

'That will only make the admiral more determined. The Army have never been high on his list of favourites, and after the list of objections and excuses they gave him today they have sunk to a new low.'

Leghorn, full of British civilians, from exiles to Grand Tourists, was just one day's sailing away. As soon as news of the capture reached the Italian mainland, it seemed every one of them wanted to visit the place. Corsica, which rarely figured on the list of places interesting to rich and spoiled travellers, had suddenly become fashionable. Markham, when he came ashore from *Victory*, landed on a San Fiorenzo quay full of babbling visitors, each one trying to negotiate accommodation and porterage with the locals. Several officers' wives had also come ashore, to be whisked away to quarters already requisitioned from the previous, now departed, French occupants.

San Fiorenzo was an occupied town, but for the British that had to be applied with a light hand, the native islanders being very touchy about their honour. Orders had already been issued that no liberties were to be taken with women or property. This applied to officers as well as the men, who were told that any perceived insult could be on pain of a knife in the ribs. The Corsicans were held to be a lawless breed, addicted to the vendetta, who would act first and face the consequences of committing murder second.

Markham, lacking clear instructions once the battle was over, could easily have gone back aboard *Hebe*. Instead he chose to seek a billet on land, in an abandoned sail loft. Rannoch and the men had quickly set to and turned the place into a home from home, while Halsey, on his officer's instructions, had raided the commissary for the supplies they needed to sustain themselves, using the confusion which still reigned to acquire rations for three times the number of men actually in the unit.

With their ship on an independent cruise, such abundance had persuaded the Seahorses to stay put; what they would live off ashore was much better than the rations they would receive aboard their host ship. But they kept themselves apart from the Hebes, while Bellamy found himself shunned by both groups, and so occupied a corner of the loft all of his own. If this bothered him, it didn't show, his black countenance a mask of seeming serenity, this no doubt aided by the ample provender with which he was able to satisfy his hunger. When Markham realised just what that consisted of, he had immediate words with Rannoch.

The Highlander was sitting over a small open

stove, heating his bayonet, before running it down the seams of his coat to kill off any eggs left by lice. He was sanguine. 'We only have to be concerned, sir, if a Provost Marshal or an angry local comes to our door.'

'Which they will do shortly, given what that pair have brought in.'

Quinlan and Ettrick, despite the strict rules governing nefarious activities, had got hold of two kegs of the local wine, plus most of the carcass of a recently slaughtered pig, several hams and a coop of live chickens, claiming that these luxuries had been retrieved from abandoned French stores.

'He knows how to stuff himself, does Johnny Crapaud,' said Ettrick, when Markham challenged them. 'Their storehouses was bursting at the seams.'

'And unlocked,' added Quinlan, who was a master at opening closed doors, his eyes angelic in their innocence.

It couldn't be true, and Markham knew it, since the locals would have stripped any warehouses, padlocked or open, the French left behind long before the British occupied San Fiorenzo. But he was loath to enquire too deeply, because what the two men had done would see them at the end of a rope if they were found out.

'You took a risk, did you not, carting this lot through the streets?'

'Never in life, sir,' protested Quinlan. 'We got Dornan to do the humping, him and that darkie you rescued.'

'Suitable work for the pair of 'em,' added

Ettrick, with a loud sniff, 'though I take leave to doubt whether Dornan, dense as he is, would take kindly to bein' ranked with a black.'

'Just make sure whatever you have got is shared equally.'

'There'll be a capital dinner for you, your honour, if'n you want one.'

'I'm dining aboard the flagship, Ettrick.' When he saw the two men raise impressed eyebrows, he continued, 'Believe me, I'd rather eat here. The company will be more congenial.'

'Right kindly said, sir,' replied Quinlan, in a wry tone. 'But given that you're goin' where you're goin', it be just as well that we rescued that marine officer's chest.'

'Abandoned, like,' added Ettrick.

'What abandoned chest?'

'The one in your billet, sir,' Ettrick replied, pointing to the screened-off corner in which someone had made up a cot. What little kit he had was in there, resting on top of a polished chest. Even at this distance, Markham could see the bare patches which had, no doubt once held engraved brass nameplates. 'As luck would have it, there are proper uniforms in there, marine ones, with good shoes and clean cambric shirts.'

'Where did you get it?'

'I told you,' said Quinlan, 'we found it abansdoned. No doubt some local tried to filch it, an' had to scarper when he saw us hove into view.'

'There was no way to identify the true proprietor, your honour. And seeing it was marine kit, and you was short on the necessaries to look the proper part, we thought we'd fetch it back for you.

If you're to dine on the flagship, it seems we've had a stroke of real good fortune.'

Bent over it, examining the contents, Markham was wondering what he should do with them. They were not his, and it wouldn't be too difficult to find the true owner, since there weren't many marine officers ashore. That reminded him of his own troubles. If de Lisle and Hanger had their way he wouldn't be a marine much longer himself. And the men would have a new officer to deal with, which for their sake was probably just as well. But thinking of appearing before a court softened his initial resolve to find the real owner.

Though hardly a dandy, George Markham liked to dress well, the evidence of which had been in the chest he'd had to abandon when he fled aboard *Hebe* at Chatham. If he was going to face a court martial, it would be nice to appear before them in smart attire. When he was acquitted or found guilty, he could return these clothes to the officer who'd either lost them, or had them stolen. He held up the red coat, a beautifully cut piece of fine, soft broadcloth, with white facing, collar and cuffs, edged with braid that, like the fouled-anchor buttons, gleamed invitingly.

That was how Midshipman Bernard found him, causing Markham to drop the coat and shut the sea-chest abruptly. A quick call for a glass of wine was necessary to cover his confusion – a temporary alleviation, as it recurred when the youngster remarked on the outstanding quality of the drink. His host, taking a deep and satisfying gulp himself, quickly demanded an explanation for his visit.

'I have tried, several times,' the boy said, 'to tell Captain de Lisle that I will not testify against you, sir. But my courage fails me at the last moment.'

'No wonder, Mr Bernard. You're risking everything for someone you hardly know.'

Bernard held his position entirely at the whim of his captain. There would be a connection, of course, some person who'd exercised the influence that had got him his berth in the first place. Markham resisted the temptation to ask the boy if that someone was powerful enough to check de Lisle's anger. If he was, Bernard would know it already and be less concerned.

'Besides,' Markham continued, 'if called before a court martial you will be asked to tell the truth. That is something you can hardly avoid.'

'I could show confusion.'

It wasn't necessary to actually lie, since what he said next had a grain of truth in it. 'A waste of time. "Spotted Dick" will call all the ship's officers, as well as the purser. I've said enough damning things in their presence to make your testimony superfluous.'

Bernard smiled at the use of de Lisle's nickname. 'He goaded you, sir.'

'It has to be said, Bernard, that it didn't take much.'

The boy stood up, trying to add as many inches to his slight frame as he could. 'I wish to apologise to you, sir, for any previous occasions when my behaviour has been less than polite.'

'Sure, I don't remember being too polite when I was your age,' Markham replied.

'Nevertheless, sir, in someone who aspires to be

an officer and a gentleman, it is unbecoming.'

'Just make sure you do become that, boyo, for it is something I have never yet managed. Answer the questions you're asked as a gentleman would, and I for one will be content. More importantly for you, so will Captain de Lisle, and the rest of the Navy you're so anxious to serve in.'

The marine lieutenant who had himself rowed out to *Victory* looked smart enough to attend a levée at King George's court. He was shaved, powdered and pomaded enough to turn the odd head as he made his passage, and again when he came aboard the flagship. He felt a twinge of guilt at his love of attention, while at the same time being well aware that his height and bearing gave others good cause to look in admiration. And dressed in another's clothes, for all the world like a theatrical costume, he set out to act his way through the forthcoming ordeal. Not least to show people like de Lisle and Hanger, who were bound to be present, that he didn't give a fig for their malice or their intentions.

'Ten minutes I was out of that damned villa,' barked a bucolic-looking marine captain, 'doing the honours in the article of meeting my dear cousin from Leghorn.'

The man half turned to include the lady, plump and overdressed, his eyes straying to his nearby fellow officer as he did so, quite unable to avoid the up and down look of a man who'd just been robbed. Markham realised suddenly that, before telling him about the chest, Ettrick and Quinlan, by means best not inquired into, must have already altered the rank insignia.

'They're a desperate crew, Metcalf, the Corsicans,' replied another guest. 'Take your eyes and come back for the holes, I've heard.'

'Corsicans be damned. The cook I inherited was absolutely certain that the men who climbed my walls were redcoats. This is the work of some thieving Bullocks.'

'Are you sure it wasn't your own man?' asked another.

'He was down at the quay, to warn me of my cousin's arrival. It was a damn shame; had he been there he would have shot the sods for certain. He hates the Army even more than I do.'

Markham had been rooted to the spot throughout this exchange, having seen the look in Metcalf's eyes. He could also see the coat the captain was wearing, a touch like his own old garment, worn in places and showing traces of the stains of battle. He turned away abruptly, only to find himself under scrutiny from a pair of pale blue eyes under a burgundy silk turban.

He'd already taken in the low cut of the matching dress, and the promise of pleasure barely concealed, when the lady spoke. 'Why Lieutenant Markham, I never thought to meet you here.'

'Miss Gordon,' he replied, bowing slightly.

There was a note of triumph in her voice when she responded, and a quick flick of her fan sent a heady dose of perfume wafting under his nostrils.

'Not Miss Gordon, Lieutenant. You must be aware that the proper form of address is now Mrs Hanger.'

Chapter nine

Jealousy was not one of George Markham's faults, but he felt a strong flash of it then. The beautiful creature before him, with the wisps of corn-coloured hair trailing from her turban had, when he'd first encountered her in Toulon, been Miss Gordon. More than that: although he'd not underrated the difficulties, he had contemplated a serious attempt at seduction. The reasons, quite apart from mere physical attraction, were still there now. That slightly knowing and superior smile, mixed with a reserve that stated quite clearly that no man should contemplate trifling with her affections unless he was considering matrimony. The thought of that now redundant word made him laugh, which brought to her forehead, just above her nose, the twin lines of anger he remembered so well.

'You find something amusing?'

'No.'

The lines deepened. 'Yet you laugh?'

'Such a reaction can be caused by despair as well, ma'am.'

'Despair, Lieutenant?' The word clearly confused her, the puzzled look staying on her face as the voice barked at her: 'Elizabeth!'

She spun round to look at her new husband. His face was puce with anger, which threw the ragged scar, behind which no blood ran, into

134

sharp relief.

'Sir,' she responded.

Hanger glared at Markham, then took her arm, and with scant gentility pulled her away. Even though he was whispering, Markham was close enough to hear his terse outburst.

'You will oblige me in future, madam, by refraining from any contact with that scoundrel. Quite apart from my own dislike of the knave, there is my reputation to consider.'

'As you wish, sir,' Lizzie replied, in a louder voice than that of her husband, and moreover one that showed no trace of apprehension. 'Though I will not forget the necessity of proper social grace.'

All attempt at control went from Hanger's voice then. 'Grace be damned, madam. That rake is out of bounds, and if I see you talking to him again, then damn me, rest assured, you will feel the consequences.'

'Husband!'

'That is what I am. And I will exercise rights other than those which come to me conjugally, if you dare to disobey me.'

Lizzie had pluck, even if she also had a quaver in her voice. 'Be so kind as to keep your voice down, sir.'

Hanger, suddenly realising that people had turned to stare, jerked at his new bride's arm to lead her away from them. Behind him, Markham was glaring at his back, as much for his mere existence as for the way he was treating his wife. He knew enough about the man to suspect he had a predilection for the whip. Augustus Hanger was a bully, a gruff, ill-mannered brute who lorded it over the weak and defenceless, while toadying to those in power. Lizzie Gordon might be a trifle snobbish in her ways, and demand attentions without surrendering anything as compensation, but she was far too good for a lout like him.

'Money,' Markham said to himself. 'Just remember, boyo, the creature is stinking rich.'

'Now just who would that be?'

Markham turned to find Major Lanester standing beside him, glass in hand, white waistcoat stretched to the limit, his plump face already flushed with drink, his eyebrows raised as though he was in ignorance of who was being referred to. Yet Markham knew he wasn't confused but amused, a fact betrayed by his inability to stop his lips from twitching.

'No one.'

'Well it certainly ain't me, son. If I was rich I'd buy myself a colonelcy, take a young and feisty woman for a wife, and bribe some government official to give me a profitable and peaceable posting.'

'No hankering after glory, Major?'

'No thanks, boy,' Lanester growled. 'I've seen too many folks like that in my years, and they are a damned nuisance to a man. Your Papa had the right notion. Get your soldiering over when you're young, then settle down in a nice lucrative billet.'

Markham wasn't sure whether to be angry with Lanester or grateful. Few people even referred to his parentage, unless intent on undermining him. And no one ever alluded to venality in his father's behaviour while maintaining a warm smile. Yet this Virginian talked as if no stain was apparent in either case, with an ease that sounded too friendly to be condescending.

'I doubt Corsica will provide you with what you seek. According to one of my Lobsters, even Seneca found it barren.'

'I know it will be barren for me, Lieutenant,' Lanester replied, looking after Hanger and Lizzie. 'And for the sake of the peace, I hope the gods deny you what you're after as well.'

As a warning to watch his step, it was as subtle as Lanester could be. Markham wondered if he could see inside his head, could detect the way his blood was racing through his veins, understand the thoughts that exhilarated him. Lizzie Gordon would have been a hard nut to crack as a single woman, requiring time and patience. But now she was Mrs Elizabeth Hanger, even if, in his head, he could not bring himself to style her so. And that, given any lack of finer feelings in her spouse, might make her an easier prospect. And then there was the delicious thrill in the notion; that as well as introducing her to a degree of pleasure he was certain she could not have experienced, he might actually cuckold Hanger.

'So what did you deduce from your earlier interview?' Lanester said, changing the subject.

'That there is as much love lost as honour shared amongst our seniors. Hood didn't show him my letter, did he?'

The round, red face creased with frustration. 'I should have known Dundas would blab.'

'I got the impression he didn't tell everyone.'

'You're right. But he dropped enough hints for

the ignorant to get the rumour mills working overtime. They cleared the cabin after you left. It was just Dundas and Hood, goin' at it, hammer and tongs.'

'I can guess what about, though not the details.'

'Ships are hell for eavesdropping, boy,' the major replied. 'All that thick oak.'

'Is d'Aubent right? Do they need the presence of General Paoli? And if they do, can they get him?'

Lanester shrugged. 'Plates will fly if he does respond. Pasquale Paoli might be revered as a saint by the rank and file, but there are those with braid on their cuff, Corsican and English, who reckon him an interfering old pest. Truth is, they're both right.'

'You sound as if you know him.'

'I do, Lieutenant.'

Markham opened his mouth to pursue that, Paoli being a very famous hero whose exploits had formed the basis of childhood adventures.

'Dinner, ladies and gentlemen.' The shout from Hood's steward killed every conversation, not just theirs. Those on the maindeck began to file through the double doors on either side of the ship that led to the great cabin. Serocold was just inside, and as soon as he spotted Markham he gestured to him.

'The admiral wants you close to both him and his Corsican guests, but on the opposite side of the high table from General Dundas.'

'What about precedence?'

'I quote,' Serocold replied. '"Precedence be damned, and if anyone sees fit to mention Markham's elevation, let them know it is by my express invitation.'"

Judging by the looks he received, many of them extremely baleful, there were quite a number of people who wished to question his place. In a situation that demanded seating according to rank and importance, the placing of a mere marine lieutenant so close to the host was a case for raised eyebrows, none more elevated than those of Captain Richard de Lisle. But he was above others too, senior officers of both services, many of whom clearly felt slighted.

Markham found himself some five places to the right of Hood, seated next to one of the Corsican officers, a General of Brigade called Grimaldi, who patently had reservations about eating aboard ship, even one securely moored in harbour. Regardless of his swarthy skin, he showed a trace of pallid flesh, particularly between ears and chin, that led his fellow diner to conclude the man was a martyr to seasickness. This was an affliction which few at the table had managed to avoid during the service life, though not one of them could be brought to consider it as anything other than unmanly. But, despite his inner disquiet, Grimaldi spoke French with fluency, and so did George Markham, so they conversed easily.

Well travelled, the Corsican general was nevertheless rather parochial in outlook, able to reduce any subject to the effect it would have on his native island. Small and wiry, with a fine black moustache, he had the dark Italian eyes of his race, a very prominent nose and a craggy quality to the remainder of his features. The excitability which seemed habitual obviously had to be kept in check at such a formal gathering, which gave his conversation a breathless air, as he tried to contain his enthusiasms.

All of these revolved around the nature of Corsican society, the beauty and probity of the womenfolk, the outstanding bravery of the men, who had tamed a landscape so alien to human habitation it was a wonder of the world, while retaining standards of honour that were unsurpassed. Sanpiero Corso was mentioned with breathless awe, a low-born islander who'd risen to become a French general in the sixteenth century, aided by his patron Catherine de Medici. (Grimaldi failed to add that Sanpiero fell to an assassin's knife, as a result of a vendetta caused by his own murder of a wife thirty-five years his junior.) Markham learned that no Corsican would bow the knee to a tyrant, permit another man even to kiss his wife's hand, let alone her cheeks, and kill anyone who attempted to steal his sheep. At the peak of this paragon society stood the puissant figure of General Pasquale Paoli, the Great Liberator.

Even though the events Grimaldi seemed keen for him to remember had happened a long time ago, before his listener had reached the age of ten, the name had a resonance for Markham. Pasquale Paoli was world-famous, a philosopher soldier who seemed to embody the ideas of Voltaire and Rousseau, a true figure of the Age of Enlightenment. Celibate, deeply religious and learned, he was rightly credited with uniting one of the most fractious races on earth, then imbuing them with a common purpose so profound that they'd ejected their Genoese overlords from the island after an occupation of several hundred years.

Fighting a corrupt and ailing city state was one thing, taking on the power of the King of France quite another. Paoli had fought long and hard, and had inflicted several stunning defeats on a succession of French generals. But eventually, fearing that the British had designs on the Corsican harbours, the French brought from the mainland enough men and material to complete the conquest of the island. Even then, it had taken bribes to make any headway, gold that detached people from their allegiance to the nationalist cause.

Paoli was finally defeated at the battle of Ponte Nuovo, and chose to flee to England rather than face capture and either death or incarceration. In London he'd been lionised as a standard-bearer against tyranny, granted a pension by the King, and had lived in comfort for twenty years, until the advent of the French Revolution had allowed him to return home in triumph to his native soil.

Delivered with brio, the tale was suffocating in its intensity. But Grimaldi was so engrossed he barely noticed that his fellow diner had given up listening. Most of Markham's attention was directed to the opposite table, where Lizzie Gordon sat, several places away from her husband. One of the few women present, she had no difficulty in monopolising the guests on either side. But she would not have had a problem regardless of competition. A beauty before, her face had filled out just enough to remove any trace of pinched ill-humour. She knew he was watching her, it was plain from the occasional flick of an eye in his direction. Her reluctance to insist that he stop, which only required one steady glare, was encouraging.

'General Grimaldi,' said Dundas, calling across from the far side of the table, some half-dozen places away. 'What opinion do you have regarding General Paoli?'

Markham could almost feel the man stiffen beside him. 'In what way do you mean?'

Dundas indicated Grimaldi's two superiors, fellow generals seated either side of the admiral, neither of whom looked entirely happy. It was Hood who spoke, his face as bland as his tone.

'General Dundas proposed that it would be a boost to your troops' morale if he were to come and join the army.'

'Indeed it would, sir,' replied Grimaldi, so heartily that it seemed to increase his compatriots' gloom. 'Why, his mere presence would be worth ten regiments!'

'Truly, an army with faith in its leaders can achieve wonders.'

Hood said this with an air of mock gravity, following it with what he imagined was a look of pure innocence aimed at Dundas. Close to the top table, their fellow diners kept up the appearance of conversation. But it was a sham. Every ear, Army and Navy, was engaged in listening, breath held. Dundas had reddened even more, taking it for what it was, a barely-disguised insult. But he responded with seeming equanimity, aiming his words at Hood's guests, rather than to

142

the admiral himself.

'That is to undermine the quality of the troops themselves, something I cannot subscribe to. It requires a combination of soldiers and leaders to achieve success.'

'Hear him,' said several officers lower down the board, men who'd forgotten they were not supposed to be listening.

'Then, of course, there is luck,' added Dundas. There was a twinkle in his bright blue eyes, though he'd introduced a harder tone into his voice. 'It was damned bad luck that the troops we expected were not there to meet us when we landed at Fornali.'

Grimaldi responded on behalf of all the Corsican officers, who nodded sagely as he spoke. 'That was most unfortunate, General Dundas. We did all in our power to get there on time. But good intentions are often a victim of war.'

'And Lacombe was lucky to get clear, was he not?' hissed Dundas, suddenly like a man whose patience was being sorely tried. 'But perhaps it wasn't all dependent on fortune. The fellow on your right has an opinion on that!'

Grimaldi turned to look at Markham, a degree of confusion on his face, as Dundas continued, 'Has Lieutenant Markham told you who he is?'

The Corsican was slightly taken aback. Hood had gone as stiff as a board, and was looking straight down the centre of the cabin, jaw tightly clenched. Markham raised his eyes to look over the General's shoulder, praying that he would say no more.

'Yes, General, he has,' nodded Grimaldi.

143

'I don't mean his name and rank, sir. Perhaps you wondered why he was placed above the salt. The fact is that he was the officer who spotted that the French were abandoning Fornali. Pure luck, as we were just discussing. He fired off the flares and raised the alarm. Ain't that true, Markham?'

'Sir!'

It was the only reply he could give, since to try and elaborate would only make matters worse. Hood obviously felt the same, since he too said nothing. In terms of subtlety, Dundas's words, particularly his way of pointing up the seating arrangements, equated to dropping a cannonball into a plate of soup. Markham, determined to stare straight ahead, only saw Grimaldi out of the corner of his eye. But he reacted like the other Corsican officers in the cabin. Apart from the two generals either side of Hood, they'd been relaxed, smiling and conversational. Now they stiffened perceptibly, and the way they avoided looking at the object of Dundas's remark was only another indication of their acute discomfort.

'The luck didn't extend to catching hold of one,' added Dundas, showing great interest in the food on his plate. 'Unfortunate, wouldn't you say?'

'Very,' replied General Buttafuco, small and portly, who sat two places away on Hood's left, a remark which produced little more than a grunt from the Corsican commander, General Francisco Arena, who sat on Hood's right as the guest of honour. He was taller than his companions, but not by a great deal, and much paler of skin, his face pock-marked with the ravages of early small-pox.

Dundas turned to Arena, his voice still hearty and amused, as though he was discussing the pursuit of some game. 'Still, I daresay he has an inkling of whom to blame. Might like to arrange for the marines to take revenge. Long memories, they have, in my experience, isn't that right, Admiral?'

'Hurrump,' was the sole reply, as Hood hid his face, as well as his embarrassment, in his glass.

Markham fought to avoid eye-contact with his fellow diners, all of whom were now staring at him. It was Arena who saved him any further discomfort, by suddenly raising his glass.

'Then I propose a toast that Lieutenant Markham will find very acceptable,' he exclaimed. 'Death to the French!'

That was a sentiment both host and guests were obliged to endorse. Even Markham found himself murmuring the incantation, while at the same time wondering if Arena's injunction was genuine or contrived. When conversation started again it was stilted and full of surreptitious looks, in his direction as well as at the Corsican generals. Grimaldi had turned to his left, to engage in conversation one of Hood's flag captains. Was he eager to regale him with tales of Corsican pluck, or reluctant to look Markham in the eye? Buttafuco was likewise engaged with his neighbour, while Arena had embroiled Admiral Hood in a discussion regarding future operations, leaving Dundas to his food.

Markham was left free to look around the table, since the diner on his left, a lieutenant-colonel of the Foot Guards, had shifted his seat, so that his back was mostly to Markham, making it perfectly plain that he had no intention of engaging such a pariah in any kind of discourse. So the rest of Markham's meal passed in almost total silence, as he considered the kind of devious mind that could make him so easily a scapegoat, as well as the possible outcome.

Had the Corsicans played right into Dundas's hands by not asking if Markham had seen anything, surely the obvious question of anyone free from guilt? Yet Arena's way of killing off the speculation could be genuine, the act of an experienced officer who knew that picking over the dead bones of closed campaigns would help no one. Against that, neither Buttafuco nor Grimaldi had looked very comfortable raising their glasses. So, the subject had been killed. But there was no way of knowing if the method of its termination provided any hint as to what had happened.

But, reluctant as Markham was to make the admission, it underlined the point that Hanger had touched on, which was this; that if one of the senior officers had taken enemy gold, the rest must at least suspect it had happened, even if they could not be sure enough to accuse. The French should never have got through to Bastia, and would not have done so had the Corsican army been prepared. The absence of their generals should have made no difference. If it did, not to alert their British allies to this fact, nor apologise, openly and sincerely, rendered them all suspect.

Slowly, as the conversation became more animated, Markham could return, uninterrupted, to his previous study. He applied as much attention to Lizzie Gordon's mannerisms as he did to a piece of battleground terrain. Each gesture was noted, every flick of an eye and finger registered. It was, to the student, a pleasant task. He had a high regard for women, especially but not exclusively the beautiful members of that sex. The dinner wound its way through the various courses, wine flowed, and finally, just before the port came round, Lizzie stood up with the few other ladies, and with a bow to acknowledge the complimentary words of the admiral, left the room. It was easy, once he passed the port to Grimaldi, to leave his place, and since no one inquired his reasons, he offered none.

He found her on the quarterdeck, wrapped in a cloak, staring out over the now crowded anchorage. The early evening air was crisp and chilly, with the sun too low in the west to give off any heat. Stars were just visible over the eastern mountains, and where the snow still lay it picked up the pink glow of the sunset. Markham stood behind her for what seemed like an age, willing her to turn round, wondering if such a message, his deep attraction, could be transmitted through the air.

She half turned to lift up the hood of her cloak, and he wasn't sure if the shudder, when she saw him, was genuine or false.

'The hood suits you,' he said, smiling, 'especially the way it frames your face.'

'You must not pay me compliments, Lieutenant. My husband has forbidden it.'

'Neither God nor the Devil could not stop me doing that.'

'I'm sure you are right,' she snapped. 'Just as I am told that you're fairly free with their distribution.'

Markham moved slightly closer, but stopped when he saw her shoulders go rigid with apprehension. 'I cannot deny that I have complimented other women. Beautiful as you are, madam, you do not have a monopoly on such sentiments.'

'It didn't feel that way over dinner, Lieutenant Markham.'

'Would you care to tell me what it did feel like?'

'No sir, I would not,' she replied sharply. 'Now be so good as to leave this deck. Should my husband come up from below, and find us conversing, he would be exceedingly vexed.'

'He is jealous?'

'I rather think his attitude to you personally is more telling than the commonplace of jealousy.'

'I'm curious.'

'Regarding what?' she responded suspiciously.

'How do you find the married estate?'

She smiled then, a hard, fixed look. 'Blissful.'

'Do you refer to the emotional or the conjugal part?'

That made her angry again. 'If I was inclined to discuss such things, which I am not, sir, you would be the last person I would confide in.'

'The very last?' he inquired, his voice full of mock disappointment.

'Yes!'

'How reassured that makes me feel.' She span round to glare at him, even more annoyed by the smile on his lips. 'There is nothing worse than to be invisible to a woman you find attractive. Even outright hate is better than indifference.'

'You mistake your position, sir. Indifference, as far as you are concerned, is my overriding emotion.'

'I had you down as a more accomplished liar.'

'How dare you?'

Markham moved closer still, hemming her in so that she would have to use physical force to dislodge him. 'You have no notion of what I would dare, madam. There are no walls built that I wouldn't scale to be alone with you.'

'Lieutenant!'

'You have married a man for his wealth, for which I cannot fault you. But you must know there is more to a full life than mere comfort. I don't profess to know you well, but I am sure of this: you cannot truly love a man like Hanger.'

The slight pant in her voice robbed her words of the force she intended. 'You seem very certain.'

Markham took two paces backwards, which surprised her, a feeling which was enhanced by his next words. 'I must apologise.'

'Apologise,' she responded, aware, judging by the blush that tinged her cheeks, that such a reply was foolish.

'If I were to say that I was overcome with your beauty, that I have acted impetuously and rudely because of it, you would scoff at me.'

'I most certainly would,' she said, her voice regaining some confidence.

'Yet it is true, ma'am. And I must warn you the sensation is not fleeting. Had circumstances permitted in Toulon...'

She interrupted abruptly, the twin furrows of

anger back on her forehead. 'I seem to remember that you were otherwise engaged in Toulon, Lieutenant.'

Markham continued as if she hadn't spoken. 'And now we are here in Corsica. I have no idea of where my duty will take me. But if I stay in close proximity to you, I will not desist from bringing myself to your notice, at every turn, regardless of what Colonel Hanger thinks.'

'And who, sir, do you think will pay the price for that?'

'Perhaps you will. I have known your husband longer than you, madam, and I have no doubt that his love of a horsewhip is as great now as it ever was. He took it to me with relish, then followed it with the butt of a musket. Had he not been drunk, I might have died from his endeavours.'

'You must not speak of this.'

'If I cannot engage your attention any other way, then I must choose the path of showing you what a monster you have wed. And believe me, ma'am, that is what you have done.'

Markham was gone before she could reply, heading down the companionway, and back towards the warmth and fume-filled air of the admiral's cabin. Lanester was outside it, pacing to and fro, smoking an evil-smelling cheroot. He stopped when he saw Markham, and looked at him in a singular way. All he got for that was a smile and a nod as the marine slid past him, entered the cabin and retook his seat. Dundas was halfway down the table, talking to Hanger. Grimaldi, who had moved close to talk to Nelson, Buttafuco and Arena, detached himself, and came back to his original place, now beaming, his small bright eyes fixed on Markham.

'Lieutenant.'

'I must apologise, sir, for General Dundas's previous remarks.'

'Admiral Hood has done enough of that, Lieutenant, never fear, and gone to the trouble of explaining why they were made. But that is past. Now that we have a chance to talk, you must allow me to congratulate you. Had we not been alerted by your prompt action, that French might have got clear without the need to fire a shot. Tell me what it was that engaged your attention, and made you so suspicious?'

Markham explained about the French torches, plus the lack of any noises of damage repair after a long and effective bombardment.

'And forward piquets, General, rarely make any sound, even to let their friends to their rear know they are safe. There was just enough noise to induce curiosity.'

'Curiosity! And that caused you to fire off some flares?'

'Yes.'

'And when they went off, you must have seen something?'

Grimaldi wasn't looking at him, but over his shoulder, as if the answer to that question was academic. Behind him, the buzz of conversation had diminished. He had no idea how many people were listening, half suspecting that it numbered nearly everyone in the cabin. If Hood had apologised, then he would have implied that Dundas was exaggerating, no doubt hinting at the general's

151

motives. Whatever, his duty was plain.

'A few indistinct figures who ran as soon as they saw the trail of the rocket.'

The eyes were on him now, black and intense, and there was just a trace of strain in Grimaldi's voice. 'Indistinct?'

'Mere silhouettes, General.' Markham held the stare, wondering if he'd been believed, aware of the increase in noise as people reanimated their exchanges. Grimaldi smiled suddenly, though as was fitting it had a grim quality.

'What a pity. A few moments earlier and you might have confounded the whole plan.'

'For the men who died in their foxholes, sir, it was more than a pity. Rather a tragedy, I think.'

Chapter ten

The arguments between the services regarding future operations took on an increasingly bitter tone over the following week. Claiming he was unable to supply his forces, General Dundas had withdrawn them to within three miles of San Fiorenzo. Hood had protested with his usual lack of tact, only to be told that if he wanted to freeze in the Colla di Teghima he was welcome to go and do so, but that the army would not.

Dundas continued to insist that a land assault on Bastia was impossible for the same reasons. The soldiers lacked the means to supply their troops over four miles of mountain road, let alone nine, and that took no account of the lack of any confidence he expressed regarding his Corsican allies. Not surprisingly, relations which had been strained after the French departure had cooled even more after Hood's dinner. There wasn't an officer present, from either side, who was unaware of how the occasion had been used to cause embarrassment.

The admiral finally attempted to pull rank, claiming to be the senior officer on the station, and therefore the man with the power of decision. Such a prerogative was tenuous at best, but having made it, Hood managed to remove the last vestige of polite intercourse between the two services. He so offended Sir David Dundas by some of his remarks that the general decided to relinquish his command and go home. General d'Aubent wasn't, as far as the Navy was concerned, much more tractable. He positively exploded when he found that the wily old admiral had been talking to his subordinate officers behind his back, trying to get them to agree to operations in which he, like Dundas, had already declined to participate.

Nelson was afire with alternative plans, determined that, with the Corsicans already holding the landward approach to Bastia, the one-time French capital city should be taken from the sea. In this he ran straight up against General d'Aubent, who had no more faith than his predecessor in the estimates given by the Corsicans of enemy troop strength. He had even less in the prospect of a landing followed by a siege, without enough troops to guarantee a swift surrender, and accused

153

Nelson of whoring after glory.

This led to more bad blood, which for the sake of the national interest had to be overcome. Compromise was necessary, even if, as everyone knew, when it was struck it would be, like all such things, unsatisfactory. D'Aubent point blank refused to provide troops, but he could not stop the marines from taking part. Nelson persuaded Hood to let him try. But once ashore he would need artillery and engineering officers, and even that small token the army was unwilling to provide.

To stall matters, d'Aubent agreed to have another look at a land assault, and various officers were sent off to reconnoitre the ground. In such a confused situation, gossip became frenzied, which is how Markham and his men heard of the ever more fanciful plans. That set them, in a semi-jocular way, wailing for another officer, since their own was far too junior to participate in staff conferences, and so bring them back hard information which they could flaunt.

Markham hardly noticed the jokes, being rather preoccupied. First, he'd been informed that, due to his disinclination to apologise, plus de Lisle's insistence, a court martial would be convened within the week, with Admiral Hood using the occasion to see through a string of complaints that had festered in the fleet since before Toulon. The greatest problem Markham had was in finding an officer, who should by rights come from his own ship, willing to defend him.

To the specific charge, he had little choice but to plead guilty, since he had no intention of allowing Bernard to lie. And that course held another attraction: it would prevent anyone, under the guise of an assessment of his character, from bringing up what had happened in the past. He'd had to face a court after the Battle of Guilford, to explain his actions, a daunting ordeal for a fifteen-year-old. He'd been acquitted, but since the matter had been heard in New York, by officers who had close links to his father, no one believed that the verdict was anything other than pre-determined.

Distraction came from working hard the men under his command. In Toulon, he and Rannoch had gone to great lengths to improve their musketry. Yet in the weeks before the Corsican landings, de Lisle had scoffed at any notion that Markham might maintain their standards by regular practice. The folly of that had been shown only too well during the recent landing, and now it was very possible that renewed action was imminent. He also had the Seahorses to consider, since he had no idea if they would remain under his command.

Training was put in hand, a set of gravel pits outside the town serving as firing butts. As before, his sergeant took the main load, being so much better at musketry, and the teaching of it, than his officer. But they marched out every morning, passing the small knot of Corsican soldiers who'd appeared outside their billet, for a mile-long march to their temporary range.

The other issue which occupied his thoughts was Lizzie Gordon. Perhaps in a more bustling location he might have been able to put her out of his mind. But not in San Fiorenzo. It was so small, really an overgrown fishing port. The locals were very clannish, excessively protective of their womenfolk, and pious in a simple way. If there was a brothel in San Fiorenzo, not one of the marines and soldiers had been able to find it. The more sophisticated occupations pursued by officers, which included cards, music and dancing as well as fornication, were totally absent, the nearest place where such pleasures could be found being a day's sailing away in Leghorn. Naturally, when the wind blew fair, leave was assiduously sought by every officer who was convinced he could be spared from duty.

Markham lacked the means to take full advantage of Leghorn, even if he had the inclination. Besides, a man who was having difficulties in producing a defendant's friend would have even more trouble in finding officers willing to share their pleasures with him. The Italian mainland held few attractions if, in going there, he would be subjected to even more condescension than he received on the island.

Recalling, too frequently for his own peace of mind, what had happened aboard *Victory,* he felt confident that his pursuit of Lizzie Gordon would not be a complete waste of time. Whether it would turn out, in the end, the way he desired was another matter, the thrill of the chase being sufficient at this moment to keep him content. Not that he had much notion of how to go about it. If he saw her at all, it was in passing, and always with her husband. But Markham knew that to fret was a waste of energy. Opportunity would present itself if the fates allowed.

Rannoch was best placed to take his mind off

both things. The Highlander was not by nature given to moaning, but when it came to the Brown Bess musket he could barely be stopped, and two days in the gravel pits had him ranting. He railed against the stupidity that allotted each man a standard pattern gun, regardless of his size and build, insisting that by merely tailoring the stock to the individual, accuracy could be improved a hundredfold.

Not that it was held to be that simple. He knew better than anyone that practice was the key, just as he knew that at anything over a hundred yards, and firing into massed infantry, even the best trained unit would struggle to hit their target regularly. Muskets were inherently inaccurate, wherever they came from. But the Brown Bess had more faults than most, being a mule of a weapon. The large calibre ball was normally fired through a forty-six inch barrel, and had a kick on discharge that could break an unwary shoulder. But Rannoch was the only one still to possess his original army-issue Land Pattern musket; the rest of the Hebes, as well as the Seahorses, now carried the Sea Service weapon, four inches shorter, and a mite easier to control. Yet many of the same faults that plagued the bigger weapon still persisted.

The flash in the priming pan, as the flintlock struck home, was right beside the soldier's upper cheek, which meant that at the moment of firing, most men using the musket had their eyes shut. After ten or twelve continuous rounds, the gun-metal barrel became very warm, and further rounds expended could render it too hot to hold. Any crosswind, with such a large ball, was another factor militating against accuracy: the one thing, both Markham and his sergeant knew, that could stop even the most determined enemy in their tracks.

And everything was made even more difficult by the varying nature of the supplies they received. Now, having taken over the Lacombe's arsenal, they'd been issued with French cartridges, containing balls that were far too small. Rannoch had immediately begun to melt them down so they could be recast, before stitching the improved balls back into their cartridge cases.

'We require a gunmaker,' said Rannoch, 'just as we did in Toulon.'

'This isn't a naval base, Sergeant, in fact it's not much of a town. You'd be lucky to purchase a pair of decent pistols here, never mind find someone who makes the damned things.'

'There must be a fellow here who can make me a better mould. We need a woodworker too, some creature who can trim the stocks to fit each man.'

Rannoch saw the look on Markham's face, and continued at speed, which for him was unusual. 'We are out of sight here from Captain de Lisle, sir, so there is no one to object. And if the rumours we hear are correct, then we have a few days spare to do the thing properly.'

'The first time we order arms on deck, he'll go straight through the maincourse.'

'And what, I ask, can he do about it? Nearly every stock needs to be shortened. He may throw a fit if he likes, and jump about like a banshee. But unless he can make dead wood grow he must live with it.'

Markham grinned, recalling his forthcoming court martial. 'I doubt I'll be there to see it.'

'That would be a true pity,' Rannoch replied. When Markham flushed slightly, the Scotsman continued, pale blue eyes twinkling with mirth. 'Just when we have got you properly schooled in our ways.'

The search of the town, in pursuit of a gunsmith, was a fruitless one. In the history of the island, both Genoese and French overlords had suffered much from Corsican insurgency. The idea that locals should be encouraged to manufacture any form of weaponry was anathema. There was plenty of activity, but it was dispersed, with each islander his own expert, who brought into any conflict a gun that had all his own features stamped on it. Markham, considering this, thought perhaps that some explanation for the lack of Corsican success could be laid at the door of such behaviour, a notion with which Rannoch was quick to disagree.

'There's many a good man working on a gun away from towns,' he said, holding up his own weapon. 'This one was fashioned in such a manner.'

'In the Highlands?'

'Not quite that far north.'

'You've never actually told me which part of Scotland you're from.'

'No, sir,' Rannoch replied, a note of reserve in his voice. 'I have not.'

'I'd be interested to know.'

Rannoch pointed to a Corsican soldier, who'd

159

been a few yards in front of them ever since they'd left their billet. 'It might be worth asking that fellow, since you speak the lingo, if there's a man in the town who works in metal.'

Markham was piqued at the way his sergeant deliberately changed the subject. It seemed like years since they'd first met, yet it was a mere nine months, and then in circumstances so un-propitious as to presage disaster. Half the *Hebe*'s crew had been real marines, with the soldiers drafted in to make up the full compliment. Bullocks serving on ships was a commonplace of every new war. What was singular was mixing them with real Lobsters in the same hull. Their mutual antipathy was tempered by only one thing, a collective hatred of him, made manifest in the way they'd practically deserted him in their first engagement.

If relations with his men were bad, they proved even worse in the case of Rannoch, any exchange between them soundly based on the man's hatred of all officers. Both had been sent to sea service by a colonel anxious to get rid of them, a dubious honour they shared with all the Hebes, men who'd had been considered rotten apples by every officer in the 65th foot. George Markham was merely an embarrassment to his regimental commander, a man who'd taken up a commission which he and the colonel had thought dormant. Given his background, he could quite easily understand his own posting. There was little mystery regarding the colonel's desire to get rid of what he considered the dregs in his ranks.

But why Rannoch? The man was an excellent

160

soldier, a crack shot and a very competent sergeant. The mutual respect which had grown between them would have been impossible otherwise. And the gun Rannoch cherished so highly, plus his skill, had saved Markham's life more than once. Action and adversity had forged a good relationship with the men he commanded, but it had been the sergeant's efforts which had made the whole greater than the sum of its parts, not least his willingness to work in harmony with Corporal Halsey.

They'd lost two thirds of their men in Toulon, a higher casualty rate than most. But, as a testimony to the Highlander's care and attention, the survivors hadn't fallen apart. Quite the reverse. Their escape from the place, by the skin of their teeth, had been a collective achievement. As far as Markham was concerned, animosity had been replaced by respect, initially grudging but later wholehearted. Perhaps there existed, within the bounds of military discipline, a near friendship, as Rannoch realised that the officer he had was unlike many of his contemporaries. But Markham couldn't refer to any of these things. Nor to his feeling that, since they'd landed in Corsica, Rannoch's regard for him had cooled.

Silent for a long time, Markham finally spoke, aware that his growling voice was betraying his emotions, 'If there is a gunmaker, we'll find him soon enough in a place this size.'

San Fiorenzo being a small port, all the merchants' shops and warehouses were crowded into a compact centre. Other disconsolate officers were trudging aimlessly about, their long faces be-

161

traying clear evidence that they too were suffering in whatever quest they set themselves. There was a tailor, but he was not the type to have either the cloth or the skill to produce a proper replacement for a damaged army coat. Likewise hats, though the leather work was of a higher standard. As to the finer things required by campaigning officers – plate, cutlery, linen wear and the very best in food – the place was bereft. Fishing nets, canvas for sails, brasswork for boats, nails, tar, turps, linseed oil and all the other chandlers' goods they had in abundance. The merchants of San Fiorenzo traded in necessities, not luxuries.

Markham wasn't searching for luxuries, but Lizzie Gordon was. And so in the dark interior of one warehouse he bumped into her, without her husband, accompanied only by an Italian maid. Fortunately he was spared any hard looks, since Rannoch had stayed out in the street.

At first she pretended not to notice him, suddenly concentrating instead on a bolt of canvas that couldn't possibly be of interest to her. The small warehouse was poorly lit, and smelt musty from goods kept too long unsold. But as he moved a little closer he could just pick up a trace of her perfume, a lemony odour that he recalled from their first meeting. That made his blood race.

'I've often thought women in ducks an attractive notion,' he said in a low voice. She didn't reply, or turn round, but he saw the slight shiver of her ear and cheek as she set her face. 'The ladies at Sadler's Wells are wont to wear them when they do a naval pageant, and very fetching it looks.'

There was a significant pause before she finally

spoke. 'I daresay you know quite a few of them intimately enough.'

Markham was looking at the Italian maid, small, dark-haired and rather plump, who with the acute antennae of her type had immediately picked up the sensuality of the exchange, the brown eyes widening as they swept from her mistress to this officer and back again.

'I won't deny that fortune has favoured me on occasions with a view closer than that from the stalls.'

'Which would go some way to explaining your reputation as a rake.'

'It would perhaps justify the ease I feel in the company of women.'

She turned slowly, her finger still rubbing the thick, cream canvas. 'So much less brutal in judgment than your fellow men.'

'Certainly,' he smiled, though there was a harsher note in his voice. 'And far less boorish when full of claret. They have such a civilised attitude, women, and not just to killing and maiming.'

Lizzie knew he was referring to Hanger, and declined to respond. She hadn't missed the maid's expression either, and her blue eyes flicked very slightly in that direction. 'You will forgive me, Lieutenant, I must return to our villa.'

'A villa?' he replied, without moving aside to let her pass. 'A pleasant situation, I trust.'

'It is.'

'Does it have a name?'

'The Villa Ancona. Occupied by a French officer before us. He took most of the comforts of civilised existence with him when he departed.

My husband wishes to entertain, but will struggle to do so without plates.'

Markham bit his tongue. The name Hanger and the word entertain sat very ill together. 'But at least your Frenchman left you a maid?'

'No. I brought Maria from Leghorn. She has the advantage of a little English.'

'How very convenient,' Markham said, with a note of deep irony, since the strain on that modicum of language was obvious. Maria was trying very hard to understand the words, as well as the mood, of what she was witnessing. 'And where is your Villa Ancona?'

She looked him right in the eye then, knowing he was asking a question the answer to which he could pick up easily elsewhere. The location of Colonel Hanger's quarters would be common knowledge. Both were aware that another small piece of her defence was being challenged. He wanted her to say it, to give an indication of her position. He knew he'd won when the eyes dropped.

'The square is termed la Place des Chaumettes, though I believe the locals give it a different, more Italianate name.'

'Then with your permission, ma'am, I will call on you there.' He paused for half a second before continuing. 'And your husband, Colonel Hanger, of course.'

That brought the eyes back onto his, and they had a blaze of anger in them. The idea of George Markham calling on Augustus Hanger was ludicrous, said only for the benefit of Maria. He could see the strain in her, as she fought back the

164

hard words she wanted to belabour him with, also constrained by the maid's presence.

'That will not be possible, Lieutenant. My husband has gone over the passes to Cardo to carry out an examination of the French fortress line.'

It was a delight to him to observe the confusion that followed those words, in a woman who wasn't absolutely sure of her motives for using them. And she could see, plainly, by the smile on Markham's face, that he was choosing to interpret them as an invitation.

'It wouldn't be seemly,' she continued, with a slight catch in her throat, 'for you to call when Colonel Hanger is absent.'

His smile had evaporated. He wanted to move in closer, to see how she would react. But Maria made that impossible. The doubts that raged inside him became unbearable – not a new situation to Markham, who had done just such a thing with many women, only to be rebuffed for effrontery. But it was one of those moments of truth, too rare in any attempt to establish a mutual attraction, an occasion when, to win an inch forward, he had to risk a complete reversal.

'I told you before this that I would feel myself under no such constraints. And if I did call upon you, it would be the act of a deep and committed friend, who holds you in the very highest regard.'

The blood filled her cheeks, and he steeled himself for a slap. But even though her fists were balled, she didn't strike him, and the air which had filled her body to provide energy for the blow slipped out slowly. The lips, which had been pressed together, parted slightly, in a very inviting way. Lizzie Gordon didn't smile, but as far as Markham was concerned she didn't have to.

'Come Maria,' she said to the maid. 'Let us continue our task, and see if we can find the wherewithal to provide a decent table for the moment when my husband returns.' She swept past him in a wave of lemon scent. 'Good day, Lieutenant.'

As he bowed, he caught once more the brown eyes of Maria, open slightly too wide, an indication of her poorly concealed curiosity. When he smiled, it looked as if it was aimed at her. But it was more of an internal than an external pleasure. Lizzie Gordon didn't trust her maid, a wise precaution with any servant. And just so Maria couldn't hint to Hanger who her mistress had met while out shopping, his name hadn't been used once. Given the means to kill his pursuit stone dead, Mrs Elizabeth Hanger hadn't employed it, which left him wondering about the internal arrangements of the Villa Ancona, as well as the disposition of the other servants that must belong to the place.

Rannoch had seen her exit, and gave him a sour look when he emerged. Markham ignored him, and they continued in their quest, eventually finding a woodworker down by the harbour who would be happy to adjust the stocks. As soon as they returned to the billet, Markham requested that Quinlan and Ettrick be required to stand by, which earned him a deeply questioning stare from his sergeant.

'Regarding that woodworker,' Markham said quickly. 'We can't send all the weapons in at once,

166

so once I've finished with these two, we must sit down and work out our schedule.'

Rannoch didn't answer. He favoured his officer with a cold stare, the like of which Markham hadn't seem for months, that had him speaking for the mere sake of it. 'Then we must make sure we have enough balls to fit the guns.'

'We will not achieve what we managed before,' Rannoch said after a long pause, during which he picked up a French cartridge. 'Even if I work all night.'

'Put someone else to it.'

'Never. There are too many sloppy hands.'

'At least let some of the other men re-stitch the cartridges.'

'You're taking away the two most nimble,' Rannoch replied, nodding to Quinlan and Ettrick, who had donned their coats and were waiting for him near the doorway. As an oblique way of asking him what he was up to, it would have been perfect if he'd been prepared, for one second, to answer.

'Try some of the Seahorses,' Markham replied gaily, as he turned to leave. 'Who knows, one of them might be a true seamstress in disguise.'

Quinlan and Ettrick had gone outside by the time he emerged himself, and were trying un-successfully to trade for some tobacco with the Corsican soldiers who were lounging about. He called to them impatiently, and they fell in quickly, staying at his heels as he made his way through the narrow streets full of locals. The men had the grace to step aside when they saw a red coat coming: the British were allies. But judging by the fierce expressions in their black eyes, that

167

was not a courtesy they'd extend to an enemy, even if that man was a conqueror.

'They're an ill-looking bunch,' said Quinlan, which was odd coming from him, given that he was no hundred-guinea portrait himself. 'Half the buggers are ever on the move, dashing this way and that, yet there are more, like them rankers outside our billet, who just stand around an' watch us.'

'As if they was waitin' for somewhat to happen,' Ettrick replied. 'Or actin' as a Runner's snitch.'

Markham was only listening with half an ear, aware that these two were a couple of proper villains, whose presence in the colours was either a timely escape or a sentence handed down by a beak as an alternative to hanging or transportation. He had seen Quinlan pick locks with ease, and the way they worked was clear enough proof that they had been a team in civilian life too. Sharp-tongued, small and wiry, both with a foxy air to their features, they were the slipperiest pair in the Hebes, adept at ducking unpleasant duties. But that didn't matter to Markham. They'd proved themselves as fighters, and that was what interested him in the main.

'That's it,' he said, pointing across the small square to the thick wooden gates of a stunted villa. 'I want the number of servants, where they sleep, and the layout of the main rooms inside.'

'That last be the hard part,' said Quinlan, his face screwed up.

'I wouldn't be surprised if there are a couple of soldiers in there too,' Markham added, with an air of innocence.

'Whose abode is it?'

'Colonel Hanger's.' Both men whistled a little, then looked at each other. They knew the occupant of the house just as well as their officer did. 'He's away at present.'

'Just as well,' hissed Ettrick, 'given his love of a-stringin' folk up on a rope.'

'I can't, of course, order this.'

'No need for that,' Quinlan chirped, suddenly all smiles again. 'Bullock servants being inside will make it easy.'

'Why?'

'Never known one yet that wasn't keen to sell his master's claret. All we need, to get everything you want, is the means to buy a few bottles.'

It was slightly embarrassing, even in front of this pair, when he produced a purse that sagged enough to show how little it contained. Markham fetched out a few coins and handed them over, doling them out like a careful parent.

'That'll do, your honour,' Quinlan said. 'They won't be tying to vend it for top coin. We's'll be buying at wholesale, you might say.'

'Two hours,' Markham said.

'Just as long as you square it with the Viking, if 'n we come back staggering. Rannoch will have our back skin.'

'You leave Sergeant Rannoch to me.' Markham watched them as they walked out into the open square, sure that they were talking, but unable to hear their whispered exchange.

'He ain't plannin' to knife the bastard, is he?' asked Ettrick. ''Cause I want no party of that, if he is.'

'He is in a manner of speaking, friend,' Quinlan replied with a giggle. 'But the blade he has it in mind to shove home for the mortal wound is more akin to a blood sausage than a knife.'

''Course!' Ettrick exclaimed. 'Old Hang 'em High went an' got wedded.'

'Can't be more'n a two-month. Not that such will put a block on Lieutenant George Tenby Markham. Our boy's a proper Irish goat an' no error. He's no sooner marked 'em than he's half inside their petticoats.'

Ettrick laughed loud enough at this pun for his officer to hear him, which left Lieutenant Markham wondering how they could be so utterly relaxed when he was in such a state.

'You take my word for it, mate,' Quinlan continued. 'That scarfaced sod Hanger will have a pair of horns to add to his head afore we see daylight again.'

Chapter eleven

To people, the idea of climbing through a woman's bedroom window in the middle of the night would appear farcical, the stuff of a cheap novella rather than real life. But looking at the sketches Quinlan and Ettrick had executed for him, badly drawn, and stained with some of the drink they'd consumed, there seemed little alternative. The whole of the ground floor, apart from the public rooms, was occupied by either servants or Hanger's military valet and footmen. There were neither attics nor basements to accommodate them, and every room they used opened, in the Roman manner, onto the main hall and staircase.

The other difficulty was opportunity. Hanger was away on a specious reconnaissance for the army, but the place he was visiting, Cardo, lay a mere nine miles from San Fiorenzo, so close that he'd left the majority of his attendants behind. That told Markham two things: he was travelling light, and he intended to return swiftly to the comforts of his new wife and the commandeered villa. He could, of course, ask at headquarters, since the movements of someone like Hanger would be noted. But that risked drawing attention to himself, especially since their mutual antipathy was a poorly kept secret.

Markham believed in spontaneity, in matters relating to sex as well as war. Surprise was the basic key to success; an opportunity observed was best exploited quickly, lest it evaporate. It had generally served him well in both situations, and the times at which it had led him into trouble tended to be buried under the slightly vain awareness of the more frequent pleasures. If what he was contemplating bordered on madness, that merely reflected his emotions. Shut off in his small cubicle, with his men preparing to bed down for the night, he shaved carefully, humming to himself a soft rendition of 'Garry Owen', his favourite marching song. His thoughts were a flowing mélage of conquests past, the faces of women he had wooed and seduced mixed with the prospects for the forthcoming adventure.

His cloak would be an encumbrance, so that must be left behind. He'd have worn civilian garments if he had them, rather than his scarlet uniform coat, and even contemplated going without sword or hat. But that notion was discarded when he realised just how singular he would look. Out of doors in a war zone, on a dark night, being unarmed and bareheaded would draw attention to him rather than deflect it. The streets he was going to traverse would be quiet, but they wouldn't be completely devoid of life, even if the generals had imposed a curfew. Few Corsicans would be out late, but the Army would have patrols, and not just to suppress an imagined enemy. There might be no brothels in San Fiorenzo, and strict injunctions against molesting the womenfolk, but that had never stopped the British Army, wherever it billeted. Men would risk a thousand lashes for an illicit drink or a hour with a woman. It was only as he raised his hand to gently pull back the curtain that Markham realised that in reflecting on them, he was to a great measure, describing himself.

The wry grin produced by that thought had to be wiped away quickly. He was subjected to curious glances from around the room, some blatant, others covert. Rannoch was cleaning his musket, an almost obsessive nightly ritual with the Scotsman. Bellamy was alone in a corner, reading a book. To the assembled Lobsters that would appear very strange, much more so than if he'd been executing some wild tribal dance. He'd removed the top of the bandage from his crown, leaving just a strip tied round his head, which looked more like decoration that anything medical.

Ettrick and Quinlan were still drinking, consuming with a few of the other Hebes claret that both he and Hanger had paid for, watched enviously by the Seahorses. Some of that emotion was transferred to him. Holding a King's commission, he was not required to explain himself, and if he chose to go out in darkness that was his affair. The curfew didn't apply to officers.

The street seemed deserted, the night air chilly, even crisp, under a clear sky that had taken any warmth off the earth before the sun went down. A slight scuffing sound made him turn to look, but the area it came from was just a dark hole, the kind of spot that could hide a dozen cats or scavenging dogs. No other sound followed, so he turned and headed in the direction of the Place des Chaumettes, still softly whistling 'Garry Owen', the rhythm of the air dictating the speedy pace of his feet.

The cobbled roadway, when he joined a wider thoroughfare, produced something very close to a marching crack from the heels of his boots. He maintained it, first because it suited his mood, and also because he reasoned that he would attract less attention by appearing to be confident of his business, and was thankful for the moon- and starlight which rendered his progress so swift and painless.

The Place de Chaumettes lay no more than ten minutes from his own quarters, and soon he was by one of the side walls, close to a clump of stunted pine trees that Ettrick had alerted him to. Mentally conjuring up images from the drawings he'd been given, he reckoned this to be the best

173

point to scale the wall that enclosed the surrounding garden. The facing was old, rendered lime with enough cracks and exposed bricks to provide ample hand and footholds.

Markham took off his hat and sword, then hesitated. Another soft sound, like a shoe clipping a stone, catching his ear, was one reason. But the main one was the nagging thought he'd had all along; that a note should have been sent to Lizzie Gordon hinting at his intentions. He'd havered over this ever since he'd first had the idea, giving her something in writing that would at least allow her a degree of choice. Markham had discarded it, not sure if he had done so because he knew she'd be bound to refuse. But that at least would have avoided the worst scenario he could imagine: that not only would she not welcome him into her private chamber, but that she would scream the place down, summoning her attendants who would then chase him off the premises.

Was that what he wanted? To so frighten her that she would be bound to inform her husband of his attentions? Publicly faced with such information, Hanger would have to challenge him, an option to a senior officer in pursuit of justice from a junior which was denied, for obvious reasons, in reverse. He had that scarred face in his mind's eye now, not Lizzie's, as he contemplated the satisfaction he'd receive from finally, in a quasi-legal setting, being given the opportunity to revenge himself for the events of thirteen years before.

Thinking like that almost made him give up the whole idea. He had a natural aversion to any situation which forced others to pay a price for

174

his actions. The new Mrs Hanger, even if she did tell her spouse, would never convince him that she had not, in some way, encouraged his efforts at seduction. She might have called him a rake to his face, but it was a well known fact that women were, for better or worse, attracted to men with such a reputation.

'In the name of Christ, Georgie, me boy,' he whispered to himself, 'will you be after making yer bloody mind up?'

The image of himself, standing so indecisively, sheathed sword in one hand, hat in the other, made him laugh, and that in turn restored his confidence. He crept forward, to hide both articles in the thick, well pruned pine, his nose rubbing against the pungent greenery as he jammed both into the branches, to a point where they could not be seen by any passer-by. Exiting backwards, in the narrow gap between trees and wall, he looked up at the sudden sound of running feet, and the sight of two dark and silent shapes racing towards him produced the dive that took him back into the bush, as much to protect his body as to retrieve his sword.

He shouted, but the pair heading towards him remained silent. All he saw in the moonlight was the flash of a silver blade.

It was the trimmed pine that saved him, being thick enough to stop the hands jabbing forward from reaching their target. But confined as he was by both it and the wall worked against him as well. He couldn't unsheathe his sword, since the hilt had become jammed round a branch. He would die if he stayed still. Even if he could get his weapon clear, the time it would take him to wield it would be more than enough for one of his assailants to plunge a knife into him.

Instead he ran his hands up the wall, feeling frantically for a hold that could lever him upwards, yelling like a man possessed to alert Hanger's servants or any passing patrol to his plight, praying that even the most subdued response would scare off the robbers. When his foot slipped George Markham guessed he wasn't going to make it. Not willing to be stabbed in the back, hanging on to a wall by his fingertips, he dropped back to the ground and dragged himself round so that his back was to the cold, crumbling masonry. The robbers had taken one side of the bush each, and were pushing in behind it to get at him. Rather than wait for both, he rushed one. As he jabbed forward with his left hand he hit something metal and sharp, though he could feel no pain.

The weight of his body took the footpad out into clear space, and he fell backwards in a flurry of pine needles, stabbing again, though fruitlessly. The point of his blade, slowed by Markham's hold, was deflected by the knotted aiguillette on Markham's shoulder. Vaguely, he was aware of sounds from the other side of the wall, the shouts of alarmed servants coming to investigate the commotion. He was also alive to the fact that the man he'd attacked had ceased to try and kill him personally. Instead he was intent on holding him so that his companion could do the job with ease. His hands pushed against the rough cloth of the coat, in a vain attempt to get clear, the smell of the man, a mixture of stale sweat and garlic, in his nostrils.

The other shout, being on the outside of the wall, was loud enough to freeze every motion. In the moonlight, what they saw was like a ghostly apparition, a dark, nearly black face with a thin white strip around the brow. Markham reacted first, getting one hand free enough to land a blow on his attacker's cheek. It lacked the force to knock him out. But with whoever had come to his rescue moving forward to engage the man intent on knifing him, it provided just enough time to get partially clear, as well as enough space to allow him to grab hold of the arm that still held a knife.

The words that passed his ear were neither French, English nor even Italian. But the boot that took him in the side was international in its language and effect. Not only did it remove every ounce of air from his lungs; it sent him rocketing sideways as the man beneath him simultaneously heaved. He rolled hard against the wall, his feet scrabbling uselessly to give him the purchase that would allow him to dodge the follow-up blow.

But the man who'd kicked him had moved away, which allowed Markham to haul himself upright and attempt to marshal his senses. Sounds began to filter into his brain, as he tried hard to focus. His attackers were yelling incomprehensibly to each other, one engaged in what looked like a duel between a bayonet and a knife, while the other was gesticulating wildly. The Villa Ancona had lights in every window, as well as servants in the garden, calling over the wall behind him to demand an explanation. Third, and most important, was the heavy tread of military boots as a British army patrol came towards them. It was that which made the villains run rather than stay. They were gone quickly, mere ghostly shadows again, by the time the soldiers entered the square.

What had been a small empty piazza now became crowded, as first the patrol, then Hanger's servants appeared. Soon every house had disgorged its occupants, everyone carrying lanterns, curious to find out the reason for the commotion. Winded, with a thudding pain in his ribs, George Markham pulled himself upright. His head, once he was erect, came up last. The black eyes of Marine Eboluh Bellamy searched his face, the large whites matching the thin strip of bandage that remained round his head.

'Lieutenant Markham,' he said, his voice carrying a trace of shock.

'Bellamy?' Markham answered weakly.

'Stand out of the way, you bastards,' demanded a gruff North Country voice, accompanied by the sound of weapon butts hitting the ground. The crowd, which had gathered very quickly, parted to reveal a barrel-chested army sergeant, wearing a provost's sash, big enough in his bulk to conceal the men following him. 'What in the name of buggery is going on here?'

Markham pushed himself off the wall and shoved Bellamy aside, the stinging pain he felt the first indication that his hand had a deep gash. The look that was needed to confirm that slowed his response. But even before he spoke, the sergeant had taken in the cut of his uniform, and the scowl on his face evaporated as he pulled himself to attention.

178

'Sir.'

'Sergeant.'

'Braithwaite, sir. Twentieth foot. Might I be permitted to enquire what occurred here, sir?'

'A couple of footpads sought to rob me.' As he spoke, he saw the sergeant's eyes flick towards Bellamy, whose red marine coat was just as well lit as Markham's. 'Had it not been for my servant here, I would most certainly have been killed.'

Markham hoped the note of sudden inspiration, so obvious to him, wasn't equally apparent to the sergeant, who was now openly eyeing Bellamy up and down. This time the man's colour worked in his favour. The curfew applied to the Negro as much as it did to any other ranker. But if a gentleman chose to take a servant along with him, and a black man could be nothing other, then that was that officer's business.

'It seems you took the brunt of matters, sir,' the sergeant responded. Clearly he'd noted the pristine state of Bellamy's garments, as opposed to Markham's, and was wondering how an officer could be so attacked while his servant stood by unharmed.

'I was on the way to pay a visit,' Markham added quickly, determined to keep talking, even though it caused him pain, 'and I realised that I left something behind, so I sent my servant back to my quarters to fetch it.'

'Chancy, your honour.' As Braithwaite said this, his men pushed forward behind him, opening up the crowd so that they too could see the sorry object in the middle. Several of the locals were more taken with the Negro than Markham, point-

179

ing to him and gesticulating. Not so the Provost Sergeant, who was also looking at Bellamy, but with narrowed eyes. 'Had we come across him out of your company, we has the right to put a ball in him, or take him up before the Provost Marshal.'

'I thought it worth the risk,' Markham responded, as the sergeant, and several of his men, sucked in enough air through their teeth to let him know he was wrong. Markham turned to Bellamy, looking at him hard, commanding him by gaze alone to join in the subterfuge. 'Did you get the snuffbox?'

Bellamy was sharp-witted enough, when he answered, not to use his normal, well modulated voice, though the patois he employed, in Markham's opinion, went too far in the opposite direction. 'No Massa. I a'heared you a' yelling, so ah comes a'running.'

'He used his bayonet to chase them off,' Markham added, as much to shut Bellamy up as to provide information.

'Just as well, your honour. I would have had no mind to come across your body, full of holes, with a darkie private running around who was your servant. Might have gone hard against the bugger.'

'The people who attacked me were Corsicans!' snapped Markham, incensed at the automatic assumption that Bellamy would have been taken as the guilty party.

'Are you sure of that, sir?'

He was about to affirm it emphatically, when the image of his attackers came to mind. What doubts he'd carried evaporated as he realised it was the same outline as he'd seen, in that split second, on the beach at Fornali fort: that odd coxcomb flopping to one side on the hat, the short, dark, tight-fitting coats. The men who attacked him were not just islanders, but Corsican soldiers.

'Yes,' he replied, adding no more.

'Do you need a surgeon, sir?' Braithwaite inquired, indicating his cut and bleeding left hand.

'I suppose I will.'

The sergeant then barked at Bellamy. 'Take that bandage off your damned head, man, and give it to your master.'

'It's all right, sergeant. If I hold it up against my chest it won't bleed too much.'

'Then if you will fall in with us, your honour, we shall accompany you to the surgeon.'

'That's very good of you, sergeant.'

'It's my duty, sir. Just as it be the same thing that calls on me to report. Something will have to be done. Can't have the locals thinking they can rob, steal and murder at will, heathen Papists though they are.'

The sergeant stepped back to let him pass, and as he did so the crowd moved. Lizzie Gordon's maid Maria was there, recognition evident in her widening eyes. It was perhaps unfortunate that the sergeant chose that moment to ask for identification.

'May I enquire your name, sir?'

He had to reply, he had no choice. 'Lieutenant Markham, and this is Marine Bellamy.'

The sergeant was looking around, as if seeking something. It was then that Markham realised he was still both hatless and weaponless.

'Bellamy, be so good as to fetch my hat and sword.'

'Sir,' the marine replied uncertainly.

'They are in that pine bush.'

Braithwaite, when he stiffened, wasn't actually looking at the wall. He just needed to raise his head so as to avoid catching Markham's eye. He was too long in the tooth, had seen far too much service in the ranks, not to be able to deduce something of what had been going on.

'I think it would be best if we got off on our way, sir.'

'So do I, sergeant, so do I.'

Chapter twelve

Major Lanester had the kind of cherubic face that even the ravages of time could not make look grave for long. And Markham wasn't sure that underneath the barely disguised strictures regarding his recent behaviour, there wasn't a hint of amusement in those twinkling blue eyes. Markham had, as requested, sent in a written report on the incident, quite deliberately opaque as to the identity of his assailants, and avoiding altogether his reason for being in the vicinity. But in an army garrison numbering less than two thousand men, the gossip was quick to conclude what a man of his background was up to.

Hard as he sought to ward off contact with the rest of the garrison, they proved impossible to avoid. Firing practice had to continue, and only he could sign for the stores they received from the commissariat. Each time he stepped past the sentries, newly posted on his own front door, he was subjected to snide looks, accompanied by whispering, from both his fellow officers and the other ranks, inevitably followed by raucous laughter.

Even in his own billet he suffered some measure of the same, though certainly better intentioned. With the possible exception of his NCOs, the Hebes were secretly proud of him, while the Seahorses didn't know him well enough to risk ribaldry. But even then it still rankled, reminding Markham that he'd achieved the worst of all worlds. He'd compromised Lizzie Gordon, without enjoying any of the concomitant pleasures; provoked Augustus Hanger, yet left him in a situation where a demand for satisfaction was impossible, since that would only confirm what was, at this point, educated speculation. And in his heart he knew that whatever price fell to him for failure, the lady was paying more, thus adding remorse to all the other troubling emotions. So a call, even from someone he considered well disposed towards him, was unwelcome.

'Sergeant Rannoch!'

'Sir.'

The crisp response surprised him until he recalled the presence of Lanester. Rannoch might hate officers as a class, but he'd never let his own down in front of another.

'Take the men to the gravel pits, if you please. I will follow on shortly.'

'Is that to include those on sentry duty, sir?'

'No, leave them be. They can come on with me.'

The crisp thud of his boots on wood was a hangover from being in the army, one that had survived his induction into the marines. Rannoch wasn't alone, and his men's forgetful nature had caused Markham endless trouble with Captain de Lisle, forever complaining about the effect such stamping had on his precious deck.

'Looks like a good man,' said Lanester.

'He's the best sergeant I've ever come across,' Markham replied. A flash picture of the old Rannoch filled his mind: mean, angry and downright insubordinate, before he'd discovered that his new officer was determined to keep his men alive, rather than searching for a glory that would get them killed. 'He's also a crack shot, even with a Brown Bess.'

'You practise your firing daily, I hear,' Lanester replied, as Rannoch, now outside, got the men into order. Both officers listened as the commands were issued. The men fell in, shuffled as they dressed their line, came to attention and marched off before Markham answered, the tone of his voice registering the stiffness of an individual who suspected that he'd just been made the butt of a joke.

'Both Rannoch and I rate good musketry very highly, sir.'

'Volley fire will do at close range,' Lanester insisted. 'It's too damned costly, in time and money, to get anything more accurate in a whole regiment.'

'We're not a whole regiment, and are never

184

likely to be part of one. And since the powder and shot we're firing is French and free, it's too good a chance to miss.'

Markham only realised the pun when it was out of his mouth, one that under normal circumstances would have produced a laugh from his visitor. Now it brought forth a pained look, leaving him in some doubt as to the reason. Was it because the joke was considered bad, or the timing inappropriate? It was a relief that the look cleared quickly.

'Such application, Markham. And you even have proper sentries on your billet, and that in an allied town. I don't wonder that most of the officers I have spoken to consider you mad.'

'Only mad?'

Lanester tried hard to suppress the grin, only partially succeeding. 'That and a few other things besides, boy. You've certainly kept the Officers' Mess entertained these last three nights, though the jocularity dies quick enough if Hanger put his nose through the door.'

'What about the Navy?'

'Even worse, Lieutenant. They are a coarse bunch of rogues compared to the Army. You can't give rank to the sons of tradesmen and minor clergy then expect them to exhibit proper manners. Having had the misfortune to spend half a year in their company, you will know that better than most.'

Lanester said this without any rancour, which Markham attributed to his colonial past. That was unlike most soldiers, who tended to get quite passionate about the fact that they had to purchase their rank. More telling, they resented the fact that naval officers were not only given their commissions, but were fed and looked after by the Admiralty while they earned them. Commonly, Army officers considered themselves socially superior, a status hotly disputed by all of what the redcoats liked to denigrate as 'Tarpaulins'.

'Having served in both, sir, I would say the differences are too fine to register. My question regarding the Navy was related to my forthcoming court. I'm having some difficulty in finding a fellow officer to represent me.'

'They don't want to be tarred, perhaps.' Lanester waited for his own pun to produce a response. But Markham was too preoccupied even to notice the Major's play on words. Finally realising he was not to be rewarded with even a chuckle, he continued.

'Well, son, however galling that might be, you can forget about it now. Your court has been cancelled.'

'What?'

'At the specific request of Captain de Lisle. From what I hear, old Hood was exceedingly happy to oblige, though he did say something about a man minding what he did with the contents of his breeches. Vulgar perhaps, typical of a country parson's son, but the sentiment is faultless.'

Markham turned away slightly. 'What would you say if I told you that I was entirely innocent?'

'I would say go tell it to the fairies, or in your case the leprechauns. There's not a man jack on the island who doesn't know what you were after.

The only thing they're wondering on is, was it the first time, and if it was how far you would have got, failing the fracas which exposed your intentions.'

'Has Lizzie Gordon, I mean Mrs Hanger, been seen in public?'

'She most certainly has. Because she knows she's got to face down the damage you've inflicted. Besides, I'm sure her husband insists on it.'

Markham changed the subject quickly. 'Why do you think de Lisle cancelled the court?'

'I would imagine he did so at the express request of a certain Army colonel.'

'Hanger?'

'The very same.'

'But that doesn't make any sense at all!'

'How good are you on the Bible, boy?'

That threw Markham. It was a subject he'd loathed, being at the receiving end of two different readings of the same basic text, the only plus to the Protestant one being that it was in English, not Latin.

'There was a king once,' Lanester continued, 'who so lusted after another man's wife that he sent her husband off to die in battle.'

'Saul.'

'This notion kinda spins that on its head. Hanger has agreed to go along with Navy and invest Bastia from the sea. He'll have direct command of the artillery and engineers, which means he will exercise some control over the siege operations.'

'Nelson wanted to command.'

'Still does. But sailors can't do everything, son,

even if I've yet to meet one who will admit it. Once they're on land, he'll have to defer to Hanger's superior tactical knowledge. What I was trying to tell you is that the landing force is all marines, so you will be investing Bastia as well. Every Lobster in the fleet has been assigned to that duty.'

Markham opened his mouth to speak, but Lanester held up a hand to stop him. 'Hanger came back from Cardo even less enthusiastic about taking Bastia than before. His report put the garrison inside the town at over three thousand. Nelson lambasted this as utter nonsense, divided Hanger's estimate by two, and is insisting on besieging with only half that number. In pure military terms, if Hanger is closer to the truth, that borders on gross stupidity.'

'It could be false information. The French are good at that sort of thing.'

'It could. It might also be too damned true, especially since our Corsican allies provided the figure of fifteen hundred, which Nelson professes to believe.'

'And you don't?'

'I'm no different from all the other soldiers, Markham, reluctant to trust any figure the Corsicans gift us. But that's bye the bye. Nelson will go ahead because Hood wants action. And Hanger, who despite your opinion is no fool, and was dead against the whole thing three days ago, is now prepared to go with him.'

'And General d'Aubent approves?'

'Reluctantly, provided certain conditions are met.'

'Hanger's not going because of me?'

'Give me another good reason why he would court what, to his mind, is almost certain defeat. Of course the Navy will bear the brunt of the blame, so he won't be too badly distressed in terms of his career. But logic dictates that he should decline to move, like everyone from General d'Aubent down. He hasn't, and from what I hear at the latest conference he helped Nelson and his enthusiasm overwhelm the gathering. You hurt him bad, Lieutenant, so bad he must have trouble digesting his victuals. And it's not a situation he can salvage by calling you out.'

'Because I'd kill him,' Markham snapped.

Lanester lost a measure of control then, his voice becoming harsh and commanding. 'You know that's not the reason.'

'No,' Markham replied softly.

'I've taken the trouble to ask a few questions about you.'

'Have you?'

'Not hard to get answers right now, of course. You'd be surprised how much envy you generate.'

'I don't think so.'

'Is that common sense or vanity?' Lanester asked without emphasis on either proposition. Markham too had realised how it sounded, and had the good grace to blush. 'Funny thing, but a lot of what all these folks say to diminish you, kinda raises you in my eyes.'

'I think Americans are possibly less hypocritical.'

Meant as a compliment, it produced exactly the opposite effect. 'Don't you believe it, son. Hypo-

189

crisy knows no borders, and is not diluted even by three thousand miles of sea water.'

Markham wanted to ask what it was that so impressed him. If Lanester knew, he was in no hurry to pass on the information. The major sat for several seconds, lost in his own thoughts, before he chose to continue.

'Rumour has it that you get a touch stretchy with your orders. That you're rude to your superiors, speak when you should stay silent, interfere in operations that are none of your concern and waste every waking moment on firing practice.'

'I could mount a defence to that.'

'But not without more than a touch of bombast, I reckon.'

'No.'

'Hanger intends to get you killed, son,' said Lanester, confirming what he'd only hinted at. 'If you're not first ashore at Bastia, you and those men you just sent off to the pits will be in the thick of whatever is going. A man's luck can only last so long, and if Hanger gets his way, whatever rumours there are about you and his wife will die along with you.'

'He's tried it before, Major. And if he does so again, don't let him fool you that it has anything to do with his wife's reputation. I'm the man that put that scar on his face, so I'm with him every time he shaves.'

'When was that?'

'That's of no importance.'

'America, then!' snapped Lanester. 'I heard a whisper you two went back that far.'

'He'd have killed me there, if he hadn't been

too drunk.'

'The difference is, Lieutenant, if he succeeds this time, most people will turn a blind eye. You didn't stand too high in folk's minds before this. Now, thanks to your nocturnal wanderings, you've sunk even lower. Where I come from, the word skunk would figure. Now I reckon that you are sorry for that, and you're the type who, had the lady obliged, would have kept your own counsel.'

'I would, of course, have done just that.'

'Those two footpads have a lot to answer for.'

'They weren't footpads, Major, they were Corsican soldiers.'

'Soldiers!'

'Do you remember what I thought I saw at Fornali?'

Lanester nodded slowly, the bright eyes now bearing into Markham's. 'I recall you weren't too sure of yourself.'

'I am now!' Markham snapped. 'The pair who tried to knife me were dressed the same way as that silhouette. It was like seeing the same thing twice. Round hats that flop to one side and dark serge jackets, tight breeches and high boots. It's not much of a uniform, but it is the only one our allies have. How many Corsican soldiers are there here in San Fiorenzo?'

'A few. Generally only those who're providing escorts for their liaison officers.'

'Personal bodyguards, in other words.' Lanester nodded. 'And how many of those were in the vicinity of Fornali the night the French pulled out?'

The major didn't reply, because it was superfluous. 'Is that why you have guards outside?'

'Yes.'

'Did you put this in your report?'

'No,' Markham replied, adding as Lanester raised an enquiring eyebrow, 'Remember Hood's dinner.'

'Hard to forget. Dundas put you and the Corsican commanders on the spot. Quite entertaining, I seem to recall.'

'Not for me. Grimaldi quizzed me when I returned from the deck. I could have explained what I thought I saw, including my doubts, though I think that would have done more harm than good. Besides, I guessed Hood didn't want it aired, so I said nothing.'

'So the locals still have no real idea?'

'I stuck to my story, trying to scotch the worst of what Dundas had said.'

'He certainly likes a tall tale. None of that brief glimpses stuff. He practically said you would remember them well enough to get revenge.'

'What did he add when I wasn't there?'

'Dundas never got the chance to add anything. Hood kept them well occupied, I presume with his apologies. When Hanger tried to talk to them, Nelson was alongside them in a flash.'

'Well it didn't do much good,' Markham added grimly. 'So this time, if you don't mind, I'll keep all the senior officers in the dark. I interrogated my men when I came back. This billet has been watched since that day. It didn't register with them, or me for that matter, and why should it. Who is going to comment on local rankers lounging around in their own bailiwick? It was only afterwards that anyone questioned what so many Corsican soldiers were doing in San Fiorenzo in the first place, when their army is investing the forts before Bastia.'

'That was nearly a week ago. Why did they wait?'

'I was never alone, Major, until that night.'

'You weren't alone then, from what I hear.'

'I was when I left this billet. Bellamy, the marine who disturbed them, was out without permission.'

'Looking for what?' Lanester asked.

'A drink, perhaps.'

'Or a woman,' said the major, with deep irony. He stood up then, and began to pace up and down, his head sunk on his chest. Markham watched him for several minutes. Finally the pacing stopped, and he fixed him with a serious look.

'I came here to warn you, Markham. To give you the option, if you like, of declining certain hazardous duties.'

'For which I thank you.'

That made Lanester impatient. Having marshalled his thoughts, he wanted to speak without interruption. 'But after what you've just said, you stand in more danger than Hanger can provide. If the Corsicans have tried to kill you once, they may well do so again.'

'Thank you, Sir David Dundas,' said Markham sardonically.

'Will you be silent, sir!' Lanester snapped. 'The old sod has gone. But that doesn't alter matters. The army command still thinks that one, maybe even two, of the senior Corsican officers is working against us and his own countrymen.'

'Then they need to be exposed,' Markham interrupted, earning himself another hard look. 'Especially if we are going to try to take Bastia from the sea.'

'And how, clever Dick, would you go about that?' snapped Lanester. 'These are officers of an allied force. Why do you think Hood spent so much time grovelling? Dundas has gone, which has soothed ruffled feathers. The merest hint that Hood suspects them of treachery, without proof positive, could be fatal. I don't think you have any idea how prickly these Corsicans are in matters of honour.'

'Methinks the lady doth protest too much,' Markham murmured.

'What!'

'Shakespeare, sir. *Hamlet.*'

'Damn *Hamlet!*'

'I merely suggest, sir, that protestations of honour are not always justified. I've known them used as a cloak by the most unscrupulous people.'

The look Lanester gave him was singular, almost enough to harden the fleshy jowls of his face. But his voice remained the same. 'That's for certain. But it doesn't alter the fact that Nelson, with you, Hanger and all the fleet marines, intends to be off Bastia within ten days, wind and tide permitting.'

'That soon.'

'Nelson contends that delay only makes the enemy stronger,' Lanester snorted. 'That from a man who won't even admit that the numbers he's been given might be false, nor allow any leeway for the fact that the Corsicans may well not support him.'

'And the army still won't move?'

'No. But General d'Aubent asked me to go to Corte, and take a request to General Paoli that he come to Bastia personally and intercede.'

'Everyone seems very sure he has the power?'

'I told you before, son, to the ordinary people of this island he's a saint. But the most vital thing is this. He will know how to expose anyone betraying the cause, or to shift them so that their effect is capped, even if it means replacing them all.'

'Perhaps a more Corsican method will be employed.'

'The knife?' said Lanester rhetorically. 'Not Pasquale Paoli. He's spent his whole life trying to rid this land of the vendetta. He wouldn't engage in the start of one himself.'

'Why you, sir?'

'Well, for a start, Sir Gilbert Elliot, the politico who deals with the old man, is not here to do it for us. After our little meeting on *Victory*, I happened to mention to both Dundas and d'Aubent that I know him quite well. So the request that I go is natural.'

'How did you meet?'

For once Lanester's face took on a look of utter desolation, the twin lines between his nose and his cheeks deepening considerably. 'Two exiles, stuck in London hankering after home, we had a lot in common. Mind you, we also had a great deal to disagree about. But that's the thing about a man like Paoli. You can differ with him violently, and still hold his respect.'

'D'you think he'll oblige?'

'Not without pressure. The man wants some peace and quiet in his old age. But when you're the only person who can unify a nation, retirement is not very likely to be on the cards.'

Markham nearly said 'like George Washington', but stopped himself.

'Hanger had to persuade d'Aubent to let him go with Nelson. That was the general's condition. Either the Corsican army has new commanders, ones we can trust, or Paoli himself. Not that failure will deflect Nelson, who's a glory-hungry lunatic to my way of thinking. He'll attack Bastia regardless.'

Markham was about to defend Nelson, who he felt was being blackened, even if there was some truth in his desire to gain glory. But Lanester had started pacing again, head on chest. If the major was right, then he was in some danger. Augustus Hanger knew how to give him dangerous duties, ones that he couldn't decline for fear of losing face. His awareness that such an attitude was stupid didn't alter things. He could swear to all the saints in the canon that he wouldn't oblige, yet knew that when the time came he'd never let Hanger embarrass him. And if the Colonel succeeded in getting him killed that way, the stain would be erased from his wife's reputation.

'I need an escort,' said Lanester suddenly.

That made Markham stiffen – though not the notion itself. In such a wild country as Corsica, which had its share of banditti even in wartime,

it was unwise to travel the country without protection.

'I'm sure your own regiment will oblige.'

'It's not my regiment, son, I'm on attachment.'

That was common enough. Many regimental
officers held their commissions for social rather
than military reasons. Given a war to fight, they
were happy to stay at home and let a more
aggressive, or a more needy, officer take their
place.

'Surely that won't matter.'

'What about you, Markham?'

He'd guessed that was coming as soon as
Lanester mentioned his requirement. Having
him on hand to tell Pasquale Paoli, in person,
what he has seen, could be just the degree of
pressure the major was seeking. It was tempting,
but Markham knew it had to be refused.

'I won't run away.'

'Even if you are given express orders to do so?'

'No such orders have been issued.'

Lanester grinned then. 'I think you should be
getting on with your firing practice, don't you
Lieutenant?'

Chapter thirteen

Lanester was back before twilight, to inform
Markham that de Lisle, invited to replace both his
marine officer and the men he led, had jumped at
the chance, while the *Seahorse* had yet to return

from its mission to Admiral Hotham. Any further protests had been swept aside. Lanester produced written orders from Hood himself, and given that the fleet marines were already being loaded onto Nelson's ships, there was no time available to make representations for a change of duty.

'Draw rations as required,' snapped Lanester, 'then get some sleep. We leave at first light.'

A fifty-mile march over mountain roads was hardly a job for marines, something Halsey had taken pains to point out. Rannoch, still a soldier despite his coat, merely redoubled his efforts with his moulds, calling on all the men to make enough ammunition to see them to Corte and back, regardless of what they encountered. Markham was just downcast. He knew that, even though he was commanded to the duty, it would be seen in another, less flattering light by those he left behind.

No direct road existed between San Fiorenzo and Pasquale Paoli's mountain retreat, and Lanester would not even consider the uncomfortable route to Corte, straight through the central belt of mountains. He'd commandeered a wagon and loaded it with gifts, the product of a serious raid on every ship in Hood's fleet. He'd also helped himself to the better class of supplies, so that, as he put it, 'his little command wouldn't starve, or want for a decent glass of wine'. Pavin, his whey-faced, wrinkled servant, had interpreted this to mean the major himself, and just possibly Markham. The Lobsters who provide the escort could eat hard tack for all he cared.

The wagon obliged the party to cross the Colla

di Teghima and skirt Bastia, a route which, of necessity, traversed the rear of the Corsican positions around Cardo. They left the last British post on the rising ground near Barbaggio, some four miles from San Fiorenzo, surprised to learn from the officer in command that French cavalry patrols were active along the route.

'I thought the Corsicans had them well bottled up,' said Lanester.

'The French infantry, yes. But the coastal routes are open north and south of Bastia. The locals don't have the manpower to close off the whole town, and they are not overly gifted with mounted units of their own.'

'Is this just rumour?'

'No, sir,' the young officer replied, pointing up the road. 'We had one of them come within long musket range not twelve hours ago.'

'Lieutenant Markham,' Lanester called, turning in his saddle. 'Keep your men closed up, and ready. Once we're past this piquet, it's not friendly territory.'

'Yes, sir,' Markham responded, with the same sour air he had worn since Lanester told him of the intended route.

The road rose and the encroaching woodland retreated, until they were traversing the open, barren landscape on which they'd camped during the pursuit from Fornali. It looked even more desolate now, devoid of the men and equipment that had surrounded them. Clumps of tough bush alternated with great wind-hewn boulders and jagged spirals of ancient rock. Deep gullies were numerous to both right and left, some big enough to house an entire squadron of cavalry, which kept the whole party alert.

The temperature dropped inexorably until, still bunched up and watchful, they reached the highest point of the Teghima Pass, hills towering on either side, a thousand feet higher than the road itself, with a lonely Corsican outpost the only visible sign of human habitation. Once inside the Corsican positions, with a junior ensign delegated to escort them, they could relax a little. After a brief stop, some food and a hot drink, they were marching downhill, in increasing warmth, the tensions which had plagued them since Lanester sprung his surprise beginning to fade.

'Might I suggest we cut the corner off the road, sir? A couple of my men can escort the cart round without stopping. That will at least keep you and me clear of the Corsican camp.'

Lanester replied in that jokey way which he'd previously found amusing. On this day it grated on Markham's nerves. 'You're not suggesting I forgo a decent dinner, Lieutenant, are you?'

'Given the lack of time, sir, I'm proposing a course of action that would be expedient.'

'Can't hear you for the rumbling in my belly, son. I believe I said plainly before that I have no mind make my way by mule track.' He jerked his head towards the Corsican ensign, riding alongside him. 'Besides, what would this young buck think if we headed off into the woods?'

Markham nearly said, 'Just don't tell them where we're going, or why.' But he stayed silent, feeling the words would be wasted. Nor could he point out what Lanester should have taken into account: that for George Markham, proximity to such an encampment was like volunteering for a spell in the lion's den, that he'd feel more secure under Hanger's orders. He was a grown man and an experienced fighting soldier. There was no way he could say to another officer that every time he spied one of those tight-fitting Corsican hats, he had to suppress a shudder.

They saw the three French forts first, well-constructed redoubts really, lacking only numerous artillery pieces to make them truly formidable. They stood high on the coastal plain commanding the approaches to the walled port of Bastia, some distance in the rear. Markham's depressed spirit rose a little at the sight. Soon the bay beyond would be full of ships, this the place to be regardless of risk from supposed friends or foe. The tinge of exhilaration didn't last long, as he contemplated the drudgery, not to mention the dangers, of the task Lanester had landed him with.

The administrative centre of French rule on the island, as it had been for the Genoese, Bastia was Corsica's largest city. It was also home, according to their escort, to a multitude of people who still supported the notion of French rule, this information imparted with a gobble of spit and an air of great sadness.

'But we will chase them into the sea, will we not, Major,' the boy said, the worry that had creased his brow clearing as his optimism was restored. 'God Save King George and the people of Corsica.'

'Amen,' Lanester replied, his eyes ranging over

the tent city that held the bulk of the island's army.

'They're pushed well forward,' said Markham, professional interest overriding his other feelings. 'If the enemy sortied out from those redoubts, they'd have scant time to man their defences.'

Asked about this, the ensign fumbled for an answer. But when his imagination provided one, it was supplied with a glow of pride. 'We want them to see the whites of our eyes, to know that we are close so that they will have great fear. Every night, they must run a hand across their throat to see if it is still whole.'

Markham was tempted to say something about sabre cuts, but stopped himself. General Arena must know the French had cavalry available, and outside the defence lines, well able to mount a surprise attack. If he hadn't bothered to take precautions to deal with it, no words of his would change anything. That attitude was less assured when they examined the Corsican front line. The battlements of the nearest French redoubt, eight hundred yards distant, were easily visible with the naked eye, alarmingly close when viewed through his small telescope. Lanester, striding along beside him, likewise examining the French defences, was scathing.

'If they'd been this hugger-mugger when we came ashore at Fornali, the whole island would be French free by now.'

'It's too close for my liking. We're practically within six-pounder range.'

'Hanger reported they're short on cannon.'

'They wouldn't need too many at this distance.'

Lanester nodded without looking at him, his air slightly bewildered. 'They sure have a funny way of making war, these fellows.'

Seen close up, and in quantity for the first time, Markham could examine the Corsican Army, and begin to consider the difficulties they faced in fighting disciplined French troops. Their uniforms, such as they were, consisted of homespun jackets that had all the variety of features which come from being made by hundreds of different hands. Boots varied in length and quality. Even the round, oddly-shaped hats were mixed, vivid colours, some embroidered and tasselled, others plain black.

Equipment was just as primitive and individual, everything from ancient musketoons to the odd, even older, blunderbuss. A few regiments were fully supplied with the muskets Hood and Dundas had gifted them, and these, being the smartest clad, were probably Arena's most experienced, and certainly most disciplined troops. For the rest, they were a militia, men called from farms, villages and tending sheep to fight the enemy. Order seemed less than perfect in their ranks, hardly surprising in a peasant army. Yet history proved that they were tough, individualistic and brave, even if they did need inspired direction to achieve success. According to the perceived wisdom, he and Lanester were on their way to see the only person in the whole island who could provide such leadership.

The idea that such an aim and destination could be kept secret turned out to be wishful thinking. Either through a deliberate leak or casual conversation, the officers of the Corsican Army seemingly knew where they were going before they arrived. Lanester, with a face like thunder, came back from a courtesy call to headquarters that had lasted for nearly an hour, instead of in the time it would take to sort out part of the camp where Pavin could light a fire, as planned.

'Damnit! San Fiorenzo must leak like a sieve. I never got a chance to tell them our destination, since they told me. I'm surprised they didn't decide to read me my actual orders for a joke.'

'Do they know why?' asked Markham, with some alarm.

'No. But by damn they probed enough. That's why I've been so long. I've managed to convince them it's just a courtesy visit, one old friend calling on another, social like.'

'Are you sure they believe you?'

'They don't give away much. I've seen snakes whose eyes move more.'

Markham looked at the fire, blazing with its third quota of logs. 'I'd like to feed the men before we move on, sir.'

'You'd best sort out some billets. We're staying till the morning.'

'What!' Markham protested. Lanester looked at him hard, then jerked his head to indicate that the men could overhear them. But Markham wasn't to be deflected. They should never have come near Cardo at all in his estimation, and he didn't care what the major, or the Lobsters, thought of that opinion. He looked the sky, grey and overcast, but still light. 'We can make another six miles before dark.'

'Too late, Markham,' Lanester said softly. 'An invitation to dine has been issued. After all I said about being social, I figured it would only excite their suspicions if I declined.'

'Did you accept for both of us?' Markham asked, matching the major's quiet tone.

'Why?'

'I can move on with the men, sir, and you can make up the distance on horseback.'

'Not on your life,' Lanester exploded. 'I'm not eating with these fellows alone.'

'Time, sir. Nelson will land in nine days.'

Lanester looked grave, and he took Markham by the arm and led him away from the men. 'For the sake of six miles, Markham, we have to chance it. It would never do to let these bastards, with their nasty distrustful ways, think we're in a rush.'

'Even if we are?'

The response to that was delivered with an impatient hiss. 'I was told you were quick to the nick, boy, and yet I find you're slow, real slow. You still haven't figured it out, have you?'

With no actual answer, Markham adopted the only sensible course and said nothing, even although Lanester's pause was more than long enough to allow it.

'Coming through here was deliberate. Do you really think we could have crossed half the island without these men finding out where we were headed? Lord save us, we couldn't have got clear of San Fiorenzo. I'm trying to allay their suspicions, boy, and that includes any they have regarding you. I aim to get us to Corte in one piece, and bring back Paoli, even if it means cutting it a little fine. Now do me a kindness: park that sour puss of yours, and acknowledge that this is my mission, and that I know what I'm about.'

Lanester and his unwilling escort thus found themselves changing into their very best uniforms, one with good cheer, the other still reluctant. Markham became steadily more morose, and he made no secret of his feeling that one dinner with the senior Corsican commanders had been quite enough. But the major's servant, Pavin, easily out-gloomed him.

'One slobber of an officer is enough for me,' he moaned, as he stabbed a needle at the torn aiguillette on Markham's coat with all the venom of a bayonet. 'An' them damned Lobsters we fetched along will be laying about having downed their supper, while I slave over their governor's needs.'

Lanester, tweaking his fresh linen, ignored him and addressed Markham, who was polishing his own boots, holding them up so that they reflected the light of a dozen candles. 'You should be grateful, Lieutenant, that it's only one dinner. If I'd accepted all that was offered, including an invite to hunt, we'd be here for ten days.'

'What do we say to them, if they probe further? They're not going to believe that our mission is purely social, regardless of how much you smile.'

'Acknowledge the truth, up to a point. No sense in denying what they'll already have guessed. Just say we're going to see Paoli to ask him to redouble his efforts to help us. Hint that we're not concerned about Bastia, but Calvi. That will make

206

sense, since the defences around Calvi are naturally stronger.'

'So we need more troops?'

'That's a good idea. If you're stuck, mention that there are several regiments sitting to the south of Calvi, outside Ajaccio, which don't seem to be doing much.'

'And my being here?'

'Coincidence, man!' Lanester barked.

'There,' barked Pavin, as Markham opened his mouth to respond, 'best I can manage.'

Markham sat for a moment, unconvinced. But a growl from Pavin forced him to take his coat, and examine the expert repair. The thick gold threads entwined across each shoulder, made from the same material as Lanester's epaulettes, were once more a perfect match, as good as new. He opened his mouth to offer thanks, but Lanester's servant didn't wait for him to speak.

'What's that Sawney Jock sergeant of yours like?'

'You,' Markham replied, acidly, 'when it comes to respect for officers.'

That brought forth a snorting laugh from Lanester, and an even deeper glare from Pavin. 'That wagon I've set them to guard with their lives has all the major's rations on it, along with his gifts for General Paoli, which is only fittin'. Others might wonder what it's doing loaded with the packs of lazy soddin' escorts.'

'They won't steal it, if that's what you think.'

'They won't, eh! Then they's the first Lobsters that I've met that ain't got sticky claws. If'n so much as a sip of claret goes missing...'

'Do be quiet, Pavin,' said Lanester, without

much in the way of emphasis, as he struggled to do up his waistcoat.

Markham had watched the cases of fine wine loaded, some for consumption on the journey, others for General Paoli. He knew as well as anyone the temptations brought on by the presence of drink, and had issued strict orders to Rannoch regarding pilfering. With his usual shrewd appreciation of where trouble might lie, Rannoch had put Ettrick and Quinlan in charge of guarding it, and the pair now stood between the rankers' tents, at permanent attention, poachers forced to turn gamekeepers.

'Are you ready, Lieutenant?' Lanester asked, consulting his watch.

'I am,' he replied gloomily, slipping on his coat. Pavin, in a propriatorial way, immediately began to brush the shoulders.

'You stay on the bloody duckboards, both of you,' he grumbled as he fussed around. 'I ain't polished them boots to perfection just so you can turn up muddy to your knees.'

Both Markham and Lanester, responding affirmatively and simultaneously, sounding like children speaking to a mother. They were then hustled out through the flap with an injunction to step out, lest they be late. The Corsican officers, a round dozen of them, not only the generals but their escorting ensigns as well, were standing waiting for them. They filled the door of the convent dining room, the largest in the cluster of buildings that comprised headquarters.

The walls were, apart from various religious artifacts, bare and white, the roof the beamed interior of the thatch which covered it. But the table, normally the communal eating place of the nuns, was well laid, with enough silver to make a decent show. And the officers had dressed for the occasion, replacing their plain brown, workaday uniforms. Now they wore dark blue coats, faced and cuffed in orange. Markham, as he was ushered to his place, couldn't help looking hard at the faces of the men who'd invited them, wondering which one was responsible for trying to kill him.

General Arena, the commander, who had rather a stiff manner to go with his height and sallow, marked complexion, set himself to be as agreeable as he could to his two guests, recounting anecdotes about the earlier battles with the French, when he had been but a junior line officer. Grimaldi, who'd told Markham similar tales at Hood's dinner, was as pleasant as ever, never leaving a British glass anything other than brim-full. The behaviour of the rest of the officers ranged from formally polite to openly friendly. Of the general officers, only Buttafuco seemed rather morose, drinking little, somewhat distracted, when he did look at them eyeing the pair of guests with little warmth. But the wine flowed, and food was consumed, so that whatever reservations Markham might have had soon evaporated. At least here, in public, he was safe, and felt he might as well enjoy himself, and swap soldierly tales with some relish.

The Corsican officers were intrigued by his service in Russia, to them a land as foreign as the moon. The Czarina Catherine had at one time offered to take over the protection of the island, an

209

act which had only served to make the French even more zealous in their conquest. He tried to describe the country and its people, the problems of fighting with an army in the tens of thousands, often through country so open that there was nothing but a few trees between you and the horizon. The Corsicans responded with tales of battles in the dense woods and valleys, known locally as the *marchetta*, where men, while they might only be engaged in the hundreds, struggled with a ferocity often bred of differing kinds of desperation.

'Our aim,' said Arena, 'was always to avoid set-piece battles, on any other terrain than that which we deliberately chose.'

'Very necessary,' responded Lanester, 'when your enemy always musters superior numbers.'

'The classic dilemma for a small nation, gentlemen,' said Grimaldi. 'The ability to win every skirmish, but how to win so major a battle that a more numerous foe will give up?'

'And give way to another conqueror,' added Buttafuco.

'Genoa gave up,' said Lanester, to cover what was clearly a certain amount of embarrassment. 'And, with British assistance, so will France.'

'Everyone has heard of Nonza,' said Markham, to back Lanester up. 'Let that stand as an example.'

That reference to the Nonza fort produced grins all round, as well as a noisy toast. It was indeed an inspiring tale, from the age before the Revolution. Nonza had been held by a certain Giacomo Casella, whose garrison deserted him after

General Grandmaison inflicted a particularly serious defeat on the Corsican forces to the south. Casella, when the enemy approached, had fired off every piece of artillery himself, plus all the muskets, shouting commands from the battlements that convinced the French the fort was still manned. They offered honourable terms to avoid bloodshed, which Casella, having consulted with his 'fellows', accepted. He then marched out, fully armed, between twin files of astonished French grenadiers, to reveal that he'd been the only man in the place. The story had spread round Europe like wildfire, and was one that could always be used to silence anyone from the French military if he became too bumptious.

That set the senior officers off on the full gamut of Corsican legends. As he listened, Markham was impressed by what these men, as well as their predecessors, had achieved. Boswell had published his book about the independence struggle and the man who led it many years previously, one of those tomes he'd promised he would read, but never got round to. But many of his acquaintances had, and they spoke of the place often enough to provide him with a vague understanding of how titanic a struggle it had been.

Even the women of Corsica, it seemed, had taken up arms against the invaders, fighting and dying alongside their men, refusing to countenance withdrawal, even when ordered to do so. Once launched into that kind of nonsense, and full of drink, their manners deserted them. It was no longer a conversation, but a lecture. They went on and on till he became bored, often repeating

211

themselves in their desire to impress, each time increasing the detail until it seemed every individual musket shot, in every skirmish, needed to be recounted. The Corsicans were brave, even, it seemed, the womenfolk, while the enemy, French and Genoese, were low dogs who never fought in a fair way. It was like all national tales, more one-sided the more it was told, the myths by which any people sustained themselves, underlying the conviction of their own superiority.

Chapter fourteen

'We fought the French to a standstill in four campaigns,' said Arena for the third time. He was now very drunk, his face no longer sallow, but red from heat and alcohol.

Lanester, fearing that he would recount every battle again, raised his glass. 'To the bravery of the Corsican soldier.'

'And the British soldier,' Arena responded, once he'd drained his own glass and had it refilled.

'Let us not forget the marines,' said Buttafuco, who'd continued to drink sparingly.

'The marines,' slurred Grimaldi, who was sitting right next to Markham. Then he leant over with a leer, pushing his goblet under his guest's nose. 'And, of course, their nocturnal adventures.'

That made Markham look at him hard. Grimaldi was grinning from ear to ear, pleased with his own wit. His dark eyes sparkled and the candlelight, coming from the side, made his prominent nose stand out even more.

'We had Colonel Hanger at this very table less than a week ago,' said Buttafuco.

'A fine officer,' said Lanester, trying to deflect the conversation away from what he suspected might be coming.

Buttafuco was not going to be put off, even if he did avoid eye contact when he continued. 'With a beautiful wife, I understand.'

'Indeed,' replied Markham stiffly.

'In Corsica, we kill men who trifle with our womenfolk. They are like traitors, these people who creep about in the night. They deserve the knife.'

Markham knew he had to remain quiet. He wanted to scream out about the men who'd died in their foxholes at Fornali, of his own near miss in San Fiorenzo. But he couldn't, and it had nothing to do with the warning look and the emphatic shake of the head from Lanester, a clear injunction to 'stay calm'. He dropped his eyes for a brief moment before looking up again. It took him a few seconds to realise that the Corsicans were not interested in him, not waiting for him to respond. They all had their eyes on Lanester. Had he, by his reaction, unwittingly confirmed what they must already suspect; that Markham had possession of some rejoinder damning enough to silence them, information that both men would be on the way to Corte to pass on to Pasquale Paoli?

Whatever else was going on behind those eyes, the mood had been totally destroyed. Buttafuco particularly became more and more morose. The speed with which the dinner broke up was almost obscene, the partings having none of the geniality of their welcome. Lanester and Markham left a room full of small knots of officers, all talking in hushed animation. Guards, in the same orange-faced uniform, saluted their passing as they left the main building. The chill of the night air was a welcome relief, Lanester holding his tongue until they were well out of earshot.

'I fear, despite all my previous efforts, that I might have given the game away.'

'You think Buttafuco set out to trap us.'

'If he did, he succeeded.'

'Might I suggest we post our own guards to-night.'

'That would be wise,' Lanester growled. 'But tell the men the password is Nebbio. I don't want them shooting some innocent local out of his tent for a piss.'

Markham woke a slumbering Rannoch and gave him his orders, and between them they placed the sentinels and worked out the watches. All around them, in the darkness, fires twinkled, and in the distance Markham could see the torches lining the walls of the French redoubts. With Rannoch on the first watch, and Halsey taking the second, he fell into a shallow sleep troubled both by drink consumed, vivid imaginings, and the loud snoring of Major Lanester, so that when he was roused by the Highlander, long before dawn, he felt as though he hadn't slept at all.

'I have been watching them for an age,' said Rannoch, his voice as level and well paced as ever, despite describing what to his officer sounded like a nightmare. Behind them Lanester's snores rose to a crescendo, so loud that even he couldn't stand it. The sudden silence, as he snorted then fell quiet, made the sergeant's voice sound louder. 'They are dressed in the local way. Two of them, creeping round as if searching for an opening. But that is all they have done.'

In just his shirtsleeves, on a moonlit night, Markham knew he'd be like a beacon. So, having strapped on his sword, he donned his dark blue cloak and followed Rannoch, who had his grey cape on, as the Highlander slid out into the chilly, clear night air. He could see the circuit of his own piquet, each man with a white cloth tied to the tip of his bayonet, but not Rannoch's Corsicans. It was easy to think of himself and Lanester as the targets, but the fate of the men at Fornali haunted Markham; the notion, one he could not rid himself of, that the very same could befall both him and his command. So when he finally saw the figures moving on the edge of their tents, he had his pistol up and aimed. Only Rannoch's hand stopped him from blazing off at what was suddenly just a hint of a floppy round cap behind a tree.

'We do not know for certain who they are.'

'I do.'

Rannoch swept his free arm in a small arc, his voice soft and insistent. 'We cannot go shooting at people for crawling around their own encampment.'

'I can when I feel threatened,' Markham hissed.

'If they do not have firearms, and we can get

215

close enough, perhaps we can catch hold of one of them.'

Markham thought for a moment before replying. 'I'd rather scare and chase them, to see where they go.'

Rannoch must have picked up the note of excitement in his officer's voice, since his own sounded worried. 'They might lead us straight into a trap.'

Markham's hand was already under his cape, the scrape of his sword leaving the scabbard covered by a renewed bout of noise from Lanester. He jerked his arm to dislodge Rannoch's grip, then stood up and began to walk deliberately towards the spot where he'd last seen that head in the flop-sided round cap. The guttural cry of alarm was followed by the sound of scurrying feet. Markham shouted 'Halt!' Rannoch, with more sense, called to the guards to fall back on the tents and stand fast.

There was no wisdom in what Markham was doing, only a fierce anger, manifested in racing blood and a stream of Irish curses, as he plunged after the men he thought were trying to kill him. Rannoch was at his heels, musket raised, fixing his bayonet on the run, pleading to be allowed to catch up. What slowed Markham was the realisation that he had no idea where his quarry had gone. But he didn't stop, he kept moving at a fast walk, his eyes ranging around the silent rows of tents, flickering low fires, the only sounds those of a camp full of sleeping men, with the odd rattle of a musket as a sentry moved his weapon in response to the password.

216

'There,' murmured Rannoch, pointing to a line of trees, tall swaying poplars at the southern end of the camp. Markham just saw a fleeting image, the same kind of silhouette he remembered so well. But the hand on his shoulder stopped him from giving immediate chase. 'They are leading us on, sir, surely.'

'Then let us follow them.'

'Slowly.'

Markham nodded and agreed, though the desire to race on was strong. But Rannoch was right. To pursue at the run would rob them of any advantage. 'Use the trees.'

They leap-frogged from trunk to trunk, weapons raised, every nerve strained to hear or see danger. It was Markham who saw it first, the very faint glim of a lantern light that filtered through the trees in a small grove of pines. He dropped to a crouch, Rannoch following suit. At his next signal, the pair crept towards the edge of the wood, picking up the first hint of voices as they reached the edge of the trees. Soft and slightly damp pine needles made their progress silent, until they reached a point where they could see some of what was happening in the clearing.

'Who are they?' Rannoch whispered.

'My guess is that the man facing you,' Markham whispered, his hand pointing to the knot of blue-coated officers, one seated, the other standing, 'is General Lacombe St Michel, the French commander.'

The hum of voices rose and fell as the slight breeze made the pines above their head sigh. Markham moved a few paces closer, so that the

217

faces of those in the lamplight became clearer. 'And facing him is one of the Corsican commanders, a man I had dinner with earlier, General Arsenio Buttafuco.'

There were several more officers in their dull brown uniforms. But Markham wasn't looking at them. His eyes had suddenly fixed on the sharp Moorish face of a man in a bottle-green coat. He'd been standing a few paces to the rear of the seated French General, but had stepped forward to say something. Even at this distance, Markham imagined he could see the cruelty in the man's eyes, the sneer that was so often on his lips it seemed habitual. But it was Rannoch who whispered the name, not him.

'Fouquert.' Then he added, after a pause. 'It would be nice to know what they are saying.'

Markham, even if his voice was low, was obviously angry. 'I think I can guess.'

'If this is a secret gathering, why are there no guards?'

Markham jerked as though he'd been physically jabbed, and he span round, not sparing Rannoch a glance as he began to crawl away. He took a different route out of the copse, using thick undergrowth to stay hidden, only stopping when one outreaching hand touched the still, warm body. Steadying himself as Rannoch bumped into his back, Markham ran his hands up the arms to the shoulder, then on to the face. He could smell sweat and the acrid odour of urine, feel the moustache and the open mouth. His hand dropped into the wetness of what he thought was the neck, which produced a gasp as he realised his fingertips

218

were dipped into still-running blood.

'Body in front,' he said trying to sound un-affected. 'Don't trip on it.'

They got far enough away, onto a clear track, so that they could stand up and move normally. Markham's mind was racing, and Rannoch had the good sense to keep his own counsel until his superior was ready to speak.

'There were guards, or at least one.'

'Dead?'

'Throat slit. Someone went to a great deal of trouble to ensure we saw that.'

'Those men led us to it.'

'Yes.'

'Who?'

'Nebbio,' said Markham, as a sentry challenged them. 'Think where we are going, Sergeant, and why. To tell General Paoli that one or more of his generals have betrayed the Corsican cause. Up till now we had no idea who, but that has changed.'

'A written note would have been easier.'

'From whom? And would we have believed it, signed or unsigned? The man who arranged this is not going to reveal his identity.'

'Because it would put him at risk.'

'We have to believe so. Instead, he has allowed us to see for ourselves. To watch Buttafuco actually conversing with the enemy.'

'Including that bastard from Toulon.'

'Why not challenge him openly, and just arrest him?'

'Could it be,' Markham asked, 'that Buttafuco is not alone?'

They made their way back up the lines as the first hint of grey tinged the sky behind Bastia. The whole party, with the exception of Major Lanester, was up and dressed, arms at the ready. Pavin was working on his fire close to the front flap of his master's tent, his copper pots and pans arranged around him; a box was open to reveal beefsteak, trussed game birds, and fresh eggs ready to be cooked. Ordered to desist he glared at Markham, his gravelly voice a soft but rude litany, aimed at the flames, regarding the pleasures of serving decent folk, instead of bog-trotters.

'Please be so good as to wake the major, Pavin, and saddle up his horse. We shall be on the road before the half-hour is gone.'

Pavin poked hard at his fire. 'That'll never be time enough to get him fed and watered.'

'Nevertheless,' Markham snapped, 'it's all the time you have.'

'We'll be seeing about that,' Pavin growled, tugging at the tie on the Major's tent flap. 'Seems to me some folks has got above their place, an' forgot the rank of the officer in charge of this here venture.'

Bleary-eyed and puffy faced, Lanester looked like a man who'd had a restless night. He looked at a sky just turning blue, and being no more convinced of the need for haste than his servant, he ordered Pavin to get on with his cooking. Looking at him, Markham felt a sense of utter frustration. He knew that dead guard would be missed. Even now the other sentinels on that meeting would be searching for him. What would happen when they found the body, as they were bound to now it was light, he didn't know. All he was sure of was that he had no desire to still be in the Corsican lines when it happened. The other thing he didn't want to do was to explain his nocturnal wanderings to Lanester.

'I cannot see that our purpose can be served by delay, sir,' Markham insisted. 'We lost enough time last night.'

'A good breakfast will put a better tinge on the day,' said Lanester with relish.

'I will, if you don't mind, forgo the pleasure, sir.'

'Gawd, boy, if it's that vital to you, let's get on the road with no more than a cup of warm coffee.'

'Your honour,' protested Pavin, pointing to a partridge already roasting on a spit.

'Warm coffee,' Lanester answered, softly but firmly, without taking his eyes off Markham. 'And get my kit packed.'

'Not till I've checked that cart,' Pavin snarled. 'Seems to me there might be a reason for all this hellfire haste.'

'I doubt that's the reason,' Lanester said, his voice still soft, and aimed at Pavin's retreating back. The Major didn't elaborate further, but the look in his eyes was plain enough. That might not be the cause, but he had little doubt that there was one.

'With your permission, sir?'

'Carry on, Lieutenant.'

Markham left Rannoch to organise everyone, and went for a last, quick look at the redoubts. He ranged his glass along the embrasures, pinging to himself as he shot each presented target,

221

like a child pretending to fire a gun. The one outline he sought wasn't there, despite his careful examination. There was no bottle-green coat, no black eyes, and no sneer.

'Impossible,' he said to himself.

'We are ready, sir,' said Rannoch, from behind him.

'I did see him last night, Rannoch, didn't I?'

'I recognised him too.'

'What is a bloody butcher like Fouquert doing here in Corsica?'

Chapter fifteen

The image of that face stayed with Markham even when the camp at Cardo was out of sight. That and the memories it engendered, acting like a persistent itch to the back of his neck, which didn't fade as they began to climb towards the central mountains, using a road built by the French to help them control the interior. To the Irishman, a creature like Fouquert represented the worst excesses of the Revolution. Initially welcomed by most liberally minded people, the fall of the Bourbon monarchy had turned into a social upheaval that had begun to eat its own, with many of the original opponents of royal tyranny, radicals to a man, suffering either exile or judicial execution at the hands of fanatics.

Such mayhem had allowed men of Fouquert's stamp to rise to prominence. They used the guillotine as a child might use a toy, delighting in the indiscriminate slaughter of innocent people, cloaking their activities in the name of revolutionary justice. Not that Fouquert needed such an instrument to kill and maim. Markham had seen his handiwork at close quarters, and knew he was just as willing to use rape, torture and mutilation as instruments of both personal gratification and oppression. Indeed Fouquert boasted that, given a sharp knife to play on an individual victim, he'd take great personal pleasure in the pain he inflicted. To appoint such a monster as the Citizen Commissioner-designate of Toulon, the man responsible for retribution when the allies were ejected from the port, was an invitation to genocide.

If the reports were to be believed, six thousand souls had died when the French retook the Mediterranean naval base, quite a number just driven to drown in the harbour as they fled the approaching nemesis; part soldiers, part the rabble from the slums of Marseille. How many had died formally, decapitated in the main square under Fouquert's personal direction, Markham didn't know. Probably a minority, since one of the ploys of the revolution was to release the worst elements in society onto the defenceless populace, the mere possession of property quite sufficient to warrant a bloody death. They'd done it in Lyon, Nantes, Marseille and every other city that resisted Robespierre and his Committee of Public Safety.

They marched all day at a steady pace along the paved highway, with strictly regulation stops, crossing the flat and fertile coastal plain. After Casamozze that changed as the forests thickened. The incline also seemed to increase as they progressed, till the approach of night found them close to the hillside village of Barchetta. They took over a barn from a rapacious peasant farmer, who insisted on a usurious rent for its use, knowing that the alternative for these British soldiers was a night out in the open. Lanester, who had not bothered to pose a question to him all day, eyed him while Pavin cooked their meal, but held his peace until it was served, and his man had gone back to prepare the second course.

'So. Now that we are well away from Cardo, and alone, was it fear of the knife that had us leave in such a hurry?'

Markham had had plenty of time to rehearse the tale, so that when he related the events of the previous night, it came out with few hesitations, to a superior who mixed scepticism with outrage and surprise.

'You saw Buttafuco in person!'

'I did. I can't be sure that he was negotiating personally with Lacombe, but there can't be too many French generals languishing around Bastia.'

'Good God in heaven!' he exclaimed. Then his face clouded, and he invoked a different image. 'Why the devil didn't you tell me this before we left?'

Lanester didn't actually say that the rest of their journey might not have been necessary, but it was there in his belligerent stare. Markham was suddenly presented with one of those revelations that come at the oddest moments; the recollection of the major's insistence that they pass through Cardo instead of pressing on, cross country, to Corte. It had been unsettling at the time. Now the thought entered his head that Lanester had brought him along as bait, quite prepared to sacrifice him to expose whoever the traitor in the Corsican command was. If nothing else, that explained how he'd managed to persuade his superiors to allot the Hebes as an escort. He questioned the notion as soon as he had it, but it was still with some difficulty that he managed to keep his voice normal.

'Because I feared that if we delayed, we might not get away at all.'

'We could have confronted them,' Lanester barked, inducing a queasy feeling in the junior officer's stomach.

'Who, sir?' asked Markham quietly.

Lanester chewed on that, literally since he was consuming the partridge he'd missed that morning. Markham was chewing on his hidden thoughts, alternately accepting and denying the possibility as he recalled each conversation. One thing was certain: if it was the truth, he'd never get the man to admit it. Fetching his thinking back to the present was difficult, but it had to be done.

The major didn't need explanations really, just time to draw the obvious conclusions. That apart from Buttafuco, there was no way of knowing who else was involved; that a traitor who'd killed already to facilitate his perfidy would have no choice but to do the same to anyone who threatened exposure.

'There's more betrayal to come,' he said finally.

225

'That's my reading of it,' Markham replied. 'The French will have been told about Nelson's intentions. If for just that one day, when they see his ships in the bay, the French can be sure they run no risk by denuding the Cardo redoubts, they'll have all the men they need to throw Nelson's attack back into the sea.'

'Damnit, the whole island would be unsafe after that kind of treachery.'

'So alerting Paoli is imperative.'

'We leave before dawn tomorrow, Markham,' Lanester snapped, stabbing at the last leg of his bird.

'The cart, sir.'

Lanester glared at him. 'Don't start in on that again, Lieutenant.'

'I'm just worried that we might be intercepted?'

Lanester's round face took on a worried expression. 'The way we left that encampment, without the ritual farewells, is going to stink in someone's nostrils for sure. And it wouldn't surprise me if we had acquired a tail. But to suddenly dump that, too early, and start double marching, would only add to their anxieties. We must appear to change nothing till we're close enough to Corte that it makes no odds. One more thing, we must send a messenger back to San Fiorenzo to let them know what you saw.'

'Yes, sir.'

'We'll need to get them away while it's still dark. Thanks to your delay in letting on about this, those men will have an extra day's journey. They'll have to retrace every step they took since this morning.'

Markham used his knife to trace a triangle on the dusty table, stabbing to indicate the three points, showing that the distance between Barcetta and San Fiorenzo was no greater than that between Hood's base and Bastia.

'They won't have lost much, sir. It would be tempting providence to send a despatch containing this kind of information back along the same route we used.'

Lanester nodded, acknowledging that they'd moved on two sides of a triangle since leaving San Fiorenzo. Their messengers would have no more than ten miles to go to get back to base, and by the direct route, as Markham pointed out, they'd avoid any risk of being stopped at Corsican outposts.

'I thought, sir,' Markham added, 'that since we don't know who to trust, we'd best trust nobody.'

Lanester glared at him. 'Not even me, it seems.'

Markham detailed a trio of the Seahorses for the duty, handing them the uncoded letters that Lanester had just written to Hood and d'Aubent, with strict instructions to deliver both, seal intact. They were allotted three days' rations, accompanied by rough-drawn map, plus an admonition to keep their eyes peeled for French cavalry patrols.

'If you do think you face capture, get rid of these in any way you can. Do not let them fall into the hands of the enemy. The tracks you will be on should be pretty wide, and on the whole, if you do need to ask, I think you can trust the Corsican peasants.'

Markham handed them the paper he'd written,

with various French phrases that they might find useful if they could find anyone who could read. But really, on what judging by the starry sky promised to be a clear day, it was just a case of keeping the sun at their backs, to know they were heading north.

The main party's march was carried out at a brisk pace, on a road that grew steeper as the day wore on, cutting into the distance they could travel. The second night they spent in the bridge-keeper's house on the far bank of the Canavafola river at Ponte Leccio. Now they were amongst high surrounding hills, the central mountains right ahead, white-capped and forbidding. The weather stayed dry, but cold, though the never-ending forest, and a sky that had become overcast, kept everything moist, especially where snow still lay in the folds of the hills.

Somehow the weather seemed to mirror the relations between the two officers. Things had changed since San Fiorenzo. Cardo hadn't helped, but Lanester, probably brooding on the way he'd been kept in the dark, had seemed to become less content at the way the lieutenant had abused his trust. He'd reminded Markham more than once that the manner in which he'd acted was high-handed. That being nothing short of the truth made the marine a trifle stiff in response. Then there were his nagging suspicions regarding Lanester's motives for travelling via Cardo, which rendered him uncommunicative, as each word spoken was examined against that disturbing thought. The Virginian noticed his reserve, which only made matters worse.

'Horses, sir,' said Yelland, kneeling to look at the clumps of mud scattered across the pave, damp earth which, judging by its shape, had dropped from clattering iron-shod hooves.

Markham had come forward and joined him when the youngster signalled, his eyes following the line where the mounts, several dozen in number, had crossed the road, east to west, to disappear into the gap in the thick encroaching woods. They'd passed many tracks traversing the road, but all gave the impression of having been used by mules. Unshod and smaller than a horse, they'd left a shapeless, muddy trail on the arched stone highway.

This was different. From his elevated position, the sea was visible in the distance, the grey, white-flecked waves matching the sky, which had remained overcast. He looked back down the route they'd travelled, a snake of a road forced by nature to bow to the features of the rough terrain. Up ahead it was worse, a twisting brown scar that zigzagged, hanging to the side of steep hills, showing occasionally through the deep green landscape, until finally both disappeared into the mountain mists.

Built as a military road, it had been, until very recently, well maintained. The blocks of pavé had a high camber to let the rain run off, while the undergrowth on the edges had been cut back to ward against surprise. Yet ten feet on either side the tangled woods enclosed them, which made Markham wonder why, with no habitation in sight, a unit of cavalry would choose to journey

229

through that, rather than use this, a much easier route.

Suddenly he stood upright and retraced their hoof clods to the point at which they'd come onto the highway, the last traces of the winter snows that edged it turned into a dark and soggy mass by their passage. Moving further into the woods, he came upon a small hollow where the wet ground had been churned up badly. Clumps of fresh droppings were just visible in the mud, broken up and mixed by stomping hooves. He searched in vain for the sign of a human boot, but could see none, even on the very edge of the clearing. The track they'd used was visible, a well-worn, churned-up mule path that dropped down the hillside. Whoever these horsemen were, they'd stopped here, but not dismounted, to wait before crossing, perhaps a halt while someone made sure the road was clear.

Markham, in his present mood would have shown caution if gifted with a tearful vision of the Virgin Mary. Now, every nerve in his body screamed danger. They were too numerous to be robbers. Besides, living as they did in the *maccia*, they could barely run to a horse, never mind a farrier. The crossing had been undertaken with care. There was only one explanation for that; they didn't wish to be seen. It then followed that they felt the need to remain concealed in hostile country.

'The only people who are hostiles here, sir, are the French.'

'You may well be right, Markham,' Lanester replied.

230

'May, sir? I can't think of another explanation.'

'I can. In my conversations with Paoli I learned that the island is a bit more complicated than that.' He had to haul on his reins to control a horse excited by the smell of other animals. 'It's not just footpads and robbers. The old man spent half his life trying to snuff out horrendous clan feuds. There are some on this rock that go back generations. Just crossing another's territory can be taken as a provocation. They're a touchy crew, as you have witnessed. Why, even the islanders travelling this route show caution when they sight us, though they must reckon when they spy our red coats that we're friendly.'

That was true. The Corsicans were suspicious of everyone and everything. This was the only proper road from the mountain interior to the east coast, yet to call it quiet was an understatement. Few locals seemed to use it for short journeys, probably preferring their own ancient mule trails, which they knew intimately. People on longer errands, or transporting large quantities of produce, did take advantage of the highway, but each wagon stopped as soon as they spotted the redcoats. The owners then stood, clearly ready to flee, until they had convinced themselves of the soldiers' bona fides. Yet those hoof-prints, given the nature of their mission, were certainly a cause for suspicion, one Lanester seemed inclined to play down.

'Provocation, sir. That would just about describe a visit whose sole purpose is to expose and remove someone we consider a traitor. Maybe they're not French, after all. And maybe the people they're hiding from are us.'

'Whoever they may be, they're ahead of us,' Lanester replied, without any trace of alarm, 'and have continued on their way. If they were a danger, and intent on stopping us, I suspect we'd know by now. It's not difficult for mounted men to catch up with marching infantry, even if they left Cardo after we did ourselves. And why use a route that's more difficult than the road?'

'We'd hear them coming.' Markham pointed straight up the hillside, indicating an imaginary route through the *maccia*, which was more direct than the twisting road. 'If they are ahead they are also above. So they have an advantage. They can see us. If they decide to set an ambush, they'll have all the time in the world to make sure we don't uncover it before it is sprung.'

'We need to get to Corte as quickly as we can, man, and this is by far the best route.'

'It is also the most exposed. And I think it was you who pointed out how much suspicion we created by the manner of our departure. What if these horsemen are Buttafuco's? What if their aim is to stop us from going anywhere?'

Markham was having difficulty understanding Lanester's attitude, even if his desire for haste was perfectly natural. A lot hung on a successful outcome. With only seven days left, speed was desirable, but so was security. Failure was certain if they didn't arrive.

'Sir, you are a Virginian, are you not?'

Lanester gave him a very sharp look, eyes for once narrowed and suspicious, which looked strange in his fat, red face.

'What are you implying, Markham?'

'Only this, sir. That I suspect you fought the native Indians before taking issue with your own countrymen.'

'I did!'

'And was the terrain not, in some respects, similar to this?'

That was a neat way of reminding Lanester that only a fool took chances in unknown territory, or assumed that a strange sign could never presage danger. The major sat on his horse, clearly ruminating, though whatever thoughts he harboured he kept to himself. When he eventually gave way his voice carried with it a trace of resentment.

'I can see by the look in your eye that you have a suggestion. Lieutenant.'

'Yes, sir. It is that we leave the road as well, and use the track they have created, which will be easy to follow. That way we stay behind them, remain out of sight for most of the time. And with men well ahead on point, it is a very good way to make sure we're not surprised.'

'Marching along a road is bliss compared to that.' He pointed with his crop to the thick forests. The local word, *maccia,* had no direct translation into English. But one only had to look at it to see that such dense scrub and pines was a hellish area to progress through. More fertile local minds would, no doubt, describe it as a place of dark secrets, of evil spirits and strange apparitions. But to Markham it represented a degree of safety.

'In addition, the men would not only have to forgo the luxury of having their equipment transported, they would also have to carry what the

233

cart has been brought along to bear.'

'I'm aware of that, sir. I'm also aware that some of what you have brought might have to be left behind. But I'd rather leave your claret on this road than my bones.'

Chapter sixteen

There was a long and pregnant pause before Lanester responded to what was, after all, a rather dramatic statement, his disapproval evident in the way he was pursing his lips.

'You have a valid point, Markham, but so do I. Speed is of the essence. My suggestion is therefore that we proceed as before. But if we see any more evidence of these horsemen, we reconsider our options.'

'There's no guarantee, sir, that any other sighting will give us such clear alternatives.'

The look in the major's eye left no room for further dispute. His words might be couched as suggestions, but they were his clear orders. By the time Markham made his next recommendation the man had already looked away.

'Extra men forward, sir?'

'They're your command, Markham,' said Lanester, nonchalantly. 'Dispose them as you see the need.'

'Sergeant Rannoch. Two men a hundred yards on point, another two at fifty, the first pair to stop at each bend, and not proceed until the following pair join them. Everyone to keep to the side of the roadway which affords the best forward view, muskets primed and ready. Bellamy, Pavin and the cart will remain in the centre.'

Yelland and Tully went right ahead, with Dornan and Hollick in between. Rannoch dropped Ettrick and Quinlan back forty paces to the rear.

'Why us?' demanded Quinlan.

'Because,' the Highlander replied, 'you pair are used to people in pursuit of you. My guess is that you have some braw trained hairs on the back of your necks. If neither the Provost Marshal nor the Beak before him could catch you at your pilfering, I doubt John Crapaud, or any local culchie, can take you unawares. Now move!'

The whole mood of the detachment changed. What had been a relatively carefree march, with the usual quantity of jokes and insults exchanged, became tense and expectant. Markham had his sword out, his eyes darting about for that single trace of something unusual which would indicate a potential hazard. Lanester, for his part, was trying to convey by his confident air that nothing about the journey had changed.

They were several miles further on, having traversed a series of long uphill bends which took them into a thin mist, when, from his elevated position, Lanester saw Yelland and Tully stop. And as soon as the young blond marine bent down, he called softly, 'Lieutenant, I believe your men on point have spotted something.'

'Halt,' Markham said, in a normal voice, holding up his hand. Rannoch and Halsey, who passed on the instruction, came to join the officers as

235

soon as it was obeyed. Quinlan and Ettrick, well trained men even if they were light-fingered, spun round and dropped to their knees, muskets aimed back the way they'd come.

'Corporal Halsey, take half the men to the rear of the cart and call in the rearguard to join you. Sergeant Rannoch, the rest in front.'

The hairs were prickling on the back of Markham's neck as he went forward, passing the kneeling figures of Hollick and Dornan, who scurried back to the main body as soon as he told them to do so. Yelland and Tully were likewise poised, eyes searching the surrounding *maccia*, ears cocked for the slightest hint of an unusual sound. Yet the birds were singing not far into the woods on both sides, a sure sign that their world was at peace. The shattered wagon rising into the mist just ahead of them, and the faint outline of dead bodies in the roadway, had no effect on the creatures' natural harmony.

Markham came abreast of his men, as they knelt in front of an elaborate peasant Calvary, the bleeding man-sized figure of the crucified Christ almost producing the kind of involuntary genuflection his mother had insisted on when he was a child. He followed Yelland's finger, which was pointing further on, and went to examine the mud-spattered roadway, as well as the verges. Two sets of prints this time, confusing since they seemed to go in both directions, the others, more numerous, just inside the right-hand trees where the thick undergrowth had been cut back. He waved to the main group, then took the two point men into the woods.

236

There was no clearing this time, and Markham could see, as he went further from the road, that the horsemen had occupied this place with some discomfort, those who'd failed to dismount dislodging quite a lot of the lower greenery. But they seemed to have come here, through thick woods, on slightly diverging mule trails. The smell was very potent, that special odour of saplings and thin branches newly parted from their host plants. It was only when he examined both trails that he realised one had led to this place, while the other was their route of departure.

'They're close, whoever they are,' said Markham to himself.

'Be nice to be a mite clearer about that, sir,' Tully whined, the tone of his voice showing his fear. He was looking about him, as if every tree and bush hid someone who wanted to kill him. That made Markham wonder if Rannoch had let slip some of what they'd seen. He doubted it, since the Highlander was good at being tight-lipped. But his men would be curious. Perhaps it was just deduction. Those who'd been on guard at Cardo had seen him and his sergeant rushing into the woods. And when they'd returned, the whole unit had been up, dressed and prepared for a fight. Then there was the manner of their leaving.

'Let's just assume they're French, Tully,' Markham replied, trying to sound reassuring. 'Yelland, go back to the major and ask him to bring the whole party up to us. You and I, Tully, need to go forward and look at what's up ahead.'

'Christ!'

That exclamation showed just how rattled the

237

man was. Asked, Markham would say that of all the men he led, Tully was the least likely to be upset by the sight of blood. He'd never seen his pig-like eyes show anything in the way of emotion, nor observed pity on the ravaged, pock-marked face. But it was there now, and Markham surmised that the marine was imagining that he was in the place of the mangled bodies they were examining.

Two elderly men, a woman and a child lay amongst their scattered, meagre possessions, each one bearing the deep open wounds caused by dozens of sabre cuts. They'd been ridden over by horses too, which had smashed their heads against the stones of the road. Corsicans, by their dress and complexion, they'd died without being able to fire off the weapons that lay beside the men's bodies, muskets primed but not cocked. Markham followed the imprints in the softer earth of the verge, seeking the point at which they'd re-entered the forest, which he found some fifty yards away from the smashed wood that had once been their cart, in a direct line to that same mule trail which the rest of the horsemen had taken.

Returning to the bodies, he turned the men on their backs. What skin was unmarked on the faces was weatherbeaten and heavily moustached; the dead eyes, undamaged, stared back at him. Trying to imagine those eyes full of life, he felt he was looking at men who would have been just as cautious as every other Corsican peasant they'd come across on the road. How could they have stood, and allowed a French patrol to get so close that they'd died without firing a shot? Had they surrendered in the hope of clemency, to men suddenly appearing out of the woods? If they had, they'd not even been given time to lay down their muskets before they'd all been sabred. But what if the men who attacked them were dressed in Corsican uniforms? Then they would not have run, would not have seen the need.

'A burial party, sir,' said Markham.

'Of course,' replied Lanester, both index fingers pressing the top of his nose in an attitude of near prayer. 'And a mark on the spot, so that if we find a priest, he can inter them properly.'

'And then?'

'Then, Lieutenant Markham,' he responded with a sigh, 'we get off this road. But just you make sure you get me to Pasquale Paoli in thirty-six hours, otherwise I might not be left with the time to persuade the old Liberator to help us.'

The trail they had to follow, made by mules and travelled by the locals for centuries, might be obvious, but that didn't make it easy, and Markham wondered how they would have fared if the horsemen hadn't partly cleared the most annoying impediments. Greatcoats and packs got snagged on twisting branches that had survived the passing cavalry, each one seemingly imbued with the sole purpose of causing mankind to curse. Major Lanester had taken to walking, his crop swinging in a constant arc as he swiped at the foliage. Pavin was using his horse to transport the most valuable items which had been on the abandoned cart, the rest loaded onto the backs of the two mules which had pulled it.

This was ancient forest of a density the like of which Markham had rarely seen: tinder dry in the summer, well watered in winter, and heated to grow in the spring, though the strong winds which buffeted the island tended to bend the trees so that many of them seemed stunted. Progress was further slowed by caution. The men on point, if they got too far ahead of the main party, simply disappeared into the abundant greenery, yet they were the people who had to warn the rest of any danger.

Uphill they struggled, coming upon the road again every so often, an obstacle that couldn't be traversed until the undergrowth on the opposite side had been checked to ensure that the horsemen ahead of them had continued on their way. Sometimes they crossed other tracks, narrow overgrown routes worn away into gullies by countless feet, routes that led God only knew where, the lifelines of old Corsica, which predated the building of the French road. Markham tried to imagine fighting in this, trying to pin down an enemy who knew his way when you didn't. But he had to abandon that when Gibbons dropped back from point, his hand up to indicate that they should all halt.

'A cluster of buildings, sir, like one or two of the little monasteries we've passed. The roadway is no more than forty feet beyond, with all the woodland cleared in front.'

Markham, taken forward to the edge of the trees, was struck by the lack of activity. He could, by listening carefully, hear the sounds of small bells, which denoted animals, sheep or goats, free to wander. But a place like this should have dogs, and they would surely bark at the approach of a stranger. A wisp of smoke rose from the central chimney on the main building, the slight odour of burning pine pleasant to the nose. That was the only thing that was pleasing. The rest, the sheer tranquillity, gave the clearing an air of deep foreboding.

'Gibbons, go back to Sergeant Rannoch, and ask him to bring the men forward and take up a defensive position on the line of the trees.'

'And you, sir?'

Gibbons had no right to ask such a question, and while Markham was aware that most of the man's concern was fear for his personal safety, there was a small amount of that same worry allotted to him. How different it had been when he first met the marine! Gibbons, along with the rest of his command, would have seen him dead without a flicker of sympathy. But shared danger had fashioned them into something very different, a unit where a ranker felt he knew his officer well enough to overstep the boundary between them. To cover any effect that thought engendered, he jammed his sword into the earth with excessive force.

'This will act as a marker. I am going round the perimeter to make sure our friends on horses made it across the road.'

The eerie silence, added to the deserted nature of the place, was somehow more disturbing than what Markham expected, which was the same scatter of dead bodies they'd observed on the road. Here there was nothing human. Little

241

paddocks occupied the space between the main stone building and the road, containing a few goats and sheep. They were grazing contentedly, or lying dozing in the straw-lined wooden bothies that skirted the forest at their rear. On the building itself, the small bell in an aperture above the studded door, surmounted by a crucifix, identified it as a religious dwelling, one of tiny monasteries of the type that dotted the island. They'd passed several of them on their way here, each a small, subsistence enclave, peopled by a few poor monks and their attendants.

The front door stood ajar, a gaping hole that invited him to enter. But Markham ignored it, crawling all the way to the highway, looking in both directions through the thin mist, which eventually became like an opaque white blanket. Still observing no sign of danger, he skipped across the road and edged along the treeline, until he came to what he sought, the deep imprints of the cavalry hooves, heading on into another set of mule trails through the forest.

Confidence restored, he walked boldly out into the open, heading straight for the door to the little monastery. It was dark inside, dingy and full of the smell of church he remembered so well. An odour of wood and beeswax, a dryness so total that it seemed the dust never moved. The residue of fading incense filled the small interior, furnished with a few polished pews facing the tiny altar that lay at one end.

It was like stepping back into his own childhood, to a world where priests stood as direct representatives of an all-seeing God, men to whom even his maternal grandfather, a highly respected doctor, deferred. He tried to contain the memory of childish pleasure, the love of the ceremony and incomprehensible Latin liturgy, of candles burning and incense swinging. But reality intruded: his envy of the boys chosen to serve at Mass, a task denied to him by his birth; the looks his family party received, discreet but unfriendly, as they entered the church, young George condemned more than anyone by the knowledge that he attended his father's Protestant church as well. The divide between his parents, both in station and religion. The wearing away of a harmony between them strong enough to withstand any censure, fraying it until it became acrimony. It was hard to conjure up the face that had so ensnared Sir John Markham, all too easy to replace it with the sad eyes and puffed cheeks of an old woman who drank too much.

'Jesus,' he said softly, his voice echoing off the bare white walls, 'there's no peace anywhere.'

He blinked when he exited, the mist having lifted enough to allow a refracted sun through, suddenly feeling that the smells he remembered so fondly were musty rather than endearing. The damp air was full of odours of earth and wood, and clean enough to wash away his memory, bringing him back to the present and its problems. As he turned the corner he felt, such was his sudden loss of breath, as though a hand had grabbed at his throat. The entire party were lined up, Lanester in the middle, their weapons laid out on the ground in front of them. Behind sat a line of caped French cavalry, every carbine aimed at a British back.

'This must be yours,' said the voice at his side. Markham turned slowly, just enough to see the braided tricorne hat above the indistinct face behind the outstretched arm holding his sword. And, of course, the officer was smiling. 'Please be so good, Lieutenant, as to pass me your pistol.'

Chapter seventeen

They were marched into the chapel, Lanester at the head, hands behind their backs, and once the men had unbuckled their packs, the whole party was led to the small space behind the altar. Their possessions, weapons, cartouches and bayonets included, were put in a cell at the far end of the chapel, as far away from the prisoners as possible. The cavalry officer who had effected their capture was a dragoon, who introduced himself as Captain Duchesne, then asked them to remove their red uniform coats.

'Do you intend to rob us as well?' asked Lanester.

His colonial twang more evident than usual, which Markham assumed was caused by anger. The captain couldn't understand him whatever accent, obliging the major to translate his own question into very passable French.

'No monsieur. But I think even a private soldier would resent being searched.'

Lanester turned round, speaking quickly, his

voice more normal. 'Right, coats off, and if you're asked, we are on our way to make a private visit to an old friend of mine.'

Markham had to admire that. Lanester had shown great awareness in first establishing his freedom to speak, then said everything necessary in very few words.

'What have you told them?' Duchesne demanded, removing his hat. He looked to be in his mid-thirties, with a bland sort of face and very little chin.

'That you are a regular officer, who can be counted on to treat them well.' Behind Lanester, men were disrobing. 'I also asked them to take off their coats.'

'Good,' Duchesne replied, gesturing to a pair of his own troopers to collect the garments.

Markham had counted thirty men in all, most now outside tethering the horses in lines. Yet more were fetching the hay with which to feed them, so only six remained inside. The two collecting the coats had left their weapons against the wall, well out of reach. And they were in the midst of the captives. He knew Rannoch was tensed up and ready, as aware as he was that if there was going to be a time to overpower them, this might be the best opportunity.

Yet Markham had to shake his head. There were four carbines trained on them, while the officer still had the captured sword in his hand. And after the first yell the rest of the dragoons would come rushing in. It was gratifying to see that as Rannoch relaxed, so did most of his Hebes, who'd been as alert as their superiors to the possibilities.

The coats were searched in front of the men who owned them, while behind them a steady stream of soldiers, now freed from other duties, brought in the articles which had been on the backs of the mules and Lanester's horse: packs containing the officers' clothes, the cases of wine, Pavin's copper pots and pans, as well as the satchel of ingredients he used to spice his various dishes. These were all taken to the same cell that held their weapons, and Duchesne followed them in to oversee the search. The only thing he emerged with was Lanester's despatch case, which, when he opened it, yielded nothing but the maps they'd used on the journey, the major's writing materials and a set of seals.

'Put this with the other things,' the captain said. He opened his mouth to add something more, but the sound of hooves cantering into the clearing stopped him.

Duchesne wasn't alarmed, which could only mean that the horsemen were expected. The dragoon captain turned to face the door, which darkened slightly as a shadow filled it. The newcomer's boots rang on the stone floor as he appeared, gazing round the chapel in an imperious way. If the sound of arriving horses had depressed Markham, that was as nothing to the sight of the bottle-green civilian coat, the tricolour sash around the thin waist, and the dark-skinned, hook-nosed face.

'Monsieur Fouquert,' cried Duchesne, 'look what I managed to pick up on the way here!'

There wasn't much light in the chapel. But Markham, every nerve on edge, was sure he saw the facial muscles twitch alarmingly. Fouquert wasn't looking at him, indeed he didn't seem to be looking anywhere in particular. The voice, when he spoke, had a hint of strain in it, which Markham put down to the fact that this emissary of the notorious Committee of Public Safety couldn't quite believe his luck.

'Well, Captain, this is a surprise.'

'All theirs, I do assure you, sir. The men who led us to this rendezvous have uncommon hearing, as well as a nose...'

Duchesne was about to go on, when Fouquert cut across him. 'Let them wonder, Captain. To tell them they could not have avoided their fate would only lift their spirits.'

Markham was sure the dragoon was confused. He wasn't. Fouquert was telling him, in as polite a way as he could muster, to shut up. Something soft was said as the civilian walked past the soldier, too quiet for anyone but the pair of them to hear. And all the while Fouquert's eyes were on him, black, glinting and full of hate.

'Lieutenant Markham. I have prayed that one day I should meet you again.'

The eyes swept along behind him, flicking slightly as he recognised a face from the last meeting in Toulon. Markham spat softly, trying to generate an air of bravado he certainly didn't feel. The Frenchman smiled, and once again Markham was struck by the way such a facial gesture chilled rather than cheered. It was like Fouquert's laugh, cold and humourless, inclined to acknowledge someone's pain.

'Insult me at your will. There was a time you did it before. I seem to recall, then, I said I would make you beg.'

'I hope you remember my reply to that.'

'Oh! yes. I wonder if you will, when I get round to you.' Fouquert span away, and barked at the dragoon captain, 'Duchesne, a word in private.'

He was halfway to one of the cells before Duchesne responded, the look on his face one of shock at being addressed like a common soldier. Fouquert shut the door behind them, slowly.

'Who in God's name is that?' asked Lanester.

Markham told him. How they'd met, what he'd seen Fouquert do, and the way they'd parted company. 'He was in that copse as well, talking to Buttafuco.'

'Which you forgot to mention.'

'I didn't forget,' Markham replied. 'It just made no difference to say so.'

'Are we in more trouble because of him?'

'I am!'

'I kinda guessed that, son.'

'He might take it out on my Hebes as well. If you could save them, I'd be grateful.'

'I don't see much chance of getting out of here.'

'If I try to kill him, or to get him to despatch me quickly, make sure no one interferes.'

The major opened his mouth, no doubt to proffer the ritual reassurances, none of which would do any good. But the door to the cell opened and Duchesne came out. His face was flushed, like a man who'd been made angry, though no sound of any dispute had come through the thin wooden door. He marched straight over to Lanester.

'Major, as the senior officer I have to ask you a few questions.'

'Of course,' Lanester replied guardedly.

'If you would not mind joining me and my colleague.' He turned to one of the men guarding them, and pointed to the pile of red coats. 'Please find the major's garment, and his despatch case. The rest can go in the cell with the weapons.'

Finding the coat wasn't hard, it being the only one with blue facings. Duchesne took it and passed it on. 'It is better for your dignity that you wear this.'

'Thank you,' Lanester said, beginning to put it on. 'My lieutenant tells me that the other gentleman has some strange ideas regarding the asking of questions.'

'He may well have, Major,' the Frenchman barked. 'But you are a military prisoner, not a civilian one.'

'Well, that is a relief.' Lanester followed these words with a bow, and an invitation to lead the way. Duchesne demurred, giving way to him, and as he followed, he growled to his men. 'Search them, every one, including the officer.'

As soon as the door closed behind him two of the guards started to move into a group of men buzzing with alarm. Rannoch was tensed and ready again, just like Markham, waiting for a chance to grab for a weapon. But the corporal in charge was too shrewd to be caught out. He called his men back, ordered them to find some rope, then told them to drag the prisoners out one at a time from the front. Their hands were tied so that they could be searched without difficulty.

Each man was then returned, once he was finished, round the other side of the altar. Markham was one of the last, his breeches' pockets producing very little in the way of possessions. He refrained from looking as the others were taken, but he heard the soft sighs of anguish, knowing what Fouquert had guessed, that there would be concealed knives, and various other articles that could be used as weapons. Quinlan's picks went in a stream of curses that earned him a clip round the ear. The only consolation was that, either through ingrained deference or forgetfulness, Markham's hands remained free.

'What now?' said Rannoch.

'Wait for Lanester,' Markham replied, biting his lip. 'There's nothing more we can do right now.'

The Hebes listened hard, unable to believe that someone of Fouquert's stamp could be dissuaded from using torture. But they heard nothing, though the wait was a long one. Finally Lanester emerged, with Duchesne and Fouquert behind him, and the blank look on his red, healthy face testified to his wellbeing.

'Your coat, Major,' said Fouquert.

Lanester took it off and threw it at the civilian's feet with a defiant gesture. Fouquert stepped forward to strike him, but Duchesne intervened, which earned him a glare. That was followed by a quiet demand, which had the dragoon officer violently shaking his head.

'What did they want?' whispered Markham.

'Who we are, where we're going. Over and over again. The soldier was satisfied the first time I answered. That bastard who hates you so went on and on.'

'Look at them now.'

The two Frenchmen were arguing, with Fouquert engaged in much pointing. Their voices, quiet at first, began to rise until first the guards, and then the whole chapel, could hear them.

'*Non!*'

The French cavalry commander's tone had grown increasingly harsh to match Fouquert's, neither seemingly prepared to give way. The subject, in such a confined space, was clear to anyone with a knowledge of French. Fouquert was demanding that Lanester be tied up. But he also wanted Markham, and a quiet room, to himself. The captain of dragoons would have none of it.

'He is no Corsican peasant. He's an officer and a prisoner, monsieur.'

'Citizen is what you call me, Captain Duchesne, not monsieur.'

Duchesne waved a hand in an airy way, as if what Fouquert had just said was true, but too bothersome to contend with. Having removed his cloak while interrogating Lanester he'd revealed his uniform, and with it, some trace of the basis of his attitude. Well cut in a period way, and discreetly trimmed with braid, it was the standard wear of a Bourbon cavalry officer, dark blue with green facings, adapted to look like a National Guard coat. While the French troops in the island might be loyal to their masters in Paris, they'd been on service here for many years. They adhered to cut and cloth, as well as traditions, that had died out in the mainland army.

'Nor, sir,' the captain continued, his tone extremely haughty, 'will I consent to him being tied up like some common criminal. He is, like Major

251

Lanester, an officer of an opposing force. And as such he will be treated with all the courtesy to which he is entitled by his rank. In fact, as I would wish to be treated myself, should I be unfortunate enough to be taken prisoner.'

'Your orders are to assist me in my mission.'

'Which I will do. But I will not go beyond that.'

'Do you know who I am?' Fouquert demanded, his black eyes blazing with anger.

'I could hardly not, since you boast of it so often, monsieur. But I would remind you where we are.' This was followed by another wave, more elaborate this time, that even in the confines of the small monastery seemed to take in the whole island of Corsica. 'We are on active duty, and that means I have the command.'

'You won't have it for long, Duchesne,' Fouquert spat. 'Indeed, if I were you, with that aristocratic tone, I'd be concerned about keeping my head on my shoulders.'

The captain replied to such an open threat with complete disdain, almost suppressing a yawn in his indifference. 'When we have completed our mission, and returned to Bastia, you may take up your dissatisfaction with General Lacombe.'

'I have a power that exceeds even that of the general.'

'Not here!' Duchesne said sharply.

'I represent the Committee of Public Safety,' Fouquert insisted quietly, his eyes ranging over the old-fashioned uniform coat in a very threatening way. 'The supreme body of the nation. And the Committee represents the Revolution. To disagree with such an august body is tantamount to suicide.'

'I would not claim to represent anything, sir,' Duchesne replied, turning and heading towards the knot of prisoners grouped behind the tiny altar. 'Except, of course, a tradition of proper military honour.'

Markham had been quietly translating this for the benefit of the men nearest him, all sitting with their hands tied. Rannoch was closest. The Highlander was listening, but also looking at Fouquert, his pale blue eyes almost opaque with the murderous thoughts that filled his mind. Lanester sat with his back to the wall, staring at the rough beamed ceiling of the small chapel.

Markham, as he translated, was running his eyes along the half-dozen monk's cells, desperately seeking a means of escape. Most of them had been taken over by Duchesne's troopers, leaving one free for their officer, plus the other where they'd questioned Lanester. He knew, from approaching the building earlier, that they didn't even have a window at the back to the outside world. With a guard on the only door, and an unbroken stone wall at their back, the British were well confined.

'Major,' said Duchesne, as soon as he was close enough. 'I would be most honoured if you will consent to use one of the cells. My men will make way, of course. That goes for you too, Lieutenant. It is unbecoming that officers should share the discomforts of the common soldier.'

'Why, thank you kindly, Captain.' Lanester replied, dropping his eyes to look at the Frenchmen.

'I will of course, require your parole.'

'I cannot give you that!'

Markham had answered before Lanester could speak, effectively shutting his superior up, the effect of which registered quickly on his round, red, now angry countenance. He was surprised the major couldn't guess at least some of the reason. Those cells had no windows, and another locked door would be no aid to escape. His only chance lay in numbers, and they were out here in the main chapel.

Duchesne's face took on a pained expression as he turned to reply to Markham. 'You must, monsieur, otherwise I may be obliged to indulge the gentleman behind me.'

'He'll indulge himself at some time, if not now. You see, I've met Citizen Fouquert before. I saw a man tied to a wooden fence a few months ago, his balls cut off so that the person you refer to as a gentleman could extract some information. Before and after that little treat, he raped and sodomised the man's daughter.' If the cavalry captain had looked pained before, he was doubly so now. 'And that's an indication of the sort of fate he has in store for me.'

'Not while you are my prisoner.'

'Which I won't be forever?'

'No,' Duchesne replied sadly. 'But then, neither will you be given any chance to escape. Your parole will merely make your confinement more comfortable. Our mission will be complete in a day or so. Then we will return to Bastia, where I am sure that General Lacombe will take the same attitude as I have.'

'I am determined to remain with my men,' Markham snapped. Then he blushed slightly,

254

when he realised how much that sounded like vainglorious boasting.

'Major?' asked Duchesne.

Lanester, when he replied, did so in a voice well larded with irony. 'How can I accept your kind offer in the face of such a display of nobility?'

Duchesne shrugged. 'Very well. You will soon be fed, and well, since there is plenty of meat in the paddock.'

He half turned, to indicate the debris from the recent search, which filled the doorway of the furthest cell. 'I apologise, in advance, but I will need to raid your own stores for more mundane items. We are travelling too light to carry anything other than basic rations.'

'Help yourself,' said Lanester, in a slightly strangled tone.

'You are most kind.'

'If you're stuck for a fellow to cook a decent dinner, my man Pavin here is a rare good 'un at the stove.'

Duchesne smiled, following Lanester's finger, to be greeted by Pavin's face, which was so puckered with disapproval that he resembled a squeezed lemon. 'You are the owner of all those pots and pans?'

'That be right.' Pavin replied, in execrable French. 'Copper the lot of them, which I hope you took right care to treat.'

'Game birds too, as well as a small urn of cream.'

'For the sauce.'

'We also unearthed an interesting selection of unusual spices. I was not aware that the English

255

ate anything other than plain roast beef.'

Lanester tapped his ample paunch. 'I'm an American by birth, monsieur, with an abiding interest in good food. I refuse to let my belly suffer just because I'm on campaign.'

The Frenchman had a twinkle in his eye, which to Markham seemed slightly out of place. 'Then the quality of the wines you are transporting is explained.'

'No point in blackstrap with decent grub,' Lanester replied, somewhat more guardedly. 'Besides, most of them are a present for that friend I told you of.'

'He must be a person you value very highly.'

'He is,' Lanester replied noncommittally.

Markham made a point of looking straight ahead then. Had Lanester really got away without mentioning Paoli? If he had, then Fouquert knew nothing of their mission, or of the problems with the Corsican command. Lanester certainly wouldn't have volunteered it, of course. Quite the opposite. It could only be due to Duchesne, interfering and stopping Fouquert from pushing too hard. And even now the cavalryman showed not the slightest trace of any desire enquire further.

'Then what a pity, Major, that we are at war, for it is a love I share. I was born in Burgundy, home to the finest food and wine in all of France. In other circumstances I'm sure we could spend many a happy hour conversing over what is produced there.'

'Hélas ce n'est pas possible,' said Bellamy. 'La guerre, malheureusement.'

Chapter eighteen

Duchesne's head snapped round to look at the Negro. 'You speak French?'

The formality with which Bellamy replied was well designed to show off his familiarity with the language. And where Lanester had an American accent, and Markham's was larded with the slang of common usage, Bellamy was so perfect in his grammar and his fluency that he could have been declaiming a poem by Ronsard.

'I have the good fortune,' he concluded, 'to have been taught French at an early age, when the facility of learning is at its most receptive.'

Duchesne was looking at his rough, grey flannel shirt, breeches and boots, clearly the attire of a ranker, wondering why such a creature should sound so like a very well bred officer.

'Are you from a French sugar island?'

'No, Captain, a British one.'

'We educate our slaves well,' said Lanester sarcastically.

'I am, sir, no one's slave.' Bellamy responded, without much in the way of respect.

Lanester pushed himself up the wall; his bulk, which hunched up had made him look small, now produced the opposite effect.

'I'd like to hear you say that in Virginia, boy. And that there look in your eye would be worth a hundred lashes all on its own.'

257

'Happy to oblige, sir,' said Sharland, with a small, slightly mocking bow. 'An' I'll sew them soup plates the sod terms lips to one another, if you so desire. That'll put a cap on his cheek.'

A ripple of laughter made its way through the rows of seated men, some of whom raised their tied wrists to encourage Sharland. Bellamy was almost shaking in his desire to reply.

'History tells us that the dregs of England's gaols were used to populate the Virginia Colony.'

'Damn you,' snapped Lanester, in a voice that left the dragoon officer, without any understanding of English, bemused. But it attracted the attention of Fouquert, who had been talking earnestly to some of Duchesne's men. Lanester was on his feet now, his fat face bright red with anger. 'If I had my crop, you'd feel it on your hide this second.'

'Odd,' Bellamy continued, his voice controlled, and full of hauteur, 'that the bloodline of indentured thieves and vagabonds, who consorted carnally with their black chattels, feel the right to lord it over men of pure inheritance.'

'I'll lord it over your flaying, you black devil!' shouted Lanester, stung to the quick. 'Your blood will flow like a river. You'll scream for mercy before I get through with you.'

Pavin had his face pressed close to that of Bellamy, his voice a harsh screech, as he pounded weakly on the Negro's chest with his bound hands.

'How dare you talk on the major so, you fuckin' arse-lickin' ape!'

'What is this about?' demanded Fouquert, of a Duchesne who could only shrug. He addressed the same question, in good English, to Bellamy.

'I was trying to remind my white brothers that we are all equal in God's eyes, though I find his tolerance of such endemic ignorance personally displeasing. Clearly, he has not read *The Declaration of the Rights of Man*.'

'And you have?' asked Fouquert.

'Most certainly. If you wish I shall recite it for you, in either French, English or Latin.'

Fouquert was standing right in front of Markham by the time he decided to intervene. 'Bellamy! Shut your mouth.'

The Negro replied with eyes opened wide, lower lip dropped, the very image of a man bemused and hurt. 'But sir?'

'Just remember that one day you might be back in a British camp. And so will Major Lanester. He's not likely to miss you in a crowd.'

'He won't get a chance to skin the bastard alive if 'n I'm there,' growled Sharland.

'Come here,' demanded Fouquert, his finger crooked at Bellamy.

'Stay still,' Markham commanded.

The kick Fouquert delivered was vicious and painful, just below Markham's knee. 'Shut up, you scum.'

'Monsieur!' cried a shocked Duchesne.

'Never mind that horsehair-stuffed dummy,' Fouquert continued. 'I will get my hands on you, never fear. And I intend to enjoy myself. You will know the meaning of the word pain. Women find you handsome, I'm told. But they will recoil from you when I am finished with your face. I'll leave you deaf, dumb, blind and a castrato. You will pay

259

for what you did to me a hundred times over.'

Fouquert was upright again, barking at Bellamy. 'You! come here! Now!'

As soon as Bellamy stood up, hands knocked his legs, so that he fell heavily amongst his fellows, all of whom, either openly or secretly, took the opportunity to fetch him a blow. It was ignominious rather than painful. Markham ploughed into the mass of bodies to rescue him, dragging him to the front, and throwing him into the clear.

'Why, our lieutenant is a saint as well,' said Fouquert, with a wicked grin, as he pushed Bellamy towards one of the monks' cells. 'Perhaps he will bear pain with the fortitude of one.'

Then he turned to Duchesne, his voice becoming harsh. 'I have had a word with some of your men, Captain, several of whom have more brains than you. At least they know about their duty to the Revolution. The officers will be tied up, as I requested. If you choose to dispute this command there are those quite willing to take your place, and complete our mission.'

Duchesne looked at his men, some of whom returned his stare without flinching. 'There is no one there above the rank of corporal. You'd be a fool to trust to such men the task we need to perform, never mind getting you safe back to Bastia.'

'They're soldiers, and therefore all I need, since they can follow my orders. You may think you know who I am, but you underestimate me. I have the power to make any man in this room an officer, which General Lacombe will be obliged to confirm, or face his own removal. The same applies to you, Duchesne, if you do not obey me.

Believe me, I will endow my choice with the legitimate authority not only to replace you, but to eliminate you if he feels your presence endangers our operation.'

The pause was indication enough that the dragoon officer would have to back down, especially since three or four of his troopers had edged forward, an eager look in their eyes. Typically, Fouquert had sought out his malcontents before he'd made the threat. But the captain had his dignity to consider. He would not give way completely. He flicked a hand towards Markham.

'And what of this gentleman?'

The grin with which Fouquert responded made Markham think of the wolves he'd encountered in Russia. 'That is a man I owe much to. But what is a day or two after several months? I can wait for my revenge, captain. It is, after all, a dish better taken cold. Now tie both officers up – in Lieutenant Markham's case, lash both his hands and his feet. And search the major carefully before you do it.'

Duchesne opened his mouth to protest, but closed it again. Fouquert, now clearly in control, nodded to the two troopers closest to the prisoners. They looked at their captain, who gave a curt nod. Within a couple of minutes both British officers were trussed up, Markham like a Christmas goose.

'Is there anywhere in this globe that you don't have enemies, Markham?' moaned Lanester, as he sought to ease the tight bindings on his wrist. 'Talk about jumping out of the skillet into the fire. I should have left you to Hanger.'

'I wish you had,' Markham replied, his eyes fixed on the back of the bottle-green, civilian coat. His experience tended to make him believe that when people delivered threats, they rarely carried out that which they promised. But that was not a view he could hold about Fouquert. He'd meant every word he'd said, which sent a frisson of fear shooting through Markham's whole being.

The tight knots began to interfere with the supply of his blood. Lanester was in a similar state, though in his case an appeal for some relief, made directly to Fouquert, produced an easing of his bonds. Markham's request was ignored, and he watched as the soldiers moved the pews and set up two tables at the far end of the room at which to eat. There had to be a kitchen beyond those cells, since the odour of cooking food filled the chapel.

Fouquert and Duchesne, sitting at the smaller of the two tables, had already started on Lanester's wine, a privilege they clearly intended should extend no further, since the troopers were drinking their own rations. They were sitting opposite each other talking, though in a stiff and formal manner. Bellamy, standing to one side, was invited by Fouquert to join them, which he did with some alacrity, causing Duchesne to stand up abruptly. He was ordered to sit down again, and did so.

They weren't still for long. The door burst open, and one of the outside guards, set to mind the horses, came rushing in. The sound of a solitary pair of hooves made it unnecessary to strain forward for the words he whispered to Duchesne.

Both the captain and Fouquert stood up, indicated to Bellamy to remain still, and then went outside, closing the door behind then. Whoever the visitor was, he didn't remain long and the sound of his departure coincided with the return of the two Frenchmen. Bellamy, in their absence, had helped himself to several cups of wine, each one gulped down.

Not that this seemed to offend Fouquert. Markham watched the way he and Bellamy talked, almost cutting the cavalry officer out of the conversation. The Negro was obviously affected by the wine, more animated in his gestures than his officer had ever seen him. His hands, once they came into play, became almost comical in the extent of their expression. And he never refused a refill. Quite the opposite; he consumed whatever wine was given to him greedily, like a man who needed to drink it, rather than one who took it for pleasure. Markham thought back to the night Bellamy'd saved him outside Hanger's villa. He'd wondered since what it was he was looking for that night. Now, watching him gulp down the rare and expensive clarets, plus the way his whole demeanour seemed to have altered, he thought he knew.

Fouquert kept pace with Bellamy, and Markham also watched him down his drink with some interest. On two occasions before he'd seen him succumb to excess at what turned out to be a critical time. He might do so tonight, and allow them a chance to effect something. But then, against that, Markham knew that drunks lose control, and that if Fouquert got too far into the bottle, he might put aside his cold-dish strategy

263

for one of more immediate purpose.

Rannoch, when the victuals came, had to feed him, Pavin struggling to do the same for a much more comfortable Lanester. As he spooned the meal into Markham's mouth, they talked quietly, seeking some way to effect an escape. But nothing could alter the fact that they were in a building with only one, guarded door. As for trying to overpower the French, they'd been stripped of everything, coats, hats, packs and all their weapons, which were stacked in the cell.

'That altar stone is marble, and has a broken edge,' said the Highlander.

'They'll hear you rubbing against it,' Markham whispered, indicating from that alone just how much sound carried in the spare stone chapel. Suddenly he pushed forward, almost into a ball, as he sought to put emphasis into the words he wanted to say.

'I don't think that I am going to survive this, Rannoch.'

'It will not help to give way to despair.'

Markham responded with a hollow, humourless chuckle. 'I'm not giving way, and if that bastard lowers his guard once, and lets me near his windpipe, I'll take him to hell with me. But you must see to the men.'

There was a pause, while Markham wondered if Fouquert would extend his revenge to them. If he did, there was nothing that could be done to stop it, and even less point in speculating about it. As far as his Hebes were concerned, he'd be best to stick to the optimistic.

'Ask Duchesne to give you my purse. God

knows it contains little, but it might buy you all some food, and help keep you alive till there's an exchange.'

Markham opened his mouth to continue, to say the ritual things about contacting relatives. But who was there, really? His father, who in any case had grown distant after his court martial, was dead. His mother was so addicted to poteen that she was barely conscious most of the day. Hannah, his half-sister, would rejoice to hear he was dead, and that the stain on the family name caused by his birth had been expunged. Perhaps Freddy, his gentle half-brother, would care. Certainly he would weep. But Markham had seen him do that too many times to be sure that it contained any depth. Oddly, the face of Lizzie Gordon came to mind, with those twin furrows on her brow that denoted anger.

'If you get a chance to pass a message to Colonel Hanger's wife, tell her that I am sorry for the trouble I caused her.'

'Look at that black bastard,' hissed Rannoch, the spoon with which he was feeding his officer pointed at the Negro's back.

Bellamy was on his feet, having finished his food, drinking with gusto, he held two of Lanester's bottles in his hands as he traipsed round the room dispensing drink and good cheer. He'd borrowed Fouquert's long tricolor sash, and wound it round himself like a Roman toga. Elaborate gestures, clearly of a salacious nature, matched his sallies. Whatever he was saying, the words lost in the general merriment, was producing great mirth, even from the normally humourless Fouquert. In contrast, Lanester was complaining bitterly under his breath, while Rannoch was near to grinding his teeth.

'I did not have time for him, but I swear I never thought to see him in betrayal.'

'Can you blame him, Rannoch?' Markham replied softly. 'Even you saw fit to club him with a musket.'

Rannoch didn't make any attempt to deny it, and his voice, always so even and slow, became quite animated. 'I will do a sight more than that should I get him near the branch of a tree. The bastard will dance more than he does now, but without the benefit of a floor.'

'Amen to that,' said Lanester, who was straining forward to hear what Rannoch was saying. 'There's no trusting the tribe of Joab, not ever.'

'I've heard good men say that about the tribe of Catholics,' Markham replied, not sure why he was still taking Bellamy's part.

'Hang 'em too, I say,' Lanester responded bitterly, challenging the lieutenant to admit to his own religious background. Even in extremis, Markham declined to be drawn. Lanester carried on, his voice full of the unreasoned hate which seemed to go with adherence to the Thirty-Nine Articles. 'We've got a room full of the swine, right here, the popish bastards. And I bet you that turd over there, the thin one that loves you so much, had it in mind to be a priest at one time in his life.'

Markham looked at Fouquert. There was an ascetic quality to the dark-skinned, fine-boned face, disapproval of sin in the thin, bloodless lips. Certainly there was fanaticism in the black, piercing eyes. Some men of the cloth shared those Jesuitical attributes. But he'd known gentle priests too, men who had given up all chance of creature comfort to tend to rural flocks of poor Irish croppies.

'Where are the monks?' he asked suddenly.

'What?'

'This place wasn't empty. It couldn't have been, not with all that livestock. So where are they, the men who lived here?'

'Who cares,' replied Lanester, his face screwed up with his own personal discomfort. 'Let the Rome worshippers fry in hell for my money. I've had too many of the swine under my own command to care much for the breed.'

Rannoch had been silent while the Major was cursing Catholics. Though they'd never discussed it, Markham wondered if that, and not the strict Scottish Calvinism, was his true religion. The Highlander spoke now, and all his hatred of officers spilled into a condemnation of Lanester's attitude.

'I daresay you have seen a few killed by your own hand, that has marched them to a death they neither sought nor deserved.'

'You cannot speak to me like that, Sergeant,' said Lanester, his eyes narrowing.

'I have spoken to better than you in the same vein, Major, and I have the scars on my back as a testimony to how they respond to the plain truth.'

'You also have that M branded on your thumb, though you try damn well to hide it.'

'Aye,' Rannoch replied, looking down at the raised letter. 'And I am surely ashamed of it. But

not for reasons the likes of you would understand. The pity of it is, that if I had only swung
my musket round, I could have killed the stupid
swine that earned it for me. Instead, a poor
innocent colonial died, for nothing more than
causing fright to a commissioned fool.'

'Where?' Markham asked.

Rannoch, who normally frowned at any enquiry into his past, smiled at him, his whole
square face lighting up as he did so. And his blue
eyes twinkled, as he jerked his branded thumb at
Lanester.

'It might be that I would tell you, sure as you
are that perdition is close. But I'll not satisfy this
one, who is no better, in the way that he betrayed
his own, than that jigging black over yonder.'

Lanester was speechless, faced with an accusation he hadn't heard for fifteen years, probably
because he steered clear of anyone inclined to
make it. And Rannoch, despite his lower rank, had
a natural dignity the pot-bellied major lacked.

'Now, sir,' Rannoch said pointedly to Markham,
'I must see to the rest of the men.'

'I'll lash them to the same wagon,' spat
Lanester, his bound hands pointing at Bellamy
and his eyes glaring at Rannoch's back. 'So help
me God if I don't.'

At the other end of the chapel it had quietened
down. The meal continued, with half the contents of the paddocks making their way to the
table. Voices rose and fell amongst Duchesne's
troopers. Judging by the revelry, it was as if there
were no war, no uniforms, no bound prisoners

268

behind the altar. The mood seemed to extend to both Fouquert and Bellamy as well. If anything, those two were consuming more than ever, this in the company of a captain who drank sparingly, and seemed content to take as little part as possible in the conversation. As soon as he decently could, Duchesne excused himself. Having checked on the guard rota, including the pair on the horselines outside, he ordered his men to bed down, ignoring the groans of those for whom the flavour of their own cheap wine had taken hold.

Soon only Bellamy and Fouquert remained, their movements slow and unco-ordinated, as they leant across the table in deep conversation. Their speech was indistinct but slurred, this obvious even at the distance from which Markham was hearing it. Not that he paid them too much attention any more. His hands had gone numb, as had his feet, with no sign of much blood left in either. It was a wry thought that they'd hurt like hell when the ropes were removed. If Fouquert had his way, the pain would scarcely be noticeable.

Eventually the two drunks fell silent, Fouquert picked up one final bottle, then staggered to his own cell, slamming the door behind him. Bellamy, after a final tip of a bottle which proved to be empty, fell forward, clearing the plates from the table with a clatter, as he rested his head on his arm.

Chapter nineteen

Numb they might be, but Markham's hands were sensitive to the touch. Nor was he sleeping properly, so that when he felt the first brush of contact, he was immediately awake. Dozing, he'd had several troubled dreams, and it took several seconds to orient himself to his actual physical surroundings. By that time, the knife was already rasping through the wrist ropes. Not being a truly sharp instrument, it took time. But when they parted it was suddenly, which produced an agonising pain that nearly made him faint as the blood rushed back into his extremities.

The hand that clasped itself across his mouth was large, with an odd and faint odour of mutton fat. There was an unpleasant blast of stale breath, sour with wine, before the voice spoke.

'You must bear the pain, sir,' hissed Bellamy, trying to press something hard into his hand. 'Cry out and we will both die.'

Markham was in agony, biting his own lips until he tasted blood, desperate for something to clench between his teeth. The bone that Bellamy jammed into his mouth created fear rather than security. But he bit on it nevertheless while Bellamy was working on his ankles, sawing away with a knife that seemed too blunt for the purpose. Soon there was suffering at both ends, as the blood began to flow back into his feet as well.

270

'Rest a while, sir,' Bellamy whispered. 'Let the pain subside. They have changed the guard on the horselines half an hour past, and those who had the early duty are now asleep. As soon as you can walk we can make some attempt to get away.'

Markham pulled on Bellamy's shirt, working to bring his ear close to his mouth, the bone dropping out as he whispered, 'The rest of our men.'

'Can rot,' Bellamy replied, in a voice that bordered on too loud.

'No.' Markham's hand was reaching down, to take the blade from the Negro, who was trying to hold it out of his grasp. 'Damn you, give it me, or I'll yell the place down.'

He had Bellamy's wrist, but not the strength in his hands to hold it. It was as though they belonged to another. The breath to plead was absent as well, taken up in an attempt to stop himself yelling for release. Bellamy pushed away from him, whatever faint light present in the chapel insufficient to show his black face. Why was there no light? Had someone failed to see to the fire and the candles? Markham lay still for several seconds, aware of loud and persistent snoring. His head swung back and forth, looking around in the darkness. It was all wrong, even for men who had drunk themselves into a stupor. Then Bellamy came close again, the sheen on his sweating forehead picking up the faint glimmer from the wads of tow flickering in sconces on either side of the single door.

'We cannot all escape,' he said, in a voice so soft it was almost inaudible. 'The horses are in the nearest paddock, with two men who can see the

271

whole front of the building.'

'We must,' hissed Markham, damning the haste which had lost him the bone. 'The guard on the door.'

Bellamy gave a low chuckle. 'A full wine bottle will fell a man so easily, and rarely break when it does.'

'Cut Rannoch loose first. Then let him see to the others.'

'Why?'

'Do it.'

It was impossible to wake and free so many men without some noise. Yet whatever they did, no one stirred from behind their closed cell doors. By the time the last man was freed, Markham had some life back in his limbs. He was able to stand, and to issue whispered commands that should be passed on, the main one being to maintain their position, as if they were still tied. The real question was, could they retrieve their arms. Uniform coats and packs were secondary. If they could get their hands on the muskets, then turning the tables on the French would be easy.

Hobbling, he headed for the furthest cell from the altar, the one that the enemy had used to stash their muskets. The door, gingerly tried, wouldn't yield, clearly locked on the inside.

Markham stood back, his mind working furiously to contrive a solution. He couldn't batter it down, since that would wake everyone in the monastery long before it produced any positive result. Suddenly he grinned, remembering Toulon. Fouquert as a hostage would guarantee them safe passage. They might not best Duchesne and his men. But they could get clear, with some security against the danger of pursuit.

He was just about to move towards Fouquert's cell when the door of Duchesne's quarters swung open. The captain, fully dressed, stood there, pistol in one hand, a lantern in the other. It was shaded, but produced enough candlelight through the thin open strip to illuminate them both. He had his fingers to his lips, and as he shook his head, he also indicated that Markham and his men should get out. A wave of the pistol underlined the fact that if they chose any other course, he would have no option but to fire it off and raise the alarm.

Markham pulled himself fully upright, and bowed, a gesture which the Frenchman matched. Then Duchesne shut the door so that only a crack remained, through which he could make sure that his instructions were obeyed. There was no choice, though the thought of hacking through that February forest in nothing but a thin shirt was not inspiring. Making his way to the outer door, he dragged the comatose guard to one side and opened it a fraction. Immediately the blast of cold night air hit him, making him shiver.

Bellamy was right, though how he'd unearthed such detail was a mystery. The two guards on the horselines were just discernible in the moonlight, as they paced to and fro in their cloaks, only thudding hands to their bodies in an attempt to ward off the predawn chill. The horses, tethered and rugged, stood in two lines. They had their heads down, one foot raised, in that half comatose state, so near to sleep, that such creatures could

273

maintain. But that wouldn't survive the exit of twenty or so men. Even if the guards didn't spot them right away, the animals, sensitive to movement or noise, would react to any sound they made. The only possible way to avoid that was to move men slowly and in small groups. He eased the door closed and went back to talk to Bellamy.

'You took care of the guard, and located the men outside. How?'

'I needed to relieve myself,' hissed the Negro, in his usual formal way. 'I clipped the guard on the door first, and while I was outside I had a chance to observe the sentries. Perhaps we could employ the same tactic.'

'Twenty men through one door would be some piss.'

'The number, sir, is your notion, not mine.'

'Get the coat off that guard you clobbered, and hit him again if he shows any inclination to wake up.'

While Bellamy obliged, Markham crawled amongst his men, sitting in silence behind the altar. He had a quick word with Lanester, to advise him of his intentions, then issued his instructions. First he ordered them to remove their footwear, take a hand each and follow him to the door.

'If you lose your boots,' he whispered, 'you'll march to Corte in bare feet.' His voice suddenly became angry. 'And when we get clear, every man jack of you will apologise to Bellamy, and thank him for getting us out of here.'

Markham, wearing the cutaway coat of a French

dragoon, started retching as soon as he opened the door, the sounds from his throat mixed with a string of French curses. He stood, one hand against the stone wall, feet splayed wide, head dropped low so that he could see the two sentries. At first they called to him, soft but rude reminders of the price of taking too much drink, as well as the lashing he would receive if he woke the others. But after a short break they resumed their desultory pacing, calling quiet jokes to each other to which he was clearly too ill to respond.

Markham counted their steps, and called to Rannoch as soon as they were at the furthest point of their beat. The orders had already been issued, so he, with a pair of Seahorses, were out of the door and tiptoeing for the treeline as soon as he hissed the command. Markham nearly retched for real, so close was his heart to his mouth, when he saw the way the moonlight picked up the reflection of both shirts and breeches.

'This isn't going to work,' he hissed. 'Pavin, Halsey, get Major Lanester out next. As soon as he's at the trees, the rest of you go in single file.'

'And if they shoot?' asked Lanester, clearly alarmed at the notion of having to run.

'Then I will be their target, Major. Now go.'

It was Lanester who set off the horses. Fat, lacking any grace in his movements, he tripped over his own feet and stumbled into the wall, throwing himself back so violently that he nearly fell over, emitting an involuntary cry as he did so. Markham's loud retching sound might have fooled the guards. But not the animals. One head came up sharply at the perceived danger, and the uplifted hoof hit the ground simultaneously, which set the beast next to it shuffling sideways to bump into the succeeding tethered animal. That stopped the sentries pacing, and they peered round in the darkness, their eyes eventually coming round to their distressed compatriot leaning on the door frame. The line of ghostly shapes crawling along the wall was as obvious as he.

'*Garde!*' they shouted together, raising their carbines.

'Run!' Markham yelled.

He stood upright and turned to face them, presenting a target at which they could aim, willing the pair to fire off the weapons without taking too careful an aim. They obliged, with a standard of shooting that was deplorable. If muskets were inaccurate, cavalry carbines, with their short barrels, were worse. But they should have been able to hit Markham at thirty-five yards even with a weapon whose main purpose was to maim at ten paces. Both shots were way too high, coming nowhere near their target. He flinched as one of the two balls, having hit the wall, ricocheted so that it span past his head.

He ran himself, glad to see that the last of his men were halfway to the woods. Behind him the interior of the chapel had come alive, the shouts magnified by the confining echo, as the troopers armed themselves. Through the ballyhoo he thought he could hear Duchesne issuing clear instructions, but that notion faded as he put distance between himself and the open door, aware that in a moment, those very men, having loaded their own carbines, would be rushing out behind him.

It was Rannoch shouting 'Down!', when he was about five yards from the trees, which saved him. Unknown to Markham, Duchesne had brought out his men, all thirty of them, in a disciplined manner, and they'd lined up in good order behind him. Inaccuracy was not a consideration when firing so many guns, so that the Frenchman allowed little time for aim. As soon as the carbines were shouldered, he ordered them to be discharged.

Flat on his stomach, still sliding forward over the damp earth, Markham heard and felt most of the balls crack over his head. One or two hit the ground in front of him, others thudding into the trees behind which his men were hiding. A scream told him that at least one had found flesh, but that was just a fleeting thought quickly suppressed by the need to get to his feet and move. The word to reload, clearly shouted by Duchesne, surprised him, since the escapees were unarmed. That lasted until he realised that the French officer, whose honour would not permit him to partake of torture and mutilation, was giving him more time to escape.

'Who was hit?' he yelled as he made the treeline.

'Major Lanester,' called Pavin. 'He's taken a ball in the chest.'

'He stayed on his feet,' spat Rannoch, holding out an arm to slow down his own officer.

'We'll have to carry him,' Markham replied. 'And you and Dornan are the strongmen.'

'Enemy preparing to fire,' said Halsey who,

good soldier that he was, had never taken his eyes off the enemy.

'Get behind...' Markham shouted. The word 'something' was cut off by the way that Rannoch lifted him bodily, and slammed him into his own broad chest. The Highlander had his back to a tree, which, judging by the sounds, took several of the carbine rounds in its trunk.

'Run,' gasped Markham.

'We're not armed,' growled Rannoch, already on his way to pick up Lanester.

'Then we have to use the forest.'

In the dark, it was truly a hellish place. Little moonlight filtered through to aid them, once they'd gone a few yards. Each man had to hold the hand of another, just to avoid getting lost. But there was one consolation. It was not a place where cavalry could follow. And horse soldiers, even dragoons who were trained to the task, had a deep aversion to fighting on foot. The dark woods would hold just as much terror for them as for their quarry. What use was a weapon when your enemy could be standing right next to you without your knowledge? The trail they were leaving would not become obvious until daylight, by which time Markham hoped to have put enough distance between them to contrive a hiding place they'd never find.

'Where in the name of God are we going?' asked one of his men, in a muffled, unrecognisable voice.

It was Quinlan who replied, easily identified, even though he was gasping, by his endemically cheeky London accent. 'To Lucifer's hell by the

278

look of this place, old mate, which is where most of us belong.'

'Quiet!' Markham called, trying to shout and whisper simultaneously, bringing the whole line to a halt by the act of stopping.

It was impossible to be sure how long they'd been going, but there was one thing of which he was certain and that was the silence around them; no breaking of wood or cries of frustrated soldiery. Any pursuit still moving through the *maccia* would have to be making a noise they could hear, and there was none. Markham realised that his own party were all close to exhaustion, and though he didn't think they'd achieved more than a couple of hundred yards, in this tangled woodland that might just be enough. By staying quiet, they'd hear the chase long before it arrived, and they could either move on themselves, or, given some light, contrive decent concealment.

'Try to make yourselves comfortable. Sit close to stay warm.'

'Here, Daisy Quinlan,' Ettrick squealed, in the midst of a great deal of shuffling, 'you mind where you place your hand.'

Quinlan's reply was delivered just before Markham could renew his call for silence, in a gruff imitation of a farmer's voice. 'You ain't no use to me, Ettrick, without you've got a fleece.'

It produced suppressed laughter. Not much, but enough to revive battered and fearful spirits. Markham, annoyed by the noise, was nevertheless grateful for their presence, as well as their inability to be serious. Chuckling through heaving lungs himself, he called out softly to locate Rannoch,

following the voice with some difficulty, not realising they were practically beside each other until
the Highlander's outstretched hand touched his.

'How's the major?'

It was Pavin who answered. 'No idea. And we
won't have till it's light. I'm afraid to start poking
about in case I cause more damage than I save.
All I can say is that there is blood, and he's
breathing enough to emit the odd curse.'

'He should learn to obey an order to get down,'
said Rannoch.

'That'll be the day,' spat Pavin, 'when the likes
of Luke Lanester take instructions from a
sergeant.'

'Try and make him as comfortable as you can.
It's a long time till dawn. Sergeant Rannoch,
there's no way of setting a proper piquet in this
place.'

'You and me then, sir.'

''Fraid so.'

They barely spoke, though such a duty had been
occasion for some intimacy in the past. But here
the need to concentrate was paramount, and
confined them to the odd exchange just to ensure
they were still awake. There were sounds in the
forest, rustlings and scrapings that were probably
moving wildlife, but could just as easily be human,
certainly enough to keep them on tenterhooks.
Not that any of the others got much sleep. Whatever bodily heat they had generated in their escape
soon evaporated, and a deep chill set in.

The first birds started to sing before the dawn
grey tinged the sky. And, in truth, so little light
penetrated their position that the sun was well up

before they noticed much change. Enough filtered through eventually to show a sorry bunch,
not one of whom, apart from Markham, could be
said to have a whole shirt. The French coat he'd
stolen had saved his own linen from a shredding,
but all the others, in their lacerated flannel,
looked like workhouse paupers. Hollow-eyed, un-
shaven, with their tattered garments, they were
hungry as well.

Markham went to examine Lanester as soon as
he could see, the dark stain of blood on the shirtfront plain even in the gloom. Pavin pointed to the
gap in the linen, and told Markham of the hole in
his chest that lay beneath it, just above his right
nipple. He described the wound as a dark, puckered hollow in the soft flesh opposite the heart.

'It's best left to a sawbones, your honour. Without we knows the track of the ball, we can't say
'ow serious it is. But it's no small matter, even if
it has missed 'is vitals.'

There was a tenderness in Pavin's voice that
Markham had never heard before, an indication
that for all his endemic rudeness he cared deeply
for the Major. Asked to give up his shirt for
bandages, Markham did so willingly. But he himself was as worried as Lanester's servant. That
wound sounded deep, painful and likely to become quickly infected if not properly treated.

'What a fine predicament,' he said to Rannoch,
as behind him Pavin tore his shirt to shreds. The
Highlander, because of his fair stubble, at least
looked something like his normal self. 'No food,
no weapons of any kind to kill some or defend
ourselves, and an enemy that will be in here after

281

us as soon as they've finished their breakfast.'

'I doubt they'll come after us, sir,' said Bellamy.

Markham had to peer hard to see the Negro, who was well hidden by his makeshift bed, which he seemed to have occupied on his own. He still had the tricolor sash he'd been wearing the previous night, and was thus the only one with some kind of covering to ward off the cold.

'How do you know that?'

'Fouquert's solution was to kill you all.'

'He still might,' growled Rannoch.

Markham put his hand on his sergeant, to calm and quieten him so that Bellamy could speak. In the background, Lanester groaned as Pavin sat him up to apply the rough bandages.

'Do you need any help, Pavin?'

All the previous irascibility had returned, and was in his negative reply. Markham turned his attention back to Bellamy.

'Tell me what happened.'

'Fouquert and Duchesne were at odds about the risks involved in holding us captive. The captain said that it would do nothing to jeopardise their mission. Two troopers could look after as many men, as long as they were armed, and the prisoners were tied.'

'He was right,' said Markham.

'Not according to Fouquert, who asked where this confinement would take place. When the captain said the chapel he called him a fool.'

'He's a saint to me.'

'They won't be staying there, it seems, nor coming back when they go, so Fouquert suggested they do to you lot what they'd done to the monks.'

'And what was that?' asked Markham, who had a horrible fear that he knew.

'Strangled them to a man.'

'And Duchesne?'

'Would have nothing to do with it. So Fouquert told him to stick to his soldiering and leave the hard decisions to him.'

'I don't suppose they told you what their mission was?' asked Markham.

'Fouquert did, mixed with what he was going to do with you. Mind you, that was when he was very drunk.'

'He was not alone in that,' said Rannoch sourly.

Bellamy tapped his head with his knuckles. 'This might not stop the butt of a musket, Scotsman, but it is enough to drink most men under.'

'What did he say?' Markham demanded impatiently.

'You must understand his thoughts were less than lucid by then, so it only emerged in dribs and drabs. He spent most of the time boasting about his position with the Committee of Public Safety, and how it would be enhanced after this. Then there were his past exploits, a lot of which were too grisly for Duchesne.'

Markham had to bite back his annoyance. Clearly Bellamy had no intention of being hurried. He wanted to string out his tale, to demonstrate how clever he'd been. Rannoch knew it too, which accounted for the low growling sound that had replaced his breathing.

'Would that be why he retired early?' Markham asked, with as much control as he could muster.

'Most certainly. Once Fouquert noticed he was

283

squeamish, he laid on the gore with a trowel.'

'So?'

'There was something about their allies in Corte, Corsicans by the sound of it.'

'Did they say that?'

'Not precisely,' Bellamy replied, emphasising the final sibilants with infuriating condescension. 'Duchesne nearly let slip something more revealing, but Fouquert shut him up. Yet once the captain was gone, and he really got into the bottle, he talked about men loyal to Paris, prepared to risk their lives to aid them. The only thing I can say with certainty is that they were not French.'

Markham was almost resigned as he posed the next question. 'And what else did he say?'

Bellamy waved one hand, his face taking on a look of some superiority. It was in his voice too, the tone of a man discussing the actions of lesser mortals.

'A great deal, some of it nonsense about how the whole of Corsica would be subdued when his mission was complete.'

'Which is?'

The *coup de grâce* was delivered with an almost foppish air, the sole evidence of Bellamy's amusement in the enlargement of his eyes. 'Fouquert has instructions from Paris to enter Corte, which he seems to regard as already arranged. Once in the town he is to arrest General Pasquale Paoli, and take him to France to stand trial for betraying the Revolution.'

'What!'

Bellamy's voice went down two octaves, and it slowed right down, so that he sounded like a man

284

addressing a moron.

'They intend to enter Corte, assisted by another faction. I think they called them Buonapartists.'

The voice changed again, to that foppish tone, as if he was discussing nothing of any importance. But Rannoch grabbed him by the shirtfront, and dragged him close, hissing in his ear what he would do to him, which, even if Bellamy did try to maintain his dignity, brought the last sentence out in a rush.

'He also alluded to the notion, a sudden inspiration I hazard, that they might dress a few of the dragoons in our uniform coats, as an added confusion to their opponents.'

Chapter twenty

'We're a day's march from Corte, Major. It makes sense to see if we can find someone more local.'

Lanester's hand moved across the bloodstained shirt, to the edge of the bandages which now swathed his chest, careful to avoid the area close to his wound. His face looked healthy enough, still red and fat, if you discounted the sheen of sweat that covered it.

'You're not carrying a ball in your chest, Markham. I am.'

'There's bound to be someone in the nearest village, even if it's only a mendicant monk, who can provide some help.'

Lanester wasn't a good patient, and if he'd been

irascible before, because of a loss of comfort, he was even worse now.

'A papist shaman and charlatan, fit only to cure a goat. And I doubt we'll find better in Corte. I'd rather go all the way back to Bastia, any day, and place my trust to a good old British Army surgeon.'

Markham was tempted to ask why. In his experience, army medical men were generally there because of their incompetence, not their ability. No one questioned them when a patient died, nor inquired why so much of the rum issued to dull the pain ended up down their throats. Any of them who could have drawn a decent stipend in civilian life would do so rather than submit themselves to the rigours of campaigning.

'We are on foot, sir,' said Markham, holding up the cutlery knife that Bellamy had used to cut his bonds. 'And probably without even the ability to rig a stretcher. Which means we'll have to carry you for some time. That wound has part of your shirt in it, and that's a sure formula for infection. We need to get you to someone who can deal with it as quickly as possible. Who is less important than when.'

'He's right, your honour,' said Pavin leaning forward to come into the Major's view. 'We ain't even got a drop of ardent spirit to be sloshing on the hole.'

'G'damn you, man!' Lanester growled. 'Obey my orders.'

This was followed by a bout of painful coughing. Pavin looked up, his eyes meeting Markham's. They didn't need words, just a nod. Lanester, in

pain from the constant movement, would be unlikely to have a clue where they were headed. Pavin
moved away when Markham indicated that he
wanted to continue in private, though the servant,
as nosy as all his tribe, stopped well within earshot.

'As you wish, Major,' Markham lied. 'But you
must rest here a little longer, while I try and find
out what alternative there is to a forced march
through this labyrinth.'

'How?'

'By heading back to the monastery. Bellamy
seems to think the French won't come in here
after us.'

'And you believe him?'

'The man just saved your life.'

'Wrong, Markham,' Lanester responded wearily.
'He saved yours. I don't recall mine being at risk
until we ran from that damned building.'

'Then you only have yourself to blame, sir,'
Markham replied acidly, though he dropped his
voice so low not even Pavin could hear it. 'Or me.
Bellamy wanted to leave you and my men behind.'

'Then I'll see him hang.'

'You won't, because I'll never repeat those
words to you or anyone else.'

There was a wheezing sound in the Major's
chest as he struggled to put force into his next
words. 'You'd take the part of a nigger against
your own kind?'

Markham stood up, wondering whether his
reply was the truth or just a convenient response.
'Nine times out of ten, yes.'

'I was told you were poor quality stock, Markham. After what I saw you do at Fornali I didn't

believe it. Now I'm not so sure.'

Any number of people could have said that without causing distress. But coming from Lanester, a man he'd initially taken to, it was wounding, regardless of what had happened on the journey. And his response was an involuntary thing, which with more careful consideration he would never have voiced.

'Am I poor enough stock to sacrifice to a Corsican assassin in the lines at Cardo?'

Lanester tried to push himself onto one elbow, but failed. 'What are you talking about, man?'

'A convenient way to shorten your journey, Major, by leaving the Corsicans in no doubt that I had information to give Pasquale Paoli. Almost an invitation to the traitor to reveal himself by sticking a knife in my back.'

Lanester gasped, as much from the effort of breathing as from surprise. His face, red and still sweating, took on an expression beyond physical pain.

'Everything I had to tell Paoli, including what you told me in private, was listed at my insistence, and in case I failed in a letter from Admiral Hood. I hope and pray you believe that to get it, they would have had to kill us both.'

That produced a sudden bout of coughing, and Lanester turned his head away as Pavin rushed to his side to comfort him. Markham stood for a moment looking at him, wondering where the truth lay, especially since this was the first time he'd heard mention of Hood's letter. The notion of getting the admiral to write something of that nature made sense, removing any temptation to make Lanester a scapegoat for subsequent failures. Part of him felt he should apologise. It was base to accuse a man in Lanester's condition of anything. But, in reality, anything said now that the accusation had been aired would be pointless.

He moved over to Halsey and gave him his orders, basically to stay still and quiet. Then he signalled to Rannoch, who followed him as they retraced their steps towards the monastery. Following the path they had created wasn't difficult, but neither was it straight. They traversed right and left across the forest, until they heard the distinctive sound of several blades chopping at thin wood.

'So much for the black man,' hissed Rannoch.

'If they're carving out a path, we have time to get further into the forest,' Markham replied.

But he was also wondering, if there was a limit to how deep they dare go with no food or water. Perhaps it would be better to try and hide any trace of their route, then just stay still and hope the French lost their spoor. He put his hand on Rannoch's shoulder to indicate retirement. The Scotsman stiffened, hearing a fraction before his officer the sound of a single galloping horse. A shouted exchange followed, indistinct but audible, indicating that the road was closer than Markham had reckoned. By his present calculation, in the dark, they'd covered less than half the distance he'd previously estimated.

'They could have spat on us if they had wished,' said Rannoch softly, having arrived at a similar conclusion.

This was imparted in his usual measured way,

his ear cocked to make sense of the outcry that followed several loud shouts of alarm. The noise of men hacking at wood ceased. That which followed, hinting almost at panic, went on for some ten minutes, then died down suddenly, to be replaced by the clamour of impatient, stamping animals. Then a clear order floated through the air, followed by the sound of departing horsemen.

'South?' Markham asked Rannoch, and received a nod in reply. He then moved forward, till he saw the faint outline of the building through the thinning trees. He moved well to his left before crawling further, listening for any sound that would indicate the presence of a remaining horse; a stamping foot or a snort. There was nothing, and when he reached undergrowth thin enough to give him a view of the paddocks, he could see that they, as well as the clearing in front of them, were deserted.

'We should look on the road, sir. I do not think it would be wise just to expose ourselves by walking in through the door.'

'Good idea.'

They stayed in the trees, going slightly deeper into the forest, using what sunlight filtered through to hold their direction. The highway itself, when they came to it, was clear in both directions, and silent, allowing them to emerge cautiously before turning back towards the opening that led to the monastery. The evidence of the French departure, at the join between the clearing at the road, was clear from fifty yards away, the churned-up earth an indication of a troop of cavalry quitting the scene in some haste.

'That saves the hide of your darkie,' said Rannoch, with a shrug. 'They had little time to fasten their girths, never mind to carry on looking for us.'

'You still cannot bring yourself to like him, can you?'

'I would not have it said that it was for the sake of his black skin.'

'You expect me to believe that!'

Rannoch, by his lights, practically barked back at him. 'I am not accustomed to being doubted by any man.'

'Then why, for God's sake?'

'It is one thing to be clever, and no doubt good in its way. But it is coat of another cloth never to let anyone within ten feet of you forget it. And he does the same to you as he does to others. Look at the way he dragged out his tale.'

'We'd best look inside.' Markham replied, uncomfortable with the way his sergeant was looking at him, challenging him to agree. 'But slowly.'

Markham raised the cutlery knife, sharp enough to cut through cooked meat and thin rope, but hardly deadly. At least the sight of it brought a smile back to Rannoch's lips.

'What can we have to fear? With such magnificent weapons we can take on the whole French army.'

The sound, as they approached the door, made them pause: a creaking, either like a door or what it turned out to be, a stretched rope. Duchesne was swinging slowly, his face deep purple with the strangulation which had killed him, tongue out and bitten, eyes half out of their sockets with the terror of death. He seemed, with the noose

291

around his neck, to have no chin at all, and more expression in his suffused features than he'd had in life.

'Oh! Jesus Christ,' whispered Markham, as Rannoch swiftly crossed himself. 'If you are judged, Captain, let it be by your last act of humanity.'

'Shall I cut him down?'

Markham nodded, then looked at the blunt knife. 'It would be easier to untie the rope. We'll lay him in one of the cells.'

Markham helped Rannoch, the two men silent over the body of an enemy who'd paid the price for saving them. But once he was laid out and covered, they returned to their task. The chapel was a deserted mess, though not through any deliberate act. But there was no hiding the fact that it had been occupied by soldiers who'd left in a hurry. All the detritus of their occupation and their departure lay precisely where it had fallen. The cells occupied by Fouquert and Duchesne were no better, full of discarded items which had belonged to their captives, papers lying amongst the smashed wood of the boxes which had once contained wine.

There were bottles too in Fouquert's cell, some full, others empty, one tipped on its side as though it had been knocked over, the stain on the flagstones showing where most of the contents had ended up, with only that in the bottle which was held back by the narrowing neck. Whatever else they had left, they'd taken the weapons and red uniform coats with them, though he found Lanester's map case under one of the cots. Likewise, they'd left the rankers' infantry packs, too heavy to carry. Markham followed Rannoch through to the kitchen, a windowless room with a chimney at the back of the building, the first thing to catch their eye the carcasses hanging from ceiling hooks, that followed by the wall full of knives, saws and an ancient rusted chopper.

'Careless,' said Rannoch.

'They were in a hurry.'

'To leave food behind, they must have been in terror.'

'Not as much as Duchesne,' Markham added.

Rannoch looked at him, strangely. 'We all of us saw that door open and shut. I was sure we were undone.'

'Duchesne was an old-fashioned soldier, Rannoch, and a cavalryman at that.'

Rannoch snorted then, though out of respect he forbore to say what he was thinking: that cavalry were stuck-up pigs who could never be relied upon to arrive when they were supposed to. It was the view of every foot-slogging infantryman, who often saw fodder for horses taking precedence over their own requirements for food. In victory, cavalry got to the spoils first. In defeat they made safety long before their compatriots on foot. If starvation threatened, they were astride their last meal. And when it came to boasting they were, to a soldier's mind, only surpassed by sailors. The troopers of the mounted regiments were bad enough, but nothing as compared to their officers.

'Odd, really. On a battlefield he'd have skewered me on his sabre with great relish. But he couldn't stomach handing me over to Fouquert, especially when he heard him boasting to Bellamy of some of his previous exploits. He'd be alive now if he'd been prepared to go further than that.'

'Then you don't think he was fooled by the acting the black man put on.'

Markham touched his neck. 'Obviously not. He might have rumbled Bellamy, but he didn't know Fouquert at all. If he had, I doubt he would have lifted a finger to save us.'

'Best to think he would have been Christian enough even then,' Rannoch responded. 'May the good Lord bless him and keep him, even if he did go to war on a horse.'

'I have a mind to get everyone back here, Rannoch. At least they can be fed before we set out for Corte. Men with a meal inside them will move at twice the pace, and with these saws and things we can rig up a proper stretcher for the Major.'

'That will slow us down, sir. He might consent to stay here, with a guard, till we can fetch someone back to tend to him.'

'I need him with us, Rannoch.'

'With respect, sir, if you need him that badly, he has to be alive.'

'You suggest it,' Markham replied, pulling a face.

The men emerged from the *maccia* like long-term prisoners coming into daylight, those not carrying the comatose Major Lanester blinking and brushing themselves as if they wanted to remove the last traces of their confinement. Markham let them drink some water, ordered Pavin into the kitchen, then sent Ettrick, Quinlan, Dornan and Bellamy back into the woods to search for bodies. They found the four men who'd kept this place within minutes. Their hands had been tied behind their back, so that they could be strangled before being tossed into a clump of bushes not forty yards from their home. They must have died within earshot of him and his men as they stumbled up the hill towards the monastery.

'Bury them,' Markham said, when he was shown the bodies, 'and Captain Duchesne as well. There's some soft ground at the back of the paddocks. There's no time to go deep, just make sure they have covering enough to keep off any animals. We'll be moving out as soon as we're fed.'

Lanester had passed out on the journey through the *maccia,* so that by the time they got him into one of the cots the notion that Rannoch had suggested seemed to make more sense than moving him again. What colour the major had was now gone. His face was pallid, seemingly devoid of blood. Since this was a decision on which his servant should be consulted, Markham went to find Pavin in the kitchen. Of course, Pavin asked the obvious question, but with none of his usual ill-humour.

'And what occurs if they Crapauds comes back this way?'

Markham shrugged, because he really couldn't answer that. He had no idea where the French had gone. Bellamy had mentioned some kind of mission that would prevent their return to Bastia. If he had the right of it, they could be anywhere.

'He'd be better not being jigged around, and that's no error,' Pavin added. 'To my way of thinking, that would do for him.'

His satchel of spices and condiments was by his hand, and, having tasted the contents of the pot, he added something unknown to the largest of his copper pans. Then he began to stir. Markham knew he was ruminating, weighing up the pros and cons, and had to fight to contain his impatience. For a moment, the noise he was making, as he poked at it vigorously, seemed unnatural, until Markham realised that Pavin wasn't the source. The sound of running feet in heavy boots was different.

'Soldiers!' shouted Rannoch.

Markham guessed that before he spoke, just as he knew he'd been truly humbugged for a second time. Fouquert had been too shrewd to chase him through the *maccia,* and he'd been too stupid to see the trap that he set instead. The French had even left their horses and come back on foot. No wonder they'd left the food, the one thing guaranteed to keep hungry men still long enough for him to come back and recapture them. The sound of the boots, clearly moving at speed, increased until they seemed to invade the whole building. As silence fell, he dragged himself out of the kitchen and, watched by his men, who stood in an attitude of fearful anticipation, went towards the door. His hand rested on the handle for several agonising seconds before he could be brought to turn it and pull.

The air outside was still colder than that in the chapel, and the light from the low, early March sun, which barely topped the mountains to the south, temporarily blinded him. He could see the figures lined up, indistinct shapes until his eyes adjusted. That and walking forward brought them into view. Looking along the line to find Fouquert, he was wondering if the cutlery knife he had put back in his pocket would do what he required, while cursing himself for not picking up something sharper from the kitchen. Even for dragoons on foot, the troopers seemed small, which he put down to a trick of the light. And the uniforms, in silhouette, showed none of their colour. But enough of the weapons were raised to catch the sunlight, and the command, in French, to raise his hands was one he had to obey.

But the voice was wrong and it certainly wasn't Fouquert's. First, it was of a higher pitch. And secondly, why address him in French, when Fouquert spoke good English? The idea that it was a different French patrol, though unwelcome, gave him some hope of personal survival, until he discarded that as wishful thinking. He took four quick paces forward, until the command to stand still could be spoken, which brought him into the shadow created by the mountains. Again that light voice spoke in French.

'You were expecting someone else, soldier.'

She was uniformed and armed, wearing the dun-coloured jacket of the Corsican army, even to the point of having a coxcomb round hat on her head. So were all the other women. If there was a concession to their sex, it was the very elaborate embroidery that decorated their caps. Much as he was taken by the novelty of what was before him, he was too smitten with the leader to spare much attention to her inferiors. She was remarkable, and in every respect except her striking face and fulsome figure, she looked the very image of an infantry officer.

But the face – dark smooth skin, full sensual lips, and black eyes – was enchanting. He guessed the hair would be black too, that tone so deep it was almost blue, the kind of topping they said in Ireland had the Spanish Armada in it. The gun she held, a long, old-fashioned pistol, looked too heavy for her slight frame. But it was steady enough. Even through the dull cloth of the uniform he could detect the swell of her breasts, and in the split-second it took to discern all this, he felt his blood race a little as he began to smile.

'Allow me to introduce myself, madame. I am Lieutenant George Markham of His Britannic Majesty's Marines.'

'In that coat!'

That stopped him in mid bow. He had forgotten about the coat he was still wearing, which even lacking a shirt identified him as a French dragoon. Absurdly, he was stuck, looking up while remaining bent over, the smile still on his face making him feel even more stupid.

'Stolen to ward off the cold, madame.'

'Not madame. Commandatore!'

Her retort at least allowed him to adopt a more dignified pose, standing fully upright. 'Might I ask your name?'

'Calheri.'

'Then you may considerably outrank me. And if the French had not stolen my hat, I would perforce raise it in salute.'

'What nonsense is this?'

'Do you speak English?'

'A leetle,' she replied.

'Then if you will forgive me, I will continue in French.'

Having now an in-built distrust of anything Corsican, he found himself being exceedingly circumspect. Particularly, Nelson and the impending attack on Bastia could not be mentioned. Markham confined himself to the line of the proposed visit, that their desire to see Paoli was purely social. He told her how they'd come to be captured, followed by a gesture towards the multiple grave. Expecting her to be shocked by the murder of the monks, he was surprised when she merely crossed herself and murmured an incantation for their souls, before bidding him continue. This was followed by the details of their escape, leaving out that which didn't matter regarding Duchesne and Fouquert, all the while searching her face both to see how she was reacting and, he was forced to admit to himself, to admire her beauty.

'You are, of course, free to step inside, and talk to my men. And you may wish to examine the grave, of course. The man in charge of our mission, Major Lanester is in one of the cells, carrying a wound. He's an old friend of General Paoli and knew him in London. If he can talk, I think he will be able to convince you more readily than I.'

She slipped past him with ease, so that the long pistol was off its aim for no more than a second. 'Call your men out.'

Soldiers, be they Lobsters or Bullocks, look the same everywhere, even in tattered garments. But they were, to anyone with an ounce of military knowledge, not cavalry. Several men, like Quinlan

299

and Ettrick, being small and wiry, could have passed muster. But no one but a Prussian martinet without brains would put a man of Rannoch's height and build on a horse. Bellamy, like half the men present, was also far too tall. His colour made him the subject of much attention from the Corsican women, who murmured and pointed. Markham was only grateful that at least he'd found the good sense to rid himself of his tricolor sash, even if he'd done so for the wrong reasons.

'We were informed there was a detachment of French cavalry here,' she said, for the first time allowing her face to show a trace of doubt.

Markham was half tempted to ask, if that was so, why they'd walked in with such disregard for the consequences, nor even noticed as they did so that the earth they were walking over was well churned up by hooves. But this was a time for courtesy, not a discussion of either observation or sensible infantry tactics.

'A squadron of dragoons. Around thirty men. They were here last night, holding us captive. We escaped into the *maccia,* which will go some way to explain the state of our dress. The French left less than an hour ago, in great haste.'

The tongue in which she barked the commands was incomprehensible. Several of her female troopers darted forward and made their way to the open door, the gait and gender openly admired by his men.

'Eyes front, the lot of you,' he barked, feeling like a hypocrite.

There was not much of a search to make. Only Pavin, who'd deserted his pot to take station be-

300

side the wounded Major Lanester, was still inside. To inspect the chapel, the kitchen and cells took no time at all, and it was only minutes before the searchers reported back, answering the questions she fired at them in rapid order.

While this was happening Markham had time to think, and to remember what he'd heard. Did the hurried departure of the French now have another reason? Was that panic induced by the knowledge that their presence here had been discovered? They must have been unaware of what force would be sent to root them out. Fouquert might well have remained if they had known.

But that didn't alter the one salient fact. Someone was able to tell them of the danger they faced, and in enough time to let them get clear. Which added some verisimilitude to what Bellamy had told him about his drunken conversations with Fouquert. And they'd gone south, in the direction of Corte, not north to Bastia, which surely should have brought them into contact with these female soldiers.

Remembering suddenly how they'd doubled back to capture him and his men, he was wondering how far they'd moved down the road. If whoever was aiding them knew the *maccia* so well, they could have turned off the highway and headed for Corte by the mule tracks.

These thoughts were interrupted by Calheri barking another set of orders, which sent two groups of four women towards the road, where they split up and went off in different directions.

'Would it help if I were to tell you where the French are headed?'

'Back to Bastia, since we didn't meet them on the road?'

'Perhaps not,' Markham replied, before shouting for Bellamy to come forward. 'Please explain to the Commandatore what you gleaned from Fouquert and Duchesne last night. And this time keep it brief.'

Bellamy obliged, speaking fluently and convincingly, Cornmandatore Calheri moving closer to him to listen intently to what he was saying. The use of Paoli's name, in this context, shocked her, as did the notion that the French would dare to try and arrest him. Markham, meanwhile, since Bellamy was talking, was able to study her in more detail, which only served to increase the depth of his admiration.

'My sergeant and I heard them leave, madame,' Markham said, as soon as Bellamy finished, 'And if you look at what is left of their tracks in the mud by the pavé, I think you will see enough evidence to indicate which way they went.'

Calheri went to look, bending down and picking up a section of compacted earth that still clearly held the shape of a hoof, following that with a long stare down the road. It was still in her hand when he returned.

'Please take your men inside, Lieutenant,' she said, her face screwed up in concentration. 'I require a moment to think.'

He was tempted to tell her she had no time for such a luxury, but held back. He'd intended to feed his men anyway, so that time used up mattered little. More important was that he convince her of both their true status, and their mission, so

302

that they would be free to carry on to Corte.

'We have food prepared, madame. If you and your troop would be prepared to join us, we can make it stretch.'

'We will see,' she replied.

Markham bowed again, and did as he was bidden, his main task to stifle the ribald comments of his men by informing them that the lady in command spoke English. It hardly served to stop Quinlan and Ettrick, who could not resist alluding to the kind of rigid salute that she would be getting from a certain marine lieutenant before the sun rose one more time.

'It'll be her hat that's a liftin', not his, Commandatore or no.'

'Quiet, damn you,' he yelled, to stifle the laughter. But on another mental plane, he could not help but contemplate the pleasure such a seduction would bring. Sharland's added comment quite spoiled that.

'Don't you go thinkin' your Croppie is going to have her? Seems to me she was more interested in the fuckin' darkie.'

Chapter twenty-one

Markham ate on the move, pacing up and down inside the chapel, wondering what Calheri was up to outside. There was movement after a few minutes, departing horses. Despite her injunction to stay inside, he couldn't contain either patience or

303

curiosity, and strode back out into the strong sunlight. She'd taken off her cap and allowed her hair to drop free. It was, as Markham had suspected, blue-black, a perfect frame for her olive-skinned complexion, as she swung round to face him.

'General Paoli left Corte this morning, for his home town of Morosaglia.'

Markham nearly choked on a gobbet of ham, struggling to remember if the place she'd named lay closer to Bastia than Paoli's capital. He'd seen it on the map, but in the mass of Corsican town names he'd looked at, it was hard to place.

'I've sent off messengers with instructions to tell him what happened here. I also told them to look out for a cart with which to transport your wounded Major. He can be taken to Corte to await the general's return. We, however, cannot wait for you, Lieutenant. We shall return to the rendezvous we have arranged with the general.'

She smiled then, which widened her cheeks, and showed her strong white teeth. The glow it brought to her whole being also made her look even more attractive. 'He is no longer a young man, and gets impatient.'

'Might I ask where the rendezvous is?'

He could see her thinking, still not entirely convinced that he was who he claimed. He called to Pavin, and asked him to bring the Major's map case, which had been put in his cell.

'We are to meet him at the Convent di San Quilico Rocci, which is just beyond Sovaria on the road to Corte. The men who have escorted him there, who are part of the garrison, will then return, while we take him on to Morosaglia.'

Markham was looking at the map as she spoke, happy to see that Morosaglia, albeit surrounded by mountains, was halfway to Bastia. 'Such a complex arrangement for escorts. He obviously fears for his safety.'

'Never!' she snapped, mistaking Markham's worried frown for criticism. 'It would take the whole French army to get within ten miles of him in his own home city. There he is surrounded by people who revere him.'

He was worried, especially at the thought that Fouquert as well as Calheri knew where Paoli was headed. 'Perhaps there are those between Corte and Morosaglia who do not.'

For the first time he saw her temper, the opposite of that radiant smile. The way her body stiffened, the black eyes flashed and the fine, slightly upturned nose dilated and paled, becoming sharp and unattractive. She turned away, stood up and headed for the door, which immediately drew Markham's eyes to her swaying hips. But for all his interest in this female, he was actually thinking about other things, namely everything that had happened on the way here.

The dragoons had used mule trails, not the road: routes which were on no map that he'd ever seen, including the one in front of him. His mind went back to the family dead on the road. He recalled the words Lanester had used about the caution of Corsican peasants, then the undischarged weapons, the way their bodies had been trampled, which indicated that whoever had approached them not only looked like friends, but were numerous.

Then there were the horsemen who'd come to the monastery with Fouquert, the previous evening. Had one of them returned, alone, this morning? Markham was sure he and Rannoch had heard a single mount. Given the response, he had to be a messenger. What if he hadn't just come to warn of approaching danger, but to tell the French dragoons that General Pasquale Paoli was no longer in Corte? What if the men who'd killed those peasants, Bellamy's Buonapartists, were shadowing the general, just waiting for Fouquert to show up?

Markham called after Calheri. 'This visit of General Paoli's, was it long planned?'

She turned abruptly. For some reason her anger had evaporated and she now sounded sad. 'One of his cousins, who fought the War of Independence with him, is dying. He has gone in the hope of holding his hand, and easing him into the arms of God.'

'When did he receive this news?'

'The night before last.'

'So his decision to go was an impulse?' Calheri nodded. 'Will the escort he has now wait with him?'

'Till he moves on. Why do you ask?'

'The French left here in some haste. Did they do that because they knew you were coming, or because they heard that the man they had come to arrest was no longer in his capital city?'

'Have no fear for the general, Lieutenant.'

'Where is the Convent San Quilico Rocci?' he said, reaching for the leather map case again. She came back as he opened it, stabbing her finger.

'And where, precisely, are we?'

That produced another stab. Markham used his finger, tracing out the long narrow triangle, the Convent at one point, the monastery they were now sitting at in another, with the town of Morosaglia some twenty miles away.

'I think the French have gone after him. They'll probably wait till he leaves your convent...'

'They'll never find him, Lieutenant.' She interrupted, waving her hand languidly towards the French-built highway. 'Pasquale Paoli is not a Frenchman. He does not need to travel by that sort of road.'

'If you're trying to tell me he's on mule tracks, I have to inform you that's how the French came to this place. And since you didn't meet them on the highway, that is how they would have avoided you.'

'Frenchmen cannot hide in Corsica. They stick out like the plague.'

'What if they murder anyone who sees them? An innocent family was slaughtered on that very road, I believe merely because they saw something.' She looked at him keenly wanting him to explain, but Markham was in too much of a hurry. 'They have been brought this close to Corte by Corsican guides.'

'I still think he's in no danger. People flock to touch him wherever he goes. You are English, you don't understand.'

'Irish!' he snapped. She looked confused, a clear indication that she didn't know the difference. 'You say he's an impatient old man. I daresay he feels as safe in his own country as you claim. Will

307

he wait for you to return, if he has the chance to press on?'

Her doubt had been growing, first in her eyes, then in the clenching of the jaw, as Markham continued. 'You are, after all, his escort?'

'So!'

'It's a clever idea to detach that escort on a futile chase, while the men they are supposed to be after leave the road and head cross-country to a point where they can intercept their quarry.'

'You have too much imagination.'

'It's a feature of my race, I grant you. But can you afford to take the chance that I'm wrong?'

Calheri thought for a moment, her tongue running round inside her lower lip. 'Are you fit enough to march?'

'Of course.'

'Then we will leave in ten minutes. Half my troop will stay here with your men.'

That was no good. There was a lot he was unsure about, but not that. Markham wanted his men with him.

'Commandatore, I...' He hesitated, not quite sure how to phrase what he had to say. 'My men have not enjoyed the comfort of female companionship for some time.'

'Nor will they enjoy it now, Lieutenant. And you may tell them so.'

Markham spread his hands in a gesture of impotence. 'Officers can issue orders. They are not, unfortunately, always obeyed.'

The smile lacked humour, if anything displaying instead a streak of cruelty. 'They will not require orders, monsieur. Just tell them that the

308

first man to misbehave will find he has three balls in his point of alliance.'

The French expression stumped him for a moment, until he realised she meant the groin. Then the directness and vulgarity of what she had said produced a smile.

'I think it would be better if they came with us. That way you can take along your full strength. And my men are good in a fight. Who knows, you might need every pair of hands you can get.'

'The only people we need, Lieutenant, are you and your handsome Moor.' That threw him too, until, with a slight stab of pique, he realised she meant Private Bellamy. 'But if you insist on bringing all your men along, I will not stop you.'

'It all depends on Major Lanester how many I leave.'

'You'll have to get me up on a horse,' Lanester said, trying hard to smile, 'even if I'm hanging over the saddle. All you have to do, Lieutenant, is find me one.'

Markham couldn't see the wound, swathed as it was in Pavin's clean bandages, made out of a surplus sheet he'd found. But he could see his superior's face, which despite the ample flesh, looked blotchy. The eyes were wet too, and bloodshot, the whole an indication of serious ill-health. And he was caught on the horns of a triple dilemma. He needed Lanester to convince Paoli to head for Bastia, but given the immediate danger the old Corsican was in, saving him from an ambush was paramount. So was keeping the Major well enough to talk, given that time was running out for Nelson.

'Even if I had one to hand, you don't have the strength. You'd fall off before we got a mile down the highway. And we can't double-march stretchering you. It will slow us all down.'

'Perhaps we can find a cart,' he replied, his voice weak.

Markham took refuge in a hastily contrived excuse. 'If the officer in command of the Corsicans can't put her hands on one, what chance do I have? Besides, I fear we might not be on a proper road for long.'

The need to know why was in Lanester's eyes long before he gathered the breath to pose the question. Certainly long enough to allow Markham to feel that he was reluctant to give an honest answer. That would, of necessity, once more involve Bellamy. On balance, he thought it better not to mention the Negro again if it could be avoided.

'The Commandatore fears that there are quite a few French sympathisers lurking around in these parts.'

'I can't fault that assumption,' Lanester gasped. 'The bastards are everywhere.'

'What we have uncovered, unfortunately, means you're right.'

'Tell me.'

'That sod Fouquert got drunk last night.'

'With your damned nigger.'

Even ill, that was said venomously. But now that he'd alluded to Bellamy, there was little point in covering up his part in things.

'He hinted to Bellamy...' Markham paused, to

310

let both pain and distaste at the name subside, 'that their aim was to arrest Pasquale Paoli so he could be shipped back to stand trial in France.'

There was some strength in Lanester's grip as he clutched at Markham's sleeve. 'If there are traitors in Corte, or even in the surrounding countryside, then they are in touch with the men who captured us last night. This morning Rannoch and I heard the arrival of a solitary rider. Within fifteen minutes, the place was deserted.'

'Apart from Duchesne.'

'I think it was a messenger, who came to tell Fouquert that Paoli had left Corte and was on the way to Morosaglia.'

Lanester sat bolt upright, his hands grasping the facings of Markham's dragoon coat, so close that the marine could see the open pores on his cheeks, the sheen of sweat, and the black stubble on his skin. He stared into Markham's eyes for a few seconds, breath wheezing, before the effort proved too much and he fell back on to the cot.

'That's why they left in such a hurry,' Markham added, picking up a cloth and mopping the patient's brow.

'Morosaglia?' he gasped.

'Yes. It's not on this road, but it is halfway to Bastia.'

Lanester just repeated the name of the town, this time in a whisper, before Markham added, 'His birthplace, I believe.'

'I'd forgotten.'

Markham explained briefly what Calheri had told him, trying to keep his voice calm, since his words were clearly having a detrimental effect on the major's condition. So much fluid was leaking out of his eyes he looked very like a man consumed with grief.

'Can you get to him, Markham?'

'We intend to try. The question is, if we can find him, what do I do, and more important what do I say?'

'You've lost me, boy.'

'Given where he's headed, which is on the way to where we want him to go, do I escort him on to Morosaglia, or try to persuade him to come back to Corte to talk to you?'

Lanester's head started to roll, as if he was approaching delirium. 'I must see him, Markham. We have to persuade him to go to Cardo. Nelson needs him!'

'Calm down, sir.'

For the first time since they'd set out from San Fiorenzo, the major looked set to agree with him. He laid back his head, jerking slowly as Markham swiftly outlined the alternative. First to make sure that Paoli was safe, second to ensure that he, Lanester, got some attention, then contrive a way to bring them to each other in the limited time they had available.

'We must make a decision now, sir. If the French do catch him, we can almost guarantee the Corsican army will not move. Every man Nelson takes ashore could be captured or killed.'

Blood had come back to Lanester's face, turning it red again. But it was not the glow of health, rather the effect of too much pain, that and the tears running down his face showing the effort he was expending. Markham sought to calm him

312

again, his voice soothing and confident.

'We're not even sure the French are after him. That messenger might have just been warning Fouquert about the approach of Commandatore Calheri.'

'Don't turn back to Corte,' Lanester hissed. 'Get him to Cardo.'

'How?'

'You don't need me any more, Markham. It was you who saw what happened with Buttafuco and Lacombe. Tell him that.'

'If there is time I'll take him to San Fiorenzo.'

'No!'

'He'd be safer there than anywhere.'

Lanester's bloodshot eyes were afire. He shook his head to and fro several times, his mouth moving like a man seeking words.

'Like you were, Markham?' he asked finally. Then for the third time he said, 'Cardo. With his troops. Send ahead for an escort.'

'I can try. But without you to sway him, what assurance do I have that he will be willing to do my bidding?'

'Hood's despatch. With the evidence of your own eyes to back that up, the letter will persuade him. It's in one of the bottles of Bordeaux. The Haut Brion 'eighty, in a sealed oilskin pouch.' Lanester groaned then. 'God, I hope Fouquert didn't find it.'

It was now Markham's turn to pose a mute question, his eyebrows raised in some surprise. Lanester, as he lay back, actually managed a weak smile. 'It was a way of passing him the message in secret, by recommending that as a wine to be

313

opened. Not that he would have enjoyed the contents, since before I waxed in the cork again, I refilled it with the local piss.'

Markham had to dash around, between his own men strapping on their packs, searching the whole chapel, and actually found the bottle in the last place he looked. It was on Fouquert's table, the one that had been spilled. It was an amusing thought that Fouquert had tasted it, then spat it out, knocking the thing over in disgust, too drunk to see what it contained. The thin oilskin roll was just visible above the level of the remaining wine, and Markham had to tip the bottle up to retrieve it. His first act was to examine the wax seal that had kept the letter from being soaked by the wine. It had an elaborate layout of Lanester's initials. Drying it off on his coat, he took it back to the major, who was lying back, seemingly exhausted.

'You'd better tell me what it says.'

Lanester blinked and sighed, as if he was having trouble remembering. Outside, Markham could hear the commands that would have the Commandatore's troop forming up.

'Hood has told Paoli what he suspects happened at Fornali and Tregima. Then he's threatened that if he doesn't take over the army himself, not only will the assault on Bastia be called off, he will seek another island as an anchorage.'

'Is that true?'

'Of course not! Nelson will attack Bastia as planned. Hood's bluffing, threatening to leave the Corsicans to fight the French on their own as a way of levering the old goat out of hiding.'

'A battle Paoli has already lost once.'

314

'Get him alone when he's read it,' Lanester gasped, raising himself again. 'Don't tell him what you saw at Cardo if anyone else is close enough to overhear.'

'Shouldn't I trust those who have his ear?'

'No!' Lanester said, before allowing his head to fall back. 'And neither should Paoli!'

Markham was vaguely aware of Pavin in the background, his face anxious as he looked at his master.

'I take it the decision has been made. That the major and I ain't goin' along with you on this jolly.'

Moving away from Lanester, Markham slipped the oilskin roll into his breeches, praying that the seal wouldn't break when he started marching.

'There may well be a cart on the way. If not, as soon as we find one, we'll send it back for you. Stay on the road until you get to the Convent of San Quilico Rocci and wait there. Who knows, Pavin, I might be able to bring one back myself. This whole thing could be a wild goose chase.'

'What have you told him?'

'A lot, but I'm not sure I've covered everything.'

'Then you best be on your way, an' leave that chore to old Pavin.'

Rannoch was in the doorway, pack on his back, beckoning him to come. There was no time for the discussion his responsibility demanded. Pavin knew the odds better than his master. Taking the major might kill him, but leaving him there could do the same. If Fouquert came back to the monastery he'd kill them both. A man who hanged one

315

of his own country's officers wouldn't shudder to string up these two. Pavin had seen Rannoch too, and he actually grabbed Markham's arm to propel him out, the look in his eyes clear proof that what the officer had in his mind was known, therefore saying it was unnecessary.

'No speed, Pavin, when the cart arrives. Comfort first for the major, and if you can find anyone at that convent who can heal him, let them have a go at getting the ball out, regardless of what he wants.'

Pavin actually smiled, which doubled the depth of his wrinkles. 'I'll bet he orders otherwise.'

'You have my permission, Pavin, to ignore him.'

The servant grinned even more, exposing long yellowing teeth. 'That, I have to tell you, is a pleasure I have enjoyed for many a year.'

Chapter twenty-two

At double marching order, with Calheri's troops out ahead to make sure their route was secure, they made good progress to begin with. The dragoons, as well as taking their coats and capes, had stolen the British marching rations. The Corsicans had none, so they had to stop occasionally, usually at a small church or monastery very like the one at which they'd left Lanester. Drink was the most important requirement, since even in March the Mediterranean sun had the power to turn the road dry and dusty. What food the priests

316

and monks gave them was filling without being abundant, and offered freely despite the obvious hardship this would visit upon their future wellbeing.

Moving so fast, they caught up with Calheri's messengers, dawdling along with no sense of haste. They received a tongue-lashing for that, as well as for their failure to find the required cart to send back. Not that they could be entirely blamed for the latter. When the French built the road, their construction had naturally been dictated by the topography. So no villages abutted the highway. They were visible, certainly, but they sat, for security, on rocky outcrops too far away to be of any use. The odd conveyance they came across tended to be rickety and man-drawn. What Markham wanted was a horse, not for Lanester but so that he could send a messenger on ahead to request Paoli to stay still. But the best the monks or priests could offer was an ass, which carrying a rider made slower progress than a running trooper.

Calheri measured her distances in leagues, and after a quick calculation Markham worked out that the convent rendezvous was some six miles distant. Some of his men were good runners, especially Yelland, with his long legs and slim frame. But they were not trained in that regard, so to send them off too early would be useless. Besides, it would really have to be one of Calheri's females, with a written message from her, since a man of Paoli's stature was hardly likely to pay much heed to a British marine dressed only in his spare shirt.

The Corsican women were fit enough, but no

more trained at running than his men, which left Markham thinking that if they'd had to fight the Battle of Marathon with this lot the Greeks would have lost. As if to underline the problem, the strain of double marching began to tell on the marines before the local females. The former, having spent most of the last three months aboard ship, had been gifted little chance to retain the excellent physical condition they'd achieved after four months ashore in Toulon. So it was with blessed relief that they saw first a tower, then the roof tiles on the buildings of the town of Sovaria, a place substantial enough to cause the French engineers to bend their road to run through it.

Coming into the town, Markham was struck by the notion that Sovaria was no bigger, and no better endowed, than places of a similar purpose he'd seen in his native Ireland. If the town had a purpose that exceeded the need to change animals, he couldn't see it. The tower they'd spotted first was a fortress like the one at Fornali, which spoke to him not of garrisons, but of armies of occupation. True, the buildings were taller and the roofs tiled and more steeply canted. But each dwelling had a dilapidated air that had not been present in the richer atmosphere of San Fiorenzo. If there was any wealth in Corsica it did not reside here in the interior, where the locals clearly lived a hard subsistence existence, just as afraid of their neighbours as they were of invading armies.

The tower was empty, long abandoned and used to house sheep, not soldiers. There was a local clan chief, of course, who'd come into the small square between the church and fortress on

318

being advised of their approach. He was swarthy, squat and elderly, with fine white moustaches, dressed in the local costume of smock, embroidered waistcoat and baggy breeches, tucked in at the knee to highly polished fine leather boots. From Caleri's elaborate greeting, carried out in a language which was neither French nor Italian, it was clear that obeisance had to be made to this individual to obtain anything. And that extended to basic hospitality, a gift not given without much head shaking.

The rest of the inhabitants lined the square, and if the inhabitants of San Fiorenzo had been lukewarm about the presence of strangers, the common folk on this part of the island were doubly so, barely able to find a smile, even for their own female soldiery. Markham, still in the dragoon coat he'd asked Bellamy to procure the previous night, was hissed at. Bellamy himself was on the receiving end of many a pointing finger, mostly from bent old crones who looked remarkably like witches.

Extracting a horse plus a mule cart from the headman took so long that Markham wondered if the time expended was worth it. Even the popularity and prestige of Pasquale Paoli had to be weighed in some traditional balance. Finally, after much haggling, a mount was produced, one with ribs that a blind man could count. The mule was little better, a scrawny creature with skin rubbed bare where the straps of the rig made contact. The drover was a toothless individual, and the cart itself had wheels that seemed incapable of moving in a circle. Calheri scribbled two hasty notes, one a receipt to the clan chief, the other handed to the mounted female, who was then sent on her way. Markham waited patiently until this ritual was completed before stepping forward, Lanester's map in his hand.

'Can you ask him, Commandatore, to indicate on here any mule tracks or paths that would bring us to Paoli's route?'

She was angry again, he could see, the nose losing half its width and all of its blood. Clearly Calheri felt that any alternatives to a straight onward march to the Convent of San Quilico Rocci was her prerogative, one that he should not usurp.

'It would be better for you, Lieutenant, to stop regarding me as a woman, and acknowledge me as a soldier.'

'But I do,' Markham lied. The very idea of women as soldiers appalled him as much as it amused him. General Arena had gone on at some length about this, boring Lanester and him rigid at Cardo. In telling his tale, Arena took it for granted that his description of the Corsican women who'd supposedly fought alongside their men would impress his guests. He also assumed that they would believe what he told them of the battle exploits of the ladies.

Markham had no idea what Lanester had felt, but to his way of thinking the only reason to put women in uniform was to fool an enemy into thinking that you had more troops available than your true strength. The idea that they should go into battle was risible. As a man who liked and admired the opposite sex, he had no desire to tie them to domesticity. There were to his mind a great many areas in which women could become as accomplished as men, even surpass them. In truth, no army marched anywhere without its train of camp followers, wives long-term and temporary, plus a majority no better than tuppenny whores.

But most such women tended to be brutes, the dregs of society. Calheri wasn't like that, of course. And neither, from what he could see, were her 'soldiers'. They didn't vary much in height, being small and compact, a description which could be applied to their menfolk as well. But in terms of shape there was as wide a variation as you would find in any group. Some were broad of beam, well endowed, quite a few with more facial hair than young Yelland. Two women were so thin they looked as if a serious blow would break them in half, the remainder being of every shape between those twin extremes.

Their skin was not the pale, carefully protected olive of their officer, more the darker hue of creatures who'd toiled for the greater part of their lives in the sun. Collectively, they would make incomprehensible jokes aimed at his men; individually, any form of proximity was to be avoided, an occasion for the head to drop and scurrying feet to carry the unwary back to the safety of her group. His men indulged in much subterfuge to counter this, all to no avail, if you excluded the odd high-pitched giggle. Starved of female company, they would have reacted to a toothless septuagenarian. Close to younger women, especially a group dressed in breeches and uniform jackets, an enticing variation of male clothing, they could barely control themselves.

But regardless of dress and behaviour, war – actual fighting, with its constant hardships, not to mention the pain and suffering of battlefield wounds – wasn't for women. And since he couldn't see them as warriors, he could not countenance the notion that their 'officer' should be deferred to in a matter of tactics. It was a subject of which she was clearly ignorant, given the way she'd marched right into the clearing in front of the monastery without any kind of preliminary reconnaissance.

Yet it was also true that he must dissimulate, treat her in a way that showed respect for her rank, and put his own agenda in abeyance. If their primary objective was the same, namely to keep Paoli out of harm's way, it was still her country and the general was her national patriarch. Besides, the women she commanded had weapons and his men did not, a situation which could only be altered if the combined force was faced with imminent action. Accustomed to flattering women, he was sure he could charm Calheri, so that she followed his tactical instincts and not her own.

'I am anticipating you, I know,' he continued. The tone of his voice sounded so false to him, he could scarcely believe it would fool anyone. 'This I do only out of impatience. You will, no doubt, have decided on the same precaution, to cover the possibility that General Paoli may have left San Quilico and headed off towards Morosaglia.'

The way she was looking at him gave nothing away, regarding her opinion either of him, or the notion he'd just propounded. And when she agreed to what was, on reflection, an obvious step, he had no idea if she had already thought of it, or was merely picking up the requirements of the situation from his intervention. Plainly, there was no point in proceeding up a road that carried no threat. If Paoli had been stopped at the convent, he was safe. The only risk he ran was plain: that, in ignorance and impatience, he would leave his Corte escorts there and set off down his ancient trails, to where Markham believed Fouquert was waiting for him.

'I have no need of this old man's help, Lieutenant,' she replied eventually, reaching out to take his map, which she held towards him as she traced with her finger. 'There is a track that runs along the river Golo. Though it is far from straight, and hard marching, it will bring us onto the Morosaglia road in less time than we would take to get to San Quilico Rocci. Once there, we can head back up the track to the convent.'

'Cautiously,' Markham added.

'Let us see if there is something we need to be cautious about first.'

Water from the well had been given freely, the only commodity the inhabitants of Sovaria were prepared to part with on those terms. Compared to the heat of the middle of the year, the early afternoon sun was pleasant. But it was still warm to a marching man, and Markham could see the sweat stains on the backs of his marines as they left the town behind. After about half a mile they cut off to the left of the road, and plunged into forest made even deeper than normal by its proximity to a fast-flowing stream.

By the time they reached the Golo, full to the brim with rushing water from the melting mountain snow, the situation was reversed. Now they were shaded from the sun by the canopy of trees. They were so dense they reached out over the riverside trail, leaving, between themselves and those on the opposite bank, only a thin strip of sunlight in the middle of the deep cutting. A fine, icy spray filled the air. Initially welcome as cooling, it soon became an irritant. Calheri's females had capes in their packs, which they were quick to use. Markham's men, after the depradations of their enemies, had nothing but their shirts, and were soon shivering.

Markham's dragoon coat was soaked in minutes, his hair matted and stuck to his skull by the icy spume. The track itself didn't offer much comfort, being at times right next to the edge of the river; at others, after a steep climb, they'd cross a slippery glacis of bare wet rock, above the natural tree line, which gave them a panoramic view of towering rock formations, worn by weather and wind into fantastic shapes, wrinkled granite that testified, like the face of a venerable sage, to the years they'd withstood the elements.

Keeping a hold on their position wasn't easy, even with such a view, since each huge rock formation was surrounded by the same kind of dense forest they were trying to negotiate. But Markham knew that they were still somewhat to the north of the river, while Corte, invisible in the distance, must lie to the south. With water dripping from his chin, he felt as he spoke just how much the spray had frozen his bones.

'Is there a crossing?'

Calheri, who'd tucked her hair into her cap, looked younger than she had previously, her skin shiny from the same source as everyone else. The noise of the rushing water made hearing difficult, forcing Markham to repeat the question, this time much closer to her head. It never ceased to amaze him how much his senses could extract from such brief opportunities: the perfection of her ear, small, perfectly formed, with lobes that he was tempted to nibble there and then. The slight down on her face, caught by wetness and a flash of sunlight. Then the smell of her body, mingling with the freshness of the mountain water. When she replied, the feeling of her hot breath on his own ear.

'There is a wooden bridge half a league distant, where the rocks rise to form a narrow gorge. We will have to move away from the river, anyway, as the road has to follow more level ground.'

'A good place for an ambush,' he replied, more to get close to her body smell again, than as a true appreciation of possible danger.

Yet once the thought was voiced, it made sense, because the potential for escape, in a trap set next to a narrow bridge, was much reduced. It would also provide added security as a place to defend, for a troop of French dragoons who, even if they did have some local support, were deep in hostile territory. Markham got even closer to her ear, so that his lips were almost touching it.

'Could the French have got to this place in the time they had available?'

Her nod was curt, as she span her head so

325

rapidly that, merely by not reacting, his lips brushed her cheek, forcing Calheri to recoil. Markham gave her his full smile, using a hand to brush back his now black hair, grey eyes twinkling and their owner relishing the ambiguity of his conclusion. 'Then I suggest we go forward carefully from here.'

Rannoch had stopped too, and was looking at the line of Corsican women with something less than admiration. His voice was so angry it carried above the tumbling rush of water.

'Not one with the sense to cover their flints,' he barked, his hand running along the line of muskets. 'If they've no dry spares, those guns will be as much use as a crofter's crook.'

'I take it we have spare flints, Sergeant?'

'That is one thing the Crapauds didn't filch from our packs.'

'Commandatore, would your soldiers consent to share their weapons with us?'

'No, Lieutenant, they would not!'

'Sergeant Rannoch.'

'Sir.'

'With maximum respect to their sex, relieve every second trooper of her musket and bayonet.'

Calheri must have picked up the sentiment, if not the actual order. She pulled back her cape to get out her own pistol. Markham grabbed her hand, and held it as his own men, with the exception of Bellamy, moved eagerly forward. The women lifted their muskets, but only one tried to pull the trigger – foolish, since the guns weren't even primed. But that had one positive result. The lack of a spark from the flints showed how right Rannoch had been.

'If the French are ahead, on that route to Morosaglia, my men will help you to deal with them. But they can't do that without weapons.'

'We do not need your help,' she hissed.

'Yes you do,' Markham insisted, his eyes no longer dancing and amused. Instead they were hard, boring into her own, so black it was difficult to tell pupil from iris. 'These men may be few, Commandatore. But every one of them has faced the enemy a dozen times. They are the best fighting men I've ever served with, and better marksmen than most of the British Army.'

It was hard to equate what he said with the line of bedraggled, dripping-wet individuals now trying to wrest the guns of the Corsican women, none of whom would agree to surrender their weapons lightly. But in the case of his Hebes, it was the literal truth, and of the remaining Seahorses, he reckoned Sharland to be a fighter. So was the third one, whose name he couldn't remember, judging by the way he wrested a musket from a struggling female while elbowing two others aside. Bellamy was an unknown quantity, and since he was a refined soul, what they were doing now was not a true test of his courage.

'There are things you do better than us, Commandatore, but making war isn't one of them.'

The spittle hit him right between the eyes, mingling with the damp spray, and he felt the pistol, which she'd produced from under her cape with the one free hand, poke into his belly.

'Let me go.'

'Order the weapons to be handed over.'

327

'No.'

It couldn't be cocked, he was sure of that, let alone loaded. She was struggling, in vain, to free the hand he'd grasped, which rocked them to and fro in a way that Markham found uncomfortably erotic. Even the way anger had altered her face was attractive, merely because of the physical nature of the challenge. That allowed him to smile again, which he knew must look very theatrical, excessively devil-may-care, Mark Anthony before the Roman mob.

'Then, Commandatore, shoot me.'

Judging by the way her eyes hardened, he had the sudden fear that she might, which put some strain on his attempts to look unconcerned. But, after several seconds, in which the whole party seemed to become frozen, she nodded sharply and handed over her pistol, then told those she commanded to do likewise.

'Sergeant Rannoch, we will be pulling away from the river shortly. As soon as we do, get the priming pans dried off and fit new flints to the muskets.'

'How many?' he asked, looking at the women who'd retained theirs.

'All of them,' Markham replied. 'Yelland, Tully, up ahead on the trail, and see what we face. There is a bridge, I'm told, a wooden affair. Once you sight that, or any kind of substantial trail which will qualify in these parts as a road, stop and wait till we join.'

'Sir.'

Calheri watched them move away impassively. Markham went to the head of the column and called to his men to follow. After a short pause, the Corsican contingent fell in behind them. It was a blessing to get away from the noise of the river as well as the spray. Within a few yards, so dense was the shielding forest, it was as though what lay beyond the trees was a benign brook. And they were at last walking on dry earth. The passing of the two marines had killed any birdsong, so it was impossible to tell if they faced any external danger. But Markham didn't want to go any further without loaded weapons, so he ordered a halt, and told Rannoch to get the muskets into good working order.

'And Sergeant, see that the ladies' weapons are fit to fire as well.'

'At a distance, sir, if you will consent,' he replied in his slow Highland lilt. 'I fear a bayonet in the vitals if I get too close to any of those creatures.'

'I'd put my bayonet in any one of 'em, half chance afforded,' growled Dornan, as he eased his pack off his shoulders.

Markham had to issue a warning then, to all his men. If a slowcoach like Dornan was getting aroused, the situation could easily get out of hand. This he did while he was removing his dragoon coat, which was weighed down with water, holding it with some difficulty as he tried to shake some of the moisture out. Bare-chested and shivering with cold, he was just about to ask if any of his men had a second spare shirt, when he looked back towards Dornan. He was kneeling, pulling garments out of his pack in a bemused fashion. But then he was often bemused, so it wasn't that which attracted his officer. It was the merest flash of gold braid that made him move towards the man, but by the time he got there, he had high leather boots to catch his eye as well.

'What in God's name is all this?'

Dornan looked up at him, his gaze as bovine as ever, the shake of incomprehension only adding to the impression of a man several biscuits short of the full day's ration. Looking at Duchesne's uniform and his high cavalry boots, Markham had not a single doubt how it had got there. And he knew what the explanation would be when he bearded Quinlan and Ettrick. It was true Duchesne had no further use for these things, but to rob the man who'd saved all their lives seemed sacrilegious to him. He turned to the two Londoners, who were beavering away, seemingly too busy with these unfamiliar weapons to notice anything that had happened.

The crashing sound of Tully bursting upon them killed his reprimand. 'Them dragoons, your honour, same lot that was at that monastery. Only a few of them, up ahead on this side of the bridge, hidden from view.'

Markham, having got hold of Duchesne's dry shirt, translated for Calheri, noting her alarm. But she'd not lost all her rationality. 'They might be waiting in vain, Lieutenant.'

Markham gave her another one of his smiles, well aware that over-use had stopped them being in any way disarming.

'You're not suggesting we leave them be, Commandatore, are you?'

Chapter twenty-three

'Is there another place where we can cross the river?' asked Markham, as he shook the still-dripping dragoon coat.

'Not in the spring,' Calheri replied. 'The water drops in summer to a trickle.'

'If we have to kill those Frenchmen, we will do so without knowing what other opposition we might face.'

The explanation which followed was swift and sparse and openly acknowledged to be speculative, interrupted by his need to get on a wet cavalry coat which was too small for him. With men on this side of the bridge, it could be the spot chosen to close the trap. But Paoli wouldn't be travelling alone, even if he had left the contingent from Corte behind. Could Fouquert be sure he had no escort? If he wasn't, he'd have men stationed on the far side, to shut the bridge off from the southern end, so killing off any chance of a rescue, a move which would allow him to get his captive away from the point of danger. Any rearguard he would sacrifice, if he had to.

Calheri was still seething over his behaviour regarding the muskets, but the situation was too grave to let that distract her from the main difficulty, which was how to warn Pasquale Paoli to turn back, without drawing down on his head the very ambush they were trying to avoid.

'I don't care how well your men can shoot, Lieutenant. In the *maccia,* this work is better left to Corsicans.'

He opened his mouth to protest, but then he saw the knife in her hand. It wasn't threatening him in any way, but it did take his mind back to a dark night in a trench, when he and Rannoch had been threatened by just such a weapon, wielded by the same sex.

'Two of my marines to accompany two of yours,' he said, moving on swiftly, anticipating the obvious question. 'If it gets wholly physical, it will need men to subdue them.'

'That may be true in England, Lieutenant. It is not the case in Corsica.' Her 'soldiers' had removed their capes, which disguised their differences, and were back to all their shapes and sizes as well as their dun-coloured uniforms. Calheri raised the knife, a long, thin stiletto with a sharp tip. 'In the *maccia,* to get close is all that is needed.'

'Tully,' he called, 'I need to be able to tell the Commandatore exactly where these dragoons are.'

'By the road, sir, if 'n it could be called that, about ten yards into the trees. They're spread out, three pair, the first right by the end of the bridge, the others no more'n ten feet apart from each other. Yelland had a good look further away from the bridge, but there was no sign of anyone about.'

'How close did you get to the men by the bridge?'

'We didn't have to risk being seen, if 'n that's what you're askin'.'

'Noisy?'

'Chattering away like they was outside their own front door, your honour.'

'Which means that they don't feel threatened,' Markham said to Calheri. 'So we have two choices, Commandatore. We can shoot them, which will raise the alarm for miles around, hoping that the noise will alert Paoli. That will draw them down on us, which means we'll have to retreat along the riverbank.'

He didn't get a chance to propose the alternative, which was to engage a force the size of which he didn't know with a limited supply of weapons and ammunition. He had even fewer troops he was prepared to rely on, though Calheri seemed to entertain no doubts as to the abilities of her 'soldiers'. The temptation to scoff had to be avoided. And in truth, he was intrigued by this demonstration of her logic. It was a chance to discover whether his low opinion of her abilities was based on prejudice, or fact.

'You are forgetting what you yourself told me, Lieutenant Markham. That is that they are not just Frenchmen out there. Some of them are Corsican traitors who need to be exposed.'

'With respect, Commandatore,' Markham replied, aware as he spoke that, even if he was playing Devil's Advocate, what he said sounded pompous, 'while I understand your emotions on this matter, they should not be allowed to intrude on a purely military problem.'

'You mistake me, Lieutenant,' Calheri said, the first smile for an age lighting up her face. He could almost see the thoughts which had produced the change, the idea that she was giving this upstart intruder a lesson in his own profession. 'I was thinking that if we tried to retreat through this, with my own countrymen pursuing us, your men would be very lucky to get out alive.'

Markham nodded, accepting the point was valid, even if the analysis was faulty. Good as his men were, fighting in this labyrinth was not what they were trained for. He felt they would acquit themselves well, though they'd still be at a disadvantage. But Calheri was making a wild assumption. All they had found was half a dozen dragoons. No decision could be made until they knew the whereabouts of the rest.

'Nor would we know if we were successful,' she continued insistently. 'Paoli is an old soldier, who may just ride to the sound of the guns. We must take the bridge and hold it, which will force our enemies, if they want to have an avenue of escape, to attack us instead of the general.'

He was terribly tempted to say 'Bollocks!', given that the lady herself had a tendency to vulgarity. But the widening smile made that unwise. And having deeply offended her, he was being gifted an opportunity, too good to miss, to raise himself in her esteem by being agreeable. Why upset her again, before he was sure that he had sound reason to do so?

'I repeat, the dragoons on this bank must be taken care of first,' he replied, trying to sound cheerful even if he wasn't. 'Until we can reconnoitre the road, we can't contemplate what you suggest.'

If she observed the cautionary note, it didn't

register. Her eyes were afire with the prospect of a fight, and her words demonstrated quite clearly that rationality had gone from her thinking.

'It would be quicker to forget silence and just shoot then. We don't know how much time we have. Once they are thrown back, we can occupy the bridge and prepare to push up the road beyond.'

'Against unknown odds?' he replied quietly, watching his esteem plummet again, at the same rate as her passion. He took her hand and lifted up the knife again. 'This is the way. I leave you to deploy your troops. My men will merely act in support until the situation is clearer.'

She didn't pick up the truth, which pleased Markham, since he found the degree of his own cynicism slightly repugnant. Regardless of Tully's report, this was a stab in the dark. If there were going to be casualties, he needed them to be her women. His men, for their fighting qualities alone, must be preserved.

Calheri had moved over to talk to her 'soldiers', picking on the less well endowed, particularly the thin pair, to follow her back up the trail, those who had muskets handing them over to their compatriots.

'Rannoch,' Markham said softly, 'two men behind each woman. They're to keep well back unless they hear a struggle.'

'Muskets?'

'To be avoided unless the French shoot first. I don't want us all put at risk just to save one soldier. Tully and I will take the Commandatore.'

'There's sentiment in this,' said Rannoch,

giving him an odd look. But he was also nodding. 'It would be, I think, unmanly to behave otherwise.'

Markham turned and fired off a quick explanation to Calheri's remaining troopers, trying to reassure them, wondering from their blank response if they understood a word he said. He then set off with Tully at his heels. Behind him, Bellamy had quickly stepped forward, volunteering for the duty, which obliged Rannoch not only to accept, but to hand over the musket and bayonet he'd acquired, since he wanted other men to do likewise. Being too old at the game, the marines thwarted this aim, and he was forced to issue orders.

'Dornan, you go with Bellamy, and try to keep silent.'

'Elephant's got more chance,' sneered Sharland. 'Why don't you climb on his back, darkie?'

Rannoch, who had been going to detail Halsey and Dymock, killed the laughter quickly. 'You too, Sharland, and take Ebden with you.'

The other Seahorse, Ebden, gave Sharland a glare, sure that they would have been spared the duty if he'd kept his mouth shut. Not that they went very far. As soon as they left the track, both men were close to being lost. Markham was in the same boat, relying on glimpses of the sun to keep his line. The women he'd been following, Calheri and another, had disappeared, both from view and sound, able to move through this impenetrable jungle with an ease neither he nor Tully could match.

Tully actually tripped over the dead dragoon's

body, the blood still pumping out of his shoulder where the long thin blade had pierced a major artery. Both men had to suppress a scream when Calheri appeared from nowhere, brandishing her evil-looking knife, her eyes full of mock hate, which turned to shuddering amusement when she saw the reaction she'd achieved. Then she turned and headed to what Markham assumed was the bridge, pushing through thick bushes, stepping over another victim, and her companion, who was busy stripping him of possessions.

Dornan and Bellamy weren't so lucky. The two Corsican women they were following had stabbed a dragoon; indeed one had sliced her knife across his throat. But if he was silenced, he wasn't dead, and he came crashing through the thick undergrowth, trying to escape, a horrible gasping sound emanating from his ruptured neck, and blood spurting over the hand he was using to try and keep it closed. His other hand held his cavalry sword, which he was sweeping back and forth to clear a path.

Dornan, surprised, didn't move quickly enough, and if Bellamy hadn't thrown up his musket barrel, the blade would have split Dornan's skull. The Negro followed that up with a knee in the groin, which dropped the dragoon on to his haunches. Then, with great difficulty, he wielded his bayonet, his personal strength compensating for the lack of force he was able to muster in the confined space. Two of Calheri's troopers appeared just as the blade went into the Frenchman's side, their eyes fixed on Bellamy as he twisted it right and left, cutting through the vital internal organs until the man was still. The Negro then looked up to see the women, eyes alight, grinning at him, though what they said was incomprehensible.

'Thanks mate,' said Dornan, who still hadn't moved. 'He would have done for me, the French bugger.'

'Get his sword,' Bellamy said in whisper. He then span round and retched into the bushes, throwing up Pavin's breakfast and the rations he'd consumed since. The Corsican women patted his back, and when he looked at them they were grinning even more.

'I've never killed anyone,' he said, looking back at his blood-soaked victim. But since he'd spoken in English, they didn't understand him any more than he'd comprehended them. The women led the way back to where they'd first attacked the dragoon, revealing the second French body in the centre of a small clearing they'd made for themselves some ten yards from the bridge.

Markham, lying flat in the bushes, could see the road, though that word nearly made him laugh. It was far from being a highway, just a wide grassy track worn down by the passage of feet, animal and human; a dark cavern covered with the thick, leafy branches of evergreen pines, no more than three times the width of the single-file trail they'd been using to get here. He gave Tully orders to go back and ask Calheri to bring the rest of the marines forward, then turned his attention to the opposite side, wondering if the man who'd taken over command after the death of Duchesne had any brains. If he had, the far side would be clear. Only a fool placed troops on both sides of a road to effect an ambush. With firearms they would end up shooting not just at the target, but at their own. But if Fouquert was in charge of the deployment, anything was possible.

'Horses?' asked Markham, as Calheri joined him.

'We are looking,' she replied, edging forward, disturbingly close to him, trying to peer up the road towards Corte. Markham grabbed her shoulder and tugged her back, his free hand indicating the coat he was wearing as he got to his knees.

The bridge itself was a pine-log affair, the sides barriers covered in moss, the base black, damp earth packed onto wood, the undergrowth cut back from it so that each end formed a small clearing. The same fine mist that had chilled them earlier rose from the stream below, too thin to interfere with any lines of sight. Markham had taken full advantage of his dragoon coat, buttoning it up so that, in the dappled sunlight, it looked better than the sorry soaking wreck it was.

This allowed him to walk forward rather than crawl. Breath held as he came out from the protection of the trees, he waited for a call from across the road – relieved when none came, since a coat that could fool at a distance would look very like what it was close up. Darting across the road, he moved up the line of trees, calling softly in French to make sure the forest was clear.

Markham knew he still had to be cautious. Fouquert must have his men on the other side of the bridge, and they would be looking south, not north. Kneeling, he examined the numerous hoof-prints in the soft grass, made by metal, not goats or sheep, deep because the blown spray had dampened a long stretch of the surface. He searched closely for the imprint of a boot, the possibility that some of the men who'd gone up this road were infantry, but could see none. Not conclusive, if the cavalry had come along behind, but reassuring nevertheless. The important point to him was that they were headed in the same direction. Behind him, the first bend was a mere forty yards away. Looking south, the direction in which Paoli would come, was better, a good hundred yards of straight road.

'No horses,' a voice called softly at his back.

So the men they'd killed were a backstop, a last line of defence should Paoli foil the original attempt to capture him. Six men out of an estimated French strength of thirty, the sort of proportion he might have used for such a task. All the horses, very likely with a couple of men to keep them quiet, were on the other side of the bridge, probably quite deep in the woods so that their scent, strong after such a hard ride, would not be picked up by anything, man or beast, on the road. Those lying in wait would be well back too, so that they could not inadvertently give things away.

Markham was in a quandary, and it had nothing to do with what he'd discussed with Calheri. Was any kind of attack necessary, or a useless waste of lives, since it couldn't be accomplished without killing on both sides? Old Paoli might still be at that damned convent and not on the trail at all, but the only way to find that out without risking his life was to go straight to San Quilico Rocci from here.

Starting an action which would force a French withdrawal sounded wonderful. But holding the bridge, given the field of fire which had been cleared around the approach, wouldn't be easy. The powder and shot they had was limited, and that would impact on their ability to stand firm. To expend all they had would be fatal. He had to acknowledge the ability of Calheri's female troopers in the thick woods, but standing up to repeated attacks in an open fight against mounted men, with just cold steel as a weapon, required different skills. And if the enemy were numerous enough, skill would not be enough.

Too much imagination was, he knew, a curse in war. But he couldn't help having one, and in his mind's eye he could see the action develop. Some of the enemy would use the cover to move forward, sniping to attract return fire, trying to establish the defenders' supply of powder and shot. Then, when they discovered their caution, the dragoons would come. Mounted men, charging down the narrow track three abreast, on horses so fired up they'd bite the guts out of anyone who got in their way. The defenders would have to occupy the clear space before the bridge, packed into too small an area to manoeuvre, bayonets out to try and stop riders who would see their mounts speared rather than slow their assault.

There would be a second clutch close behind, ready to fan the opposite way from the first, so that the defence would be confronted by a line of six pairs of flaying hoofs. The dragoons, if they had husbanded their own ammunition, would fire carbines first, hoping to hit enough of the packed defenders to crack their solidarity. If the horsemen fell, the next trio would push past them to engage, hacking with sabres at his men and Calheri's women until they'd cleared a space. Once a single horseman broke the line, they'd be in amongst infantry too tightly packed to wield their weapons, on stamping horses that would trample men and women alike underfoot, as the men who rode them slashed left and right. And behind them would come the rest of the dragoons, trained to fight on foot as well as mounted, accompanied by an unknown number of Corsican traitors, to engage an enemy who would very likely, by now, be decimated, the few remaining unwounded in flight.

The alternative, of a long fight in the woods as they retired, stirred up equally lurid and unwelcome images: of trying to move in single file along a track, soaked to the skin, muskets useless because of wet flints. It would be hand-to-hand combat, against pursuers always trying to get round and ahead of them, with his men as the rearguard suffering the most. But how else, could he get Fouquert to withdraw, and quickly?

'It won't do,' he thought, looking at the churned-up surface of the road. 'There has to be another way!'

Chapter twenty-four

He got himself, Bellamy, Rannoch and Commandatore Calheri across the bridge without being seen, heart in mouth, helped by the fact their opponents had to concentrate on the possibility of an approach, shifting uncomfortably as they sought to contain their fear. It wasn't sympathy that made him consider that it must be equally nerve-wracking for his enemies; just his own knowledge. For a soldier facing a fight, to stay still and silent was hard. The mind was given free rein, just as his had so recently been, and all sorts of terrors were conjured up, demons that disappeared as soon as action was joined.

Calheri hadn't argued with his intentions; she'd merely insisted on coming along. Perhaps time to contemplate, and the use of her knife, had tamed her enthusiasm for pitched battle. Asked to cut camouflage for his men, she and her troopers had put their stilettos to good purpose. An odd note was struck when she, close to Bellamy, had cut off a strip of her own white shirt, still clean from being tucked into her breeches, and tied it round his head, as she said, for good luck.

Halsey had charge of the men remaining in the woods. Gibbons and Leech were now crouched on the north side of the bridge, using the upright barriers and odd bits of foliage to disguise their presence. The orders he'd given them were simple.

At the first sight of a horseman approaching from the south, they were to fire off repeatedly to drive them back, taking any target closer that presented itself, but to remember that rate of fire was of more importance than accuracy.

Then they were to run, Corsicans and Lobsters, taking the track they'd come on, without trying to fight, and hope that the sheer pace of their withdrawal would give them a breathing space. Under no circumstances were they to wait for him and the party he had brought across the bridge. Rannoch was annoyed that he'd chosen Bellamy to come with them. But a Negro, even one with a white tie round his brow, was a positive asset in deep foliage, Halsey as left with the unenviable task of trying to exert authority over those who remained behind. He knew he could manage the Lobsters. It was the *women* who worried him.

Once on the south side of the Golo, the quartet stayed close to the riverbank until they were at least a hundred yards from the bridge, dropping down into a sudden valley that, opening into a clearing, took them close to the river again at a point where it formed a deep, slower-moving pool. Sheer on the opposite bank, it shelved like a shallow beach here, and was bathed in sunlight. A place for a swim on a hot day, Markham thought, with a beautiful woman, the tumbling sound of water further upriver a pleasant background. He realised, suddenly, that he was staring at Calheri, and tried to concentrate on the task ahead.

The trail through the pine needles was clear. In such strong light they could even see the wet line of water spilt from the sutler's buckets. It was so

344

easy to follow, up a gentle, leaf-strewn slope. But not one of them was deceived by the tranquillity. Their muskets and pistols were aimed forward, and they were moving with the minimum amount of noise.

The forest closed round them again before long, more darkly brooding and still because of the preceding light. The undergrowth was so deep that the track of the men fetching water for their horses was soon lost, leaving them sniffing the air like dogs as they tried to pick up the scent of drying equine sweat. Calheri insisted on being in the forefront, and Markham had to admit to her skill in this environment, as she found a route that, though less dense than it appeared at first, was sufficient to hide them from anyone more than ten feet away. Bellamy and Rannoch, carrying muskets, found the going harder than the officers, who could tuck their weapons in their waistbands and leave both hands free.

If any distance opened up between them, the forest swallowed the body. The Commandatore was definitely aided by the dark brown of her uniform. Not that the other three were too disadvantaged. Bellamy and Yelland had on grey flannel, now as stained as their breeches, while Markham's coat, being dark blue with green facings, blended quite well into the surroundings. A verdant mass like this produced odours of its own: thyme and myrtle were strong, as was the sharp, throat-catching scent of pine. But the stink of a hard-ridden horse, added to the reek of fresh dung, was powerful enough to rise above even that. Calheri half turned, her nose twitching as she pointed silently half right. Markham came forward to join her as she whispered to him.

'The ground must dip again, into a hollow, I think. They will have their mounts in a clearing that gives easy access to the road.'

Markham nodded, then fell in behind her again as, on hands and knees, she led the way, his face too close for comfort to the tight breeches she wore, producing unwelcome thoughts. Stopping suddenly, she motioned him alongside, a command he passed back to the others. The ground in front of them dropped sharply, a barren face, as if a section of earth had been recently dislodged. Three temporary horse-lines were strung between trees, each dragoon mount tied head up so that they wouldn't try to graze on the pine needles. Though their girths were eased and stirrups raised, they were still saddled, ready for a swift departure.

The cavalry mounts, by far the bigger of the two types of horses, occupied two of the lines. Two dragoons, carbines slung across head and shoulder, were making their way along the line, holding leather water buckets to the animal's mouths, rationing the intake of each so that their performance wouldn't suffer from overindulgence. The other, smaller mounts, sturdy island ponies, were unattended, on longer halters that allowed them more freedom of movement, their shuffling noisy enough to still any sound of birdsong, so that the approach of Markham's party had gone unnoticed.

Calheri pointed to their right, indicating the route by which the riders had made their way on

346

foot to the road, ground well disturbed by marching feet.

'Forty-five horses and ponies,' Markham whispered, without adding, because it wasn't necessary, that there were at least fifteen Corsicans keeping watch on that road, as well as the thirty Frenchmen. 'It would be nice to know how close they are.'

'There is no time. Let us shoot those two French pigs and stampede the animals.'

The 'No!' was loud enough to make all three of the others cringe, and they pulled themselves slightly back to the safety of the bushes. Markham kept his eyes forward, so that they could all hear his whisper.

'Those men have to be dealt with in silence, and it makes no difference if they are killed or just clubbed. Any noise, too soon, and we'll have the whole force to deal with.'

'Paoli!' hissed Calheri.

She didn't like to be checked, that was obvious from her glare and the way her eyes narrowed. Nor did she much like what he said next, made all the more telling by the low growling tone of his voice.

'I think if I hear that name once more I'll yell blue murder. I haven't even met this paragon and already I'm sick of him.' She looked set to respond in kind, but he cut her off. 'But I will save him, if indeed he needs it. Die even, but not uselessly. You've proved you're good with that knife. Do so again. Take Bellamy round to the other side, while Rannoch and I come down off this ridge by the path that leads to the road.'

'Why there?' she asked, suspiciously, since what he proposed put her much closer than him to the dragoons.

'If that path is too narrow and dark, we'll never get the animals down it at anything like enough speed. If you'd ever tried to get a horse into a dark stall you'd know that. Some of them might have to be led in there, so that when they go, the rest will follow.'

She nodded as he added, 'And I don't know how far away the road is, do you? Let us come from that direction, and get our guns on them. You can then take them from behind.'

Markham grabbed Bellamy as she slithered away, pulling him close, aware for the first time that the odour of his body was different. 'No guns till I say so. Club her if she tries to use her pistol.'

'If she orders me?'

'You are a marine, Bellamy,' Markham interrupted. 'You obey me, not her. And if you doubt the wisdom of doing so, then just think of staying alive.'

'If he does not go he will lose her,' growled Rannoch.

Markham pushed Bellamy away, indicated to his sergeant to follow, then, on his belly, crawled off in the opposite direction, keeping the edge of the ridge on his left. Soon he was heading downhill, at an angle so steep that he needed both hands to hold himself. He felt Rannoch, encumbered by his musket, slide into him, which pushed him faster than he wanted to go, and forced him to grab hold of a sapling to stop both men tumbling to the bottom of the slope in a noisy heap.

'We would be best to go down on our arse,' muttered Rannoch, his measured way of speaking causing Markham to wonder if the Highlander had ever gabbled a sentence. 'That is, if we want to arrive with some dignity.'

Back on flat ground, life was easier, if no less scary. They were close now to the road; Markham could sense it, even if he couldn't see it. The path that led to it was, as he had suspected, an overgrown track, so dark that no horse would go into it unless driven. So little light penetrated the thick arc of cover that he slipped across it without the slightest danger of being seen by the horse minders. Rannoch followed and they stayed upright as they made their way round the perimeter of the clearing, to a point just far enough away from the horse-lines to avoid spooking the animals.

The two dragoons had finished their watering, and were now looking to their own needs, opening saddlebags to produce bread, a flask, pipes and tobacco, the sound so like rustling hay that every horse's eye was on them. Their carbines were still slung across their shoulders, which would make it impossible for them to get them off, over their heads, and presented in under five seconds, then a threat only if they were loaded. So preoccupied were they, so secure, that the pair didn't notice the two intruders until they were within ten feet. An accidental scuff of Markham's boot made one turn round, his gasp doing the same to the other. What they saw caused confusion: one giant blond in just his shirt, another man, who would have looked tall next to anyone normal, wearing one of their dragoon coats. What they didn't misread was the two weapons aimed right at their chests.

As they turned to face the muzzles, hands raised, Commandatore Calheri walked out of the trees behind them, stiletto in her hand. Yet she herself was taken by surprise. A figure in Corsican uniform appeared at her left before she'd covered half the distance to the dragoons she intended to knife. Having been hidden in the trees, the third man's view of both the marines and the dragoons had been obscured: he must have seen their upraised hands as he rushed forward, judging by the surprised flick of his eyes. Calheri, turning in shock, rocked back on her heels. Her attacker took advantage of her lack of balance and knocked her over. She fell, arms spread out, and as she sprawled on the ground he whipped out his own knife.

Then Bellamy stepped forward, and froze. For reasons only the Negro knew, his musket was pointing towards the ground, and his face was shocked and pleading rather than angry and full of resolve. He stopped when he should have come on, which earned a curse from Rannoch, one that was redoubled when he swung his musket, pulled his trigger, and was rewarded with nothing but the crack of flint striking flint, as the musket misfired.

Both dragoons went for their carbines as soon as they heard that sound, only to hesitate when Markham moved forward, pistol extended. Calheri's assailant was still standing astride her, knife out, but his gaze fixed on a Bellamy who

350

appeared to be no threat. The Commandatore lunged up with her stiletto, plunging into the man's lower belly so hard that it sliced right up to his leather belt. He should have screamed then, yet he didn't. His eyes stayed on Bellamy as the black marine stumbled forward, slowly raised his weapon, and pushed the man to the ground. There he lay, twitching and groaning, one hand raised, pointing towards the Negro's head.

Calheri jumped up and ran, her knife taking the first dragoon in the small of the back, ramming hard upwards towards his heart. Her other hand was a little late, and he got off half a cry before she smothered it. His companion stood, transfixed by terror, looking as the light of life died in the eyes of the man beside him. Rannoch moved forward and clubbed him with his useless musket, a blow the victim, mercifully, didn't see coming.

'Ponies first,' snapped Markham. 'Just untie their lines from the trees and leave them on their halters. Commandatore, relieve those two men of their carbines, and Bellamy, once you've untied the ponies, make sure your musket will fire.'

While they complied he was looking at the animals closely, with that practised eye that every Irishman prided himself on. In all equine groupings, there was a hierarchy. Man might think he'd tamed horses, but they were still full of wild instincts. One of these ponies would be respected by the others, not so much a leader in the true sense, but a mount that inspired confidence. Where he went, they would follow. There was no time for deep analysis. First they had to be kept under control, and second, the sound of sixty hooves was bound to carry. He thought he detected one less frisky than the others, a roan-coloured stallion that had an air about him as he pawed the ground without fear.

'Right,' he said, moving forward and taking the reins. The animal tried to move sideways as he tightened the girth, but soothing words stilled it, and kept the beast there while he lengthened the stirrups. 'Cut the cavalry horses loose on my command, and then blaze way with everything we've got.'

'Lieutenant,' Calheri demanded, standing in the middle of the clearing, a carbine in each hand, the very image of the kind of bandit queen so beloved by dramatists. 'How do you know which way the horses will run?'

Markham leapt into the saddle with ease, grabbed the reins and rode to the very entrance of the tunnel-like path. The roan jibbed of course, but he held it steady and, spinning round, said in a joke that was wasted on her, 'Sure, they're like my men, Commandatore. They'll bloody well follow me anywhere.'

It wasn't just the horses that came to life when the guns went off. The whole forest did. Birds that had sat in silence while their territory was occupied shot out of the trees and into the sky, squealing and squawking. More distant animals, pig deer and boars probably, broke cover and ran. But nothing compared with the horses, who, even trained for war, panicked immediately. Markham had yelled and dug hard with his heels at the very point of discharge. Threatened from the rear, and with one obvious avenue of escape available, the pony he was riding shot into the gloom, followed by the others, who while they ran were rearing and bucking to break their tethers. Rannoch and Bellamy were holding one end of each line, so that they ran out through the loops, and set the beasts free.

Within a minute, that dark, narrow path was full of striving horses. He was on the road in no more than ten seconds, hauling on the halter to get his pony round and heading north, a stampede behind him that, given the larger cavalry horses, threatened to overwhelm him. Suddenly the road was full of men and animals, some dragoons, others Corsicans in blue caps. Those behind didn't help, firing off their weapons to add to the general mayhem. The few humans between him and the bridge threw aside their guns and held their hands up in vain, their efforts only succeeding in channelling the frightened horses, rather than stopping them.

Ahead of him, Markham saw Leech and Halsey run from the bridge to the safety of the trees, as they'd been instructed. His problem was to do likewise, no easy task considering he was sitting on a pony wild with terror. All horses run naturally, and all want to be in front. He had two cavalry mounts alongside him by the time he was in stone-throwing distance of the bridge. Callously, he headed his pony over, so that the one on his left was heading straight for the pine logs that formed the uprights that lined the side. That forced it to rear and stop, and to shy away towards the trees to avoid plunging into the river.

Markham held his mount on that line, so that nothing came between him and the side rail. He had to raise his left foot out the stirrup to avoid his leg being crushed, which made his next task more difficult. Control was hard enough without purchase on one side, but he threw his body weight that way, and hauled hard on the reins as they reached the northern bank. It only slowed his pony a fraction, and he had no time to judge the wisdom of his departure. He only knew how fast he was going when, having leapt clear, he hit the ground, off balance, tumbling in a heap into bushes and saplings, his momentum carrying him clear of the flailing hooves of the rest of the stampede. Hands grabbed him and dragged him further into the undergrowth.

Clods of earth flew high and wide as the rest of the horses streamed by, watched from a recumbent position by the main body Markham had left behind. The question of what happened next was crucial, the whole point of his action being an attempt to get Fouquert and his support away from this part of the Morosaglia road. In his absence, his men had been busy with more camouflage, everyone with a weapon now concealed within yards of the road, so comprehensively that it would be hard for a person standing on top of them to see anything.

'Here they come,' he said. 'Pass it on.'

If they stopped to wonder what had happened to the men who'd been left to hold this side of the bridge, it would cost the enemy dear, exposed as they were on the open road to fire from point-blank range. That would mean a fight, but the muskets would even matters up, and might, with decent shooting, put the odds in his favour. But Markham was relying on the cavalryman's need for his horse, plus the thought, which would filter through to the most ignorant brain, that without them, this far from base, they were at the mercy of any sizable Corsican force they encountered.

The pounding of feet didn't register till they were very close, since the thudding noise from the horses was still audible. As the red-faced dragoons ran by, waving their various weapons, shouting and cursing to horses deaf to their pleas, each one was at the mercy of a musket barrel. The same applied to the Corsicans, who like the Frenchmen had eyes only for the pursuit of their mounts. Fouquert was in the middle of them, his face set, jaw clenched so tight it seemed his teeth would crumble under the strain.

The last man to appear was a corporal, his arms full of weapons that his men had dropped in their eagerness to pursue. He looked right at his hidden enemy, unable to see them through the skilful camouflage, calling out names, presumably those of the men they'd killed. The eloquent shrug that followed testified to his belief that they too had deserted their posts, and were in pursuit of their horses.

'They will catch them, Citizen Fouquert,' the corporal shouted, to a man probably too far away by now to hear him. His voice had a pleading tone, well suited to addressing a man who'd hanged his officer that very morning. 'Horses don't run for ever. They'll stop as soon as they find some decent grazing. We could be back here within the hour.'

These words were followed by a deep sigh, another shrug, before the corporal, mumbling to himself, trudged away in the wake of his troop.

Chapter twenty-five

'Tell the general to remain at the convent,' said Markham, as Calheri's women formed up. 'We will be there some time after dark.'

'I cannot *tell* him anything,' she responded. 'As soon as I give him news of what happened here, he will probably return to Corte.'

'He can't do that!'

'Why not?'

It was on the tip of his tongue to say. After all, they had fought the French together. But Nelson's intended attack on Bastia, now no more than five days away, was a subject he wanted to avoid. The injunction from Lanester to trust no one was wise advice he intended to follow. Unlike the major's assertion that he could carry out the task of telling Paoli what was required himself, an idea that became less appealing the more he considered it.

'The whole future of Corsica depends on it. Major Lanester needs to speak with him, urgently, just inform him of that. You must send a cart and some escorts to pick him up. Don't, for God's sake, let Paoli go himself. And if those men from Corte have left, it would be wise to get them back again.'

Her eyes flashed, preceding the anger in her voice. 'Does it not embarrass you, as such a junior officer, to issue so many orders?'

'Requests, Commandatore, they are requests,' he replied, trying to be emollient.

'Then that is what I will pass on, Lieutenant.'

She span on her heel and marched to the head of her troop, who immediately took up step to follow her. Markham kicked a clod of earth out of the ground in frustration, which was a bit overdramatic considering the way his hopes had been realised. The trap was no more, the enemy had withdrawn towards Morosaglia, and neither he nor Calheri had suffered a single casualty. The only thing he was doing now was using up time that could not anyway be put to good purpose.

'I did not understand a word of that,' said Rannoch, 'but would I be right in thinking you have not got your own way?'

The Highlander was looking up the track, at the backs of the Commandatore and her marching troopers. Had there been any alternative but to send them? The Morosaglia route had to be held till they knew Paoli was safe, and in a situation in which infantry must face cavalry, this was the best place to do it. And given a choice between his men and the females, there hadn't been much in the way of an option. But there was also the nagging suspicion in the back of his mind that, in the time available, they would be able to fetch Lanester, and provided he was well enough the major would be able to undertake the task with which Hood and d'Aubent had entrusted him.

'Thank God there are no women in the marines, Rannoch.'

'Does it not occur to you, sir, that the whole skirmish was a waste? If their man had been coming he would surely be with us by now.'

His officer nodded. 'It does occur to me, Sergeant. But there's an old saying that goes like this: "It seemed like a decent idea at the time!" Right now, the best thing we can do is take up our positions.'

'Yelland,' Rannoch called, 'up to that first bend and keep your eyes peeled. The rest of you, into the woods and find enough wood to bar this bridge to those bastard cavalry.'

They worked on through the rest of the afternoon to build a barricade. Rannoch had the men lay kindling all along the base, which could be lit to make it a fiery obstacle to men on foot. Four feet high, it was not beyond the power of a dragoon horse to jump. But any rider who attempted it would be forced to do so singly, which would leave him at the mercy of the defenders. To Markham it was precautionary. He didn't think Fouquert would return. But if he did, he would have to risk losing most of his strength. The Lobsters had all the powder and shot that had previously been available to the dragoons, no need to shoot until they were threatened, and good individual skills, especially firing from solid cover at short range. Unless there was something Fouquert wanted that he knew nothing about, it couldn't be worth the price he'd have to pay.

Markham, working alongside Rannoch to raise the barrier, suddenly laughed, which caused the

Highlander to give him a look.

'I was just thinking how nice it would be, being present when that corporal does a roll call of his men and finds how many are missing.'

Rannoch shook his head slowly, his face grave. 'That Fouquert is not a man I would like to be giving bad news to. The corporal you speak of, if he has any regard for his skin, will want to come back to be sure.'

'I wouldn't let him,' Markham replied, lifting one end of a twisted pine log. 'He's lost six dragoons without knowing what has happened to them. For all Fouquert knows, he faces walking into a trap himself, just like the one he set for Paoli. I would swear he values his hide pretty highly. It's not something he will risk, even for such a prize. My bet is he will retire, and if he thinks his purpose has been discovered, all the way to Bastia.'

'I hope that you are right.' Rannoch wasn't sure that they should stay here at all. The circumstances hadn't changed; they were still outnumbered, albeit in a better state to mount a defence. And being the kind of man he was, he'd let his officer know of his worries.

'Call Yelland back in, Sergeant,' said Markham, as soon as the work was complete.

'It is going to get cold now we've stopped toiling, I think,' Rannoch suggested, 'and I am not sure I am going to be right fond of this forest in the dark.'

'Don't worry,' Markham replied, grinning. 'We've chased the demons away.'

Many sounds disturbed the forest as the sun began to dip in the sky, but they were those of nature. This bridge, at this time of year, according to Calheri, was the only crossing of the Golo for miles. Markham trusted that only so far, especially since Fouquert had Corsicans with him. He put a piquet out on each flank, with orders to keep one musket loaded and cocked, with a finger on the trigger, his words regarding Fornali guaranteeing that his order would be obeyed.

'We'll be pulling out about an hour after dark, so anyone not busy, get some rest.'

With so few men, providing that was difficult. The previous night had been uncomfortable, the day a long one of hard marching, and now they were standing watches, grumbling mightily. And Rannoch was right, they were going to get cold, with what heat the sun could produce cut off early by the surrounding trees, and his men still in no more than shirts. Hunger, too, would do nothing to make a night march easier. Rannoch was pushing at an open door when he asked that the situation be remedied and, having been given leave, sent one party off for water, and two more to hunt and kill some food.

The embankment above the clearing that had contained the enemy horses was a rabbit warren, where the skills of the countrymen like Yelland and Leech came to the fore. Ettrick and Quinlan, clodhoppers who were told to get out of the way, responded sniffily that their mates wouldn't be quite so handy in a town. Bellamy, along with Dornan, was useless at hunting, so these four were left to man the barricade, as their mates first gathered, then began to spit-roast, what they had caught.

'Stand to,' called Quinlan, without raising his voice any more than necessary.

Rannoch was asleep, having had less rest than anyone the night before. But he was on his feet a fraction after his officer, musket up and over the top of the logs. Halsey had a pole under the makeshift spit, ready to break it up, while Dymock picked up one of the leather buckets that had been left by the dragoons, preparatory to dousing the fire. The rest were at the musket stack in quick time, and at their stations a few seconds after their sergeant.

Quinlan spoke out of the corner of his mouth. 'Corsican bastard, with a blue cap, I reckon. Just the one, your honour.'

'There will be more,' said Markham.

'I might be able to shoot him,' said Rannoch, patting the unfamiliar weapon.

'How long till that food is ready?' called Markham.

'Some it is there now,' Halsey replied.

'Right then,' Markham barked. 'Grab what you can, and eat, then man this barricade. Sergeant Rannoch, be my guest.'

'Sharland, Ebden,' Rannoch called. 'Two more muskets here, one either side.'

He didn't lay his own weapon back on the top of the logs, but instead found a gap he could aim through, keeping as much of the muzzle hidden as he could. Markham looked at the track, gloomy now and getting darker by the minute. He guessed Rannoch would try for the horse first, then the rider, wounding him so that if he wasn't alone another target might be presented when his companions tried to rescue him. In the event, Rannoch was denied that. He fired just as the blue-capped horseman hauled on his reins, the shot going wide of the mark, removing a branch not far from the animal's flank. By the time he'd got upright, grabbed Ebden's musket which was on his right, and fired, his target was on his way, astride a horse even more eager to find cover than its rider, and the sole result of his second discharge was another felled branch.

'Useless,' Rannoch spat, holding out Ebden's musket. 'How can anybody, man or woman, expect to score a hit with these?'

'Eat, Sergeant,' said Markham.

'Do we stay?' the Highlander asked softly.

'We don't know how many there are,' Markham replied, as Leech lifted one of the leather buckets up, using his mess tin so that his officer could take a drink.

'If he was local, he might know just as much about these woods as your lady officer.'

Markham was staring at the side of the bucket, water dripping from his chin, in his mind the place they'd got to that morning, where the men looking after the horses had drawn their water. Calheri was right about this being the only crossing at this time of year. But that, surely, only applied if you didn't mind getting wet. The pond he remembered was swimmable, and anyone who could lower themselves down the cliff on the far side had a fair chance of getting safely to the opposite bank.

'Get all the wood we have on the fire well

spread out, and gather more, green stuff that will smoke. I want a blaze that will last.' Markham grabbed the remains of a rabbit from the hand of Gibbons and threw it into the embers. 'And let's get the smell of cooking filling this forest.'

The men moved to obey too quickly, and he had to order them to act normally. He was looking anxiously over his shoulder to the Morosaglia side of the bridge, knowing that they'd have someone up a tree by now, high enough to see over the barricade, able to tell those on the ground what was happening. If he went too soon, before they deployed to find an alternative crossing, they would simply charge the barricade. If he delayed too long, they might get across the river and take him in the flank. He had to judge the light as well. Retreating at leisure through a dark forest was one thing. Running in fear of a horse, a creature with better natural night vision, was quite another.

He waited for ten agonising minutes before he spoke again, slowly explaining the situation as he saw it. His Hebes had become accustomed to this, the Seahorses less so. Both Bellamy and Sharland were prone to ask questions, the calls for them to shut up loud enough to override the way they growled at each other.

'If I've got it right, we will separate them from their mounts long enough to give us a head start. And they won't pursue us on foot, which increases the margin. Everyone stay in the woods till the first bend, then we can use the road.'

The light was going. Now the track between the trees at the first bend was barely visible. The green wood was placed on the fire, which was hot

363

enough to produce quickly billowing smoke. As soon as it began to blow about them, Markham gave the order to each man personally, so that they slipped out of sight singly to form just inside the line of trees. They moved fairly quickly, covering the hundred yards to the first bend without exposing themselves. Then they were back on the track, Markham at their head, not actually running, but keeping up a good trot, on a path that twisted and turned, rose and fell as it followed the contours of the country. It was hard to hear when you were moving fast, because of the sound of your own breath, but every ear still strained to pick up a hint of a pursuing horse.

'Take them on, Corporal Halsey,' shouted Markham, as they rounded a tight bend that marked the end of one of the few long straights, jumping to one side to let them pass. The sky above his head was going from blue to indigo, and this would present his last chance to shoot at anything with any hope of seeing it. 'The last four, halt.'

Rannoch was bringing up the rear, and the other three were Bellamy, Leech and Dornan. Not the best shots by any means, but then accuracy was not what he sought.

'You've heard something?'

Markham shook his head, and grinned. 'I'm going to wait here just two minutes, Sergeant. I'll take a wager on it.'

In the event he was wrong: it was five minutes or more before they heard the sound of hooves. Not galloping, but moving fast, aware that even if time was running out for a pursuit, on the open trail they were sitting ducks. Markham waited

364

until the first outline of the enemy was visible before calling his men out to fire a salvo. He used his pistol, and had the odd feeling as they let fly, and the glade was lit by the streaking flames of the discharge, that not all the weapons had fired.

He would have liked to listen to the confusion, in his mind's eye imagining rearing horses, men trying to wheel and flee, a degree of chaos. But they had to run, the job of slowing their pursuers done.

But it wasn't. The narrow track suddenly seemed full of sound, the thud of hooves loud even on the yielding earth. They all stopped and turned, Rannoch swift to whip out his bayonet and fix it, discarding any attempt to reload on the move. Leech was halfway to the same state, but Dornan dropped his and Bellamy just stood with his mouth open. All Markham had was a pistol to throw.

A single horseman, determined to get to them while their weapons were unloaded, came round the twist in the track, his head low over the pony's shoulder, blue cap just visible and a sabre extended enough to pick up what light was left in the sky. The sound of a musket going off by his ear, plus the orange flash, firing into the air, startled Markham. It also made the charging Corsican sit up and slightly check his mount. That was a split-second which was fatal to him, for Rannoch charged forward, bayonet extended, swept aside his sword, and rammed the blade home into his chest.

Markham had followed his sergeant. He grabbed the animal's bridle, pulling down to stop the beast rearing as he allowed it to drag him in a circle. Then he let go, stepped out of its path and gave it a mighty slap on the flank as it went by, speeding back the way it had come, to show the rest of the Corsicans the inadvisability of mounted pursuit. In the meantime Rannoch had got hold of Bellamy by his shirt, and practically lifted him off the ground.

'Why did you not fire before, you black sod?'

Markham punched him on one huge shoulder, his order to get moving obeyed, though the look in Rannoch's eyes was murderous. A dozen more twists brought them to an anxious Halsey, visible now only by the white of his shirt, who had halted at the sound of gunfire. Markham was just about to berate him, but he was sure he could hear hooves approaching again, this time from the other direction.

'On your knees the men at the front, the rest stay standing.' Chest heaving, he stood, trembling hands trying to reload Calheri's pistol, as the sound grew louder, cantering horses that he'd never expected to hear from that source. His voice, when he gave the order to present, was no more than a gasp.

'Stand by,' he yelled, as he saw the first glow of the torches. That strengthened until they rounded the bend, the flames lighting the embroidered cap on Calheri's head, which brought forth a hurried shout to 'Shoulder arms'.

She was astride one horse, holding aloft a torch in the same hand with which she was leading another pair, and came to an abrupt halt when her torch revealed what faced her. Then, sure

366

that the muskets were raised, she started to move forward, a smile on her face.

'General Paoli is safe,' she called. 'He retired to Corte with my troopers as soon as our messenger reached him.'

Her face fell at the snarled response. And she was more offended that Markham wouldn't even tell her what had happened. He merely grabbed her reins, turned her round and set off at his own pace, dragging her mounts with him, his Lobsters bringing up the rear. If she could have heard the words he was muttering under his breath, most of them relating to her hero Pasquale Paoli, the riding crop stuck into her boot might have come into use.

They had to slow to a walk eventually, unable to keep up the pace, hoping that the pursuers, from fear of being drawn too deep into country in which they were exposed, would call a halt. Markham never knew if it was that, or the distant, tolling bells of the Convent of San Quilici Rocci, calling Vespers, which gave them a sense of safety.

Calheri, once they'd slowed, took her chance to speak. 'The General wishes to see you as soon as possible, Lieutenant, as well as the man who provided the information on which we acted.'

'Bellamy!'

'Yes. He requires you to leave your men at the convent to come on by foot, while we make as much speed as we can on horseback.'

Markham, feeling more secure, had mellowed somewhat. But the words, which sounded very much like an order, still managed to rankle.

'Requires? I requested that he stay at the convent and wait for me. I don't recall being obliged.'

'You cannot refuse such a man.'

'Where is Major Lanester?'

'He wasn't at the convent when I left.'

That was worrying. The carter had had ample time to get to the monastery and back. Had something happened to the major? The oilskin tube he'd extracted from that bottle was in his breeches, forgotten in all the actions of the last twenty-four hours: he was acutely conscious of it now.

'You told me his condition when we left was poor. Unless he has had attention since then, he may well be unfit to travel.'

That angered him, although she was only mirroring his own thoughts. 'I don't suppose anyone bothered to send a fast horse to find out.'

The 'No' she replied with was muted.

'Then I'll have to go myself.'

'Impossible. General Paoli demands you go to Corte. You have information that is directly related to his wellbeing.'

Markham stopped, and glared at her. 'He could have waited for me, if he was so bloody concerned.'

That shocked her. 'And exposed himself to even more risk?'

'Sure, I believe even generals are obliged to occasionally,' he responded sarcastically. 'It's a feature of war.'

That really made her boil, so much that he wondered where she'd put that pointed knife she wielded so effectively. He'd known all along he'd have to oblige, and it was nothing to do with what Bellamy had overheard. Now, looking at her changed face, it seemed a good time to accept the inevitable.

'Sergeant Rannoch,' he shouted, as she opened her mouth to curse him.

'Sir!'

The Highlander came abreast of him, musket in hand. Markham told him about Lanester, then waved a nonchalant hand towards Calheri, still on the verge of spitting at him.

'Seems the big chief wants to see me. Our Commandatore here wants Bellamy and me to go on horseback, while you follow on foot.'

'Then I hope you do not meet anyone who wants to harm you, with only a woman and that darkie in tow. I asked him why he didn't use his bayonet in the clearing, nor fire when ordered. Do you know what he said?' Markham shook his head. 'It seems he has found that he does not like the killing, which he discovered when he bayonetted one of those dragoons.'

'He fired quick enough when that fool came after us.'

'That was panic,' Rannoch sneered. 'And everyone knows it. And now you are proposing to put him on a horse.'

'Not me, Sergeant. That idea belongs to the Commandatore.'

Markham's spirits, already low, sank when they reached the convent. Lanester still hadn't arrived, and it was very doubtful if the carter would travel by night. The more time the major spent away

369

from the security of his escort, the greater the risk. Where was Fouquert now? He didn't know, and neither did anyone else.

'I want someone sent immediately,' he insisted.

The nod he received in reply lacked conviction, which was reflected in his last orders to Rannoch. 'Crack of dawn, Sergeant. If there's no sign of the major and Pavin, get back to that monastery yourself and fetch him on.'

'Sir.'

'And take care, man. You never know who might be lurking in that bloody *maccia*.'

Chapter twenty-six

Dawn found them approaching Paoli's capital. Markham was exhausted and felt filthy, so that when he actually saw the main church spire, as well as the taller buildings of Corte, it was with some relief. The city was distant, of course, but nevertheless a beacon. There was some comfort in the fact that he was approaching a place where he could rid himself of the burden he carried, knowledge that he could not act on, but Paoli could, mixed with his anxieties about pulling it off without the help of Lanester. The story was reeling around in his mind now, like a recurring nightmare.

But there were things to distract him even from that. It rankled that the beautiful Commandatore Calheri seemed to take more interest in Bellamy than him, despite his best efforts to make up for his previous rudeness. She had called the Negro forward to ride alongside them, as an equal. Unwisely, in Markham's eyes, the black marine private played up to her shamelessly. If he was aware of the discomfort he was visiting upon his superior, he gave no sign of it. For the first time Markham could see a hint of the arrogance that so offended the men he served with. Bellamy was like a cartoon rake, with his overblown sallies and arch wit, all delivered in blissfully fluent French.

Eavesdropping, Markham learnt more about the man than he ever had from direct conversation: about his birth in the Sugar Island of St Kitts, and his luck in being the offspring of slaves purchased by Jeremiah Bellamy's father, he being described as a whip-wielding tyrant, in contrast to his saintly, good-natured son. Having selected Eboluh as a promising case, Jeremiah had provided tutors to teach him, and several other boys, everything that would be vouchsafed educationally to a well-bred Englishman.

Markham was watching her face as Bellamy boasted, arms moving expansively to underline each point, relating how astounded his teachers had been at his application and intelligence, marvelling at the way he left his compatriots behind as he absorbed their lessons.

'French, Latin of course, though I confess I struggle to this day with Greek. And it does amaze me that having such a facility for mathematics, I seem incapable of holding on to any kind of money, coin or bill. Still, pleasure above all would line my coat of arms, should I ever be granted one.'

Bellamy, laughing, had leant across to say this, pushing his horse close to Calheri like a man bent on increasing the degree of intimacy. For the tenth time Markham saw her features change, especially the involuntary sharpening of the nose. On one level this made him think that she'd be an easy woman to attempt to seduce, since you would never be in any doubt where you stood. The other half of his mind was consumed with the temptation to tell Bellamy not only to shut up, but to move away as well.

'We must make more haste,' she said, spurring her mount.

'I remember you said how impatient the old man was,' said Markham.

'You would be too, Lieutenant, if you had his concerns.'

He couldn't resist the jibe, even although it was clearly the wrong thing to say. 'Concerns, is it? He has those all right, and that after you telling me how safe Paoli was. Revered, was the word you used, I think. Yet he can't ride out ten miles from his own capital for fear that one of his own countrymen might knife him.'

'Be content in the knowledge that you do not understand Corsica,' she replied sharply.

'You must forgive me, Commandatore Calheri,' he said, with deliberate irony. 'I've been here for two weeks, and it gives me no pleasure to say to you that I probably understand Corsica only too well.'

Both men having blotted their copybooks, they were relegated to a position well to her rear. It was some time before they realised how much attention they were paying to her trim buttocks, rising and falling rhythmically in time with the canter of her mount, made shapely by the tight corduroy of her riding breeches.

'A better view, sir,' said Bellamy, 'than the arse on the back of your average Lobster.'

Markham was annoyed at the over-familiarity. Though not excessive in his regard for rank, he knew that without it only mayhem could ensue. Bellamy seemed incapable of remembering that he was employed to fight, not amuse. Right at this moment he wasn't doing either.

'You're not much given to acknowledging hierarchy, Private Bellamy, are you?'

Meant to check the Negro slightly, and to remind him to whom he was speaking, it failed abysmally.

'Those at the bottom of a pile have no time for such malarkey, which is the preserve of those sad creatures who aspire to something they will never have. How fatal it is to be of the middling sort, forever casting an eye to the rear in panic, while bowing a knee to the front in hope. That is not a dilemma afforded to a black man, however handsome or intelligent.'

Bellamy grinned then, showing those large white teeth, and his eyebrows arched to increase the size of an already large face. He waited just long enough for Markham to purse his lips at the vanity before adding, 'Nor, I daresay, to officers whose reputation amongst their peers it not of the highest.'

'I have just been slapped down?' Markham

asked, amused in spite of himself.

'It is hardly my place to do such a thing,' Bellamy responded, not attempting to disguise the irony. 'I merely seek to point out that my station, while it has limitations, also has freedoms.'

'Education has surely done a great deal to remove some of the limitations.'

'And imposed others, sir, like jealousy and mistrust. Hate I can comprehend. But if a white man is kind to me, what is his motive? I can never be sure. Is his charity not prompted by a need to compensate for the colour of my skin? Do people hang on my words because of their quality, or because they cannot believe wisdom emanates from such a source?'

He flicked a hand at Calheri's posterior. 'If the lady ahead of us, with the so-attractive *derrière*, succumbed to my charms, and proved amenable to a touch of dalliance, would it be because of my wit and my erudition, or mere curiosity about the supposed physical endowments of my race? I am like a very rich man who never knows whether people like him for himself, or for his money.'

'Which, in my experience, makes rich men mean.'

'It only makes me boastful.' Bellamy saw Markham smile, and nodded once more towards those bouncing buttocks. 'I find it is healthy, as do all philosophers, to know one's own faults.'

'To hell with philosophy,' Markham replied, his gaze following in the same direction.

They had to drop down into a deep valley before they could make the final leg of the journey up the steep incline to Corte. The road wound over several rushing spring torrents, which Markham recalled from his maps were either the River Restonica or the higher reaches of the Golo. The town itself stood on a thousand-foot outcrop of jagged rock, a walled citadel, fronting on an escarpment shaped like a noble Roman nose.

The main citadel looked, from where he first sighted it, like a boat without sails, but bearing buildings as cargo. Turrets marked the corners of this, one looking down to the round tower of the original castle, pushed well forward over the cliffs to command a view of the approaches. The city, dominated by a tall Romanesque spire, had spread outside the walls of the old town, spilling down the hillside. It was a place of which Commandatore Calheri was inordinately proud. When she talked of Corte and its history, she reminded Markham of General Grimaldi and his tales of Corsican heroism.

Founded by the indigenes, it was unlike all the other cities of Corsica, which were of Roman or Genoese origin. Hardly surprising, then, that it was the seat of the first independent government and the home of Corsica's first university. It looked like an impregnable fortress, yet the list of people who had captured the place was long: some foreigners, others island heroes who'd re-taken the place. Looking at the terrain, broken, irregular hills between steep valleys, all covered in dense forest, Markham wondered how any of them had managed it.

But then he looked at the citadel itself, a brooding presence even in its light, sunset-coloured stone. It spoke to him of treachery, of secret arrangements that opened gates that should have remained closed. From leaving Cardo, through all the forests and fights, and even in his dealing with Fouquert, the name of Corte had sounded like a haven. Now that he could see it, it didn't feel that way at all.

Few people came to watch them ride through the narrow streets, made dark by the deep shadows, which cast most of the lanes they rode through into gloom. This, along with shuttered windows, added to the chill caused by the lack of sunlight. Up and up they rose, through steep, winding streets, criss-crossed by even steeper alleys. Then, quite suddenly, they rode into a decent-sized square, bright with sunlight and lined with buildings made imposing by the meagre surroundings. All were of light-coloured sandstone, with generous windows and imposing entries. The other feature they shared was a number of bullet holes etched into their soft stone walls, the edges worn by time.

'The Palais National,' said Calheri as she dismounted, proudly pointing to the biggest building, which filled one end of the square.

'Home of the general?' asked Markham.

'Home of the government of Corsica,' she said, her chest swelling out with enough pride to drag his eyes away from her face. She must have noticed the direction of his gaze, since her tone changed abruptly. 'Please dismount.'

He did so, stiffly, not having spent much time in a saddle for six months. He felt it showed when he walked, and that if anyone asked him to stop a pig, it would escape easily through his bandy pins. Bellamy, who could not have been on a horse himself since joining the marines, moved with an ease that added another sliver of resentment to Markham's appreciation of the Negro.

They made their way up the steps, into a deep, colonnaded portico, the first hint that people occupied the building the buzz of conversation, echoing off stone walls, passing out through the open double doors. Once through those, they found themselves in a crowd: all men, knots of people talking in an animated fashion while glancing anxiously at the other door, guarded by two smart sentinels, which stood at the far side of the main salon. Markham was surprised, having expected the place would be deserted at this early hour.

Calheri marched forward, her boots thudding on the stone floor, creating a path for herself by sheer force of character.

Someone had noticed Markham's French cavalry coat, kept on despite its provenance to ward off the chill when they were out of the rays of the sun. And Bellamy, of course, drew automatic attention. With his shining black face, one eyebrow raised, he examined the locals with a disdain that would have done credit to a Prince of Wales. People began to edge towards them, some growling, others pointing, until Markham took the coat off, and threw it at the nearest pair of feet.

'Abuse it if you wish, gentlemen,' he said in English. 'It is, after all, the garb of our common energy.'

That stopped the forward movement, and

377

Bellamy showed great presence of mind in translating Markham's statement into French. Looks were exchanged as he spoke, nods added when he identified his officer as a British ally. One man, standing near the coat, leant over and spat on it. This was an act soon followed by everyone present, as though it was necessary for each of them to prove their adherence to the Corsican cause, which left Markham wondering just how many of them were being truthful.

He hadn't noticed the guarded door open the first time, as Commandatore Calheri made her approach. But he did see it open for the second time, above the heads of those assembled, not least because all those who'd already partaken of their ritual abuse span round to look. He sensed the crowd parting in front of him before he saw any physical evidence. But finally they did, creating a clear space, and George Markham had his first sight of the paragon himself, General Pasquale Paoli.

He'd expected an upright frame, but age had spoiled the perfection of that. The hair was snowy-white without benefit of powder, the face lined with wrinkled skin the colour of parchment. Somehow he was disappointed, even though he'd known long before he arrived that the general was an old man. A portion of that feeling evaporated as he came closer, so that Markham could see the steady, bright blue eyes; observe that a lot of the wrinkles had been caused by mirth rather than frowns, and that the man had natural grace in abundance. The bow with which he greeted the general was therefore given as much through respect for what he saw, as for the legends that he'd heard.

'Lieutenant George Markham, General Paoli,' said Calheri. What she added to that was obviously for the benefit of the crowd. 'Who has come from San Fiorenzo, via Cardo.'

There was a shuffling in the crowd as Paoli came closer, but no one spoke as Markham opened his mouth to present his own greeting. The finger, which came speedily up to the lips, surprised him, as did the look on the older man's face, but he obeyed the injunction to remain silent.

'You will walk with me for a while, Lieutenant.' Paoli paused while Markham nodded. 'And accommodate me by saying nothing while we do.'

The voice was commanding without the least trace of harshness. There was no option but to obey, and no anger in being obliged to do so. Despite his earlier cursing, such an order from such a source seemed the height of reason. Paoli had his hand held out, indicating that he should come closer, and as Markham joined him he began to walk, pacing round the outer rim of the salon with his hands behind his back. It spoke volumes for the majestic nature of his presence that not a soul even dared to cough while this was taking place.

Every so often the general would stop and look at him, examining his face for a few moments before stepping out again. These halts and inspections were unnerving. Markham felt those bright blue eyes, steady and unblinking, could see into his very soul. Yet if Pasquale Paoli could so do, nothing of what he saw showed on his face. Calheri was watching, her eyes more intent than

379

the others, as if this was some kind of cabalistic ritual which would reveal hidden secrets without the need for speech.

They paced around in silence for some fifteen long minutes, the only sound the echo of their boots on the stone floor. The room was cool yet the atmosphere seemed oppressive. Opposite the door through which he had arrived, the General finally stopped, turned to face him, clasped both the British officer's hands in his own, and said: 'Welcome to Corte.'

That was a signal for conversation to recommence, and the buzz of it filled the high-ceilinged room.

'Please, Lieutenant, come into my private quarters, and bring your Numidian companion with you.'

Chapter twenty-seven

To Markham it was like sitting before the Star Chamber, worse by far than a court martial. Not that Pasquale Paoli sought elevation. He sat at the same level as his visitors, listening carefully. But the room, high-ceilinged and panelled, had just the right degree of oppression, the white flags drooping at the rear providing the only relief. On both sides of the general those important enough to qualify for attendance, numbering about twenty souls, stood silently, like courtiers. And all this for a man supposedly retired from active political life!

First of all, he reiterated his concerns for Major Lanester. Then, for public consumption, Markham trotted out the story relating to the mission he and Lanester had been sent to perform, the need for more troops. If this old man, with steady bright blue eyes that never left his face, considered it eyewash, he kept that knowledge hidden from his own countrymen. Yet Markham suspected they knew it was a cover for something else as well. Why send a file of marines, and two officers, to deliver a request that could have come by single mounted messenger?

The general continued to listen without interruption to a filleted story of what had happened at Fornali, agreeing the escape of the French had been a misfortune. He showed slightly more concern when Markham went on to speak of the situation at Cardo, agreeing in a sage but noncommittal way about the lack of Corsican strength, allied to the danger posed by the positions they had adopted. He did not enquire who had made this decision. In fact, no names were mentioned by either man, not Arena, Buttafuco or Grimaldi.

Yet Paoli was no fool, and even if he claimed to have relinquished power, the evidence of Markham's own eyes showed that he had it in abundance. He must have sources of information that reported back to him, independently of the titular commanders. What had happened at the Teghima Pass had been a disgrace. Yet, with an informant in front of him who could shed light on the failure of the whole operation round San Fiorenzo, he posed not a single question.

381

That left Markham high and dry, since he'd banked on curiosity to lead him onto more murky areas. He had no intention of producing Hood's letter, telling the truth about Fornali, nor of mentioning what he'd seen at Cardo, as long as others were in the room. But he would have been quite willing, with a little probing, to disturb the air of complacency which seemed to prevail in this gathering.

Paoli, speaking for the first time since they'd sat down, suddenly changed the subject. He mentioned the proximity of the French patrol, which at least stirred the audience from their torpor. That was followed by a series of questions on how they had come to be captured. It was clear, when Markham answered, that those present were less than impressed. Paoli came to his defence, acknowledging that the trap Duchesne had sprung showed cunning. He mentioned the original inhabitants, the monks, offering a plea for their souls, and frowned when Markham, responding to another enquiry, reported how they'd been found in the *marchetta*.

'I can only assume that was the work of Fouquert.'

'This, I am told, is the man who has come from Paris to arrest me,' exclaimed Paoli, to a murmur of anger.

'He is also the man who claims to have men faithful to him inside Corte.' That caused uproar, as each person present assured the men next to them of their complete faith in their loyalty.

'Bellamy,' said Markham, stepping back.

The Negro started speaking, in his clear fault-

382

less French, which shut everyone up. They listened intently, tensed up for denial, as if each one expected to be named. Tempted to stray off the point, Bellamy was rudely returned to it by his officer, and cut off abruptly when it came to describing the escape.

'This man you talk of, this Fouquert, is a priest-killer.'

'I believe he is. I cannot think Captain Duchesne had a hand in it,' Markham continued. 'He paid with his life for saving me. A man of that type does not kill innocent priests.'

'It is a great sadness, but hardly uncommon, Lieutenant, even for French officers who are themselves sons of the church. You must understand that nearly every man of the cloth in Corsica supports the desire for independence. This is not like mainland Europe, where bishops live in towering palaces and the monasteries hold great tracts of land. The priests of Corsica come from the same stock as their parishioners, and share a life that is equally hard. Rome to them is a distant place, less of an authority than their loyalty to their own kin. Without their help, I could not have pacified and united the island. They were with us when we fought Genoa, and it was with their help that we rallied enough to hold the French at bay for a decade. The consequence of that allegiance has been to expose them to the kind of reprisals you witnessed.'

He nearly replied that there was no sign of a struggle, or any spilling of blood, and that was part of the reason they'd walked into the French trap: the place was so very peaceful. But he stopped himself, knowing it would imply an insult he did not intend.

'You were lucky that you and your men got away from this Fouquert.'

Paoli could know nothing of the extent of Fouquert's intentions regarding his visitor, so didn't know just how lucky Markham felt. Nor did he want to tell him, since thoughts of that tended to induce a degree of terror. He went on to describe the escape, pointing out Bellamy and detailing his contribution.

'Luckily Major Lanester was the only casualty we suffered.'

'Yes, Magdalena,' said Paoli, with feeling. 'We must make sure Lanester will be safe.'

'Cavalry from the garrison are already on their way.'

The use of her first name was welcome. She had been stiff and formal since their last stop, and it served to make her more human. It also revealed an intimacy with the old man that went beyond the bounds of military attachment.

'Good. I would hate anything to happen to Lanester. He has suffered enough in his time for the choices he has made.'

'No more than you, Uncle.'

Paoli smiled, a slow warming affair that made his eyes glow. He was looking at Markham, rather than the woman now revealed to be his niece.

'But I have gained what I desire, Magdalena, whereas poor Lanester, for choosing a king over a congress, lost everything he'd striven for.'

'Which was?'

'A sizable fortune.'

384

'Money cannot be compared to the independence of a nation.'

Markham, looking around the blank, impassive faces, was beginning to get annoyed at the air of unreality which permeated this gathering. There were traitors, who must be of high rank, in the Corsican army, assassins on the loose, enemies of Paoli riding around the country within ten miles of Corte, not to mention French dragoons who had crossed half the island without so much as a skirmish. He had the feeling that not just Paoli, but everyone in the room, knew things they were keeping to themselves.

All had reacted with theatrical horror to the threat to arrest Paoli, yet it had seemed so stagey and unconvincing that it would have shamed a Greek chorus. It was an act of dissimulation, not fear, which made him wonder just how many of the worthies with enough influence to make the inner sanctum were loyal to their leader and their country. Even Duchesne had let something slip in that regard before Fouquert had shut him up. It was something he was inclined to believe. If there were traitors in other parts of the island, why would there not be the same in the capital city?

While perfectly prepared to keep his word to Lanester about Hood's letter, he had an overweening desire to let these smug Corsicans know just how badly they'd failed at San Fiorenzo, and just what he'd witnessed at Cardo. He wanted to see their reaction to an accusation of treachery and base murder. Never blessed with much in the way of patience, it took a titanic inner struggle for Markham to keep his mouth shut.

'You are still in danger, General,' he said. 'I'm sure your niece must have told you so.'

'From one troop of French dragoons?'

Markham looked from one to the other. Judging by the stiff face of Magdalena Calheri, he was sure that she'd indeed passed on everything he'd said about Corsicans being involved in the attempt to capture him. But it was equally obvious that Paoli either didn't take it seriously, or was disinclined to discuss the matter in public. The anger that had risen in Markham began to subside, along with the realisation that Paoli knew very well that there was betrayal around. If he wasn't probing, it was because he didn't want open answers. Instead of being obtuse, he was remarkably astute.

Lanester's gift of wine, his way of passing the message from Hood, didn't now seem the piece of tomfoolery he'd initially imagined. The major had foreseen this, known that he would not easily be able to see Paoli alone. That in turn led him to wonder just how much both senior British officers, and the major, knew about the nature of Paoli's court. Perhaps there was something in that despatch that Lanester hadn't told him about. After all, Markham was too junior to be included in the councils of the mighty. The question was, lacking any secretive bottles of Haut Brion, what was he to do about it?

'I wonder, General Paoli,' Markham said boldly, 'if it would be possible to speak to you alone.'

'Why?'

It had been there, the very slight flash of approval in the older man's eyes. 'I have something

386

I want to say that is for your ears only.'

But Paoli was also a consummate actor. The white bushy eyebrows rose slowly, as though he was deeply shocked at the suggestion. The accompanying angry buzz from the others present only underlined what he was implying by his reaction; that the honour of the leading citizens of the island was being impugned.

'I am amongst friends here, Lieutenant,' Paoli said, with an expansive gesture of the arms aimed at faces just as angry with him as Markham, men who considered he was indulging in sophistry rather than doing what he should, which was to flatly refuse. Paoli had the sense to keep his voice normal, aware that false anger would probably make them more suspicious. 'Equals, as well. Some of them are elected members of the National Assembly, whereas I am not. How can I exclude men chosen to govern Corsica from any deliberations I, as a private citizen, may have?'

'I must insist. And I also assure you that you'll not regret it.'

'Does this include your companion?' Paoli asked, to stifle the protests of his own kind.

'Yes. Private Bellamy knows nothing of what I want to impart.'

A hand waved slightly towards his niece. 'It is so great a secret that even my own flesh and blood must be excluded?'

Markham looked around the room, at the scowling worthies, before settling on Magdalena Calheri. As far as he was concerned, given her hero-worship of the man, she could have stayed. But to relent on one would only invite more

387

objections to the exclusion of others.

'Having heard what I have to say, General, you then have every right to share it with whomsoever you choose.'

'I trust my niece Magdalena as much as everyone else present.'

'No doubt, having known her for years, you do.' Her eyes flashed as she picked up the drift of his words, a clear indication that she anticipated what was coming next. 'I, on the other hand, only met her yesterday morning. As to the gentlemen assembled in this room, I know nothing of them at all.'

That was like a collective slap on the face, and Markham wondered what would have happened if the towering presence of Paoli hadn't been there to dominate proceedings. The general thought for a moment before looking at his niece in a slightly pleading way, a plain request for her to oblige. If she went with some grace, then the men present would possibly feel less slighted. She was angry, controlling most of it well. Yet she could do nothing about the way her face changed, a physical reaction of which she was probably unaware. She felt, like these powerful citizens, that to be excluded at the whim of a mere messenger was intolerable. Her nod of agreement was sharp and unfriendly, but it was decisive. One or two of them protested, only to be silenced by Paoli, who asked them, with great politeness, to vacate the chamber.

Magdalena Calheri was the last to exit, and refused to be easily beaten. Her parting shot was delivered on a slightly husky note, which proved that although she dressed and behaved like a cavalry officer, she was also a woman, one experienced enough to have noticed the slight frisson between the marine officer and his Negro private.

'Come, Eboluh Bellamy,' she said, 'you are my lucky talisman. It is time you were shown some proper Corsican hospitality. You need to bathe, don clean clothes, eat some food, and tell me more about your past.'

'Wait outside, Bellamy,' Markham ordered, not sure what prompted it: a need for discipline, or sexual jealousy.

The voices of the men faded as she shut the door behind her, and it was some time before Markham could be brought back to thinking about the subject that had brought on this display.

'What I am about to say to you, General, will not make pleasant listening.'

Paoli put his fingers to his lips again, then, handing Markham a cloak, indicated that he should follow him. They went through a door which led to a balcony overlooking a steep drop. The sun was on the other side of the Palais, and the chill air made Markham shiver. Once outside, with the door shut behind him, Paoli nodded for him to continue.

Markham passed over Hood's letter and stood, trying to contain his shivering, as Paoli tore at the wax seal. Having broken that clear, he unravelled the oilskin, took out the parchment and read it. As soon as he finished, Markham began to speak.

'I am not privy to the contents of that letter, sir. Does it tell you of British intentions regarding Bastia?'

'It does. It seems your assault is imminent.'

'It is also in grave danger of failure.'

Markham wished he'd read the letter. Did he need to tell the General about Fornali, then the events which had marred the dinner aboard *Victory*, followed by the attempt on his life, or was that all written down? Lanester had been so vague about the contents, perhaps justifiably so because of his condition. Tired from the exertions of the previous two days, it was easy to see his task of persuading Paoli as impossible. And deep down, his real worry was that he would fail so comprehensively that any support Lanester might provide when he arrived would be wasted.

He had to speak, but knew he couldn't start with what he'd seen at Cardo. Besides, he felt he needed to husband some information, quite sure that this old man was doing the same. Paoli knew more than he was saying, and would not quibble to make his visitor look foolish. He would hold to himself what he had while extracting everything from this garrulous informant. The act was instinctive rather than rational, but Markham wanted to shock this old fox, and show him that cunning was not solely a Corsican prerogative.

'About Fornali,' he said.

'Yes, Lieutenant, please tell me about that.'

Yet again he was listened to in complete silence, something he found slightly disconcerting. Paoli didn't even look as though he was curious, never mind pose a question. Was he prone to shock? Not even a flicker of a silver eyebrow disturbed his air of serenity, and he listened as Markham related details of the attempt on his life in such a still pose that the marine wondered if he was being believed. Details of the meal at Cardo finally produced a reaction, but that was only a thin smile related to the level of boasting to which the British officers had been subjected.

'In short, General, and it gives me no pleasure to say this to such as you, treachery seems to be widespread.'

'That implies a great deal, Lieutenant.'

'Your niece, no doubt, has told you of what happened when she arrived to look for the French dragoons.'

'You claim a messenger. But you have no evidence that whoever came to see them was Corsican, or came from Corte.'

That made Markham angry. 'Then how were they on the route to Morosaglia, waiting to entrap you? Why did we have to risk annihilation, your niece and I, to stop them?'

Again that infuriating unflappability. 'That you have propounded a reasonable supposition, I cannot contest. But you have no evidence.'

'No. But taking everything together.'

'Beginning at Fornali?'

'Yes.'

Paoli fell silent again. Markham, having told his tale, had expected to be interrogated, anticipated that Paoli would make the same deductions he had. With his host showing no signs of obliging him, he was drawn into doing so himself.

'Major Lanester's last words to me were to get you to Cardo in time for our landing.'

'He would have had a reason?'

'Well you'll be safe there,' Markham sighed,

making no attempt to keep the irony out of his voice. 'At least, that is the received wisdom, because the army adores you. It is my opinion that you would be just as much at risk.'

'Why?'

'There can be no doubt that one of your senior commanders is in league with the French.'

The reply was infuriatingly unmoved. 'If you wish to assume that, I cannot stop you. Tell me, does Admiral Hood think so too?'

'You have read his letter, sir, and in all honesty he could hardly do otherwise.' That earned nothing but a slow nod. 'It's not just Fornali or the attempt on my life. You must know, General, that the dragoons we fought would need help to get as far as they did without using the road. I doubt there is a Frenchman born who knows his way along the mule trails of the *maccia*. We found a family on the road, dead, the weapons of the menfolk not even primed. They died because what they saw they trusted. No Corsican peasant would allow a French patrol within a mile of them. But men in Corsican uniform, perhaps.'

'How much do you know of the history of this island, Lieutenant?'

'Not enough,' Markham replied, with a trace of impatience. The General observed his reaction and gave him a disarming pat on the shoulder.

'Indulge an old man, and let me tell you. I do not impugn other nations when I say that Corsicans have a higher sense of honour than most people.' Paoli smiled, noticing Markham's raised eyebrows. 'It is not because they are more virtuous. It is more to do with the abiding fear of treachery. So what would pass for a humorous sally elsewhere, could be the start of a blood feud here.'

'A vendetta.'

'An Italian word I hate with a passion. A trick of the weak Genoese government, young man. If you cannot impose your will by either ability or force, and have no real desire for justice, why not encourage the Corsicans to kill themselves? Bribe one, then tell a rival that he has taken your gold. Engineer a murder, then when it is done, turn a blind eye – but make sure the family of the victim know the identity of the perpetrator. Arrest the men of a family, then let another steal the sheep and rape the women while they are absent. Set clan against clan, in a series of feuds that become so tangled the original reasons for the spilling of blood gets lost. That way the men who would fight you die at the hands of their own. Should someone arise and threaten to unite the nation, pay one jealous individual to stick a knife in his back. That was the way the Genoese ruled Corsica.'

Paoli's voice had risen slightly as he spoke. Yet it was still under control, as if he had said these words a thousand times to many people, the beginning of a plea to put aside their quarrels.

'And the French?'

'Royal France began better. But our demand for independence meant that Bourbon gold was just as liberally spread as their predecessors'. They were, to their credit, less fond of the knife than Genoa, having some sense of legality. But they were no more able to allow us freedom, which is what the majority of the people want. The Revolution was supposed to change all that.

393

But power has turned the heads of those lunatics in Paris.'

'Who want you arrested.'

'They insisted that we invade Sardinia, an idea that appealed to certain local firebrands, but not to me. I had one Buonaparte in Paris insisting that I act, and another here in Corsica, who thought of himself as the new Alexander, demanding to be allowed to lead the attack.'

'He wasn't called Napoleon, was he?'

That did cause surprise. 'Yes.'

Markham explained the circumstances of their meeting in Toulon, as well as the success the Corsican had enjoyed. 'He struck me as a trifle obsessed.'

'He's a madman,' Paoli hissed, showing deep emotion for the first time. 'But times are troubled, and people like him will prosper, if they can keep their heads. The other one in Paris, who is more sane, is Lucien. If their father was alive, he would be ashamed to look me in the eye.'

Markham heard the catch in his throat, an indication of deep feeling from so controlled an individual. 'He was at my side in the French wars, a trusted companion. And now his sons fight me, on the side of tyrants who cut off heads for pleasure.'

'Does it occur to you that Fouquert might lose his head if he doesn't arrest you?'

'An interesting notion. It would certainly make him tenacious.'

'He intends to have your head, I'm sure.'

'That, young man, is a thing Paris has desired for some time.'

'Why?'

'They believe I betrayed them. I came back to Corsica through Paris. I stood before the National Assembly and pledged myself and this island to their principles, the same notions for which I had fought all my life. That men should be free to think and act; that governance was not the prerogative of kings. Now, in order to preserve their own power, they are worse tyrants than any Louis. They do not understand that it is they who have betrayed the purity of their revolution. So they look elsewhere for cause, and their gaze alights on me. From pedestal to proscription in less than a year.'

'"And when he falls, he falls like Lucifer, never to hope again",' said Markham.

Paoli smiled. 'No. Shakespeare coined those words for Julius Caesar. They do not apply to me, though I admit to a hope that they will to Robespierre, who is close to the devil incarnate.'

'Will you join your army, as Admiral Hood requests?'

'Do you know the contents of this?'

'Major Lanester told me of that part. He may well have kept concealed anything else.'

Paoli didn't respond to the invitation to be open. Instead he lifted the letter, and waved it without much fervour. 'This is a demand, young man, not a request. It is also, very possibly, a blatant piece of bluff.'

'Hood doesn't strike me as the bluffing type.'

'The good ones never do.'

The pause that Markham allowed was part of the pleasure. But it was difficult to be offhand,

and he was unsure if he struck the note of insouciance he intended.

'Then General Buttafuco will be free to act against you.'

'Buttafuco?'

'Yes!' Much as he tried to speak slowly, the words tumbled out: men he thought were assassins disappearing like chimeras; himself and Rannoch skulking through the camp; the password, Nebbio. 'I saw Buttafuco with my own eyes, in negotiation with a French general, whom I took to be Lacombe. The British are preparing to land at Bastia, which is only viable if your army occupies the French at Cardo.'

'You saw Buttafuco in secret negotiation,' Paoli said, raising his finger to indicate the need for precision.

'Yes.'

'And so you conclude it was he who failed to close the Teghima Pass?'

'He is a very senior commander,' Markham replied, unsure where this was leading. 'You could find out in an hour if his troops had the lead role in that affair.'

'And, no doubt, you will also deduce it was his men who murdered the marines at Fornali.' Paoli smiled slightly, then changed the subject slightly. 'You say you felt threatened at Cardo.'

'Yes,' Markham replied uneasily.

'Yet you go wandering through the camp, with only your sergeant as company, and just happen upon a secret meeting which is taking place beyond the perimeter of the bivouac. The guards posted to stop that happening are conveniently removed, a fact you only discover by chance. I think some people might say that either you are making this up, or that there is something more you have missed.'

'I did not make it up.'

'I believe you, Lieutenant. What I'm curious about is the identity of the man who led you to witness something you would never have been allowed to stumble upon unaided.'

Markham, feeling foolish, sensed that his mouth was open, but that he had no words to say. But Paoli hadn't finished speaking.

'And you say you did not hear any spoken exchanges, so you only have a visual impression of what was taking place.'

'You think I'm mistaken.'

'I don't know. But I wonder who wanted to send, through you, a message to me.' Paoli continued without waiting for him to reply, holding up the letter in his hand. 'You say Admiral Hood is unlikely to bluff. What is he like when it comes to apologies?'

Markham visibly shivered, even although he tried not to. 'I don't think it's something he enjoys, General.'

Paoli noticed his discomfort. 'I have kept you out here too long, and after such adventures. You must get some rest. My house is at your disposal.'

'And?' asked Markham, pointing at Hood's letter.

'A decision on that will wait a few hours.'

'Sir, Nelson lands in five days from now!'

'And I, young man, have ridden the length of Corsica twice in the same period. I understand

397

your impatience, but you must also take into consideration my concerns.'

'I must know, sir. If need be I am obliged to risk a fast horse back to San Fiorenzo to tell Admiral Hood.'

'Something which I would happily provide.'

Those words chilled, indicating that he'd probably failed. 'In a few hours, sir, perhaps Major Lanester will be here to help you decide.'

'Let us hope so.' He opened the door, ushering Markham in, an avuncular hand on his shoulder. 'I am glad that you were protected from that knife you so feared. Too many men have died by the blade in Corsica.'

Chapter twenty-eight

Bellamy was waiting for him, as instructed, holding open one of the white Corsican flags. He turned and grinned when Markham appeared, and pointed to the head of the Moor which was the main device. In profile, the black face, with one white eye, stood out sharply. Looking at it now made certain things obvious: the reaction of the citizens of San Fiorenzo in the Place de Chaumettes, when Bellamy'd saved him from assassination. Likewise the way Magdalena Calheri had taken a strip off her own shirt to bestow on him. The Corsican moor had a bandage round his head, and though blacker even than Bellamy, had a profile which was not dissimilar.

'Independent Corsica, Lieutenant,' said Calheri, emerging from the shadows. 'No cross of St George or Bourbon lilies, just the head of the Moor.'

Markham pointed towards the thin white line at the neck. 'Is that jewellery he's wearing, or the sign of decapitation?'

That jibe earned him another dose of Corsican folklore.

'It could be either. Ugo della Colonna defeated the Saracen King Nugalon at the Battle of Mariana. That was the first time we threw off a foreign yoke. My uncle chose it to symbolise the idea that, having been successful before, we could be so again.'

'You'd best be careful, Bellamy,' Markham replied. 'They might take their lucky talisman too far, and don't rely on a Corsican to be open about which alternative they'll choose.'

'You don't like us much, do you, Markham?'

She'd rarely used his name, sticking to black looks and his rank. Nor was the accusation delivered in a harsh way; if anything her voice contained a note of sorrow.

'I'm tired, hungry and cold, Commandatore.'

'I am waiting to escort you to my uncle's house.'

'Then please lead on.'

'What did you talk about?'

'You must ask him that,' Markham said.

That removed any trace of sympathy from her features. He then looked at Bellamy, sure that he'd related his part of the private conversations already. Markham was fed up with both of them: her coquetry, friendly one minute, angry the next; his playing to her moods, not to mention the endemic insubordination. Yet his sense of gallantry was too ingrained to leave matters there.

'I'm sure if General Paoli will tell anyone what we discussed, it will be you. His trust, as far as you're concerned, is almost as great as his justifiable pride.'

Did he detect a responsive tinge of rouge in her cheeks, or was it just a gust of wind, swinging the lantern light to deceive him?

'The house is in the square, if you will follow.'

The luxury of heat, to aching, tired and cold limbs, could not be exaggerated. Paoli had ordered a hip bath placed in his chamber, which was on the first floor of the general's residence – a tall building that looked tiny, until it was entered, and its true spacious dimensions were revealed. With a servant to pour the blissful hot water over him, Markham was as near to heaven as he could be.

Given the travails of the past few days, he fell asleep, that kind of deep slumber that was total, and very necessary to a soldier, who never knew when he would be called upon to fight. Woken by the water cooling, he felt distinctly refreshed, and any new chills were relieved by a rough towelling before a roaring fire. There was a razor, soap with which to lather, and a proper mirror. Clean linen had been laid out, and while he slept his breeches had been cleaned and his boots polished. 'Garry Owen' was in his mind again as he combed his hair, and tied it back with a black silk queue.

'Enter,' he said, in response to a soft knock.

The door opened to reveal a very different

400

Magdalena Calheri. No longer in uniform, with the blue-black silky hair brushed out, her appearance was transformed. He spent so much time staring at her face that it was an age before he could take in the clothes she wore; blue lace over orange silk, cut low to reveal a smooth olive neck and bosom. Over one arm she had a scarlet coat, which looked distinctly military.

'I was hoping it would be a message from your uncle,' he said, before he realised how dismissive that sounded. What he added had a lame quality. 'With news, perhaps, of Major Lanester.'

'We have no information regarding the major as yet. My uncle, however, is on his way to eat with us.' Then she held up the coat. 'He wondered if you'd consent to wear this, Lieutenant. It was presented to him while he was in London by King George's First Regiment of Foot Guards. They gave him an honorary commission.'

Markham took it off her by the collar, and let it fall open. It was outdated, of course, a uniform more tailored to the American War than the present day. But it induced an odd sensation. As a youngster in New York, surrounded by glittering officers, he'd wanted a coat like this more than anything. The Irish in him longed for a cavalry regiment, but the romantic saw the Foot Guards as the very pinnacle of British military prowess. Their officers were richer, grander, wittier and braver than anyone. Just the place for an impressionable boy.

It had been one of the experiences that taught the foundling out of Ireland exactly where he stood in the wider world. The First Regiment of

Foot Guards would eat at his father's table; they would drink his wine and laugh at his jokes, even accept hints from the rough old General that led to pecuniary advantage. But nothing would induce them to grant a commission to Sir John Markham's bastard son.

'I'd be delighted,' he replied. There was no choice, regardless of bad memories. General Paoli had made a kind gesture, one he must accept.

'Then put it on, Markham,' she said, 'I have never seen you in anything other than your shirt, or that horrible French thing.'

The swish of the silk lining slipping over his body was matched by the sound of her breathing, audible even above the crackling fire. He looked at her breasts, rising and falling in the tight bodice, pleased to see that the rate of movement hinted a degree of excitement.

'It suits you, the scarlet. Please hurry, the food will be ready in a matter of minutes.'

The way she was dressed, the meal would no doubt be formal, and he felt guilty. There was no time for this. On leaving San Fiorenzo he had thought the span he and Lanester were allowed for their task to be tight, and the major's attitudes had eaten into that long before the misfortune of meeting Fouquert. Now it was getting very close to a crisis: Lanester still missing, Paoli dithering and Nelson already under sail, his warships and transports crammed with troops and equipment.

There was a desperate desire to move matters on, to insist on a conclusion. But that, he knew, was an emotion he'd had in the past, especially before a battle. To say he'd learned to control it would be an exaggeration. But at least he'd come to recognise the fact, so that he could try to convince himself that certain things were beyond his control. This was one of those occasions, and all he could do was make the next hour pleasant for all concerned. So he held out his arm, smiling.

'Then, Commandatore Calheri, the most beautiful officer I've ever served with, you would do me great honour by allowing me to escort you to the table.'

'Delighted, sir,' she replied, curtsying just enough to draw his eyes to her cleavage.

But he was all innocence by the time she rose again, and she slipped her hand chastely over his red sleeve. Both kept a respectful distance as they exited the room and made their way down the hall to the top of the wide staircase. But decorum was no proof against elemental force, and George Markham felt as if his body had been invaded by some rushing demon, which seemed able to ebb and flow from him to her and back again, through that very slight point of contact.

'My dear, you look wonderful,' said Paoli. His eyes flicked to Markham, causing him to smile. 'And you, Lieutenant, look ten times the warrior I ever did in that coat.'

Eboluh Bellamy was standing at a respectful distance, as well dressed as Markham, but in civilian clothes. The plum-coloured coat and yellow waistcoat suited him admirably, since he had the necessary air of insouciance to carry it off. Catching his officer's eye, he favoured him with an elegant bow, one that only lacked an eyeglass in his hand to turn him from marine private into salon rake.

'I dressed Bellamy in this fashion,' added Paoli, 'so that you would not feel discomfort sharing a table with him.'

'I'm most obliged to you, sir,' Markham replied, taking a step on to the first tread, certain that there was nothing else he could reply. But the look he gave Bellamy was singular, and noted. It said behave yourself; no gabbling or showing off, and no attempt to play the wise man while casting me as the fool.

The next two hours had a surreal quality, as if outside the four walls of the house, all was harmony. At least he wasn't subjected to a repeat of the dinner at Cardo. Paoli had an urbanity that his generals totally lacked, and a breadth of interests that seemed to span the whole cosmos. He had, in his time, met or corresponded with all the leading figures of the age. Rousseau, Voltaire, Davy Hume, Burke, both the Elder and Younger Pitts, even Markham's old commander, the Czarina, Catherine of Russia.

Bellamy tried to cap him by mentioning Mozart, Haydn, Schiller, Kant, Washington and Jefferson, only to find that Paoli knew them too. He had more luck with Boswell, the man who'd brought Corsica and its leader to world notice. Bellamy'd shared his company, and no doubt his fondness for drink, on more than one occasion, but was astute enough to draw a veil over his whoring. To move on to Johnson was inevitable, and the great lexicographer was dissected sympathetically.

'Did he not say, Uncle, that you had the greatest

404

port of any man he'd ever met?' exclaimed Magdalena who, having drunk glass for glass with the men, was in a very alluring mood.

'He did indeed, my dear,' Paoli replied, before adding modestly, 'That is, according to Boswell. But I think it was Lanester who warned me, in quite an amusing fashion, that one must have a care with Doctor Samuel Johnson.'

'He was acquainted with the doctor?'

'He was,' Paoli replied, 'quite a man about the town after his ejection from North America. He was a seeker after pleasure, his chief love being conversation. I used to chide him for his love of the tavern, which was only surpassed by his addiction to the salon and the card table. I daresay you have Boswell in common, as an acquaintance.'

'Odd that I never came across him,' Bellamy said, 'either by name or reputation.'

'The revolution in France changed him, a subject on which we had our greatest disagreement. I freely admit that I did not foresee the Terror.'

'And the major did?'

'Not in precise terms. But he knew, from his own past, that revolutions eat their own children.'

'Hardly amusing,' said Magdalena.

'No. But he also informed me that for every compliment Sam Johnson throws out, he has a pair of barbs to go with them.'

A female servant emerged from behind a screen and, with a shy bob to the master, came up behind Magdalena's chair to whisper in her ear. She immediately looked at her uncle and said, 'Gianfranco.' Paoli nodded and waved his hand.

Standing up, she proffered an apology. 'Forgive me. My youngest child.'

Markham was nodding sympathetically, wondering why he had assumed Magdalena to be unattached. She must have a whole tribe of children, if this Gianfranco was the youngest. That in turn meant a husband somewhere.

'The boy has dreams,' said Paoli, indicating to an attendant that he should pour more wine. 'Bad ones, full of blood, which is a sadness in one so young.'

'How many children does Magdalena have?'

'Three, all with her beauty.'

'Of course,' Markham replied.

'The two girls will need careful watching, or they will start a blood feud by the attention they command. I would have sent them abroad for their education, but times do not permit of such luxuries.'

'They could go to England, sir,' said Bellamy.

Paoli smiled again. 'I wish to tame their wild natures, Mr Bellamy, not freeze them to the marrow.'

'The boy's dreams, does he have them often?' asked Markham.

'Every time he has visions of his father, my nephew, Luciano.' The old man's eyes suddenly became watery, as though the memory had the same effect on him. 'He died saving me, old, weary and useless Pasquale Paoli, which was a very foolish thing for a young man to do. Especially one who would have risen to be a leader to his country.'

Neither guest spoke. They just sat and watched

as the tears began to run down the general's cheeks. 'There are many joys to a celibate life, gentlemen; the suppression of jealousy, the time to pursue great causes. But to lack an heir, which seems so unimportant at thirty, becomes a sad gap at forty, and a positive curse in old age.'

'You say he died saving you?' asked Markham.

'Did I not say to you, Lieutenant, that too many of my fellow countrymen have died by the knife? Luciano was one such. An enemy wanted me removed so, in time-honoured fashion, an assassin was employed. Magdalena's husband distracted him from his task, and paid the price instead of me.'

'I take it the son was there?' Bellamy inquired.

'He saw his father die.'

Whatever General Paoli had been going to say next was killed off by Magdalena's return. She moved into the candlelight which filled the table, with Markham looking at her in a new way. The mood of the gathering had changed as a result of her absence, though it wasn't gloomy, just more introspective as they discussed how and why the bright hopes of liberty had died in France. Paoli, with his long political experience, knew the faults of men in the public eye, the way some competed to be holier than their neighbours, losing the capacity to forgive in the process.

'I thought of going to France after my benefactor died,' said Bellamy, 'believing for a moment that my situation in such a society would be improved.'

'It would have been under the Bourbons, sir,' Paoli replied, 'though I hate to credit kings for

407

anything. But not under the Revolution.'

'How can people lose sight, so badly, of their cause?'

Paoli leant forward. 'Is it St Francis Loyola given great power, gentlemen, or the Inquisition applied to government. Robespierre and his friends, like flagellant Jesuits, vie with each other to prove that their brand of revolutionary purity is the most sincere. And in order to establish, with the mob, that their care for the rights of man are correct and paramount, they kill even more human beings than their rivals.'

That mention of the founder of the Jesuits made Markham think of Fouquert, and at the same time Lanester's incisive identification of that trait in the Frenchman. Yet he thought Fouquert different. His stand on killing contained less hypocrisy than that of people like Robespierre and St Just. They did it at arm's length, for political advantage. He did it close to, for pure pleasure.

'I have made you all sad talking of this,' said Paoli.

They all murmured negatively, denying what was palpably true. The conversation had driven them all to their own unpleasant thoughts: Magdalena about the corruption brought on by the search for power, Bellamy of a world that despised him, and Markham imagining Fouquert at work.

'It is my habit to take a turn around the square,' said Paoli, 'to breathe some air after eating.'

Magdalena smiled. 'A filthy English custom.'

'Which I acquired while a guest in English houses,' her uncle replied, in a way that firmly

408

labelled the exchange as a family joke. 'When I insisted that I continue it in London, my friends forbade it, saying crime was too rife.'

'They were right, sir,' said Markham, who had lived in the middle of the metropolis himself, and was well aware of the number of villains it housed.

Bellamy cut in. 'Was it not Horace Walpole who opined that it was safer to take ship to Gibraltar in wartime, than to cross London after dark for dinner with a friend?'

'I presume Corte is safer than that?' said Markham.

'Much safer,' said Paoli, standing up.

He let Paoli and Bellamy get ahead on purpose, pleased that Magdalena kept pace with him. In front they could see the Negro, who had drunk more than anyone at the table, gesticulating away as he made some histrionic point. The general seemed perfectly content just to listen, while he aimed an occasional nod at his fellow citizens. They were discussing the value of an Erastian Church set against the central rule of Rome, which was a subject that would have bored Markham rigid, even if he'd had Medusa on his arm.

It was impossible not to treat Magdalena differently. Here was no unkissed maiden, all a flutter at physical contact. She was a mother and had been a wife.

'Your son is better?'

'He is asleep again.' Markham took a fraction off the distance between them, one that she made no attempt to restore. 'That is not difficult when I am here. But when I am absent, he does suffer for his visions. Gianfranco thinks he will not live if I am not there to comfort him. He thinks his father will come back and kill him.'

It was impossible to mistake the bitter note in her voice, nor the surprise in his when he responded. 'His father?'

'We were in Bonifacio. My uncle was doing everything in his power not to invade Sardinia, while making the kind of bellicose noises that keep the more ardent souls happy. That was not a strategy which fooled people for long, especially the Buonapartes.'

'They tried to kill your uncle?'

It was her turn to close the gap further, by taking a tighter grip on his arm. 'In Corsica, Markham, things are never that simple. You must often guard against your professed friends, as well as your obvious enemies. Whatever, the assassin came, and got within feet of Paoli. My husband tore Gianfranco from my arms – he was but two at the time – and threw him at the knife to distract the assassin.' That brought forth a sharp intake of breath from Markham, and by now he was close enough to feel her shaking at the memory. 'The man was a murderer, but he had compassion, or perhaps a son of his own. He moved the knife aside just enough to spare Gianfranco. Then my husband went for him.'

'And died.'

'In great pain, Markham,' she spat. 'But not great enough.'

She was trembling from head to foot. He span her round and pushed her gently into the deep shadow formed by the flying buttress of a church, pulling her body close to his so that she could rest her head on his shoulder, whispering in her ear, his lips close enough to make contact.

'You mustn't,' she gasped eventually.

'Wrong,' he growled.

It took all her strength to push him away, but she managed, then slipped past him until she was on the other side, back in full daylight. 'I cannot, ever, have another man.'

'What?' he said, genuinely surprised.

The words tumbled out, garbled by her confusion: of brothers who would kill anyone who touched her; of her husband's family, still addicts of the vendetta, who would knife him for an inappropriate sideways glance.

'What you're telling me, Magdalena, is this. That if I try to take liberties with you, I'll gain myself some enemies.'

'Deadly enemies!'

'Jesus, girl,' he replied, 'I've got dozens of those already. A few more won't faze me.'

She got him walking again, the distance restored between them and her uncle. 'You must not even look at me so. I would remind you I'm living in my uncle's house.'

'I wasn't planning to ask him for anything.'

'The servants,' she replied.

Markham needed no further explanation. When it came to improper liaisons, he'd had more trouble with servants than he'd ever had with their mistresses, or the husbands of the house for that matter. Nothing could happen under their roof that they didn't know about. And it wasn't just a case of relying on one or two. You had to trust them all, right down to the lowest kitchen skivvy who scrubbed the sheets.

Paoli's voice floated across the square, asking them if they'd had enough. Markham's response was whispered to himself.

'Holy mother of Christ, we haven't had any.'

Chapter twenty-nine

Any attempt to pin down Paoli regarding his intentions was swept to one side, politely but firmly, and once back in his room and feeling the effects of good wine, Markham soon succumbed once more to the need for sleep. The bells of the church woke him, great pealing strokes that called the workers from their toil and the faithful to their evening prayers. The last of the sun had faded outside, and he thought he could hear, faintly, the sounds of sentinels calling to each other.

It was nice to lie there, warm, imagining Magdalena's body under the same sheets, perhaps lying with her back to him, until that became too uncomfortable and he threw himself out onto the wooden floor. There was no fire in the grate and the room was chilly. So was the water in the jug, which was refreshing.

Few people can resist the sound of marching boots, and certainly no soldier. He threw on his breeches and the scarlet coat, and dashed out into the hallway. There was a shuttered window, and it opened on to the square before the National As-

412

sembly building. The torches lining the portico revealed Rannoch and his Lobsters marching towards it, packs on their backs. A shout made them halt, and once he was out of the door he was presented with a disgruntled group of men covered in dust.

'I take it you've been marching all day, Sergeant?'

'Most of it, sir,' Rannoch replied bitterly, 'only to find the bastards would not open the gates after sunset to let us in.'

'Did they expect you to spend the whole night out there?'

'They did. Under the walls, freezing our parts off. If I had possessed my own musket, I would have shot the sentry.'

Markham, suffering from some degree of guilt, noticed that all his men were eyeing the scarlet coat, the braid of which picked up the torchlight. It was Rannoch who voiced the question, which had undertones of perfectly understandable resentment.

'Had a bit of good fortune in the promotion line, sir?'

'A loan, Rannoch. I'm not a Foot Guards colonel, it's just that they don't like French coats round here.'

'Nor British marines, it seems.'

'Follow me. I'll see about a billet and some food.'

At that moment Eboluh Bellamy appeared, still wearing the plum-coloured coat and yellow waistcoat. He didn't look quite as grand as he had earlier, since his clothes were somewhat creased,

413

and his face looked puffy and pale, if you could say that about a black man. Markham had left him at the table, very close to the port bottle, and it looked as though he'd indulged himself.

'Holy Christ,' said Rannoch, 'would you look at that black bastard.'

The way his men were looking at him, Markham knew he was close to forfeiting whatever trust he'd built up these last months. The prejudice against Bellamy was widespread, his manner multiplying the feelings about his race. To men who had just spent an uncomfortable day on the road, the sight of him, clearly the worse for drink, dressed like a gent, was infuriating.

'Bellamy,' Markham barked, with a slight feeling of shame. 'Get that damned kit off and rejoin the unit.'

The 'sir' was slow and slurred, partly by drink, but as much by confusion. What had happened to that amusing companion of the meal? Then he observed the hate emanating from the rest of the men, and that made him scurry to comply.

'Where's Major Lanester?' asked Markham suddenly.

'They couldn't find a trace, sir. Major Lanester has disappeared.'

Markham organised food and a billet for his men, and sent a message to General Paoli requesting an immediate interview. The news of Lanester bothered him deeply, but he was at a loss to know what to do about it. He lacked both time and any knowledge of the terrain to go searching for him. But he'd ordered Rannoch to return when he was ready to do so, and give him more details of what had occurred.

Fed and warm in the general's kitchen, Rannoch told his tale. First the scrawny carter had turned up at dawn, empty-handed. He had been about to set out himself when the Corsicans sent by Paoli turned up. Given their greater mobility it made sense to let them go to the monastery. This they did, only to find no sign of Lanester or Pavin. A search of the surroundings produced no trace either, so they'd returned to San Quilici Rocci. Rannoch, on his own initiative, knowing that his officer would want to be informed, had upped sticks and marched out.

'Had I known what mean-spirited swine I would have to deal with, I would have stayed where I was, or at least brought those cavalrymen back with us.'

'They didn't even come and tell me,' Markham replied, his mind full of images of Lanester and Pavin swinging from the branch of some tree.

'That would be because they denied your exist-ence, if I understood one word in ten of what they said.'

'Did you mention Commandatore Calheri?'

'I did. All that produced was laughter and ribaldry.'

'I thought you didn't understand them?'

'The laugh produced by men slighting women is the same the world over.'

Markham's anger on her behalf was deflected by the way Rannoch suddenly looked over his shoul-der, and shot to his feet, which made his officer turn round. Paoli, dressed in civilian clothes and

415

looking very benign, stood in the doorway smiling. It was a testimony to his presence that the Highlander, who often had to be dragged to his feet in front of most British officers, had spotted right away that this man deserved his respect.

'Lieutenant.'

'Sir. Allow me to introduce Sergeant Rannoch.'

Paoli stepped forward. He was a tall man, but he still had to look up into the Scotsman's eyes. 'You fought on the Morosaglia trail, sergeant?'

'I did, sir!'

The General held out his hand, showing a fine sensitivity to the nature of United Kingdom politics. 'Then I shall thank you in the British manner, and shake you by the hand.'

Rannoch grasped the outstretched limb and shook it, his eyes open more than usual, evidence of his surprise. 'You will have brought Major Lanester to us.'

'No, sir,' Markham replied, before passing on Rannoch's explanation. A cloud descended immediately over Paoli's features, a clear indication of deep distress. It was one Markham only partially shared, but he spoke to reassure the General.

'He was a soldier, sir, as we are, and took a soldier's risks.'

'That may explain a loss, Lieutenant. It does not, however alleviate it.'

'Major Lanester may be safe, sir. Indeed he may well have decided to return to San Fiorenzo and expand upon the despatch he sent Admiral Hood.'

'Which one was that?' Paoli asked, absentmindedly.

'After Cardo, sir, and what we had seen.' That got the General's attention, and as he continued Markham found himself looking into the old man's penetrating blue eyes. 'We felt that Admiral Hood should be apprised of any information we had.'

For the first time since meeting Paoli, Markham was exposed to the rod of steel that upheld that elderly frame. It was hardly surprising it was there. No man without it could have even begun to tame the Corsicans. But it stood as testimony to his skill with people that it was so well concealed.

'You did not tell me of this?'

'I'm sorry, General. I took it for granted that you would guess.'

'It is my fault, Lieutenant, for not inquiring,' Paoli replied, managing to look as though he meant it. 'But what you and Lanester have done is a mistake. Can you tell me precisely what the Major said?'

'No sir. I told him what I saw, he wrote the despatch and we sent it off, in a sealed packet, with three marines.'

'How far did they have to travel?'

'A day's march, perhaps more than that if the terrain was rough.'

'And they left you when?'

'Four days ago.'

Paoli sucked in a great quantity of air, which he released slowly. 'We must leave at once, Lieutenant.'

'Why, sir?'

'Because the situation is grave.'

'You think Admiral Hood will withdraw?'

417

The reply, given Paoli's habitual behaviour, was quite sharp. 'No! I told you he was bluffing. But from what little I know of Hood he is strong-willed. He may act on that information and precipitate a crisis.'

'Surely, sir, if he acts on what we have told him he will avert one. General Buttafuco will at least be neutralised.'

'He will condemn an innocent man, and in doing so he will allow the true traitor to flourish.'

'Buttafuco is innocent?' asked Markham with disbelief.

'If Arsenio has taken French gold, and sought to betray us, I hope God sends a plague to rid this island of all human life. I know of no man more patriotic than him.'

'Then what was he doing talking to the French?'

'That is not the real question, Lieutenant Markham.'

'Well what is?'

'I have already told you. Why were you allowed to see him doing so? Whoever arranged that will be the real traitor. How soon can your men be ready to march?'

Markham looked at Rannoch, whose opinion was likely to be more accurate than his own. As usual, in what appeared to be a crisis, the Highlander answered slowly.

'We have no coats, your honour, and we have returned the guns and ammunition.'

'Given those?'

'We are ready as soon as you want to leave.'

'Lieutenant, organise your men while I find my niece. I will get her to take you to armoury and

418

see you fully equipped.'

'Do you have any British weapons there, sir?' asked Rannoch.

'Twenty stands of Brown Bess muskets, Sergeant, with bayonets and cartridges.'

Paoli turned to leave, but Rannoch wasn't finished with him. 'From which manufactuary, your honour?'

'Birmingham.'

'Hirst and Waller?'

'You know your guns, Sergeant.'

'It helps me survive, sir.'

Markham, still slightly shocked, suddenly returned to the real world. 'Clothing, General Paoli.'

'Will have to be Corsican, since we have no others to provide.'

'Do we march for San Fiorenzo?'

'No, Lieutenant. We go to Aleria, which is on the east coast.' He could see the question in Markham's eyes, and paused just long enough to stretch his eagerness to know. 'In that despatch you brought, Admiral Hood offered me a ship to save time. There is a Royal Navy sloop at Aleria, waiting to take me to where I need to be.'

Paoli turned to leave, but Markham's voice stopped him. 'I have to know, General, would you have undertaken this journey without that despatch?'

'I cannot say, Lieutenant.'

'Why?'

'Because I do not know the answer.'

They were back through the gates within two hours, Paoli ahead on his horse. Magdalena was

419

Commandatore Calheri once more, in breeches and short dark jacket, with a carbine over her shoulders, Markham's troops, dressed in the same uniform, marching along behind. It had been a disappointment to the marine officer when the General designated his niece's female soldiers as his main escort, instead of the male garrison of Corte. His men, however, were as pleased as punch. Some of them had even got a smile as the two groups formed up, and harboured high hopes of turning those shy grins into something more substantial before the journey was completed.

Aleria was straight down the valley of the River Tavigiano, which twisted along a valley floor hemmed in by huge mountains, the foothills coated with the inevitable *maccia*. As they marched the old man was able to relive the battle they'd fought on the Morosaglia trail. The details of the action produced cries of wonder from his lips, with an inordinate amount of praise bestowed on his niece and her troopers. It was an indication of how struck the Lobsters were with the idea of rogering the lot of them that they didn't resent this.

'Uncle, we must move further into the forest,' Magdalena said, on one of the frequent stops.

'Of course, my dear.'

'Lieutenant,' she said stiffly, 'please ensure that your men stay on the road.'

Markham just nodded, and watched them file down a path, looking for a place private enough to double as a latrine. 'Why don't we stop in the towns?'

'Two reasons, Lieutenant,' the old man replied.

'I cannot enter any Corsican municipality without being afforded a reception. Given that, I have to stay and show that the hospitality is welcome. To show gratitude, in other words. Speeches are called for, drink is consumed and if I am not there till after dark, insult is taken.'

'Which means you cannot travel fast enough?'

'Nor discreetly enough. The camp at Cardo would know of my coming before I had gone twenty miles.' Markham opened his mouth to speak, then hesitated. The old man gave him that knowing, sometimes infuriating smile. 'You have something you wish to say?'

'Yes. Bellamy was told, in no uncertain terms, that there were traitors active in Corte. What is to stop one of them using the road, which is a faster route even if it is longer, to get to Cardo before us?'

'The gates of Corte were shut behind us, young man. The garrison, which I think you would have been happier to bring along with us...'

'I ... em...' stuttered Markham.

'I saw your face when they formed up. Magdalena you welcome, and I will not inquire why. But her soldiers.'

'I didn't know it was that obvious.'

'If a little self-regard may be allowed, I have trained myself to observe men's moods. I have had to hone that skill in order to survive. I think that I was the only one who noticed. Anyway, the garrison will keep those gates shut, and patrol the walls to ensure that no one leaves without declaring themselves.'

'Is that protection enough?'

'Probably not. I regret to say that the society of this island is not like that.'

'Whatever possessed you, sir, to form female units?' Markham asked.

'We are short of men, a situation made more acute by the actions of clans like the Buonapartes. Our women are fighters, Lieutenant. Don't ever make the mistake of seeing them as lesser mortals.'

'Certainly not in the *maccia*. They use their knifes well. But in open battle?'

'They will fight, Lieutenant. And what makes you think, anyway, that we face a battle?'

'There were French dragoons close to here two days ago. And whatever precautions you have taken, news of your journey is bound to leak out.'

'True. But those who might betray us will be informed that we are on our way to Ajaccio, to confront the Buonapartes.'

'They would have watched us heading down the Tavigiano valley.'

Paoli smiled. 'And assumed a bluff. This is a double bluff.'

Markham had to smile too. This old man might be serene and celibate, but he was also one of the most devious sods that George Markham had ever met. Not that he thought they could relax. An accidental encounter with French cavalry was always possible, the risk increasing the closer they got to the coast. When Magdalena returned he tried to engage her in conversation. But she shied away from him, her look having none of the warmth of the previous night.

'Right,' he barked, 'on your feet, let's get moving.'

The sound of Bellamy groaning, loud and clear, cheered him up a little, and putting him on point restored some of his lost prestige with his men.

'Yelland, you go with him. Sergeant, two men to drop back, muskets loaded, fire off if anything troubles them.'

'I think I know of just the pair,' he replied, and the moaning from Quinlan and Ettrick that followed testified to who he'd chosen. It wasn't the duty that bothered them so much as being separated from the two women they had their eye on.

'That moon-faced one with the bit of a 'tache has been giving me come-on eye, and no error,' said Ettrick. 'So none of you sods so much as look her way, do you hear?'

'Trust you to pick the ugliest one,' replied Dymock.

'You stick to your slim beauties, mate, and you'll be glued to your right hand when it's dark. Not like me. I'll be cosy, and with a face like that, she'll be grateful.'

Tully waited till they fell back before speaking. 'Hey, Dornan, I reckon that one with that black hair on her lips has a likin' for you.'

Dornan searched the line of women, until he located the one Tully meant. Then he smiled, and flushed when the woman responded.

'See, what'd I tell you?'

'Typical,' hooted Gibbons, 'All that mooning to Ettrick and as soon as he's gone he's a cuckold, the hairy strumpet.'

'Wait till he finds out it's a man,' crooned Leech.

'Will you lot belay,' growled Halsey.

'Just 'cause your nuts are dried out, Corps, don't mean ours are.'

Halsey grinned at Leech. 'Said like a man who wants to stand two watches tonight.'

'I take it back, Halsey,' Leech replied. 'You've got the bollocks of a bull.'

The women didn't march like that, constantly exchanging insults. They weren't exactly silent, but they tended to speak in low undertones, exchanging small smiles rather than broad grins and jokes. Markham was up with Paoli and his niece, still trying to rekindle some of the previous intimacy, and failing miserably. He prayed it was the presence of her troopers that made her so distant, and that she'd melt a little once they reached their bivouac.

Chapter thirty

Their destination, Aleria, was thirty miles away. It could, by forced marching, be made in one day, but they had set out in the small hours of the morning and marched all day and now, having reached the flat coastal plain, with the sun dipping behind the mountains, Markham insisted on a halt. To keep going didn't, to him, make sense. Marching in darkness, even moonlight, was a murderous business, and he took pains to remind Paoli that this was a military escort, which had to be able to fight should they come across an unexpected enemy.

Naturally, the old man was in a hurry, fearful that events might have moved on to a crisis point. They'd avoided towns of any size all along the route, even skirting villages where they could, a wise precaution since every time they were obliged to pass through some hamlet, the inhabitants, old and young, came out to touch the Liberator's hem. That provided another cause for haste; the certainty that news of his presence would travel round the countryside like wildfire, and not always to the ears of people that esteemed him.

Fully equipped now, both units set up camp some six miles from the east coast, with a stream in the middle, a tributary of the Tavigiano, just deep enough to discourage casual crossing. The food was prepared by Calheri's troopers, which was a blessing, there being not a man in Markham's unit who could do anything but drop whatever came to hand in hot water or spit-roast it. Paoli, Markham and Magdalena ate together, which helped to thaw her attitude somewhat. The old General seemed to relish the hardship of sleeping in a tent, regaling them with tales of past campaigns. Because he listed all the things which had gone wrong, entirely due to his failure as a military commander, he was extremely amusing, rather than repetitively tedious.

'Every time I was put at the head of the army, I was amazed we got to where we were going, never mind fought a battle. Luckily, my brother was another Sanpiero Corsa, so I left all that side of things to him, and stuck to preaching the virtues of freedom.'

'What do you regret, Uncle?' Magdalena asked suddenly.

The answer was quick and typical. 'The enemies I've made, whom I would rather have had as friends. The affections I have squandered, so that I have lost the love of another human being through what appears to be arrogance, which is just, instead, idleness.'

'How can you say you are idle after such a life, sir?'

'With great ease. As a general I fought a war without hardship, safe in the distance issuing stirring commands. Did I stay here and face the sanctions of the victorious Bourbons? No! I fled to London and lived on a royal pension. I should have been like that Scottish hero Boswell told me of, "the Bruce", and taken to a cave to keep up the struggle.'

Paoli paused for a moment, some of the pain of the years of struggle evident in his expression. Then he smiled suddenly, and added, 'Children, Magdalena! I certainly envy you your children.'

'I wonder, Lieutenant?' she asked suddenly, 'whether you would object to marching under our flag tomorrow. It would be pleasant to parade into Aleria under the Moor.'

'I would be delighted,' Markham replied, pleased that their relations had thawed enough to permit the request. 'And might I add, I have just the man to carry it.'

Paoli gave a poorly disguised yawn, apologised for it, then said, 'Riding tires me now. In the old days I used to live in the saddle.'

Magdalena reached over and touched his face,

426

with a tenderness that made Markham envious. 'Then rest, Uncle.'

They both left his tent, and to Markham's surprise it was she who suggested that they walk down the riverbank. Though it was encouraging, he sensed that being tactile would be a mistake, so he kept his hands firmly clasped behind his back.

'It is pleasant being out here, Markham.'

'I've done too much campaigning. Give me a warm bed any day.'

She stopped suddenly and turned to face him. 'What is it you are offering me, Markham?'

Wisdom, or at least advantage, dictated he lie. And asked a variation of the same question by other women, many times, that was precisely what he'd done. There had been the odd miscalculation, but in the main the deceit or self-delusion had been mutual, and any wounds easily salved. But he knew, instinctively, that he could not lie to her. Quite simply, it was not what she wanted. But he took his time, and they were close to the tree-lined bank of the Tavigiano before he finally responded.

'The honest answer, Magdalena, would be nothing. I'm a penniless bastard with nothing more than a marine lieutenant's pay. My prospects are dismal. And tomorrow, or the day after, I could be put aboard a ship bound for India, the West Indies or the frozen North.'

'I have little actual experience of this. But is it not usual for a prospective lover to talk of the future, to paint dreams?'

'Let me be your lover and you can have all the dreams you want.'

'But that is all they will be.'

He stopped and so did she. 'Yes.'

She set off again. They were in the trees now, getting further and further away from the camp, and the fires that lit it.

'In Corsica, they stone women who are unfaithful to their husbands.'

'You are a widow.'

'It still applies. I am supposed to don black and mourn till I die.'

'You're not that type.'

'I may have to be. Luciano's family will never consent to my marrying into another clan, and I will never accept one of his cousins as a husband. On the other hand, my brothers will kill anyone, including a foreigner, who even looks at me outside wedlock.'

'Then you are in for an unhappy life.'

'How often, Markham, will I get the chance to have a little joy with someone, when it can do me no harm?'

'Which is why you asked your uncle what he regretted.'

He pushed her against a tree, but it required no strength, and as he leant against her Magdalena's hand went inside his short coat, pulling at the shirt so she could get to his skin.

What followed was brutish, noisy and short, and very beautiful for all that.

Markham had gone to bed happy, and woke even more so. Whatever the reasons that persuaded Paoli to make for Cardo, the result would be the same. And with two full days to spare, and a Royal

428

Navy sloop waiting to make the short journey up the coast, he could be sure that the old general would be on hand when Nelson came ashore. Wetting his finger, he felt the wind, but then dismissed that as no problem. Cardo was close enough for the Navy to row them to a point on the nearby shore.

It soon occurred to him that he and Magdalena had not been the only couple to take advantage of the opportunities presented by a night in the open. Judging by the number of nudges and winks, plus the sudden silences when he approached, the Corsican notion of inviolable chastity was a bit threadbare. Breakfast, when the two groups came together to eat, was, for the first time, full of laughter and shared jokes. Not that they could talk much, but sign language sufficed to produce the kind of endless giggling that hinted at shared intimacy.

'See if you can get this lot into some form of order, Sergeant.'

'Sir,' Rannoch responded, with a grin. The Highlander's own eyes were bleary, though whether that was from overnight excursions, or futile attempts to put a stop to them, wasn't clear. 'We are like the moorland stags at a certain time of year, are we not?'

Markham didn't really want to reply to that, considering what he and Magdalena had done was very close to rutting. He hoped that was a secret, though the way Bellamy had looked at him at first light left the notion open to doubt. And he was still on edge since, satisfying as it had been, it served to whet rather than satiate his appetite.

And here they were within a few hours of the port of Aleria. Once they were inside that town all the passion which had surfaced last night would have to be suppressed, and when Paoli took ship for Cardo or San Fiorenzo, Markham would go with him.

The camp was struck before the sun tipped the horizon and they were on their way, along a wide track that ran alongside the river. Here on the flat coastal plain this was no torrent, rather a meandering watercourse, without either drama or much in the way of scenery, if you excluded the numerous clumps of trees. After two hours, with the sun still low, the first buildings came into view, a cluster consisting of a dilapidated barn next to a farmhouse. This induced mixed emotions. Most longed for rest, the lucky ones from the previous night instead ached for a bit more time.

'Cavalry!' said Rannoch, pointing a few degrees off north, to the opposite bank of the Tavigiano.

'I thought you said this was a secret, General?' asked Markham. 'How many people did you tell?'

'None,' Paoli replied. 'I told you that I hinted I was on my way to Ajaccio.'

'That's on the south-west coast.' That produced an arched and disdainful eyebrow at the superfluous comment. 'And we left heading east.'

Paoli smiled, though the situation that confronted them hardly warranted it. 'I am held to be a devious old fox, prone to subterfuge. Obviously, Lieutenant, that is not as true as I supposed.'

Either someone had read Paoli's hand, or this

430

was just bad luck. He couldn't avoid his fame, and nor could he help it if there was a French cavalry patrol close enough to pick up rumours of his passing. He could see them himself now, riding hard, sending up a great trail of dust to their rear.

It was as if they'd ordered up special low-morning sun to light their breastplates, and knowing it was coming had applied enough polish to blind anyone looking in their direction. A line of heavy horse some forty in number, within half an hour they'd forded the river and were lined up across the road back to Corte. Arranged in close order, they were patently ready for action, and just waiting for the small force before them, who'd gained as much distance as they could, to attempt to run.

Markham had spent the time looking around at the flat landscape, before ending up in a small tree-filled copse, a mixture of pines and live oaks. Clumps like this were dotted here and there at intervals, wooded areas into which he could retire to break up a charge. But they ended long before the town, which lay on a flat, dried-out marshland estuary. The ground close to Aleria provided no cover for a good mile. To stay put and fight in the trees might make the cavalry cautious. But to proceed, and get caught in the open, would give them no place to mount a defence against a determined charge, even from horses that had already been ridden hard.

'Quinlan, up a tree, and see if you can spot the masts of a warship in the harbour.'

'Tree-climbing?' Sharland hooted. 'Job for the black man, that!'

431

The reaction to that surprised Markham. Instead of a general murmur of agreement, or a laugh at his feeble joke, Sharland got quite a few angry looks. Quinlan, meanwhile, helped by Ettrick, had got high enough on a live oak to reach the lower branches. He shinned up from there at speed, until he reached a point where the wood bent with his weight.

'Can't see much for the buildings, your honour. There's boats, but I take leave to doubt there's a mast in the place big enough to be a sloop.'

Markham anxiously wetted his finger again, until he recalled his ignorance of matters nautical. But, subject to tide and wind, the boat could easily be late. The decision was a difficult one, but the object was simple. They had to get Paoli into Aleria, then keep the French out so that the ship could come in and pick him up. Whoever stayed out in the open was going to risk a great deal, yet sufficient force had to be left to defend the town until the old man's transport arrived.

'Commandatore, leave everything but your weapons and water bottles. We will form line here until you are two hundred paces back. Then we would like you to give us something to fall back on.'

'Can we not stand and fight them?'

It was Paoli who answered, pointing downriver to the low, sun-bleached buildings of the unwalled port, dominated, like every other Corsican town, by the church tower.

'We must get to Aleria, and they will know that to be our destination. To fight heavy cavalry in the open is difficult for a small force. How can we

432

present an unbroken front and no flank? We are too few for that.'

'Then why retire? We might as well fight them here.'

Markham smiled, thinking that she was a beautiful woman, a passionate and exciting lover, but a lousy soldier without a forest to work in.

'When they charge, we will try to slow them down by musketry. If we can put a check on their advance, then we can run for your line, then you can do the same, repeating the manoeuvre to gain ground. If the man in command is not the type to sustain casualties we might just get you close to the outskirts of the port without loss. At that point you can run for cover.'

'And then?'

'Buildings, so the positions are reversed. We have the advantage.'

Markham used the word 'we' deliberately, though he doubted if it would apply in practice. The only way to stop the horsemen mowing down running troops was to place something in their path. That something had to be him and his Lobsters. Calheri's female troopers would never hold against heavy cavalry, and he had severe doubts if his men could either. Useless sacrifice, of which he had seen too much in his time, was something he hated. But he'd always known, since the first day of taking up his commission, that the moment might come when life was the proper price to pay for the desired outcome.

'General, I suggest you remount your horse and ride to Aleria as fast as you can. If we are mistaken, and Admiral Hood's sloop is in the harbour, get aboard and leave us here.'

'I think not, Lieutenant. I may be a poor general but I am not given to running away from a battlefield.'

'I was thinking of Corsica, sir, not your pride.'

Paoli pulled a two-barrelled pistol from inside his coat, and reached into his saddlebags to extract powder and balls to load it.

'I will retire with my niece.'

'Sir, the whole purpose of this march is to get you to a boat.'

'Which I will achieve in the company of my escort.'

Markham was thinking that Paoli's claim to be a poor commander was not, as he'd thought, self-deprecation, just the plain truth. But he didn't say so.

'As you wish. But for the sake of Christ get on with it.'

The response to that was quite sharp. 'Profanity will not serve your cause, young man.'

'The Moor will,' said Magdalena, gesturing to one of her troopers to come forward with the sheathed pole. Then she looked questioningly at Markham, and when he nodded, the flagstaff was handed to Bellamy. The Negro hesitated before accepting, but only for a second. Once he had the shaft in his hand, he dipped it and she removed the leather cover. 'You carry the honour of the island, Eboluh Bellamy.'

The reply, delivered in his normal cultured voice, was larded with double meaning, and a sideways look at his own officer, as he raised the standard to let it fall open.

'I can think of few greater compliments you could pay me, Commandatore.'

Sharland's voice was low, but the venom didn't suffer for that. 'Like givin' the true cross to Lucifer, that is.'

Halsey made no attempt to lower the tone of his response. 'Will you give over, you miserable bastard. You never stop.'

Markham, still blushing slightly from Bellamy's knowing look, was again amazed to see at least half the heads of his men nodding in agreement. And when the Negro wrapped another white bandage round his head, so that he looked like the Moor on the flag, the buzz of approval from men who had spent weeks cursing him was palpable. Wondering what had brought about the change, he had to drag his thoughts back to what needed to be done.

Chapter thirty-one

Rannoch was looking at the retreating Corsicans, his eyes full of doubt, his voice even more gentle than usual. 'Do you think, if they get through, the girls can keep them occupied, sir?'

'Why not?' Markham replied, grinning. 'They managed to keep most of you lot occupied last night.'

'Dip before you die, I always say,' quipped Ettrick, a joke that was met with a variety of looks and very few laughs, proving that not many of his

435

men were in any doubt about the task they had been elected to perform.

'And not too fussed about the port of entry,' Tully wheezed.

'I can always learn new tricks from a bilge bugger like you, Tully.'

That did produce humour. Halsey laughed along with the rest, but he had never taken his eyes off the cavalry.

'Why ain't they moving, sir?'

'I don't know,' Markham replied. He looked over his shoulder to where Magdalena Calheri's troopers, having made their distance, were lining up. 'Yelland, back to the Commandatore. Ask her to retire at the same pace as us, and keep the distance. We will engage only if the enemy attacks us.'

It was cat and mouse from then on, as Markham fell back and the cavalry moved up, never getting into range of even Rannoch's musket. Aleria loomed large in both their vision and their thoughts, though it didn't look like much of a port, especially when they reached the barren marshland that formed the final approaches. The dilemma was whether to cut and run or to continue this slow retreat, the latter likely to favour the horsemen less.

'What does this remind you of, Sergeant?'

'Herding sheep into a pen.'

'Are the French in Aleria, Quinlan?'

'There was no flags flying that I could see, your honour.'

Still confused by the French behaviour, Markham continued his retreat across the featureless landscape, Bellamy in the middle, white flag aloft, while all around him the others cursed the irritant of the cavalry. When they'd covered half the distance, the front they had to defend began to narrow. On their left the sea had encroached to form a salt-water lake, edged with reeds. That would be soft underfoot, bad for men, worse for heavy animals. On their right the river had broadened out, too deep to cross.

The cavalry suddenly became more active, prancing and moving as if getting ready to engage, which was puzzling. Normally horse soldiers liked as much space as possible. But whoever commanded this lot had waited until the attacking ground narrowed. It was never a good idea, by Markham's way of thinking, to rate your opponent a fool, even if he was making what seemed like basic errors. Better to assume a deliberate plan. But the question remained how to respond, whatever the quality of the enemy.

Common sense dictated good husbandry, since the time was approaching when Calheri could run with some hope of making the small farmhouse and barn. Was it the Irish in him that was loath just to let that happen while these Frenchmen remained an unblooded threat, or just the certainty that he and his Lobsters were going to have to fight them anyway, in order to cover the withdrawal?

'Form up properly,' he called, to a line which had become very ragged. 'Let's see what they are made of.'

Bellamy just stood still, and the Hebes were in place quicker than Ebden and Sharland, who

437

seemed more nervous than their fellow marines. That highlighted how many of his men were ex-soldiers. This was what they'd been trained for, fighting with solid earth under their feet instead of the pitching timber of a ships' deck.

'Bayonets!'

The steel rasped out of the scabbards as the butts hit the ground, and Markham listened to the rhythmic clicks as they were clipped on to the muzzles.

'Present!'

He saw the reaction immediately, in the way the riders were handling their mounts. By stopping he had surprised them. They weren't prancing about now, but getting ready to respond with a close-order charge, three-quarters of the command, with ten men and an officer as reserve. Markham wanted them to do that, just to break the deadlock, to get off a round or two of musketry and dent their insufferable superiority.

'Sabres,' said Rannoch softly. 'No guns.'

'Real Prussian stuff,' Markham replied, a remark which mystified most of his men. But he'd studied war, its history as well as its future. This was the doctrine of Frederick der Grosse. No carbines or horse pistols, just boot-to-boot shock tactics to drive the infantry under, a good tactic against poor troops. Dressed as they were, like Corsicans, the Cavalry commander would rate their courage high, but their training low.

'When they come, everybody aim for the left of centre. We can't hit them all, so let's try and hit a few and open up their formation to our advantage.'

438

He aimed this at his Hebes, assuming that the remaining Seahorses still lacked the skill necessary to zero in on the right spot for cavalry, right between the animals' ears. High, that would take the rider, and low it would kill the horse. They would aim for the animals' chests, and perhaps they would get lucky and strike something vital. But a musket ball, even a big round from a Brown Bess, would have little chance of stopping a charging cavalry mount. Only luck would damage a swiftly moving leg so badly that the horse would fall.

Charging forward at speed, their herd instinct high, they were a formidable weapon of war. In full flow, they would come on even if they were hit, absorbing the punishment inflicted into their heavy shoulder muscles. It was necessary to hit them mid-forehead, and the safest method of all was to kill the rider. Markham had seen men die from stabs and sabre slashes, delivered by a mounted soldier on an animal so wounded that it was sinking to its knees, blood pumping out of the jugular groove.

They started to trot, a solid line, thirty wide, of hard flesh, each horses' flank practically touching the next. There was a sudden shout from the rear, floating across the fields, probably an injunction to withdraw. But it was too late for that: the cavalry were in motion, at the trot, the thud of their hooves growing louder by the second. Trot, then canter, so that the rhythm of the sound changed.

'Hebes, take aim.'

Markham knew that whatever else happened,

the cavalry were in for a shock. Not the kind of blow that would destroy them, but a standard of musketry they'd probably never experienced. Every one of his men was using sights, something almost unheard of in the British forces. He knew that, squinting along their muzzles, the Hebes especially would have picked a rider, and not be deflected from that as the horses' tossing heads obscured their target. Markham waited, calling the range down inside his head. One-fifty, one-twenty-five, one hundred, seventy-five. He was also watching for the moment they spurred into a gallop, that second of real elation for a horse soldier, and the very second at which he yelled, 'Fire!'

True to his command, every ball was aimed at the six men left of centre, each gun firing slightly low to allow for the upward kick of the forty-six-inch barrel. Like the Brown Bess muskets themselves, every ball in the muzzles was regulation British Army issue, which if it wasn't as good as Rannoch's own, was at least a great improvement on half-sized French balls. The salvo scythed into the line, several shots taking one man in the chest, thudding against his breastplate with such force as to knock it back into his vulnerable ribs.

He and two others disappeared over the back of the mounts, several of which had taken a ball, but not in a vital spot. The effect on both human and animal gave Markham what he'd prayed for. The closest, seeing the results of the volley, were shocked enough to react, putting a check on the headlong rush of the charge. One or two of the horses changed their stride so that the line began to expand, especially to the right, daylight opening up between each horse.

They were no longer the shock chargers of a few minutes ago, but disorganised cavalry in the kind of order they'd use if they were up against a running foe. Their confidence was, quite rightly, still high, because they were closing the distance so quickly on what they thought to be troops of low quality. Against such men, shepherds and farmers, they would never have had to face another salvo. But these were British marines, who'd been schooled by Rannoch, a man who'd scarcely give his men the pleasure of firing a gun if they couldn't reload in twenty seconds maximum.

'Aim right,' Markham shouted, gratified to see every muzzle swing round together. The dozen men nearest the reed beds were so close they could see the foam on their horses' lips; so near that the moment of discharge and the moment of striking seemed to be the same. The four who didn't pull up ran into a fretwork of a dozen bayonets, something which did affect their wild-eyed mounts. Faced with a threat they could see, the horses gnashed and tried to bite, reared and attempted to kick, only to be slashed and stabbed in their vulnerable bellies.

'Fall back left and reload,' he yelled, praying that Paoli and Magdalena had taken the chance to run, happy at least in the knowledge that he'd cut the pursuing cavalry force in half. But they didn't go after the others; instead they seemed intent on pressing home the attack on him.

That made what he'd thought a relatively safe manoeuvre, wheeling round to retire through the reeds, deadly dangerous. The safety of soft ground

441

and water, sodden earth through which horses couldn't charge, was too far away. And they were faced by men who'd had a shock, but had yet to sustain a scratch. And the reeds slowed him down more than he'd anticipated, breaking his own line up so they no longer presented a solid front. Markham knew he was going to sustain casualties now, the cavalrymen attacking him incensed enough to throw any idea of caution to the winds, his only reward the time he was buying.

Hauling their horses round, the Frenchmen spurred to gain momentum. The ragged fusillade which took them in the flank surprised him as much as them. And in truth its effect was in the mind rather than the body. Paoli on his horse managed to look magnificent, even if he was old and frail. But it was the sight of twenty women of all shapes and sizes, screaming as they charged, which put the riders off their stroke. And once they lost forward movement, unable to decide who to fight, it was easier to wheel and retire than to press home the attack.

'Run!' Markham yelled, as soon as he saw that everyone had reloaded their weapons. Magdalena Calheri yelled just as loud at her own troopers, and they began to trot back to the spot from which they'd advanced.

The need for the cavalry to withdraw and regroup, on horses that were more than a little blown, gave the whole of Paoli's escort a chance they hadn't had before. Not that it was easy. Whoever commanded the enemy was stung enough to order a fresh assault long before his men were truly ready. This meant that those he kept in reserve got ahead of the others, and by enough distance to be slightly isolated.

Paoli had the authority to command both groups, and it was he, able to get ahead on his horse and turn to see events unfolding, who gave the order to turn about face. Those ten cavalry troopers found themselves facing a solid line of thirty-odd muskets, all with bayonets fixed, on ground that restricted their ability to wheel right of left. The Hebes stuck to their training, but for the rest there was no aiming at breastplates. But such was the concentration of the fusillade, fired low at mounts not yet at full speed, that it had the black horses tripping and rearing, to form a barrier that prevented those following from coming through with anything approaching a disciplined charge.

Markham got off two rounds to Calheri's one into a mêlée of beasts and men, some mounted, others trying desperately to avoid being trampled by their own animals. Paoli's next command had them running again, heading for the farm buildings, stumbling under the black face and white single eye of the Corsican Moor.

Paoli was cock-a-hoop, waving his hat as though they'd won a great victory instead of a stalemate skirmish. The cavalry were too disordered to pursue, quite a few having dismounted to put themselves to rights. Markham could feel the tension draining from his body when the first musket opened up from the windows of the farmhouse.

The sight of blue Corsican caps, flopped to one

side, behind the cloud of smoke, nearly stopped Markham in his tracks. And he wasn't alone, since several other muskets opened up. Two of Calheri's troopers went down, as well as Ebden from the Seahorse, Sharland, who'd paused to help him, getting a furious shove in the back from Rannoch for his pains. Bellamy, either through fear or the elation of battle, raised the Moor's head flag higher and screamed. Certainly the Highlander knew that to stop between the cavalry and the barn would lead to a massacre. Perhaps the Negro understood that too.

Markham was shouting individual names, telling half his men to poke their bayonets through the farm windows, while the rest were ordered to get the walls at their backs and reload. Calheri's troopers were milling about around Paoli's horse, which was spinning in a circle, presenting the rider as a target almost impossible to miss. It was fortunate that no shots were aimed in his direction – indeed, none of the Corsican women were coming under any fire.

Magdalena did the right thing. She hauled her uncle, without any ceremony, off his horse and pushed him towards the small barn, her troopers following her, one dragging on the bridle to bring the animal in. Some had reloaded, and fired off what they could just to keep the cavalry confused. Then it was butts on the barn door, smashing it down so they could get into some cover.

'A trap!' Rannoch spat.

Markham was so breathless with running he could barely speak, his words coming out in gasps. 'No wonder ... damned dragoons ... why charge?'

444

'No grenades,' Rannoch responded, jerking his head towards the open shutters.

The Lobsters were all lined up on the farmhouse wall, backs flat to the mud and lime as they reloaded their muskets.

'Rannoch, take half the men,' Markham barked. 'Fire without aiming through the windows.'

The Highlander reeled off names and orders, his voice crossing that of Markham, who was calling on others to crouch low. Within half a minute, at Rannoch's command, his men span off the wall, and poked then discharged their weapons into the building. As the muskets came out to reply they ran into a volley from Markham's party, who were kneeling under the line of the sill. Each man used the protruding barrel as a point of aim, knowing that there was a man right behind it, a high-pitched scream from the interior demonstrating the effect of their efforts. Able to load faster than the enemy, Rannoch's men delivered a second volley, this time stepping several paces away from the wall to increase their angle of fire.

'The door must be round the back, Halsey,' Markham shouted. 'Take two men round there and worry them.'

'Here they come,' shouted Tully, pointing his bayonet back to the road they had just vacated.

Half the cavalry were mounted again, sabres raised, coming on at a trot. They wouldn't need to charge, the object being to pin their enemies against the outside walls of the farmhouse and finish them off. Having just employed the recent tactics, Markham had to keep his men's backs to the wall, or risk exposing them to fire from the now wiser Corsicans in the building.

Magdalena Calheri rescued them for the second time in a quarter of an hour. Her troopers had reloaded in the relative security of the barn. Now they rushed out to take the cavalry flank on, kneeling to increase their accuracy, and firing off as one a salvo of musket balls that tore into the sides of the enemy horsemen. It didn't halt them completely, but it did provide enough time for the Lobsters to reload and deliver a second fusillade that broke up their continuity.

Horsemen hate to be alone in the midst of infantry, since no one man can cover every flank of his horse. Without mutual support they were vulnerable, so the cavalry began to pull back. Then Markham noticed the muzzles disappearing from the farmhouse windows. The best of his men were already reloading, some a bit slower than others, so the command he gave was confused. Not all the people he wanted to remain stayed still, instead they followed him as he ran round to join Halsey, who was crouched against the wall by the farmhouse door, the wall beside him being peppered occasionally with inaccurate fire. Just as he shouted a warning the door opened and a muzzle poked out. Dymock, on the opposite side to Halsey, protected by a stack of logs, grabbed the barrel and pulled, and as the man attached to it emerged, Halsey spun his musket and clubbed him hard on the side of his head.

Both then jumped back to avoid the shots that came through the door, followed by a salvo through the windows by his men on the other side. Sense would have made the blue-capped defenders surrender. Instead they panicked and just ran out, presenting easy targets to Markham and his men. Seven fell and were then subjected, by men who had no time for finer feeling, to a frenzy of stabbing bayonets. One Corsican, with a luck that no man could hope for, got away unscathed by ball or blade, running in a zigzag line, yelling his head off in fright, preventing his own side from exacting revenge by cutting across their line of sight.

Once inside, Markham found two more casualties. From their blue caps he presumed them to be Buonapartists. One had taken a bayonet through his eye, and was dead, while the other was hunched over a smashed shoulder, carrying a wound that was certain to cost him his arm. He had to shout to avoid his own men firing into the gloom, and then ordered them to get inside themselves, fully expecting at any moment another cavalry charge. But whatever mistakes the commander of those troops had made up till now, he wasn't stupid enough to follow them up with one so crass. A horseman attacking a man safe behind a wall was asking to die.

'They're dismounting,' said Rannoch.

'Try and keep them still, while I go and check on the general. Halsey, four men by the back wall. Knock out some holes in case they try and retake this from the rear.'

'Do you think there's many of them, sir?' Gibbons asked. Having detached his bayonet he was jabbing at the wall.

'I think I'm about to find out,' said Markham, hauling the door open, then stepping back to kick it shut: a loud series of thuds followed, as several balls smashed into the stout oak. He smiled. 'Perhaps that's not the best route.'

Gibbons grinned, but it was Ettrick, also stabbing at the wall, who said the words. 'You should try the window, your honour. I hear you're a dab hand at the casement lark.'

Laughing made Markham realise just how thirsty he was, and since Ettrick had made the crack it was his water he took, pleased by the pained look on the man's face, a mixture of concern and anger. He threw his head back to swallow hard, then spat a stream of vinegary red wine halfway across the room.

'Present, your honour,' said Ettrick, all innocence. 'From the lady with the 'tache. Wouldn't do to turn down a gift from a friend, would it now.'

'Sergeant Rannoch, Marine Ettrick is on a charge.'

'Sir!' Rannoch replied, without any emphasis at all.

'Now stand aside and let me out the bloody window.'

The distance to the barn was no more than thirty feet. But it was a deadly area to cross, the only bit of cover the low wall around the well, and given that fire would come from both sides and every gun the enemy had that could be trained on it. Since his men had finished their fire holes, he didn't need to say any more. They knew what to do, so he jumped through the window, following a fusillade aimed at the dismounted cavalry, and ran for the barn door, trusting his own men to fire at the Buonapartists as soon as they showed themselves. Judging by the number of balls that whistled past him, they must have been well concealed.

Inside the barn, Magdalena had done the same as his men had to the farmhouse, knocking out holes in the soft walls to make firing points. There was an old cart by the door, and a loft full of hay bales. And animals, two pigs and a cow, evidence that the men who'd held this place had never expected to lose it.

'If we push that cart out and tip it over, it will provide extra cover,' said Magdalena.

'Get those bales of hay down too,' Markham added. 'There must be enough there to make a line between here and the farmhouse, then we can get to the water, and each other, in safety. Firing from that height will help to pin down the enemy too.'

As he was speaking, he was looking around for Paoli. He saw him finally, amongst women working furiously to turn the barn into a redoubt, his head forward and his face filled with sadness. He tried to smile as Markham approached, but it failed to lift the mood of gloom that seemed to assail him.

'We're safe here for now, sir.'

'They knew we were coming, Lieutenant. This was a snare.'

'Yes, sir,' Markham replied. He'd realised somewhere along the line that was the truth, but had been too busy to examine it. As a proposition it didn't bear too much of that. Now it was obvious why the cavalry hadn't attacked. Their task had been to drive them to where they were going any-

way, and remove any possibility that circumstances might allow them a change of mind. They
attacked only when Markham stopped, when it
looked as though that aim was in jeopardy.

Paoli pulled Hood's despatch from his coat
pocket and waved it. 'How could that be? Does
your admiral want me killed too?'

'No, sir. He wants you in Cardo, leading your
troops.'

The hands went up in a gesture of despair.
'Then who has betrayed us both?'

'There is work to do, sir, to improve the defence.
I must concentrate on that, rather than allow
myself time for speculation.'

Chapter thirty-two

'Can he talk?' said Markham, leaning over to
examine the wounded Corsican, who was lying
amongst whole and broken jars of olive oil.

Bellamy nodded, but the look in his eye was
confirmation that treatment for this man was
essential. Markham could see that for himself:
the skin was waxy, covered in a thin film of sweat,
the lines between nose and cheek deeper than
they should be, the eyes, when they were open,
full of pain. He leant forward and began to talk
in the wounded man's ear, softly, asking questions which were answered by nods and shakes,
so that those watching, who included a good half
of his Lobsters, muskets loaded and pointing in

both directions, were left with only half a tale.

The man admitted he was a Buonapartist, or at least nodded when that easily discernible word was posed. The name Ajaccio formed by Markham's lips was also comprehensible. The shakes of the head corresponded to inquiries regarding numbers and names of his commanders. Then Markham leant closer, his voice even softer, which had his men straining forward for a half note to which they could attach some certainty.

'Fouquert,' said Yelland, hissing the name to the men nearest him. 'He's asked him about Fouquert.'

'Bastard nodded, too,' croaked Gibbons.

'He's got to be here,' moaned Dymock, in a hushed tone. 'Bad penny ain't in it.'

'No ship,' whispered Halsey, who so forgot his own standards as to join in, taking his eyes away from the window he was posted on. 'The frog word is *bâteau,* and he shook his head.'

'Why ain't the Viking here,' moaned Leech. 'He can read old Shaft-em's mind.'

'He's out there digging trenches, you useless bollock,' snapped Halsey, who felt he'd missed some vital clue because the marine was speaking at the same time as Markham. Then self-discipline resurfaced and he barked at them all, 'Attend to your bloody duty. Like old women, you are.'

'Kettle calling,' responded Yelland, so that Halsey couldn't hear. To the men he was Daddy Halsey when obliging, Old Fanny Halsey, a Seven Dials trollop, when cross.

'We will need to get a white flag out,' said Markham, standing up and stretching to ease muscles

451

that prolonged bending had strained. 'This man needs a sawbones, or he's going to die.'

'Good fucking riddance, I say,' called Sharland, who'd been allotted the lonely task of keeping watch on the far side of the farmhouse, and so had heard nothing.

Bellamy responded with a confidence which, especially where Sharland was concerned, had hitherto been lacking. To Markham it was further evidence of his changed stature, which had yet to be explained.

'There speaks a shining example of the benefits of universal education.'

'You cheeky black...'

'Sharland!' snapped Markham. 'Get ready to go out, under a truce flag. You will ask for an opportunity to return the wounded prisoner. You will also request that the French, or whoever is running this affair, take in our casualties, since we do not have the means to care for them.'

'What, like Ebbie?'

'Ebden, and the two women who took wounds.'

'They're dead.'

'We don't know for certain. Corporal Halsey, go and ask the general to join us.'

The straw bales and the overturned cart provided some cover, which Rannoch was busy adding to by digging shallow trenches. But it was still an uncomfortable journey for a man his age, who found being bent double a strain. Once he was in the farmhouse Markham had a quiet word, then led him to the wounded prisoner. Much to the annoyance of those within earshot, Paoli began to talk softly to the Corsican in his own, incomprehensible tongue.

Markham understood, when he heard the name, that the general had introduced himself. More interesting was the reaction. The invalid's eye opened in wonder, finding himself talking to a paragon of whom he could only have heard. Pasquale Paoli spoke gently but insistently, to Markham's mind like a priest giving last rights. There was a hypnotic quality to the voice, low and seductive. The man he was addressing was an enemy, but whatever Paoli said produced first tears, then a flood of stuttering information.

Finally the old man wiped his perspiring brow, and leant forward to kiss him on the forehead, that followed by a nod to Markham. Another whispered conversation followed, still maddening for those who couldn't understand. But they could see that Paoli had elicited more information than Markham, and that none of it had done anything to cheer either man up.

'Improvisation,' said Markham, thinking about that oilskin pouch, sealed with wax of course, but in such a way that it had no device to identify it, all seemingly to no avail because Paoli had decided to leave for Morosaglia. No wonder Lanester had looked like a man at death's door. 'From that first day at Fornali, it all seems to have a gimcrack quality.'

'There's no absolute way to find out if that supposition is correct, Lieutenant.'

Markham nodded, though in truth he had no interest in Paoli's pedantic way of looking at things. He called to Sharland, ordering him to get ready, then added with a commanding hand that

453

Bellamy should come close. That led to more whispering, the only sound that made an iota of sense the Negro objecting to whatever task Markham was giving him. But it was clearly an order, and as Sharland readied his truce flag, Bellamy got himself prepared to follow him out of the door.

Sharland glared and gave a sharp gesture with his thumb when he realised what was being proposed, the tone of hatred in his voice matching the sentiment in his look.

'I ain't goin' with this ape.'

Markham was tired, suffering from a lassitude caused by too much action, the need to think and give orders, plus the depression induced by his recent conversations. They had to get out of here, and right now he would happily have elected to leave this man behind. He was about to bark at Sharland, but the marine saw the look in his eye, and buckled immediately.

'Whatever you say, sir.'

There was a pause while a flag was waved outside one of the windows. That, in turn, had to be translated and passed on to whoever was in charge of the combined French and Corsican force besieging the farmhouse. A cavalry bugle eventually blew to signal acceptance, and Sharland could then open the front door, confirm the arrangement and walk out into clear daylight with Bellamy at his side.

After some ten minutes two men arrived with a stretcher to take away their wounded friend, both avoiding even the slightest eye contact, treating the British Lobsters, and the Liberator, as if they were the Devil incarnate. Markham stood just inside the door, watching Bellamy. When the Negro, after what seemed like an age, turned and waved, he finally spoke.

'Halsey, gather up all the oil and combustibles you can find. Yelland, be so good as to go over to the barn. On the way tell Sergeant Rannoch to stop digging and come back inside. Then request Commandatore Calheri, along with her troopers, to take up positions between the barn and the farmhouse. Everybody is to get ready to move out as soon as the general and I have finished.'

'Sir!'

'Discreetly, Yelland,' Markham added, as the youngster ducked to exit through the hole in the side wall. 'I don't want the enemy to know.'

Rannoch had listened carefully while Markham gave him his orders, nodding slowly, though there was doubt in his pale blue eyes.

'The lady will not take kindly to accepting such instructions from me.'

'Then tell her they are from her uncle,' Markham replied, making for the door.

He took a last look over to where Pasquale Paoli sat in a corner. In the fading light, which made it hard to pick the old man out, he was looking at the floor, in an attitude that would have seemed strange to anyone who knew him well, but which had been there since he and Markham had finished their quiet conversation. Such a figure as the Liberator could never draw the description 'broken', but no-one could doubt the deep sadness that filled him, evidenced by his complete unawareness of anyone around him.

'General,' Markham called, and returned the smile he received as the old man stood up.

'Right, you lot,' said Rannoch, 'let us be getting ready.'

That it was dark in the farmhouse was natural, even if it was still a strong twilight outside. Certainly when the man Markham had asked to see stepped forward from the cover of the houses on the very edge of Aleria, he produced a gasp from the sentinels which was a compound of anger and fear. They looked at each other, then at Markham, whose face was rigidly impassive as he stepped forward and reopened the door. The walk to the agreed spot, halfway between the positions, took no more than a minute, Markham thinking on the way that the light did a great deal to favour the hue of the scarlet, gold-trimmed, coat.

'I was half tempted to demand to talk to Fouquert.'

'He's not here.'

'A lie,' thought Markham savagely. The wounded Corsican had confirmed the Frenchman to Paoli. But he smiled nevertheless.

'Good.'

'Besides, he wouldn't have come if you'd asked him. I think you scare him almost as much as he scares me. There's no way he'd come out from under cover with you around.'

'How very wise.'

'It was damned cheek you sending that nigger to demand I come out, Markham. It nearly caused me to refuse.'

'Lie two,' he thought, the word improvisation recurring in his brain.

The face was red, fat and, despite the circumstances, still jolly. Indeed, as he'd approached Markham, he had his arms held out as though he was welcoming a prodigal son. There was no evidence of a wound on the man who'd been lying at death's door a few days before. Pavin, looking even more gaunt and wrinkled in the dying light, stood near the first house that marked the boundary of the town of Aleria. The events of the last weeks flashed through his mind: what had happened outside the officer's mess tent at Fornali; the inconsistency of behaviour; and the fact that he'd never actually seen the wound.

'Made up,' he said to himself, 'the whole damn thing made up.'

'What d'you say, Markham?'

'That night at Fornali, Major,' Markham said. 'I should have spotted that wet sand on your boots.'

Lanester smiled, though from the look in his eyes it was clear that he'd no more realised the significance of that clue to his involvement than Markham. 'Daresay you would have done if you'd seen them after.'

'It doesn't bother you that those men died?'

'They were soldiers, Lieutenant.'

'Who, I think, have a right to expect their officers to be on their side.'

'You have a streak of sentimentality, Markham, that is about to get you killed. I had it once, pledging loyalty to a cause, until I found that commodity only goes one way.'

'It won't get me killed today though, Major. You don't have enough men to mount an attack.'

457

Lanester sneered at him, telling him not so much a third lie, as a very necessary piece of exaggeration. 'Oh! we do. It's never a good idea to underestimate your enemy.'

'What changed your mind, Lanester, about having me killed?'

'Who said I changed my mind?'

'I've just been talking to a very wise man,' Markham replied, changing the subject, eyeing the fading twilight, determined to keep him talking. 'And he and I think you might have managed to underestimate your friends.'

'That I don't follow.'

'The horse soldiers. Our shepherds got too hungry.'

'Cavalry, Markham. Had they just done their job we would have had you cold. You can never rely on them. Christ, they're worse than tarpaulins.'

'What price renegades?' The major behaved as if Markham hadn't said that, or at the very least, as if such a description didn't apply to him. 'It's not the first time they've let you down. We were never supposed to meet Duchesne, were we?'

'With your friend being such an unforgiving bastard, it cost him his life.'

'Not before he'd played out that farrago at the monastery. I should have known that with Fouquert around, gentle interrogation was out of the question.'

'He was acting to save his neck. What was that thing Sam Johnson said about hanging concentrating the mind?'

'The price of some sense of decency.'

'There you go being sentimental again. Who do

458

you think garrotted those monks you buried if it wasn't Duchesne?'

'It would be nice to see you hang for the men at Fornali, hopefully within sight of the place they died.'

'You're planning to go back there, are you?'

It was such a stupid question that Markham had answered, 'Of course,' long before he realised that it shouldn't have been asked.

Lanester threw his head back and laughed. 'You should worry about your own skin, Markham, not mine. If you thought you were up to your chin in ordure when we left San Fiorenzo, wait till you get back. Not that you will, of course.'

He couldn't ask, but then he couldn't avoid looking curious either, and the major was too keen to tell him to hold it back for later advantage.

'Your orders,' Lanester hooted.

'What about them?'

'They don't exist. Gawd, I've had to be subtle with people in my time, but you were easy. You're so goddamn vain you actually believed what I said about Hanger. And such a dupe that you marched out of San Fiorenzo without asking for confirmation from your own superiors.'

'I was supposed to go,' Markham responded, trying not to sound too doubtful.

'Oh yes. I borrowed you to escort me to the Cardo outposts. But de Lisle was expecting you back within the next day.'

'De Lisle!'

'He'll want to court martial you even more now. You're absent from *Hebe* in a battle zone. I

459

shouldn't even think about going back, because he would have the right to request that you hang from his own yardarm, with his good friend Hanger holding the rope.'

Lanester was about to go on, to drive home the message to a clearly depressed Markham, who was struggling to convince himself that this was just another improvised tactic. Instead, the major looked over the marine's shoulder, his eyes opening just a fraction.

'I don't know that the truce will hold for him.'

Paoli was coming as arranged, though given how loquacious Lanester was being it hardly seemed necessary.

'Make it!'

'Why should I?' demanded the Major with a shrug.

'Because,' Markham lied, enjoying the sensation of improvising himself, 'Sergeant Rannoch has a musket aimed at the very centre of your forehead. And it's not dark yet. If he is even threatened by a mis-aimed ball, you die.'

Markham could see Lanester working himself up to a complaint, and cut him off. 'And I don't think, Major, you are in a position to question my notions of gentlemanly behaviour during a truce.'

It was the threat of Rannoch that shut off the protest, a man he suspected might take pleasure in shooting him even if he hadn't betrayed anyone. He span round and made a sharp, insistent gesture, that there should be no shooting.

'Just before he arrives, who is the traitor?'

'For me to know, Markham. Neither you nor Paoli will ever find out.'

'Major Lanester,' said Paoli.

His voice was strong, and Markham knew without looking that whatever his inner turmoil, the old man was presenting to this friend who'd betrayed him his habitual strong personality. The conversation they'd had in the farmhouse could not help but be depressing. The question Paoli feared to ask was how long Lanester had been in the pay of his enemies. Had he harboured, as a close friend, a man who had betrayed him for nearly the entire length of his exile?

'General Paoli,' intoned Lanester, adding a small bow.

'I said to Lieutenant Markham, not ten minutes ago, that if he'd called you a Virginian at any time in my hearing, I would have been able to sow a seed of doubt in his mind.'

'Quebec, Markham.'

'So I gather.'

'French father, English mother. Not really a secret, just a slight change of emphasis to avoid certain discomforts.'

Paoli interrupted, his tone bitter. 'Like huge debts?'

'Odd how the English can forgive even American rebels, but still harbour a loathing for any soul who carries in his blood a trace of Quebec.'

'Come, Lanester. You betrayed them too.'

'I did not!'

Markham was only half listening to what was a meaningless debate. Lanester was a traitor claiming to be a patriot, though he couldn't quite nail the cause to which he adhered. Paoli, so upright, was relentless in his strictures, but clever enough to make the major defensive, so that information came out as hearty justification, not feeble excuses. The Virginian label, he'd adopted in the American war, to ease his activities as an English spy, and hung onto it when forced to flee to England.

'It was I who brought that slug Benedict Arnold to General Clinton's notice, me who set up the meeting with André.'

'Perhaps it was you who betrayed them too.'

'Damnit, I wish I had! That pack of gabbling lawyers might have paid me a decent stipend, instead of leaving me, like King George did, on the streets of London to starve. Six thousand pounds and a pension was what Arnold got. He lived like a lord while I was made a pauper.'

Markham had come out here to trap Lanester, to lull the man into a false sense of security. But right now, having heard what the major had said, he was trying to assess the damage it had done him. The despatch, supposedly from Hood, was a forgery. What had he put in the one he'd sent back after Cardo? Not that it mattered. There were enough people around prepared to think badly of him. A hint that he'd gone absent would be only too readily believed.

But for all the trouble that would cause him, his mind was operating, simultaneously, on the required level. The consequences would never interfere with his will to survive. From this closer distance, he was trying to fix in his mind the layout of the enemy positions. They were outnumbered by the force that had them trapped, but not by many, especially if they could, by moving fast, negate the cavalry, who were on the far side of the farmhouse.

Speed was the key, though he knew taking them wouldn't be easy. But once they were through, the French and their Corsican allies would be surrounded by a hostile, instead of a passive, population. Every village they'd been forced to go through had gone wild at the sight of Pasquale Paoli. The wounded Corsican had refused to answer Markham, but faced with the towering presence of the Liberator, he'd been more forthcoming. The population of Aleria would surely react the same way.

What happened after that was incalculable. His mind was full of possibilities – ships, escape routes and killing – until the name Fouquert concentrated his attention.

'I said he was a Jesuit, didn't I, Markham? Can't seem to accept that half a cake is better than none.'

'What's the whole cake?' asked Markham.

'Don't go flattering yourself, son. It ain't you, though it's odd to think you'd be dead now without he saved you. No, it's the general here, the Hero of Corsica, taken in a tumbril to meet Citizen Robespierre, before a final soirée with Madame Guillotine. Fouquert won't give up on that. Not being a soldier, he can only see so far. Hardly surprising. He really doesn't give a damn about Corsica.'

'And you do?' asked Paoli.

'My mission was simple till that Jesuit came along. Now it's got more complex. But it don't matter none, it will end the same way.' Lanester turned to Markham and fixed him with a hard look. 'If it wasn't for your feud with our friend Fouquert, I'd tell you to dump the Liberator and save your skin.'

'And I tell you to go jump in the harbour.'

'God,' Lanester replied, with deep irony, 'I can't abide honest men.'

'Half a cake?' asked Paoli. 'What does that mean?'

'Guess, Pasquale, you were always good at that,' Lanester said.

Paoli opened his mouth to continue, but Markham cut across him. The light was fading fast, the sky taking on that brittle blue quality that precedes full night.

'We must discuss terms.'

'There won't be any,' Lanester snapped.

'I suggest that you let us retire to Corte, without further fighting. I suggest we meet tomorrow at the same time, to discuss our proposal.'

'A waste of breath.'

'So much better, Major,' Paoli sighed, 'than a waste of life.'

The walk back was no more than fifty paces, made in silence, Bellamy standing by the edge of the farmhouse holding the flagstaff. Haste had to be avoided, especially now, since Markham suspected he had a double reason for getting Paoli to Cardo. Only the old man beside him could convince those who bore him ill that he had been as much a victim as they had of Lanester's machinations.

The major had let things slip, but they were conundrums not clues. Cakes; half cakes. Plans laid, made more complex, and spoiled. The outrageous fact that Fouquert, in pursuit of a higher prize, had spared Markham's life, taking Duchesne's instead, for what was no more than an error made out of ignorance. But he knew, or at least suspected, that Fouquert and Lanester must have different agendas. The major had almost said that.

It made no difference now. As he approached the farmhouse door, he slowed to let Paoli through. As soon as the old man disappeared, he held out his hand, and was obliged by the feel of his pistol. Turning, as if to take a last look, he could just see faintly that the enemy was still disorganised, still behaving as if the truce was in place. Strictly speaking they were right, but with men like those he faced, breaking his word as an officer was a duty, not a crime.

'Bellamy, the flag.'

As it unfurled, in the last of the light, cracking open on the evening breeze, the white silk seemed luminous. From behind the straw bales and the upturned cart, Calheri's troopers and his marines emerged. There was no yelling, no great shout to signal the charge. A party left behind went to work with their flints, rasping at oil-soaked straw which only caught light slowly. They'd gained ground by the time the first enemy musket fired, and were halfway to Lanester's line before anything like an organised defence was mustered, close enough to get in amongst them before the fires they'd set rose enough to silhouette them.

Markham yelled then, and so did Magdalena. Behind him, in a phalanx of his marines, Pas-

465

quale Paoli, protected from harm, felt his Corsican blood race, and even he, as he raised his double-barrelled pistol, managed a war cry.

Chapter thirty-three

Deciding they had to break out was one thing, and achieving it quite another. However disorganised they had been, the forces opposing them rallied quickly. But one vital ingredient was missing, something the defenders had banked on. By acting as they had, they'd completely fooled the cavalry. If they'd stirred they hadn't arrived on the scene. And the fire Markham had started was beginning to take hold, a blaze that would in time consume the barn, the farmhouse, and the oil-soaked lines in between. The horses would shy away from that, further slowing their riders. So Markham and Calheri could concentrate for quite some time on those in front of them, without having to worry about their rear.

Counting on that lost advantage, the Buonapartists hadn't bothered to do anything other than man points in the buildings that gave them cover. Markham was surprised, though elated, by the fact that no real attempt had been made to block the streets leading into the town. They had left gaps, ones which with the advent of night became very obvious. Markham didn't want to fight them, but bypass them, so had suggested that they head for the areas that lacked gun

466

flashes. Rannoch and his Lobsters, with one exception, obeyed. But Magdalena Calheri and her troopers, with their flag and Eboluh Bellamy in the middle, had charged the guns, seemingly intent on taking the strongest point on the town perimeter, a low set of cattle stalls, which provided natural and linked cover for defence.

'Rannoch,' he yelled, as they made an opening that was obviously some kind of street. 'Once you've got the general safe, form up on the corners and see if you can suppress some of that fire.'

'Those horse soldiers will not be long,' the Highlander gasped, pointing at the flames beginning to roar, quickly consuming the dry straw. 'They'll come round if they can't get through. And an open street is as bad as a field.'

'Not if we can block it.'

The yell from his rear killed any idea of getting hold of Magdalena and dragging her away from her own private battle. The shape that loomed up at the head of a counter-attack was identifiable. Fat, Lanester still ran at the head of the men he led, swinging his sword right and left, trying to get behind them and close off the route to the port. The whole area had taken on the glow from the flames, making Lanester's coat radiant. Pavin was by his side, jabbing with a pike, trying to beat down the opposing bayonets.

The flaring of sparks, which silhouetted the positions they'd just left, increased the available light. But they also indicated the danger, showing as they did cavalrymen dragging the bales of straw aside, creating a gap they could ride through. It was stupid considering, as Rannoch had pointed out, the option existed to ride round the conflagration. It mattered little; they would be involved in the fighting within minutes, and if he and Calheri could not present a solid front by blocking one of the streets, they'd be in real trouble.

Markham fended off a stab with a sword, ducked under a wielded axe to skewer the bearer, then disengaged, falling back to where Bellamy stood rooted to the spot, the flames shining off his black skin, holding the black and white flag. How he'd survived was a mystery, pennant carriers being primary targets for the enemy in any battle. But he had, and his officer grabbed him and dragged him towards his own men, yelling to Calheri and her troops to follow him.

It was the flag they obeyed, not him. That square of silk seemed to exert a strange hold, inspiring them to crazy valour. Certainly they'd fought well, and if they hadn't taken the cowsheds, they stopped any of the defenders from getting out. What he wanted now was for them to occupy Lanester and his foot soldiers, so that he could get his Lobsters some space. They needed to reload and take careful aim on the cavalry as they came through the gap between the blazing buildings.

They had to be stopped. If they couldn't be, then the idea of making an escape into the town was doomed. Stepping over a dead Buonapartist, Markham picked up his weapon, a heavy cleaver, and pushed it into Bellamy's hand.

'Use it, damn you,' he screamed, pushing the Negro right to the front of his fellow Lobsters, happy to observe that even if he didn't like killing, he hated the idea of dying even more. Bellamy had strength, and the cleaver was for him a perfect weapon, fortuitously found. Flagstaff firmly placed to give him leverage, the way he swung it had Lanester taking a jump backwards. A shove from behind sent Bellamy after him, and a lucky cut from his cleaver took Pavin under his lantern jaw.

Markham had no time to see what developed after that, busy as he was trying to pull his men back to create a space for Calheri's troopers to take over. Suddenly he realised he was beside Magdalena. She'd lost her cap, her eyes were alight, and she was searching for a victim to stab with her knife. She looked magnificent, with the light of battle so strong on her features. Her chest was heaving too, and her legs were parted to give her balance. He wondered where it came from, that blood lust. But that word, in his mind, also had Markham querying how he could think of sex at a time like this.

Fortunately Rannoch had kept his head, and his eyes on the progress of the horsemen. He too was pulling men back to form a line, shouting at them to get their muskets loaded. Markham, watching him, didn't see the man trying to club him with his gun. It was only when General Paoli fired both barrels past his ear that he turned to see the danger.

'We must run, Markham.'

'To where?' the marine demanded, as aware as the general of their situation.

'The church,' Paoli gasped. 'We can defend that.'

'One prison for another.'

'Better than dying like a dog in the street.'

The old man was right. They lacked the strength to stand, or even to retire at a pace that suited them. It was a case of one volley then run, and hope that they could slow the cavalry down enough to get clear. He knew Rannoch would do his part without orders. The difficulty was to get everyone else moving. He grabbed Magdalena, and spinning her, threw her towards her uncle. He would have to explain. Then it was that flag again, once more in the midst of a heaving block of fighting bodies.

His throat was so dry, and the sounds around him so loud, he had no idea if a shout actually emerged. But the retreating flag, as he collared Bellamy and hauled him out of the mêlée, had some effect, since gaps opened in the jostling combatants. In fighting, whatever the weapon, it is always desirable to go forwards rather than back. Even Calheri's troopers were trained to that degree. So getting them to run wasn't easy, and he took a cut on his arm from trying to save one of the thin girls and get her on her way. She paid a higher price than him, as two men speared her with bayonets, her body pushed sideways to protect Markham.

The volley of musketry, loud in everyone's ears, produced a split-second pause which he used to good effect. Then he was running, swinging the flat of his blade to keep anyone in front of him from turning round. The sudden disengagement left Lanester's men looking for orders. Once they were given they pursued quickly enough, but that hiatus had given the fleeing soldiers a breather. They soon caught up with Paoli, hobbling as he tried to get legs that rarely walked to function. Rannoch threw his musket to Markham, and with one sweep, lifted the old man bodily and sped ahead with the general on his shoulder.

The enemy knew where they were going, and Markham was sure he wasn't the only one who could hear stamping horses. What he couldn't observe, unable to turn round, was that his back was being protected by his own enemies, who so filled the street that the cavalry couldn't get through. The square in front of the church, opening up, gave them more room. But by that time the first of the runners had reached the church doors, which yielded to a mighty kick from Rannoch, still with Paoli on his shoulder.

The commands were garbled, the responses mixed, but enough order was in place to form a line of defenders at the door as a shield to protect those rushing into the sanctuary. The horses' hooves were on stone now, sending up sparks as they sought to climb the steps that would bring them into the well of the church. But the space had narrowed again, now more than ever, and they found themselves hemmed in by walls and columns, fighting off men and women who seemed to want to tear them apart.

How they got the doors shut, Markham never knew. He was just aware of pushing, with his own men all around him, some with hands on the oak doors, others with their shoulders supporting their struggling mates. In the middle, Bellamy still swung his cleaver, ensuring that in the gap between the door edges, no hand could interfere.

'Magdalena!' Paoli cried, from the spot where Rannoch had dumped him. 'Check for other exits and if you find them, bar them.'

When silence came, it was swiftly, with nothing more than the odd echoing boot, as various people rushed around securing any possible point of entry. Markham was, like most others, leaning on something trying to catch his breath. They'd made the church, only to become besieged once more. But there was some gain in this, only at this stage Markham had no idea how much.

Nearly everyone had a wound of some kind, but to his amazement Markham found he had all his men in the church. Not so Magdalena who, through her decision to attack the strongest point, had suffered half a dozen losses. If they hadn't been dead when they fell, they would be now. Altar cloths were used for bandages, with various pairs in dark corners assisting each other.

Magdalena, having got her uncle to try and sleep, lying on a pile of hassocks, helped Markham off with his coat. The cut was shallow enough, but the bruise that surrounded it was huge and black. Looking round, seeing they were not observed, Magdalena leant forward and kissed it.

'Without medicines, it is all I can give you.'

'There is more,' he replied, 'and you know it.'

'In a church?'

'I'll tell you this for certain. If God is all forgiving, he'll not make a last night of pleasure before you die a sin.'

She looked at her uncle, asleep beside the flag that Bellamy had finally relinquished. 'I want to put the Moor on the highest point of the church spire. Will you help me?'

They'd be alone up there so, exhausted as he was, he nodded readily.

'What about guards?' she asked.

'Why bother? They know we're not going anywhere.'

There was a ladder, which stretched above the bell chamber. Markham shinned up, and found a slotted air vent right at the very apex of the spire. Getting the flagstaff through wasn't easy, but he managed, using his swordbelt to secure the pole.

Back on the platform under the great metal bells, in total privacy, they lay down. There was none of the frenzy of the previous nights' half-clothed rutting. Now they were naked, each bruise and abrasion a point to kiss. She tried to stop him as his lips slid down over her belly, a slight air of fear in her grasp.

He took her hand and held it away, knowing that whatever rituals of dutiful sex she'd enjoyed with her dead husband, they had not included much in the way of variety. He had one night to show her what she had missed, and every intention of doing so.

'Thank you, Markham,' she said, warm and locked into his body, her head in the crook of his shoulder, her hand gently stroking his groin, and beginning to revive his erection. He wanted to say that her cries of pleasure had probably out-rung the bells above their heads, but stopped

473

himself, knowing how ashamed that would make her feel.

The crack of the flag woke them up, as the morning breeze coming in off the sea made it fill out. The chill of the air was hardly kept at bay by their short jackets, and both Magdalena and Markham were shivering. It was the sound of footsteps ascending the staircase that warmed them up, a loud heavy tread that had them scrabbling for the rest of their clothes. Rannoch's head appeared, pale blond hair, the innocent blue eyes of a man who knew he'd made enough noise, and allowed enough time, for a semblance of decency to be contrived.

'A party in the square, sir. And would you believe it, Fouquert is there, along with that traitorous Major.'

'Have they sent in a message?'

'With the priest, who is saying Mass for General Paoli and those who wish to cleanse their souls.'

'And?'

'Surrender. The general wants to talk to you before replying.'

Markham climbed the ladder and looked through the slats. He could see the men in the centre of the square, their troops lolling around at the perimeter, the cavalry covering the approach from Corte.

'I can't surrender. Not to Fouquert.'

'Odd, do you not think, since the bastard, saving your presence, Commandatore, must know that.'

'I think this should be a decision for the whole town.'

Markham ordered two of his men to stand by on the bell ropes, and as the great doors opened, he placed Paoli in the centre of the entrance, and nodded to them to pull. The bells pealed out, not in any sequence so beloved of clerics, but in a cacophony of discordant sound, which somehow, given the circumstances, seemed very appropriate. Above, on the spire, the flag of Independent Corsica fluttered, and Magdalena had her women yell from every doorway that the Liberator was here in person.

'So much for the brave people of Corsica,' said Markham sarcastically, when no one appeared.

'Wait,' said Paoli.

He was right, Markham wrong, the first sign that this was so the sudden activity around the fringes, as the men besieging them stood up, looking warily down each street. Then they began to back away, muskets held up to threaten an invisible foe. Paoli, sure now he was safe, stepped further out onto the platform which surrounded the church, raising his arms in greeting to a square rapidly filling up with silent people.

Fouquert and Lanester had swung round, the Commissioner gesturing wildly for the French soldiers to come and protect him. One brought him a horse, which seemed from this distance to confer a feeling of security, even if he didn't mount it. Lanester was talking to him, earnestly, bending forward to speak into Fouquert's ear. That he was having little joy was obvious by the angry look on the Commissioner's face, and the way he swept his arm to indicate the crowd of Alerians come to support their flag and their leader.

475

Markham was out beside Paoli now, secure that the positions had been reversed. The locals weren't armed, but they were so numerous, and had such a look of determination on their faces, that the besiegers had become the besieged. Fouquert made to mount, and Lanester grabbed his bridle, in an angry gesture. The flash of steel was too quick for any but the most practised eye, but the look of horror on Lanester's face was proof enough, compounded by the way he fell to his knees.

'This man has only one reward for failure,' said Paoli softly.

'What do we do now?' asked Markham, indicating the trapped enemy. Fouquert was now mounted, and so were the rest of the cavalry, milling around as if trying to decide which way to go.

'The people are unarmed. If they try to do anything dozens of them will die. Let them go.'

'No, uncle!' cried Magdalena, who'd come to join them.

'One shot from us will precipitate a massacre. Every Frenchman and Buonapartist would need to die before it ended. Regardless of how much we help, it would not be us who paid that price, but the people of Aleria.'

'Tell them to surrender.'

'Look into that man's eyes, Magdalena,' Paoli said, pointing at Fouquert, 'and tell me he will surrender without blood.'

Rannoch's voice came from behind. 'I have a musket on him.'

It was as if Fouquert heard, since every carbine the cavalry had suddenly came out to be aimed at the church steps. Paoli waved, then called for the crowds to part. Fouquert smiled, took one last look at Lanester, crouched over holding his belly. Then he looked at Markham, and the smile disappeared, to be replaced with a look of malevolent hate, before hauling on his reins to turn his horse away.

'Lieutenant,' Paoli said as the crowd surged forward, 'it would be a Christian thing to do, if we could seek to save Major Lanester.'

The local doctor took one look at Lanester's slit belly and shook his head. Paoli had been with him all the time, ignoring the crowds in the square, holding the major's hand and talking to him. Suddenly, whatever the dying man said made the general sit up, and he gestured to Markham.

'Sir.'

'Major Lanester. Would you repeat to Lieutenant Markham what you have just told me?'

There was no faking wounds now. The face had lost all of its shape, seeming flabby. Lanester was bleeding to death, and he knew it.

'The landing at Bastia happened today,' he gasped. 'Nelson will already have tried to get ashore. He's probably dead by now. You're too late.'

Markham grinned, which took some effort. 'I don't know whether to admire you, Lanester, or damn you for the endemic liar that you are.'

'I'm telling you the truth, Markham.'

'Why start now?' It took a great effort for Lanester to curse, but he managed it. 'If I'm given the choice of two potential lies about the date of

477

Nelson's landing, I'll take the first one.'

'Your funeral.'

'No, Major, yours.' He saw the flash of fear in the man's eyes, and wondered if Paoli or the doctor had told him how close he was to death. 'I'm not much for faith, but it's a bad idea to meet your maker with a lie on your lips.'

'I told that stupid swine Fouquert. We didn't have to kill anyone, or even take Paoli. All we had to do was keep you bottled up for a day or two.'

'Why was he so insistent?' asked Paoli.

'You don't understand how badly they want you in France, General.'

'I think I do, Lanester.'

'And then there was you, Markham. He wanted to kill you so much he could hardly sleep. And having spared you twice, once at Cardo and once at that damned monastery, he hardly spent a minute without that knife in his hand, and your skin in his mind.'

'Buttafuco?'

'The French asked for terms. Fouquert set it up. He arranged the meeting.'

'Who arranged that I should see it?'

Lanester shook his head, though whether in pain or refusal, Markham couldn't tell. Instead he looked at Paoli.

'We must get to Cardo.'

The old general nodded. But he refused to move until Lanester expired. Markham saw a tear leave his eye as the man who'd betrayed him slipped away.

Chapter thirty-four

The fishing boat stank, not just of its function, but also because it was crowded with non-sailors, most of whom were violently sick on what was nothing more than a gentle swell. The attempt to look brave, by flying the black and white flag again, instead made them look slightly ridiculous on such a vessel, a fact of which only Markham seemed aware. Even he felt queasy, though whether that was to do with the jerking motion of the small vessel or the all-pervading odours, he couldn't tell. All he did know was that he reeked personally of them all, and that had him offering a silent prayer that, when he went aboard one of His Majesty's ships, that would not provide another stick to beat him with.

So when they spotted *Hebe,* some ten miles south of Bastia, his heart sank. Any hope that he might slip by and get through to another ship, was dashed when she put up her helm to come and investigate. A fishing boat would have been ignored normally, but one flying the Moor's-head device deserved an interrogation. Naturally, when they were hove to with the frigate along-side, it was he who had to go first up the side.

'Clap that cowardly bastard in irons,' yelled de Lisle from behind a row of officers – a place, Markham thought of some safety.

'Best hose him down first,' said Bowen, the

premier, who hated Markham almost as much as the captain did. 'Sod stinks.'

'That's his normal smell, sir,' added Fellows, another lieutenant, 'only you're too much of a gent to pick it up.'

'Are you quite finished?' said Markham.

'Damn you, sir, it is you that is finished!'

Markham smiled. 'You will forgive me smiling, gentlemen, but the thought of you all on half pay amuses me.'

That got their attention, being, as it was, a constant source of worry. 'We have coming aboard General Pasquale Paoli, whom I'm sure you will wish to greet in the appropriate manner.'

'What nonsense is this?'

'If you choose to insult the Corsican flag, and anger Admiral Hood in the process, I cannot stop you.'

Paoli, probably through impatience, started to come aboard, climbing from the fishing vessel onto the frigate's deck. If anything, given that he was dressed in better-quality clothes, he looked even more disreputable than Markham. He certainly smelt the same. But he did have such natural dignity that he was able to force de Lisle to drop his stare. Then the purser stepped forward to whisper in the captain's ear, which made his tiny black eyes bulge.

'I wonder if you could indulge me, Captain, with a change of clothing and the means to wash? I must join my army, and it would not do to arrive smelling like a long dead tunny.'

De Lisle's mouth moved, but nothing emerged.

'Sir, is Captain Nelson off Bastia?'

The chance to bark at Markham restored his voice. 'He is. And so should you be if you were not a coward.'

'Please do not call this man a coward, I beg you. I have rarely come across such courage and sagacity in one breast.'

Jaws dropped then, but Midshipman Bernard was smiling broadly.

'I won't say you had me in a stew, Markham,' said Nelson. 'But I was concerned, especially with de Lisle and Colonel Hanger after your blood.'

'I'm surprised he's not aboard *Agamemnon*, sir.'

That merited a raised eyebrow, as Nelson looked up and down an officer now returned to his proper red-coated estate. 'He won't come aboard unless specifically requested. Prefers to sling his hammock in one of the transports, anything rather than sup with the likes of me.'

'You don't sound too sorry, sir.'

'Can't say I am, Markham,' Nelson replied, giving his guest an arch look, 'though his wife would certainly grace our table.'

'His wife!'

The door opened after a perfunctory knock, and Allen, Nelson's servant, appeared. 'Colonel's boat has put off, sir.'

'Right. Best rout out the old General.'

Hanger stopped dead when he saw Markham, while his wife blushed to the roots of her hair. Pure mischief on Nelson's part, of course, evident from his expression – fish-faced was the best way to describe it. By the time the colonel was introduced to Paoli and Magdalena he'd re-

481

covered some of his sangfroid.

'You know the lieutenant, of course, don't you? Markham, do the honours with the wine, will you.'

He felt like a bird watched by a cat, as he took a glass of wine to Lizzie Gordon. Two cats, since Magdalena Calheri was quick to pick up the undertones. Nelson was enjoying himself, only Pasquale Paoli seeming to be in any way relaxed. Hanger could ease a bit as they discussed the forthcoming landing, but Lizzie was left out of that, to be entertained by Markham and Nelson's officers. They tried to engage Magdalena's attention too, and got short shrift. By the time they sat down to eat, it was like a Hanoverian family royal dinner, icy in the level of mutual loathing.

'I must land when you land, Colonel. To make my presence felt too early would undermine the Army commanders.'

'Feeble,' thought Markham, giving Magdalena a smile, pleased to see, when that lady responded, a slight upsurge in attention from Lizzie Gordon.

'I would also like Lieutenant Markham as my escort.'

'I think he would be better placed serving with his fellow marines,' growled Hanger. Then he barked at the subject of the request, 'Don't you think, Markham?'

Paoli cut Markham off just as he was about to reply, giving him cause to curse his openness on the fishing boat. But then, everybody was open with this old man.

'It would grieve me to insist.'

'Have him, sir.'

'And his men, of course.'

Hanger nodded sharply, then he stared at the tablecloth, as though he wanted to say something other than what emerged. 'You'll have to forgive me, Nelson. I must have found the trip over upsetting. I can't do justice to your food and I must, in any case, return to my work.' He stood up, throwing his napkin down with some force. 'I'll leave you to see the general here ashore, shall I?'

'If you wish.'

'Right. Come along, my dear.'

Lizzie Gordon rose slowly, in a way that clearly infuriated her spouse. 'Thank you, Captain Nelson.'

'Pleasure, ma'am.' A round of curtsies and bows followed, then they were gone, leaving a deep silence, until Nelson filled it. 'Exemplary manners, Colonel Hanger, don't you reckon?'

Markham could not understand Paoli. Why march into the camp at Cardo flying his flag, so that those who were betraying his cause would know of his arrival? All the senior officers assembled to greet him as he made his way down the cheering ranks of the army. If any of them were nervous, it didn't show. Not one of his generals did anything else but meet Paoli's eye squarely; Markham was greeted stiffly but with punctilious correctness. Nor did they demur when he suggested an attack against the redoubts to back up the British landing. Arena, tall and sallow, tipped his pockmarked head in agreement. Grimaldi agreed enthusiastically, and

Buttafuco gave one of his habitual glares.

'I have one more request to make, gentlemen?'

'Name it,' said Arena.

Paoli pointed to Markham. 'This officer has done Corsica such signal service, that I would wish him to escort our standard forward tomorrow at dawn.'

'A foreigner?' demanded Buttafuco.

'Yes.'

'What service has he done to deserve this?' asked Grimaldi.

'He unearthed several plots against us, hatched by a villain called Fouquert, and another officer you entertained at this very table, Major Lanester.'

'What!' said Grimaldi.

'Impossible!' said Buttafuco.

Arena stood in stupefied disbelief.

'All the plots have failed, the tendrils are known. Let us then lay them to rest.' Paoli raised his wine glass. 'To the morrow.'

Markham went searching for Magdalena, and found her in the company of two officers, both short, dark-skinned men with black hair. His cheerful greeting to her was met with deep frowns and hard, exchanged glances.

'Lieutenant Markham. My brothers, Alfredo and Guilio.'

He bowed, a gesture which was not returned. In fact they began to talk to their sister in such a way that their bodies cut him out. But they conversed with her in French, telling her in no uncertain terms what they would do to any one who trifled with her affections. Markham took the hint, and left.

The following morning saw them up before dawn, the redcoats given pride of place, not on the right of the line, but in the centre. Bellamy again held the flag, surrounded by the rest of the men, listening to the cheers as Pasquale Paoli rode along the line. Out in the bay the bombardment had started, great clouds of smoke rising to obscure the topsails and battle flags of Nelson's squadron. Markham could imagine the boats already in the water, surrounded as he had been at Fornali with shot and shell. What they were about to do carried as many risks, but with earth under his feet rather than water, he was a happier man.

'Rannoch?'

'Sir?'

'What happened to change everyone's attitude to Bellamy?'

'I do not rightly know,' Rannoch replied guardedly.

Markham knew he could press, knew it wasn't personal. 'Tell me. Now!'

There was hesitation, but not much. 'That night we made camp outside Aleria.'

'Yes,' Markham replied. He had a vision of Magdalena, her back against a tree, her legs wrapped round his waist.

'Well none of us parley the language, so getting to know the ladies was hampered.'

'And he helped.'

'He lacks charm in the English, sir. But he must have it in the French.'

'Lieutenant,' said Paoli, hauling his mount's

485

head round to face the enemy. 'Please lead us forward.'

'Mr Bellamy,' called Markham. The Negro responded to the courtesy with a huge grin. 'At your pleasure.'

The drums beat as the Corsican army fidgeted behind them. Immediately there was movement on the walls of the redoubts. Bugles blew, and flags began to shoot up and down the staffs. Bellamy, in the middle of the Lobsters, waved the device of the Moor back and forth. Paoli, from atop his horse, signalled a general advance, which brought forth a great cheer as the troops surged forward at a slow walk.

The French might be surprised to be attacked, but they were not going to give up easily. What cannon they had spoke as soon as the Corsican line moved, spewing forth round shot that scythed into the massed ranks of infantry. With only six hundred yards to cover the enemy had no time for another such salvo, and turned to case shot, the shells bursting above and behind the Corsican flag. Markham saw the staff cant over, and Bellamy staggered as he rushed forward to aid him. The Negro wasn't wounded, just thrown off his stride by a ball hitting the standard. Bellamy marched on, and it was only then that Markham realised he had his eyes closed tight, and was mouthing a desperate prayer.

Soon the Lobsters found themselves enveloped in the smoke from the guns. The line behind them was now ragged and torn, but if he had ever doubted the quality of the Corsican peasant soldiery, it was laid to rest now. They marched

486

on, taking anything the enemy could throw at them with admirable steadfastness, closing the gap on the redoubts to the point where they could begin to break into a run. The redcoats signalled that, clearly visible even in the murk. And the standard of their race, the Moor's head, which tipped forward as Bellamy kept pace, raising a huge and terrifying cheer that must have chilled the blood of the defenders.

There was a trench line in front of the redoubts, full of Frenchmen, all with their muskets aimed along the wooden parapet. But they must have known that the force coming at them was irresistible, since the volley that could have decimated their attackers was ill-disciplined, and immediately followed by an attempt to withdraw. Suddenly the Lobsters were amongst them, Markham slashing right and left at the enemy, Rannoch yelling his heathen Highland cry as he jabbed forward with his bayonet.

But that was as nothing to the savagery of the Corsicans. This was war as they understood it, close-quarter stuff where a knife was the equal of any other weapon. The French infantry tried to fight them with bayonets, but against their quick-silver reactions seemed to lose every time. And there was no quarter once they were through the enemy's guard, the depth of hate these people felt for their oppressors in every knife that cut, sliced and skewered.

Markham was on the glacis now, hard-packed earth set at an angle to deflect shot, scrabbling like his men to make some way up the slope. Again the Corsicans proved themselves, as they raced barefoot up the ground like mountain goats, even managing to keep their footing when engaging the defenders. The Lobsters might have been left at the bottom if it had not been for the flag. But the men of the island wanted that with them, and the redcoats found themselves pushed and dragged until they were on the ramparts.

Men were fighting in and around the wooden embrasures, some tumbling back down the slope as a Frenchman, more secure behind his palisade, took advantage of his bayonet's length. This was familiar territory to Markham and, shouting at the top of his voice, he managed to get enough of his Lobsters together to form a cohesive group around the flag. Discipline, rather than Corsican brio, was needed now, and as he called out the orders he was proud to see how his men ignored whatever was going on around them to obey.

'Present!' The muskets levelled, all aimed at a trio of embrasures manned by knots of Frenchmen getting in each other's way. 'Fire!'

The Lobsters were charging as soon as the balls flew, bayonets extended to take in the smoke an enemy that had survived their fusillade. Markham led them, jumping onto the palisade and waving for his men to follow. This they did willingly, fanning out on the other side to clear defenders right and left from the walkway. It was nip and tuck to begin with, the weight of the enemy greater than the force they could bring to bear. But fighting the Lobsters left them open to the knives and bayonets of the Corsicans, and behind the first line that the marines were fighting Frenchmen were dying.

Markham was between Leech and Dornan, who, if he was indifferent with a musket, revelled in the close-quarters use of the bayonet. The stoop was narrow, and open at the rear, so half the men Dornan engaged ended up as casualties because they fell under furious assault. Markham couldn't slash, just jab, and against a weapon six feet in length was at a disadvantage until, as one defender lunged at him and missed, he grabbed his musket, dragged him forward, clubbed him with his hilt, and removed the man's weapon. That was just before the soldier died under the blades of the Corsicans who were now pouring through the gap he and his men had created.

Noise was the key, even if it seemed impossible that any human ear could tell if it was diminishing. The defence was crumbling because the cries from the Frenchmen were futile pleas for mercy, rather than shouts to raise their valour. They couldn't break off the action, there was no room, so they had a stark choice: to jump and maim themselves, or die where they stood. Most jumped, and suddenly the stoop was clear of blue coats, and full of cheering men in red Corsican caps.

Behind the redoubts the walls of Bastia stood, high, white and formidable, another obstacle that would have to be conquered. But the space between was full of retreating Frenchmen, who could hear the bombardment from Nelson's ships, and some of the crack of musketry from the southern shore. Men who must know that the town they had tried to hold was now in the grip of a siege that could only end in surrender.

The Lobsters didn't need to fight their way to the beach. Even those who had opposed the landing had withdrawn, and the Navy was once again busy shipping cannon ashore. Nelson, surrounded by other officers, stood on a gun carriage, telescope to his eye, chest out and rightly proud as he surveyed the extent of his success. When he saw Markham and his men plodding towards him, he lost all sense of his dignity as a post captain in His Britannic Majesty's Navy, and waved like a child would to a long-lost friend. The likes of Serecold laughed, but de Lisle and Hanger frowned, and glared at the object of this greeting.

'We have done some sterling work today, Markham.'

'General Paoli sent me to inform you, sir, that the redoubts at Cardo have been driven in, and that the French have retired into the city.'

'Excellent.'

'I take it your men are available for duty, Lieutenant?' Hanger demanded, his scarred, ugly face as close to happiness as was possible. 'I can assure you there is still warm work to be done.'

'What,' cried Nelson, before Markham could reply. 'You would not remove my own guard detail from me, Colonel, would you?'

'Guard detail!' Hanger barked.

'These are my marines,' said de Lisle.

'Not any more, Captain. They are transferred.' Nelson's eyes were twinkling. 'I think my dignity as a commodore allows me a file of marines to guard my quarters, sir. Just as it allows me to convene, provided I have enough captains present, a court martial.'

Both men knew immediately what Nelson meant, and it showed on their faces. With the odd exception like de Lisle, the commanders in his squadron were hand chosen by him. He would select who sat on the court, and those picked would be unlikely to bring in a verdict that would displease their patron.

'Lieutenant Markham.'

'Sir!' he replied, pulling himself to stiff attention.

'Be so kind as to return to General Paoli, with my compliments, and ask him if he would care to inspect our positions.'

He found the Liberator in the convent building at Cardo, in the very room in which he'd dined a week ago, surrounded by his jubilant officers. Markham had a quick look around the faces, particularly those of high enough rank to be close to Paoli. The Liberator, with a mark of respect that was as genuine as it was deep, stood and came to greet him.

'You seem to be light on the odd general, sir,' Markham said quietly.

Paoli replied in the same way, so that his officers would not hear. 'Generals Arena and Grimaldi departed last night, we believe for the safety of France.'

'You should have hanged them.'

'Ah! Markham, you do not understand. They have family. If I kill them then their relatives must kill me. It is the vendetta.'

'Which I thought you'd wiped out.'

'No. The vendetta will never leave Corsica. It is

491

in our blood.'

He led Markham to the door and indicated the redoubts, now with the flag of Corsica flying on the palisades. The wind was strong from the north, and the Moor's-head device was visible to the naked eye.

'But as you see, our honour is redeemed, Lieutenant Markham, and for that I have to thank you and your Lobsters.'

The publishers hope that this book has given you enjoyable reading. Large Print Books are especially designed to be as easy to see and hold as possible. If you wish a complete list of our books please ask at your local library or write directly to:

Magna Large Print Books
Magna House, Long Preston,
Skipton, North Yorkshire.
BD23 4ND

This Large Print Book for the partially sighted, who cannot read normal print, is published under the auspices of

THE ULVERSCROFT FOUNDATION